Hot Pursuit

*Also by Christina Skye
in Large Print:*

Going Overboard

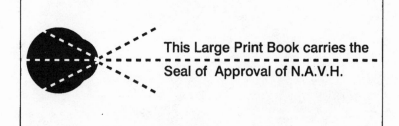

Hot Pursuit

Christina Skye

WHEELER
PUBLISHING

Published in 2003 by arrangement with Bantam Books,
an imprint of The Bantam Dell Publishing Group, a division
of Random House, Inc.

Wheeler Large Print Romance Series.

The text of this Large Print edition is unabridged.
Other aspects of the book may vary from the original edition.

Set in 16 pt. Plantin by Myrna S. Raven.

Printed in the United States on permanent paper.

Library of Congress Cataloging-in-Publication Data

Skye, Christina.
    Hot pursuit / Christina Skye.
      p. cm.
    ISBN 1-58724-447-0 (lg. print : hc : alk. paper)
    1. United States. Navy. SEALs — Fiction. 2. Stalking victims
— Fiction. 3. Women novelists — Fiction. 4. Large type books.
I. Title.
PS3569.K94H68 2003
  813′.54—dc21   2003045058

Acknowledgments

Huge and hearty thanks to some real lifesavers:

to Georgia, for providing fascinating research on current developments in genetic engineering (and also because she's my sister and she's brilliant!);

to Earl, the expert who once again helps keep the weaponry and technical settings accurate;

to Justin, who helped me up the slippery slope of climbing terms and techniques, while giving an insight into the climber's mind-set (climb on!);

to Peggy, for beating the clock brilliantly when deadlines loom;

to Judy, for creative communication, laughter, and the best imagination in town;

You are all the greatest!

THE RULES, ACCORDING TO TAYLOR O'TOOLE:

Change the names to protect the innocent. Even when they aren't so innocent . . .

Chapter One

FROM TAYLOR'S BOOK OF RULES:
Be prepared. Always pack antacids and an eyelash curler.

Taylor looked south to the distant sprawl of San Francisco. Why had she ever decided to take up rock climbing, especially when it involved hugging a granite slab two hundred feet above the ground?

The simple answer came first: She was preparing for a new book. Authors did crazy things when they were testing a new story, desperate to chisel out the reality of a new character.

But the truest answer was subtle and far more unsettling. You did dangerous things when your life changed and you lost every anchor you'd taken for granted while you were growing up.

When you found out your childhood was a lie.

Taylor wiped sweat off her top lip and sighted up the cliff. Four feet to the next ledge.

She took a breath and crouch-walked up the angled slab, ignoring the pain in her arms and shoulders.

"Watch your moves below that next bolt." Her climbing instructor, a buff twenty-

7

something from Santa Barbara, stood below and uncoiled rope as she called out orders. "You won't have much of a foothold, so stay balanced and dig in hard with your sole."

"Got it, Candace." Taylor was glad for the warning when her foot began to slip. Panting, she leaned away from the rock to restore traction, then pulled herself to the next hold, yanked up the slack on her rope, and caught a loop in her teeth before clipping into the bolt.

Cold wind snapped across her damp face. She tried to remember exactly what Candace had been discussing.

Right. Help with a cheating boyfriend. "If he's cheating, forget him, Candace."

"I can't just walk away. I need to know what's happening to us and why. Harris has been pretty stressed lately because he's working a lot of overtime at his lab on some gonzo project he has to oversee personally. But we always worked things out before." Her voice wavered. "Now he's different. It's almost like he had a personality transplant."

"People change," Taylor called as she tractioned up the steep rock face. "These things happen, Candace."

"Not like this. And I can't stop thinking about him, Taylor. Everything used to be so wonderful," she said wistfully.

Taylor thought longingly about the thermos of Starbucks Caramel Macchiato out in her car.

Don't look down.

Don't think of anything but the rock.

Yeah, right.

She stretched out a kink in her shoulder. "So what turned your friend Harris into Frankenstein all of a sudden?"

"That's just it — I don't know. None of it makes sense." The gusting wind toyed with Candace's voice, making the words drift and fade. "One day he said he wanted the whole deal — life with me, a big house, and a mortgage. He swore he was going to leave his wife, father my children, start being responsible. All that heavy stuff."

Taylor turned her head to look at Candace. "You didn't tell me that Harris was *married!*"

"He was up front about that, Taylor. He never lied about her. He explained to me how they've been having all these problems over the last year. He's been making plans to tell her about us."

Yech.

Taylor got ready for her next move, trying hard not to hate Candace for thinking this was an easy route for Taylor's first outdoor climb.

They had met several months before, when Taylor had noticed her neighbor carrying climbing equipment onto the elevator in their apartment building. Immediately plot ideas had begun to stir. After writing a dozen books, Taylor knew a story kernel when she saw it. The two women had become friends over coffee and croissants at a local bakery, where

9

Taylor grilled Candace about every detail of climbing. As the book's plot took final shape, Taylor realized she would have to make a climb herself to nail down the rich details of the experience, white knuckles and all.

Which was how she came to be standing on an unforgiving piece of cold granite, obsessing about how it must feel to crack your spine in two.

She pushed away the gory vision of her death and cleared her throat. "I still don't understand how I can help."

Candace frowned, playing out more rope. "I can't afford a private investigator. Even if I could, it would feel . . . sleazy. Harris and I have been through a lot together, and he deserves better."

Taylor clipped in at the next bolt and stopped to catch her breath. "Candace, I still don't —"

"We may have had our problems, but I love him, Taylor. I need to find out if he's seeing another woman or if he's in some kind of trouble." Her voice sounded shaky. "I know it's a lot to ask, but could you follow Harris for me? Maybe if I know he's with someone else, I can finally break free." Candace gave a wan laugh. "Of course, then I might have to kill them both."

"Murder is just a little illegal, remember?" Taylor dug into the canvas bag hanging off her hip and worked chalk dust over her fingers. She didn't think Candace's friend was worth all this angst and soul-searching, but everyone saw love differently, she supposed. Meanwhile, she was trying hard to forget the opening scene in *Cliffhanger*, where a frightened climber plunges to her death. All Taylor's climbing friends had assured her that a buckle couldn't really snap during a climb, and that the movie was a complete howler, full of ridiculous errors.

Tell that to my racing heart.

Taylor took a deep breath and sighted upward. "Climbing," she called out grimly.

"Climb on."

As wind whipped off the rock, Taylor forced herself to breathe slowly, well aware that hyperventilating could trigger bad judgment and serious accidents. She picked out her next foothold, calculated her reach, then swung her weight fluidly over the granite face.

Stay calm. Stay balanced. It's supposed to be fun, remember?

Gritting her teeth, she tractioned a few more steps up the slope, then stopped to rest. "What's the other problem you wanted to discuss?"

"I'm afraid, Taylor. I need some ammunition in case things get . . . difficult."

Taylor worked her way over the slab, cursing the day she had ever thought of writing a book focused on a rock-climbing heroine. "Difficult how?" she panted. "Are you taking Harris for palimony?"

11

Candace laughed weakly. "Hardly. I get by just fine with my temp work and my private climbing lessons. But I'm afraid Harris could be in some kind of trouble. Last week three men followed us. They had guns, Taylor. They yelled at Harris and pushed him back against the car, searching all his pockets. Harris looked really scared and gave them something. When they finally left, he looked shaken. I mean, really, *really* shaken."

"Have you ever seen those men before?"

Candace shook her head.

"What do you think they wanted?"

"I couldn't hear. Harris told me to wait in the car."

Taylor blinked into the wind, trying to concentrate. She'd seen Candace's friend Harris Rains around the apartment building before, but the man hadn't seemed particularly interesting. "Do you think they want money?"

"No." Candace smoothly belayed the rope as Taylor found the next bolt, pulled slack, and then clipped in. "When I asked Harris what they wanted, he . . ." Her voice caught.

"He what?"

"He knocked me around."

Taylor froze, her head snapping downward. "Harris hit you?"

"A little." Candace's voice wavered.

The crud. The utter, creeping scum.

Taylor revised her plan to promise anything, then vanish as soon as she set foot back on terra firma. "How bad, Candace?"

"A few bruises." She stared off at the Golden Gate Bridge, glinting like a city of dreams to the south. "One tooth got knocked loose," she said softly.

"The miserable, scum-sucking *bastard*."

"Look, I'm okay. But Harris was different after that. He told me to forget what I saw or we'd both be in serious trouble. Now I think someone's following me, and I don't know who else to ask for help, Taylor. You write about this kind of thing and you're always so in control. That's why I thought you could tell me what I should do next."

"Leave the rat."

"I can't, Taylor. Not until I understand what's happening."

Taylor rested, catching her breath, trying to think clearly. "Then you need professional help. These men sound dangerous."

"No." It was a flat, worried sound. "I don't want to hurt Harris."

Taylor sighed. "I suppose I could speak to some people at the local precinct."

"You mean the police?" Candace sounded startled. "Harris would be furious."

"I don't think you should be worrying about what Harris thinks. Besides, these are friends. They'll do what's right for you."

The younger woman blew out a breath. "Okay, fine. Do whatever you think is best. I'm really sorry to bother you about this,

13

Taylor, but I can't just pack up and leave Harris. At the same time, I'm completely spooked."

Taylor's resolve hardened. Candace knew things were sour, but she was still afraid to leave the relationship. Right now she needed all the support she could get. "When are you supposed to see Lover Boy next?"

"Nothing definite. He said he'd call me Friday for dinner." Her voice fell. "Meanwhile, I could swear there's a silver Lexus SUV trailing me whenever I go out."

"Did you get a plate number?"

"Gee, I never thought — should I write it down next time?"

"That would be a start." Taylor studied the cliff to her left, where she would have to make a slow ascent, moving almost horizontally. She *hated* traverses. They demanded perfect form as you worked sideways, with footwork that required constant focus.

She felt herself begin to hyperventilate and took a deep breath. "Climbing."

"Climb on" came the immediate answer.

Taylor stepped out and skimmed the rock, shifting her center of gravity until she snagged a new handhold. She took a breath of relief as she clipped into the next bolt. "You checked all our gear? No broken buckles, right?" The question was half-joking.

"You're fine, Taylor. Trust me, I've never blown a bolt and all my gear is brand-new.

Forget about that rot in *Cliffhanger*. Things like that don't happen in real life."

Taylor grunted, praying her young neighbor was right. Suddenly something tugged at her rope. "What's wrong? I felt the rope snag."

"Slow down. It's just a tangle." Candace's voice seemed far away. "Funny, Harris was fiddling with my stuff last night. The idiot was trying to figure out how it works." Her voice wavered, and then she took a sharp breath. "Look, you're fine. I checked all the lines myself this morning. Just watch your footwork at the end of that traverse. Even if you do wipe out, it's no big deal. That's why we have ropes, right?"

Taylor forced herself not to look down. "Sure."

Don't think about falling ninety feet. Don't think about broken bones and copious amounts of spilled blood.

"Climbing." She swung her weight sideways, ready for the final moves of the traverse, as wind gusted off the summit. Somewhere, a bird cried shrilly, and Taylor blinked as grit and dust blew in her eyes, breaking her concentration.

Her toe slipped on its ledge, the rope jerking against her leg. She worked her feet hard, fighting for traction, but her balance was blown and she snapped sideways into free fall, spinning wildly.

Rock and sky ran together in a terrifying

15

blue-gray blur as the rope jerked again, then tore free from the wall. Taylor screamed, tumbling out of control.

The last thing she saw was the cliff wall spinning up to meet her.

Chapter Two

Limping to the elevator, Taylor pushed the UP button.

It was a complete miracle her bones weren't scattered over the bottom of a cliff. After more than four hours in the E.R. with Candace, she was queasily aware of how lucky they had been. Her neighbor had taken a tumble and now sported a nasty gash along her back, while Taylor had received four stitches above her right knee, a cut on her face, and about a thousand bruises.

But they were both damned lucky the fall hadn't been worse, and Taylor was pretty sure it was no thanks to a bottom-feeder named Harris Rains.

Under the influence of two Darvocets, Candace had come up with the only humor of the evening: "It never Rains, it bores. . . ."

Wincing, Taylor shuffled off the elevator and dumped her climbing bag on the floor outside her apartment, searching for her keys. Only then did she register the amazing smells of food emanating from the nearest apartment — which was very odd since her neighbor was a Cal Tech geek whose idea of a well-rounded diet was a blonde in a thong and two six-packs of Dos Equis. The man probably hadn't opened his oven in months.

Taylor took another lingering sniff.

Lasagna with really good cheese. The spice smells could be pumpkin pie. She closed her eyes in silent homage to the unknown chef.

Despite her growling stomach, she resolutely ignored the open door. With a new book in progress, eating came at odd moments when the words weren't flowing. Even at the best of times, Taylor was no cook. Scrambled eggs and coffee tested the limits of her skill. Her favorite kitchen utensils were a telephone and a take-out menu.

Another whiff of tomato sauce with fresh basil and oregano drifted down the hall. Taylor felt like weeping.

But she had a can of soup inside. She'd shower and heat something up. For dessert she'd have the smashed protein bar left over after the climbing trek from hell.

Behind her, boots scraped on bare wood. A long rail of unfinished pine shot out of her neighbor's doorway.

And holding it steady was the most amazing, delicious, *outstanding* male body she had ever set eyes on.

"Coming through."

Taylor watched in stunned silence. Van Damme shoulders. Kung-fu torso.

Could you have a hot flash at thirty-five?

The geek must be doing an apartment makeover. His handyman clearly had a girlfriend happy to throw together a six-course meal on short notice.

With a body like that, the man could have *any* food group he wanted, anywhere he wanted.

He studied Taylor as he hefted the board easily onto one hip. "You live in 7B?"

Taylor realized she was staring. Staring glassy-eyed. "Uh . . . yeah. That's me."

"I hope the noise isn't bothering you. I'm putting in a new kitchen cabinet today."

"I didn't hear anything." Taylor cleared her throat. "I — I just came in."

"Jack Broussard. I'm your new neighbor." Mr. Fixit held out a hand covered with sawdust. "Pleasure to meet you."

Taylor swallowed. Her eyes kept drifting down that muscled chest to lean hips. "Taylor O'Toole. What happened to the prior tenant?"

The man shrugged. "Some kind of research grant came up at Cal Tech. In exchange for cheap rent, I agreed to update a few things in the apartment."

His gray eyes narrowed on her knee, bandaged just below her spandex climbing shorts. "Take a tumble on your bike?"

"No, from a cliff up in Marin. It was my first outdoor climb."

He shifted the plank of wood. "And you fell?"

"The rope pulled free." Taylor shivered, blocking the memories.

19

"It must hurt." Her new neighbor leaned the wooden plank against the wall, muscles flexing smoothly. "You couldn't get me up on a cliff without a gun at my back."

Taylor didn't even have enough energy left to brag. "You probably won't get *me* up there again either. One of the bolts broke and the rope pulled free." Even now she couldn't suppress a shiver. "Free fall at ninety feet isn't exactly my idea of fun."

The cool gray eyes flickered over her bandaged knee again. "Sounds ugly. Sure you're okay?"

"Four stitches, but it could have been worse." The lasagna smell was killing her, but she tried to look nonchalant while managing not to trip over her climbing bag.

Her neighbor ran strong, calloused fingers thoughtfully down the rough plank. "Does that kind of thing happen a lot when you're climbing?"

"What kind of thing?"

"Bolts pulling out. Free fall."

Only dogged pride kept Taylor on her feet, as exhaustion warred with pain from the stitches. "I don't think so. Then again, some people have a warped idea of extreme fun." She picked up her bag. "I'd better go and let you work on your studs." She winced. "Nuts. I mean beams. Whatever you call them. Tell whoever's cooking that she's got my vote for the James Beard award."

She was pretty sure she heard him laugh as she closed her door, but her legs began to shake and she didn't stay around to find out.

An hour later, fresh from a steamy bath, Taylor padded into the kitchen and stared into her refrigerator. Optimism turned to disgust. All she had was a wilted head of lettuce and two half-eaten cartons of yogurt.

Lasagna was her favorite food in the world, followed closely by chestnut ice cream from Berthillon's in Paris. Unfortunately, it was a long way to Paris.

Shaking her head, she headed down the hall to her office. In a few seconds she was deep in a scene involving two women climbers, a swift-moving bank of fog, and a sheer wall of granite.

Taylor lasted fifty-three minutes and four pages. The fog fled, the rocks simply evaporated. So much for being creative.

The final straw had been the chocolate fragrance filling her apartment. She paced the living room like a rabid animal and finally threw down her notebook.

You are a total disgrace. In fact, you have the willpower of a slug.

But what did pride matter when bittersweet chocolate was involved? She straightened her shoulders, stalked outside, and banged on the door.

Her neighbor answered on the fourth knock.

Same stellar abs. Same Van Damme shoulders on a body that belonged in a museum.

Taylor looked up swiftly. "I know this is rude, but is that bittersweet chocolate I keep smelling?"

He had a towel draped over one shoulder and sawdust dotting his chest. Taylor had a wild image of her fingers brushing aside the fine powder and tracing those warm, rigid muscles.

She managed to restrain herself.

"Ganache." His mouth twitched. "Belgian chocolate."

"Dark chocolate? The really good stuff?"

"The darker the better. The éclairs are almost done."

She smiled weakly. "Would you consider a trade? How about my firstborn child and a dozen active credit cards for one éclair?"

His brow rose. "I didn't hear any children at your place."

"I don't have any — yet. I'll get started right away if it will help." She flushed when she realized what she'd said. "So to speak."

"Save the children." He stepped aside and held open the door. "Take your pick of the éclairs. You want some lasagna to go with it?"

Suck it in, O'Toole. Don't drool. "Lasagna?" She managed a casual laugh. "Is that what I was smelling?"

"It's an old family recipe." He gestured at a big living room outfitted with sawhorses, tools, and dozens of boxes. "It's a mess in here, so be careful. Especially watch out for that saw in the corner."

Taylor sidestepped a hammer and nails, glancing at one of the boxes. "You seem to have a lot of equipment. How much renovation are you planning to do?"

"Replace the counters. Resurface the drawers and cabinet doors. Maybe change the floor. A deep red saltillo tile would be nice."

Sawdust drifted. Taylor watched him shift another plank of wood with practiced ease. Why did the image of sweat and manual labor suddenly seem so sexy? "No offense, but I hope it won't be too noisy. I work at home."

"What kind of work?" The question was casual as he pulled the lid off a big ceramic baking dish.

Lasagna smells filled the air and Taylor's knees threatened to buckle. "Writing. Suspense — heavy on characters and a solid hit of romance." She waited for the snicker, the frown, the twist of the lips.

He simply nodded. "Sounds interesting."

"It has its moments. Some days you enjoy matching a nasty face with a lethal bullet."

Her neighbor chuckled, measuring a piece of lasagna with his knife. "How about this much?"

Was the Pope Catholic? "Gee, I don't want to be greedy."

"No problem. I made plenty."

Taylor felt her jaw go slack. "*You're* the cook?"

He slid an éclair onto a plate and added a decadent amount of Belgian chocolate sauce. "My dad always said if a man wanted to eat, he owed it to himself to learn to cook. As a matter of fact, he could cook circles around my mom." He smiled. "And she liked it just fine that way."

Taylor forced her mouth closed. Mr. Five-Star Biceps could *cook?*

"Have some while the sauce is still warm."

She stared down at the plate he'd thrust into her fingers, pretty sure she was on the verge of disgracing herself. "Well, I don't —"

"Go on." He leaned back against the cabinet, grinning. "Don't tell me you're one of these women who watches every calorie." There was a glint of challenge in his eyes.

"Well, no, but —"

He slanted a look over her legs, now encased in fake leather capri pants.

Taylor registered the faint look of challenge, and that was her undoing. She took a big bite of éclair — and nearly staggered with the decadent force of the rich chocolate and whipped cream. "Not bad," she said huskily, licking white froth off her finger.

Her neighbor didn't move. "If you let me watch you eat," he said slowly, "I'll give you a few more."

Suddenly the room felt hot. Taylor picked up an electric charge that hadn't been evident seconds before. Maybe she was hallucinating from carbohydrate overdose. "No thanks, I'd probably drool. But I appreciate the food, really. If you ever need some cappuccino, just drop by. Coffee is about the only thing I can manage in the kitchen."

He crossed his arms, revealing ripped muscles. "I'll keep it in mind. Let me know if the noise bothers you."

"Sure." Taylor headed back to the door on autopilot. As she turned to say good-bye, she saw him silhouetted against the big picture window, light falling over his back. His face was in shadow and he didn't look like a carpenter.

Now he looked cool and dangerous.

"Did you say carpentry was your regular job?"

"You have something against carpenters?"

She stared at him in silence. The cool edge of challenge was back in his face.

"Look, Mr. Broussard, the question wasn't personal. It's just habit for me to watch people. As a writer, part of my work is noticing how people talk, how they move. You look like an athlete. Or maybe a soldier. Definitely not a carpenter."

He picked up a hammer and shoved it into the tool belt riding low at his waist. "I didn't know that carpenters had any particular look. But trust me, you'll know that's what I am when the banging starts."

Jack Broussard closed the door and frowned. He heard feet tap down the hall and a door close. Quickly he walked into the bedroom and lifted a cardboard box, revealing a state-of-the-art surveillance system and two sets of head-phones. He slid on the smaller headphones and fiddled with a dial.

He heard the dead bolt slide home next door, followed by shoes scraping across a wooden floor. Every sound was magnified by the pow-erful system he'd just installed in the wall ad-joining the two apartments.

Dishes scraped in the kitchen. Water ran briefly. A refrigerator door opened, then closed.

Broussard considered her explanation about the bandage on her leg. A bolt that pulled free at ninety feet? The woman was damned lucky she wasn't bloody hamburger in a ravine some-where. He had to hand her points for courage, if not for intelligence. Rock climbing wasn't like chalking up fifteen minutes on a StairMaster twice a week.

Amateurs never understood that you had to train for danger full time or the training didn't stick. But *was* she an amateur?

He considered the question as he pulled a cell phone from a nearby drawer and punched in a set of numbers that would appear in no phone directory anywhere.

The phone clicked once and the call was re-layed to a new location.

Jack entered his password. Silence fell, fol-lowed by a pleasant female voice telling him he had reached a nonworking number. He knew the drill so well that he didn't skip a beat. He gave his name, asked two short questions, then listened intently.

The envelope was still waiting on the edge of her desk. Taylor didn't have to look to see the neatly typed label and the expensive gray paper.

She put the lasagna she had taken on the counter and went in search of silverware. Next came spring water with a wedge of lemon. An Irish linen napkin. Her knee ached as she raised the blind, giving a brilliant view of hilly San Francisco streets and a distant glint of water.

She turned.

The envelope was still there on her desk, mocking her, making something turn over in her chest. She didn't have to see the papers inside to know what they said.

You are encouraged to keep the department or this agency informed of your current address in order to permit a response to any inquiry concerning medical or social history made by or on behalf of the child who was the subject to the court action terminating parental rights.

(a) Section 9203 of the Family Code authorizes a person who has been adopted and who attains the age of 21 years to make a request to the State Department of Social Services, or the licensed adoption agency that joined in the

adoption petition, for the name and address of the adoptee's birth parents. Indicate by checking one of the boxes below whether or not you wish your name and address to be disclosed in such a case:

Below were three simple lines.

❏ *Yes*
❏ *No*
❏ *Uncertain at this time; will notify agency at later date*

The last line was checked.

Taylor closed her eyes. Someone had conceived her — whether in lust, boredom, or dread, she didn't know. Nine months later she had been pulled shriveled, red-faced, and terrified from a stranger's body and she probably would never know the reasons why. Taylor felt an explosion of fury at the woman who had turned her head, ignored her cries, and handed her over to a stranger. She hated whoever her mother was, wherever she was, whatever her reasons. She hated — and yet her heart was a ragged, seeping wound, torn in two by regret and a vast longing.

With shaking hands she reached for the legal document, which had been shoved unnoticed and misfiled inside a collection of forms returned after the death of her family's longtime lawyer. One call and she could initiate the search that would strip away thirty-five years of lies. One call that would open yet more wounds.

Her fingers shook. She strained, trying to touch the envelope, her heart pounding.

On her desk, the phone rang. Taylor froze, her hand still outstretched. She took a breath in and out, slowly, as if her life, her whole future, hung in the balance. Then her eyes flickered to the small digital screen and she read the number.

Pick up the phone. Say one word. Say yes and they'll start searching, trying to open the records and find your mother.

Your other mother.

But Taylor couldn't move. Tears came as the phone went on ringing, each peal a new assault bringing a fresh stab of indecision.

If she didn't say yes, she'd never know the truth of who she was. She was entitled to a background history at least, with a reasonable assessment of genetic risks and medical concerns. If she didn't fight for answers, the holes in her past would grow larger every year, until the anger and uncertainty overwhelmed her.

But she couldn't move, tears hot and slick on her face, knees shaking, heartsick.

The phone finally stopped ringing and the silence settled around her. She thought about a baby crying in the night and she thought about the mother she'd never known, and then she slid slowly back against the counter, her wet face pressed against her hands while harsh, racking sobs consumed her.

It was Candace's call that roused her nearly an hour later. After a cautious glance at the number, Taylor answered with a voice that wasn't quite steady.

"Taylor, what's wrong?"

"It's — it's my leg, Candace. The stitches. You know."

"Tell me about it." Candace gave a shaky laugh. "I've thrown up twice today, and I *never* throw up." She took a sharp breath. "But you're okay, right?"

Taylor forced her thoughts away from the envelope on her desk. "I'm fine. We walked away and that's what counts." She hesitated. "Are you certain you gave me all the climbing gear we used?"

"Absolutely. Not that I'd ever touch those things again. The rope really took a beating. But why —" Candace hesitated. "God. You really *do* believe that Harris arranged this, don't you?"

"Let's just say I want some answers."

"But it *had* to be an accident, Taylor. I checked every inch of that rope myself, along with the bolts and carabiners. Everything was in tip-top shape this morning."

"I'm sure it was." Taylor was determined to have the gear examined by an outside expert. If Harris had tampered with anything, Taylor was going after him big-time. But until then, she was telling Candace nothing about her plan. "So what have you heard from Lover Boy?"

"He called a few minutes ago. He asked how things were going and if we'd had a good climb."

"What did you say?"

"Everything's peachy. That's what I should have said, isn't it? Not tell him the truth?"

Taylor rubbed her forehead, where a slow throb was building to a major headache. "Don't tell him anything. Next time he calls, just hang up." Taylor still couldn't figure out why Harris would try to get rid of Candace. Was he tired of her, angry with her, or was he afraid that she knew too much about some kind of trouble he was involved in? "I still think we should call the police."

Candace made a low sound of protest. "Not until I know what's wrong. All of this could be a mistake."

"Have you seen the silver Lexus again?"

"I haven't gone out since I got home, but I'll get the license number if it shows up. Meanwhile, I just wanted to say how sorry I am. Your first outdoor climb should have been fun and exciting. Instead it was . . ."

A certified nightmare, Taylor thought grimly.

But she kept her voice level. "Forget it, Candace. We'll deal with Harris if he was involved. I should be thanking you. With all these aches and bruises, I have no energy left for anything but writing, which is what I should be doing anyway."

"That makes me feel better. And good luck with the new book. It's a sequel, right? With a heroine who is a novice climber?"

Taylor felt her headache grow. "That was the plan, but for some reason I can't get any of my characters to do what they're supposed to do. The good ones keep turning bad, and the bad ones keep redeeming themselves."

Actually, Taylor's creative flow was at a standstill for the first time in her life. She knew it had nothing to do with the climbing accident and everything to do with the big gray envelope lying on her desk. "Speaking of which, I'd better get back to it."

"Of course. I'll call you with that plate number. Meanwhile, maybe you should relax, go get a haircut and a pedicure. You know, let yourself be pampered."

"That's the best idea I've heard all day. But first I have to finish another chapter. So many murders, so little time."

Candace chuckled. "That's funny, considering you're the least bloodthirsty person I know."

If Rains kept up his nasty tricks, Taylor decided she might develop a taste for bloodshed. But until then, she had work to do. She hung up, gritted her teeth, and padded to her office, determined to wrestle six characters into abject submission.

Chapter Three

Taylor's hands were covered in green glop.

She stared at her nails, submerged beneath cold gel. Seventy-five dollars an hour, and you got green glop. They could charge you an extra fifty dollars for aromatherapy vitalizing essence, and it smelled nice, but it was still dish soap as far as she could see.

After two days at home, her bruises had healed to the point of being a minor irritation. The stitches were progressing more slowly, and every tug brought back memories of her wild tumble before the lower bolt had caught, gripping her rope and breaking her fall. But she'd shoved down the terror and plunged into her work, emerging with twenty new pages. As a reward, she'd headed off for an hour of R and R at the expert hands of her old friend, Sunny de Vito.

Candace was right. Pampering was definitely in order.

Right now Sunny was staring at her, and Taylor realized she hadn't heard a word her friend had said. "Sorry, I wasn't listening." Taylor blinked at her stylist, whom she'd known from her reckless high school days near Carmel.

Sunny waved her styling scissors. "Forget

about your climbing accident. We've got more important things to discuss. I said, Do you want layers?"

"Sure." Taylor frowned. "But no dye."

"Whatever." Sunny went to work, and hair flew. "You've always been a daydreamer, ever since I met you back in ninth grade."

"Daydreaming is good. Actually, it's half of what a writer does. And don't remind me of high school, please."

Sunny grinned. "I'll try not to, although that skirt you made out of duct tape comes immediately to mind. But I'll shut up while you try one of those Belgian truffles."

Taylor eased her teeth into a decadent treat that left her toes curling and thought about Harris Rains. A simple search on the Internet had revealed that the lab Rains worked for did $12 million a year in recombinant DNA research. No information was available about their specific clients or projects.

The fact that she'd glimpsed a silver Lexus SUV at a cross street outside her apartment had to be a coincidence. Meanwhile, she had considered the situation from every angle, and sometime near dawn she had come to a conclusion.

Harris Rains deserved to have a stalker. Nothing overt to make him paranoid, of course. Just enough to find out what he was up to. Taylor had also called a friend and made an appointment to turn over Candace's climbing gear for his expert assessment. If she hadn't been facing a book deadline, she would have done more research herself, but such was life.

She considered her half-eaten truffle and smiled nastily. She was looking forward to some part-time surveillance on Harris Rains. After writing books on the subject, it would be a snap.

"Stalk who?" Sunny stared at her from behind a pair of styling scissors.

Taylor realized she'd been muttering. "No one."

Her friend took a step back, not fooled for a second. She shoved a hand on her ample hips, a vision in black Lycra and magenta chiffon. The nose ring added the final touch of North Beach hip. "You aren't going to fight me about the highlights, are you? You *need* highlights."

Like she needed a nose ring. "No highlights, Sunny. Just a cut."

Her friend snorted. "Highlights would help, you know."

"Help with what?"

"You're looking whipped, my dear. Too much running around and not enough Pilates."

Taylor turned to glare at her image in the mirror. Sure enough, there were disgusting dark circles under her eyes. Taylor scowled. Book deadlines were hell, as every author knew. It was wonderful to *have* written, but the actual process unfolding in the real, live present tense usually sucked.

Especially when the dreaded *b* word came into play.

B-l-o-c-k.

Taylor closed her eyes at the mere thought. Fortunately for the reading public, writing was like childbirth: You forgot all the agony when you held the finished product in your hands, exhausted but radiant with a delirious sense of completion.

She sighed. Only 427 more pages to go. Meanwhile, she had to do something about her dark circles. "Okay, maybe a facial, but no highlights." Every time she came here, Sunny talked her into going a shade lighter. Now her hair was right on the edge of strawberry blond, and there was no way Taylor was going any further.

"Something in a nice ash tone would work."

"Absolutely not. Highlights, but *no color.*"

"What are you so afraid of?"

"I'm afraid of nothing."

"Fine, then we'll go for the strawberry." Sunny gestured to a man behind a cabinet full of bottles. "I need New Passion #54, Jerome."

Taylor stood up. "That's it. I'm gone."

"My, but *someone's* snippy today. Not enough Vitamin B12, I imagine. What you need is some lovely wheat grass." Sunny nodded to another ascetic-looking young man working a juicer at the front counter. "One Green Goddess over here, Sanford. Double chlorella."

Taylor felt a gag reflex starting. "Scratch the Green Goddess."

Sunny waited gravely.

"Fine, fine. Forget the green slime, and I'll take the highlights."

Sunny smiled benignly. "They always do." She crooked a finger, leading Taylor to a station with combs, curlers, and twenty sizes of foil. "So what's happening with your next book? I can't wait to see how you follow up on *The Farewell Code.*"

Taylor hid a grimace. "Oh, the writing's going great." *All twenty-four pages and two paragraphs of it.* "Slow, but great."

Sunny frowned. "Isn't your book due in May?"

"Hey, everything's under control," Taylor lied smoothly.

"This from the queen of last minute? You know that kind of stress is hell on your system. Let me see your fingernails."

Taylor grimaced.

"Just what I suspected. They're bitten down to stubs. Why don't you start writing sooner? How much research does one book take?"

Taylor's eyes narrowed. "Do I tell *you* how to cut layers or handle a curling iron?"

"Try it and die."

"I rest my case."

"I was just offering a little advice." Sunny tossed a cover over Taylor's shoulders and pushed her down for a shampoo. "So what's your angle this time? Embezzlers, immigration scams? A white slavery ring? You know, my uncle was just telling me yesterday that he couldn't wait for your next book. He has his whole reading club waiting for it, too."

Taylor swallowed. "Your uncle Vinnie has a reading club?"

"Just a few guys from the old days. You know, back in Little Italy."

A transplanted New Yorker, Sunny's uncle Vinnie was now famous in certain parts of San Francisco, namely police headquarters. He had a rap sheet the size of a city block, and thirty years ago he would have been a dead ringer for Tony Soprano. Even now when he walked into a room, women felt a frisson of excitement — and grown men felt their insides churn. He was as "made" as you could get and not be floating in the Hudson River.

"Gee, that's . . . nice. Tell him I said thanks."

Sunny stabbed at the air. "You have any trouble with anyone, Uncle Vinnie says to let him know. He's serious. He has ways to handle problems." She made two fingers into a gun.

Taylor squirmed on the imitation velvet chair. "I'll pass on the hit, Sunny."

"Hey, you never know. If Vinnie can't help you, my cousin Giovanni will. He lives in Vegas, but he's got business interests all over, if you know what I mean." Sunny finished the shampoo and tossed a towel around Taylor's head.

Taylor squinted around the towel. "Actually, I could use some information on a man who works in a lab in Pacific Heights. He may be in some kind of trouble."

"And?"

Taylor chose her words carefully. "And he may be threatening a friend of mine." *He may also be threatening me.*

Sunny said something in Italian, tossed down her comb, and pulled out a cell phone. Today it was magenta, to match her blouse. "Let Uncle Vinnie handle this. He's got finesse, you know."

As far as Taylor could see, Vinnie de Vito had about as much finesse as Robert de Niro in *Raging Bull*, but she decided not to mention it when Sunny was being so helpful.

Her friend punched in some numbers. After preliminary family chitchat and the usual questions about when she was going to give up the beauty business and settle down with a nice Italian man and make a big family, Sunny got down to business. "Taylor's here, Uncle Vinnie. Yes, of course I gave her your love. Yes, I told her you're waiting for the new book. The thing is, she needs some help." Sunny winked at Taylor. "No, not that kind of help, Uncle Vinnie. Just some information. She's working on her next book, and she needs to check on a local lab." She gave him Harris Rains' name and the lab name, listened for a moment, then covered the phone. "He says he'll mail you a cashier's check for a thousand dollars if you send him the pages for his reading club as soon as you're done with the book."

"I wouldn't dream of —"

Sunny spoke into the phone, then looked up. "He says five thousand."

Taylor swallowed. "He'll have the first copies, no money asked."

"You're on, Uncle Vinnie. No charge for the pages. So, can you make a few calls about Harris Rains and his lab? We'll be here at the salon while Taylor gets some color. Blonde," she added firmly.

Taylor glared.

Sunny ignored her. "Within the hour? Great. I knew you could do it. We'll be waiting." Sunny cut the connection and rolled back her sleeves. "Let's get to work."

Taylor watched foil squares flutter in the air currents, listening to Sunny's latest gossip about who was getting hair extensions and BOTOX injections. At the same time, another part of her brain was running through plot possibilities.

The writer's curse: always being two places at once.

She sat up tensely when Sunny's cell phone rang. Sunny made notes on a pad, then hung up. "Harris Rains, this is your life," she announced. "Vinnie got everything: home address, home phone, cell, and fax numbers. You also have his driving record. My uncle said to tell you this guy could be a little flaky, judging by his credit history."

"He got all *that?*"

40

Sunny shrugged. "Banking records, too. He's made some bad stock investments, it seems."

It had taken him, what, twenty minutes to snare a stranger's complete life story? So much for the sanctity of banking laws and institutional privacy.

Taylor frowned, wondering how easy it would be for someone to get all the details of *her* life, birth records in particular.

One demon at a time. "Is it accurate?"

"Trust me, my uncle never gets false information," Sunny said gravely.

Taylor could believe *that*. Giving Vinnie de Vito false information could get you fitted for a cement tuxedo and a nice permanent berth beneath the Oakland Bay Bridge.

"So how's Rains' credit?"

"Six cards. All maxed out."

"No kidding." So much for Candace's assurances that Harris was rolling in cash and expecting a huge stock bonus any day. Stocks didn't always equate to liquid assets, as any survivor of Wall Street's latest roller-coaster antics could warrant.

Sunny unfolded the first piece of foil and stared gravely at Taylor's hair.

"Well?" Taylor waited anxiously. "Please tell me I'm not going to have hair like Pamela Anderson's."

"Of course not. Her hair's long, and yours is short." Sunny opened another foil section. "Interesting."

Anxiety skittered into panic. "Interesting as in

41

why-is-she-trying-to-look-like-Pamela-Anderson-but-with-short-hair?"

Sunny glanced at Taylor's chest. "Sorry, but you're out of luck in the breast department, too." She unfolded another piece of foil. "Stop worrying. When I'm done, you're going to knock people dead."

Taylor closed her eyes. Knocking people dead was exactly what she was afraid of. When she looked up, Sanford of the Green Goddess drink was standing beside Sunny, holding out a large basket lined with green paper. "A messenger just dropped this off up front. He said it was for Taylor O'Toole."

"Flowers 'R Us? That means a secret admirer for sure." Sunny did a snappy high five with Sanford, followed by some sharp finger moves. "I just love stuff like this."

"I don't *have* any secret admirers. And no one knows I'm here."

"Stop being so cynical and open the gift."

Taylor took the basket from Sunny, then tugged at the gaudy metallic bow. "I don't know about his taste." She removed the ribbon and dug away three layers of green waxed paper, then stopped cold.

She swallowed, taking another reluctant look. "Judging by this, I think we can forget about a secret admirer."

Chapter Four

FROM TAYLOR'S BOOK OF RULES:
Breathe fast. You might not feel it.

"Let me see." Sunny shoved her aside. As she did, the basket tipped and half a dozen black blooms spilled onto the floor. "Is this some kind of joke? These are black. For *dead* people." Her voice rose shrilly.

Taylor's heart hammered as she shoved the fallen flowers back in the basket, where they spilled over an intricate funeral wreath of black irises, tulips, and lilies. "See if the receptionist got the name of the messenger service." Taylor stood up awkwardly, half in shock. "But first tell me where your service entrance is."

"Past the bathrooms and through the storage area. Be *careful.*"

Taylor didn't need a warning. The situation had turned nasty, and she was taking no chances on a direct confrontation. With any luck she could get a name, description, or a truck number to be traced later. Someone was going to pay for this sick little joke.

She hit the back door at a run, scanning the sunny parking lot. Two Jaguars. Red Beemer. A young Hispanic man stacking cartons near a Dumpster.

No floral delivery truck.

No messenger.

Taylor felt oddly surreal. Things like this didn't happen in her safe, ordered world. The Hispanic man, whom she had often seen cleaning up for Sunny, was staring at her, and Taylor realized her whole body was shaking.

"Hey, lady, you okay?"

Was she? How were you supposed to feel when someone sent you a funeral arrangement as a demented and very cold-blooded warning?

"Are you sick or something, lady? You like me to get a doctor?"

Taylor shook her head. "No — I'm fine." Not in a million *years* was she fine. "I just need to . . ." *To stop panicking. To stop shaking.* "I need to sit down."

"Here, use this box." The young man frowned, shoving a sturdy box in front of her. "Had a bad day?"

Taylor sank blindly onto the box. "A bad week, actually."

"Yeah, I've had plenty of those. What happened? You lose your job or something?"

"Worse." Someone had just sent her a death threat, clear and simple.

It still felt surreal, like a nightmare happening to someone else. She had been followed and warned off in clear terms, and she could think of only one person with a motive.

Harris Rains. She was involved now — *dangerously* involved.

44

"Have you seen a truck or a deliveryman out-side the salon?"

"Not in the last fifteen minutes. I don't know about before that." The young man moved back a step, looking worried. "Maybe you should see the police."

He was right, of course. Taylor would have to do that next — as soon as her legs stopped shaking long enough for her to stand up.

Just then the back door shot open, and Sunny sprinted outside. "Find anything?"

Taylor shook her head.

"The receptionist didn't get his name. He was wearing a blue uniform, but she doesn't re-member the company."

"It was probably a phony name anyway."

Sunny braced one hand against the wall. "I'm not feeling so good."

Taylor took a deep breath. "We don't have time to be sick. We've got to think."

"About what, the sleaze that would do some-thing like this?" Sunny's eyes narrowed. "Don't tell me — Harris Rains."

"Harris Rains is looking very likely." Taylor had a sudden, horrible thought. She dug in her purse for her cell phone and punched in Candace's number. "Candace, where are you?"

"At home. Why —"

"Are you okay?"

"Of course. What's wrong?"

Taylor puffed out a breath in relief. "I just got a little present delivered to me, and I sus-

45

pect it came from your dear friend Harris." Taylor heard the words in an echo that seemed very faint, like a television heard from a nearby room.

"What kind of present?" Candace asked nervously.

"A funeral arrangement." Taylor stopped as Sunny shoved something into her hand.

It was the gift card that had been taped on the outside of the arrangement. "He sent a message, too. 'In memorium.' " Taylor stared at the neatly typed card. No way to trace that. "Your friend Harris is starting to seriously piss me off."

"But you can't be *sure* that Harris sent it. Maybe I should call him and —"

"I want you to stay *away* from him," Taylor said grimly. "If he calls, hang up. If he knocks at your door, throw the bolt and call the police. I'm serious about this."

Candace didn't answer. Taylor had a bad feeling that she wasn't really listening.

"Candace?"

"I hear you, Taylor. I — I appreciate your advice, but I'm confused and I need to think, okay? I'll call you later. And — and I'm sorry." There was a *click* and the line went dead. With a sinking feeling, Taylor realized her friend hadn't agreed to anything. Candace still loved the scum, even now. Harris had *really* done a job on her.

She put away her phone and followed Sunny

back inside. The basket was still on Sunny's chair.

"I'm taking this to the police."

"Wait." Sunny gripped her hand. "The police won't do anything except file a long report and make you sign in triplicate. You need help *now*. Let Uncle Vinnie handle this."

"What can he do?"

Sunny reached for the phone. "Plenty. Trust me."

Taylor wanted to argue, but she was starting to feel like throwing up. She realized her hair was still wrapped in dozens of foil rectangles, being stripped of all color even as she spoke. "Okay, call him. Maybe he can ask the right questions in the right places. But if he gets nowhere, I'm going to the police."

"Reasonable enough."

Taylor stared at the flowers, wondering what she would do next. "Can you finish my hair, Sunny? I've got to go."

"What are you planning to do?"

"First, I'm going to throw up," Taylor said. "After that, I'm going to dose myself with caffeine, then go stalk Harris Rains."

"That sounds dangerous," Sunny said slowly.

"Don't worry, this is strictly a fact-finding mission. The man won't even know I'm there. But I'm not giving up, Sunny. Not until I find out exactly what's going on."

Cars streamed in a noisy rush down Market

Street forty-five minutes later as Taylor sat parked in afternoon traffic, facing a glass-and-chrome skyscraper. Thanks to several comments Candace had made, she knew Rains had worked on the fifteenth floor for the last three years.

People came in and out of the front door, but none of them was Rains. Taylor summoned up the image of Candace's friend, whom Taylor had seen once or twice in the building. The man wasn't exactly movie-star material. Energetic smile, but a definite underbite. A thin nose and something aggressive in the eyes, as she recalled.

She kept her eyes trained on the front door, which was the building's only entrance except for the loading area and the lower-level parking garage. If Rains came out on foot, it had to be through this door.

She flipped on her car stereo and tried to avoid her reflection in the rearview mirror, painfully aware that her hair was too bright, with too much gold and copper. But the layers were nice and Taylor had tugged on a black beret to cover most of her new iridescence.

Just as well that Mr. Fixit had been nowhere in sight when she'd left her apartment. If he'd been baking fresh bread, she might have wrestled him to the sawdust and had her way with him.

She glanced at the passing traffic. No police. No cars circling. So far, there had been no sign of a Lexus SUV either. If only Rains would put in an appearance.

As the minutes crept past, caffeine withdrawal began to set in. Taylor glanced at her watch as she scratched her knee where the stitches were starting to pull.

Still no sign of Rains.

After writing half a dozen books on the subject, Taylor knew surveillance inside and out. On the passenger seat were a bottle of water, sandwiches, and a notebook. The telephoto lens on her camera would document everything Rains did. But as the afternoon dragged on, more people came and went, and none of them was Candace's boyfriend. Novelty turned to boredom, then irritation, and finally Taylor tried calling his office number, but the secretary said he was in a meeting.

Muttering, she cranked up Radiohead and watched the front door some more, reasonably certain that none of the businessmen in Armani couture was Harris Rains.

Taylor tweezed one eyebrow and glared at the copper strands spiking out beneath her beret. She fidgeted, then tried calling Candace, but there was no answer. By now her cell phone battery was almost dead, so she pulled out her notebook marked *surveillance* and wrote *buy car adapter* in big letters.

After that, she ate her last sandwich and wrote *buy more egg salad*.

Then she sat some more.

She had eaten most of a bag of corn chips, without any sign of Rains, when she decided the magical coffee sign shimmering across the street could no longer be ignored. She was halfway across the intersection, carrying an extra-large steaming moccachino with double whipped cream, when her target finally showed.

She took a quick drink of her coffee, moaned as her throat suffered third-degree burns, then tossed the rest in a nearby garbage can and sank to a crouch behind a dusty Suburban while she staked out Rains. Walking beside him were two men, and one of them was the top science aide to the governor of California. Taylor didn't recognize the other man, but he walked as if he was important, too.

Taylor stayed out of sight as the trio passed, talking quietly. The two men shook hands with Rains, then left, and Rains continued walking. In no particular hurry, he stopped to buy a paper. Barely ten seconds later, three men got out of a parked car and moved up beside him. Rains looked startled and began gesturing a lot, which made the other men move even closer. Taylor sidled closer, too, straining to hear the conversation, but they were talking low and fast and she couldn't pick up any details.

As she continued to watch, Rains tried to pull away, but one of the men caught his arm, forcing him down the busy street. People passed, but no one seemed to notice Rains' fear or the tense group of men flanking him. Taylor followed, staying several cars back and out of sight. One of the men gripped Rains' shoulder, talking fast, while Rains bobbed his head, his face a sickly gray.

Suddenly Rains called out a name. Taylor saw that the governor's aide had appeared and was walking directly toward Rains, who forced a smile and pulled away from the angry men circling like sharks in chum-filled water. When the aide was a few feet away, the other men smoothed their ties, turned, and vanished down a side street.

Candace's boyfriend closed his eyes, going slack with relief. If he hadn't been such scum, Taylor might almost have felt sorry for him. Just what kind of trouble had he gotten into?

In a matter of seconds, the scientist seemed to regain his equilibrium, joking with the aide as they walked toward a nearby parking garage, where the aide got into his car. The instant he was gone, Rains pulled out a cell phone.

Taylor closed the distance between them, trying vainly to overhear the conversation. When Rains walked down the street, she stuck right behind him. Five minutes later she was still on him like glue when he walked into a convenience store, talking quietly on the phone. Taylor shoved on sunglasses, pulled a newspaper in front of her face, and followed at a cautious distance, determined to hear what he was saying.

The store was quiet as Rains walked down

the snack aisle, still speaking quietly on the phone. Taylor stopped near the checkout area where he wouldn't see her, and leaned on the counter. "I'm looking for imported chocolate and feminine hygiene products."

May as well kill two birds with one stone.

The Asian man at the counter looked at her blankly, and she repeated the question, ignoring the sound of the door opening and the big man in a torn sweatshirt who strode inside to buy coffee at a nearby machine.

Taylor tried another tack. "Do you speak English?"

The old clerk's expression didn't change.

The door opened again. A chunky man in a denim jacket entered, heading straight for the beer cooler.

Taylor sighed. Rains was at the back of the store now, staring at one of the shelves as if it had grown horns. He had a frozen look of fear on his face, and his cell phone was dangling from his fingers.

Behind Taylor the door opened again, and another man entered. Suddenly she realized it was unnaturally quiet in the store.

She leaned closer to the clerk. "Hygiene? Paper? You know — women's things."

When the clerk showed no sign of comprehension, Taylor gave up and ducked into the nearest aisle, intensely aware of the growing silence. The chunky man was standing beside Rains, who looked even paler than before.

52

Taylor inched back down the aisle. Coming after Rains was probably a bad idea. His nasty friends on the street had looked like people who played by their own rules.

She circled back to the checkout area, planning to head for the door.

But before she could pass, the clerk motioned to her and leaned forward.

"Help," he whispered, his lips barely moving. "You leave quick, miss. Then you call police fast."

Chapter Five

He watched her from across the street. She was hot and sweaty, her hair glowing gold in the sun, black leather hugging trim curves.

The woman had great legs, no mistake about it.

Jack Broussard couldn't help a flash of raw male speculation before his mind snapped back to work. He'd been tracking Taylor O'Toole under close surveillance since she'd left her apartment. During the jaunt, he'd noticed Rains' altercation with a group of strong-arm men whom he knew to be Argentinean nationals. Jack had called in a situation report and was assured that his intervention was unnecessary because federal agents were already monitoring the scene.

But to his infinite irritation, Taylor had calmly followed Rains inside the convenience store. The woman was stalking him, without a hint of a doubt.

Jack glanced at his watch, scowling. Taylor O'Toole was everything her file had said — brash, stubborn, and smart. The file had told him all about her twelve best-selling books, the sister near Carmel, and the coastal resort that had been in their family for three generations. He also knew her shoe size, food preferences, important friends, and shopping habits.

But files didn't tell you how a woman moved, how she smelled up close. Taylor O'Toole got five-star reviews on both counts.

Jack felt no guilt at this intrusion into a stranger's privacy. As a SEAL, he knew damned well that the U.S. government didn't set up surveillance on civilians without justifiable cause.

Not that Jack wanted this surveillance assignment. Demolition and bioweapons work was his real expertise, and he'd been in the middle of a training mission in the jungles of Puerto Rico when a chopper had landed, pulling him in for briefings about a top-level Navy scientist who'd gone missing with secret lab documents. Jack didn't know what his attractive neighbor had to do with the kidnapped scientist, but as a SEAL, he wasn't paid to know all the details.

Right now his mission was to stay on top of Taylor O'Toole 24/7. If she was contacted, he was to document all details. If her involvement raised any red flags, he had orders to take her into custody. If she came under attack, he was to yank her out of harm's way fast. Rumor had it that Taylor's brother-in-law had pulled more than a few strings to ensure her protection, and Sam McKade had plenty of friends in high places after his act of heroism the prior year.

But certain things continued to bother Jack, starting with Taylor's fall from the rocks the day before. The explanation she'd given didn't hold up. Jack knew that experienced climbers checked their gear and fixed protection obsessively, since their lives depended on it. Ropes didn't just pull free, and bolts didn't snap for no reason. Either her instructor had slipped up — or the equipment failure was no accident.

Most people would have put the fall down to simple carelessness, the kind of thing that could befall any amateur, but Jack Broussard wasn't most people and he never left questions unanswered. Being prepared had saved his skin a dozen times while walking point through a steamy Colombian jungle or prepping for a subzero dive in nightmare waters beneath a North Sea oil rig. Standing watch as part of a top-secret Navy operation involving experimental biological weapons and a missing Navy scientist meant you went by the book more than ever.

Jack scanned the store again. Through the big front window he caught a glimpse of Rains, standing near a stocky man in a denim jacket. A third man had moved to the front counter, where he appeared to be buying cigarettes.

A bus passed in a cloud of exhaust fumes, and a man in black spandex raced past on in-line skates. A few feet away a very pregnant woman crossed the sidewalk, pushing a collapsible shopping cart. Taylor O'Toole was still at the checkout counter, talking to the elderly clerk, and she looked up when the pregnant woman walked inside.

As the door opened, the big man in the sweatshirt turned and angled his elbow across the front counter, studying the two women intently.

Jack frowned, speaking quietly into the wireless mike at his collar. "Izzy, do you read me?"

His hidden earphone crackled. "Loud and clear. What have you got?"

"Standard surveillance so far. Taylor O'Toole seemed to be in pursuit of Harris Rains when he entered the Great Asia Convenience Store approximately two minutes ago. Over the last few minutes three males have entered, along with a pregnant female. The clerk, an elderly Asian male, is wearing a dark gray uniform. But something feels wrong."

"Say again?"

"Something's wrong, Izzy. Suddenly no one's moving in there." Jack watched the door, feeling another warning jab between his shoulders. "Check with the cops and see if a silent alarm has been reported at this location."

Jack rattled off the address impatiently, and his partner on this operation wasted no time on questions. Fast and thorough, Ishmael Teague was a man whose services didn't come cheap, but so far they'd been worth every cent.

Static hissed briefly. "No alarms called in."

"I still don't like it, Izzy. Everyone looks too tense."

"What about Rains?"

"He's standing near the front of the store

now, but he's not moving. Neither are the two women." Jack shifted carefully, looking for a better line of sight. "Wait a minute." He stiffened as someone flipped the front door sign. "They just closed up."

"Barely two o'clock," his partner said grimly.

"So I noticed." The SEAL looked around at the busy street. "Where are the Feds? They're supposed to be baby-sitting Rains."

"Last I heard, they were in a Brown Taurus across the street."

Jack took a quick look. "No Brown Taurus. No sign of any Feds either."

"I'll request an update on their status, but it may take some time."

"Something tells me we don't have a lot of time."

Inside the store, the stocky man moved closer to Rains. Jack stripped off his nylon jacket, reached under his shirt, and eased the safety off his Beretta. "I'm going in, Izzy."

"Copy."

Jack was crossing the street when his tiny earphone crackled again. "Broussard, S.F.P.D. just received a silent alarm from your location. Robbery in progress — I repeat, robbery in progress. The Feds appear to have left the scene, so you are clear to move. I repeat, you are clear to move. Keep your head down and your powder dry, buddy. That's an order."

Taylor stiffened as rubber soles squeaked behind her. She looked up to find the stranger in the torn sweatshirt moving closer.

"Leave?" He leaned across the counter, frowning. His sweatshirt was stained and his eyes burned with angry energy. "Why would this beautiful lady wish to leave so soon, old man?"

Taylor cleared her throat. "Because he doesn't have what I asked for." She tried to sound casual.

"And what did you ask for? Maybe I have it." The man's voice ran over her like greasy fingers.

Uh-oh. "Water," Taylor said coldly. "Pellegrino water, I mean. And good chocolate. The Belgian kind," she added. "Dark, no milk chocolate."

Once it was clear they didn't have what she wanted, she would head for the door. Then she could call 911 on her cell phone.

But the big man in the sweatshirt had other plans. He gave a little upward twitch of anger. "Water, old man. The lady wishes for the bubbly kind, yes?" As he spoke in accented English, he glanced toward the side of the store. The stocky man in the denim jacket had moved up behind Harris Rains.

"Water, we have." The clerk stood doggedly by the register. "But American kind only. And American chocolate only. Better the lady goes now."

Without warning, the man with the sweatshirt shoved the shopkeeper against the narrow counter. Taylor saw his hand slip into his front pocket.

Not a gun. People pulled guns in the books she wrote, in scenes summoned from her imagination — not in living, breathing reality, inches away from her. The worst crime she'd ever witnessed up close had been an old woman trying to stuff Manolo Blahnik heels into her purse during Nordstrom's annual summer sale.

Toto, I think we're a loooong way from Nordstrom's.

At the back of the store, the man in the denim jacket was speaking quietly to Rains, whose face was sheet-white.

Taylor watched in shock as the man caught Rains in a wrestling hold and shoved him against the wall, searching his jacket. Taylor didn't move, feeling the outline of her cell phone deep in her pocket as the man in the torn gray sweatshirt gestured angrily to his accomplice at the back of the store.

"Finish it now," he ordered. "We must go before they use the silent alarm." Sweatshirt glared at the elderly Asian, shoving him against the counter again. "Is that right, old man? Did you just hit the alarm button?"

"No alarms here." The old clerk shook his head forcefully.

"On second thought, American water will be fine," Taylor said quickly. "Any kind will do." As she spoke, she smiled and fingered the cell phone in her leather jacket. 911 calls via cell phone were automatically traced, and she prayed that the conversation would be audible through her pocket. "I'll just take two of these little bottles right here on the shelf and be on my way." She set two bottles of water firmly on the counter. *Business as usual. Ignore the psycho glaring at you.* "Can you ring that up, please?" she asked the frightened clerk. "I really need to get going."

Sweatshirt Man wasn't having any of it. He hit the water bottles, knocking them to the floor. "Nobody will go anywhere until we're done."

At the far side of the store, the man in denim gripped Rains' arms and searched his pants pockets.

Sweatshirt looked at Taylor. "A pretty lady like you should have whatever thing she wishes. I will help you, no?"

Taylor stiffened. "Oh, I wouldn't want to trouble you."

The odd, restless eyes scanned the store. There was intelligence behind the cold energy, Taylor realized. There was also a plan at work. "Maybe you like to take a trip."

Taylor took a quick step back, only to feel a display case behind her. "Stay away from me." When the man kept coming, she reacted without thinking, hurling her purse wildly toward him. But in her panic, the purse flew wide, sailing through the air and striking Harris

61

Rains on the shoulder.

Across the room, the pregnant woman fainted, knocking down a row of soda cans, which exploded across the floor. The man in the sweatshirt scowled, nodding at the third man in sunglasses, who pulled out a knife.

The old man shot forward. "*No*. Leave her alone."

Everyone's attention flashed to the clerk, who was brandishing a baseball bat which he had pulled from behind the counter. To prove his seriousness, he slammed the bat into a plastic candy display so that M&M's shot through the room.

Taylor noticed that the stocky man was on one knee, where he had stumbled on a soda can. Rains was now hiding behind a big plastic garbage can.

Sweatshirt lurched across the aisle and began grappling with the clerk, who struggled to hold on to the bat. But the older man's burst of energy was fading, as Sweatshirt yanked hard, straining for control.

Taylor decided now was the time for her to leave. Once outside, she could call for help. As she turned, the bat clattered to the floor behind her.

A hand gripped her elbow. "You come too. We can use some company on the long drive ahead of us."

Taylor felt her stomach dive to her toes. "No way."

Just then the front door swung open, its discreet electronic chime announcing a new visitor. The man in the sweatshirt jerked Taylor in front of him, cursing as a tall man stepped in off the street. The new arrival was wearing sweatpants and a University of California T-shirt, looking as if he'd just come from a hard jog.

When he turned, Taylor realized she was staring at Jack Broussard, her neighbor. She tried to get his eye, but he was nodding at the elderly clerk. "Afternoon."

The old man nodded slightly but said nothing.

Sweatshirt Man shifted, holding Taylor so his arm was hidden by a display of lotto tickets. "We're closed," he said harshly. "Inventory to finish. Didn't you see the sign?"

"No problem. Two beers and I'll be out of your hair. Only take a minute." Jack strolled along the racks filled with snack food, oblivious to the tension in the room as he tucked three bags of barbecued potato chips under his arm. After careful deliberation, he added a can of black bean dip.

Why didn't he look up? How could he not notice the tension in the store?

"Something fall down over here?" Jack shoved aside several cans, then frowned as he saw the pregnant woman, who was just coming awake on the floor. He crossed the aisle and bent down beside her. "Are you okay, ma'am?"

The woman looked around the room, then nodded tensely. "I'm — fine."

Jack helped her to her feet, then patted her hand. "Glad to hear it. You need some help?"

"N-no thanks. I'll be okay."

Jack stood up slowly. He seemed oblivious to the stares as he walked silently down the middle of the store. He swung open the big cooler door and studied the array of foreign and domestic beers.

In the glass, Taylor saw the whole room reflected in eerie detail. She wanted to scream a warning, but she didn't dare, because the man in the sweatshirt was right behind her now.

"Take your beer and then go," Sweatshirt ordered. "Hurry up."

Broussard nodded calmly, then pulled out a single can of beer. He tucked it under his arm with the bean dip. "No problem. Almost done."

Taylor tried to step away from her captor, but hard fingers gripped her arm, tightening painfully as sirens whined in the distance.

Jack turned, scratching his neck. "Anybody hear a siren?"

Outside the singsong drone grew louder. Taylor stumbled as Sweatshirt jerked her back along the checkout counter, and something metal jabbed her side.

"Start walking backward" came the low hiss. "Any noise and I kill you, understand?"

Taylor understood perfectly when the gun muzzle dug in harder.

As she walked, she cradled her cell phone, keeping the line open and praying that someone was listening.

Harris Rains was still crouched behind the garbage can as Jack strolled back up the center of the store with his purchases under one arm. His hands hung loosely at his sides, and some part of Taylor's mind noted that he seemed unnaturally calm.

Center of gravity low. Weight perfectly balanced.

A martial arts stance, Taylor realized. But even if she was right, what could one man do against three armed thugs?

At that moment Jack turned. His cool gray eyes raked her face. "Going somewhere?"

"To the ladies' room," Sweatshirt cut in. "This is not your concern."

Her neighbor shrugged, tossing the beer can casually between his hands. "Anything wrong, ma'am?"

Taylor swallowed as the gun muzzle dug into her ribs. "No, I'm fine. Just looking for the ladies' room, the way my friend said."

The beer can snapped back and forth in a lazy rhythm. "Sure. No problem."

Sweatshirt twitched angrily. "One more word and she will get a bullet." He pulled Taylor down the small corridor leading to the restrooms. As she rounded the corner, Taylor heard the sound of voices somewhere out on the sales floor, followed by cans crashing noisily.

"Aleksandr?" Sweatshirt yelled. "What is happening?"

There was no answer.

Cursing, Taylor's captor shoved her through the open door to the manager's office, just as Jack moved to the edge of the corridor with weapon leveled. He looked entirely cold, entirely professional.

Sweatshirt jerked Taylor in front of him, holding her as a shield while he slammed the office door and threw the lock with his free hand. "If he comes looking for you, he will soon be dead." He gave her an angry shove. "Up there. Now."

High on the wall a single window overlooked what Taylor guessed was the back parking lot. "But that's too high. I can't possibly —"

Her captor hooked a chair with one foot, dragging it closer. "Shut up."

Stall. "What if it's locked?"

His gun spat, and the window disappeared in a rain of gray glass. "So much for locked. Start climbing."

Taylor felt fury battle with fear. She wanted to kick him, but what would that accomplish, except getting herself shot by the gun pointed at her head?

She climbed onto the chair, trying to avoid scattered glass fragments, then stood up. Tugging off her leather jacket, she wedged it over the jagged shards in the window frame. If this misfit made her ruin her *favorite* Michael

Kors jacket, she was going to rip his eyes out.

Assuming she was still alive.

One leg went up. She winced as glass cut through her pants. Ignoring a trickle of blood, she worked her way up until she was poised in the window frame with a view of the parking lot below her.

A police cruiser was parked twenty feet away. An officer in black tactical gear crouched near the back tire, his rifle leveled on her chest.

Thinking desperately, Taylor signed *help*, using sign language she'd researched for her seventh book.

"What are you doing?" Sweatshirt was climbing up behind her.

"I — I cut my hand. It hurts."

He gripped her arm, balanced on the chair, where he was still too low to see through the window. "Is someone there?"

Taylor stared down at the rifle fixed on her chest. "Just a woman walking a dog."

"No police?"

"None that I can see." She shifted, blocking his view.

"Lie to me and you too will be dead. How far to the ground?"

Taylor leaned forward and winced. "At least eight feet. And I'm bleeding here." That was no lie either. She continued to sign *help*, then added *behind me*.

Sweatshirt's gun jabbed hard in the small of her back. "You will jump when I tell you. We go out together, you understand me?" He was on the chair now, trying to force her to one side. Any second he'd see the police car and the SWAT officer.

"But there's only cement and blacktop down there. I can't —"

"You will *jump* when I tell you." The gun jabbed her again, and her captor squeezed in closer. Taylor took a breath, preparing to jackknife her body forward before he could stop her.

Better to break both legs than take a bullet in the head.

Chapter Six

Jack listened tensely to the wail of approaching sirens.

Izzy should have passed on his description to the locals by now. Getting his head split open by one of Frisco's hotshot SWAT snipers would make a perfect lead-in on the evening news.

He secured his Beretta, making certain it rode snug at the small of his back, and blocked out the room mentally. One assailant out of sight in the manager's office, with female hostage in custody. Second assailant down, thanks to a swift blow to the back of the head. Third assailant struggling with Rains.

Jack circled silently until he was directly behind Rains and his captor. When he was in position, he threw the can of beer hard in the opposite direction, drawing instant fire. During the momentary distraction, Jack shot the weapon from the man's hand, then drove him to the floor, cutting off his curses with a blow to the neck.

Now for Taylor.

He closed in on the frightened clerk. "What's back there?"

"An office. The freight dock, too."

"Any windows in the office?"

The old man nodded. "One. Very high."

"Could a man fit through?"

The clerk frowned. "If the man is not so big, yes."

"What about two people?"

"Very difficult, I think. You will save the lady?"

"I'm going to save the lady," Jack said tensely.

He headed for the back corridor, running through shooting scenarios. Hostage situations were a SEAL specialty, and Jack had trained for every version. Usually he wasn't handling the situation from inside the perimeter, however.

The pregnant woman began to cry quietly as glass shattered somewhere at the back of the building. Something struck the back door.

Jack brushed a small pin on the collar of his worn gray shirt. "Izzy?"

"Copy."

"Two assailants unconscious on the sales floor. Harris Rains, the clerk, and a pregnant customer are frightened but unharmed. Taylor O'Toole is being held in the manager's office by one remaining assailant. Store is otherwise clear."

"Copy" came the low voice at his earphone. "Police are on the scene." Izzy's voice was clipped. "Stick with Rains."

"What about Taylor?"

Izzy took a sharp breath. "The Feds are tied up tracking Rains' South American pals. Your orders are to stick with Rains until they take over."

Beyond the window Jack heard the bark of a bullhorn, and then the front door burst open. A SWAT officer emerged with rifle leveled.

There was loud cursing from the back room, then the sound of a chair falling over. Crouched out of sight behind the coffee unit, Jack watched Rains throwing up into a big garbage bin.

Someone's purse was on the floor about four feet away from Rains' quaking body.

The nearest SWAT officer scowled and motioned to the medic who had followed him in. "Everyone flat on the floor," he ordered. "Do it now."

"S.F.P.D. is here, Izzy. I'm going after Taylor," Jack said quietly. "Tell the locals."

"They won't like it."

"To hell with liking it. Just tell them. And give our descriptions so they don't decide to take us out as perps."

"Copy."

Two more SWAT officers pounded through the front door, followed by a second medic. All were wearing masks.

Hell. Masks meant tear gas, and that meant his time was running out.

Jack crouch-walked silently toward the rear corridor. His weapon was level when he kicked open the door with his foot.

The man in the torn sweatshirt was balanced

on a chair against the far wall. In a blur of movement Jack swept the room and sighted on the base of the man's neck for a clear takedown. High up in the window, Taylor took advantage of the distraction and kicked free, dropping forward out of sight, and as she did her captor spun around, shooting wildly.

At the same moment the door to the rear loading area banged open, tear gas smoking through the corridor.

Only seconds left, Jack thought. Taylor's assailant scrambled toward the window, cursing and fighting his way up to the ledge, and Jack fired, putting three fast shots into the back of his head, ending the curses abruptly as the first cloud of tear gas billowed into the room.

"There is the man I tell you about. He is *big* hero. He save my life, destroy that piece of dog meat before he can kill all of us."

The old Asian man came tottering in pursuit of Jack. He had some bruises from his ordeal but was otherwise unharmed, smiling broadly as he pumped Jack's hand. "You Number-One Hero, mister. Should have medal for you."

"No medal needed. I just happened to be in the right place at the right time," Jack muttered.

The wrong place at the wrong time. The last thing he needed was publicity during a mission.

But the old man was having none of his modesty. "A hero," he insisted. "Why they treat you like criminal and ask so many questions?"

Jack shrugged. "The police have to do their job."

The clerk frowned at an officer in black body armor. "Is bad job. Stupid job." He looked around the crowded parking lot. "Where is lady in leather jacket? Is she okay?"

Luckily Jack hadn't received a major dose of tear gas, and he'd made it his business to find out Taylor's condition as soon as Izzy had checked in with the police. "A few cuts, but she'll be fine."

The old man picked up Taylor's purse and centered it on the counter. "Thanks to you."

Outside, the pregnant woman was being treated in an ambulance for stress. Rains was currently in the men's room vomiting his guts out while two Federal agents waited outside, looking grim. Whatever happened, Rains was no longer Jack's business but theirs.

A SWAT officer motioned to Jack, his face expressionless. "We'll need your weapon, sir."

"In my waistband. Center of the back. Beretta." Jack knew better than to go for the weapon himself. After guns were fired, police tended to get touchy.

The officer moved carefully behind Jack and removed the Beretta. "You came on the scene while the robbery was in progress?"

Jack nodded.

"I suppose you have a permit to carry this." The officer looked like he was trying to read something in Jack's face.

But Jack made sure there was nothing to read. "In my wallet. Back pocket."

The elderly clerk was listening to every word. "What you question *him* for? I have three guns — ask for *my* papers. Go on, arrest me first."

The SWAT officer paid no attention, calmly flipping open Jack's wallet and scanning the ID. "Jack Broussard. Civilian consultant, stationed at Monterey."

Jack nodded. The ID was fiction, but damned good fiction. "You can contact my superior for confirmation, sir." Jack rattled off the nonsecure mission HQ number and a contact name.

"You took down three men in less than three minutes, Mr. Broussard. You got off three head shots in a tear-gas situation, with limited control and visibility." The officer's eyes held curiosity and just a hint of respect.

"I do some target shooting on occasion." Jack didn't mention that he'd gone hunting in far worse conditions. He knew his window of exposure for the tear gas, and there had been time to spare before he was incapacitated.

"We'll need to take a statement, Mr. Broussard. If you'll follow me, we can handle that right now."

Jack nodded, noticing that the officer hadn't given him back his wallet. Probably a deeper background check was already in the works. No doubt about it, he was going to have his ass chewed royally for drawing all this attention.

But what choice had there been? Both Rains and Taylor had been threatened, and he had been the only man on the scene.

The clerk followed the officer outside, waving angrily. "Why you treat him like criminal?" His face was turning red. "This man save all our lives, then try to save life of lady hostage. You give him medal, that's what." He glared at the other SWAT officers near their squad car. "He like John Wayne. Like Bruce Wayne. Wayne Gretzky, too. You not treat *them* this way."

"Look, it's no problem," Jack said gruffly. "This is probably routine procedure." Jack thought of the man he'd killed. The death didn't register now, but it would soon. And sooner or later he would face the cold, painful examination of whether he could have done anything faster or smarter to avoid that death. The questions would start in his head and in his gut, then continue at a mission-review session.

Hindsight could be a stern teacher.

The clerk shook his head. "Forget routine. You deserve medal. Big medal for big American hero."

Jack flushed as the old man pumped his hand.

Through it all, the police officer waited calmly. "Let's step away for a moment, shall we, Mr. Broussard?"

Crossing the parking lot, they passed a man

in coveralls lying on the ground, writhing in pain. "Who's that?"

The officer's mouth twitched. "That's the genius who was supposed to drive the getaway car."

"What happened to him?"

"Lady in the leather jacket happened. She was signing for help when she came through the window and she saw him waiting behind the Dumpsters, where the officer on the scene couldn't see him. She hit the ground, rolled, and sucker-punched him from behind with a brick, then we took him down without a single shot fired." The officer smiled faintly. "Must hurt like hell," he added. "She called 911 on the cell phone in her pocket, too. Damned interesting lady."

Jack found himself smiling for the first time that afternoon. "I'd say *she* deserves the medal."

When he looked up, Taylor was standing by a squad car, laughing with four officers. Even though her knee was cut, her pants were torn, and her face was bruised, she was still a knockout.

Jack took his time enjoying those killer legs in tight black pants. Just watching her made the air feel supercharged and full of life. How could the woman look like a million dollars after falling through a window? And when had she gotten so comfortable with the S.F.P.D. SWAT team?

Jack had the sudden, uncomfortable suspicion that there was more to Taylor O'Toole then he'd first thought. "What happened to her jacket?" he asked the officer beside him.

"Tore it on all that glass in the window."

Not that it mattered. With Taylor O'Toole's legs, she'd look damned good in anything.

Or in nothing.

Whooah, sailor.

She looked up and waved when he neared the squad car. "Hey, Jack. I —" She took a sharp breath. "Just — thank you."

"No problem."

She shoved a mass of bright hair off her face. "Wait. I need to talk to you."

"I'm kind of rushed right now." Jack gestured to the officer beside him. "I need to answer some questions." Not to mention that any minute the reporters would arrive, and he definitely didn't want to be around for the media circus that followed.

"But how can I thank you? You took on that creep alone. If not for you —"

He tried to ignore the emotion in her voice. "You did your own hostage recovery, Ms. O'Toole. There's no need to thank me." He glanced at the officer, who was clearly impatient. "I think I need to go now."

Taylor frowned at the officer beside Jack. "Are you arresting this man?"

"No, ma'am. Just completing our report, the way he said."

"You'd better *not* arrest him. Mr. Broussard

saved my life, and I want that on the record. No matter what he says, he saved my life." Her voice broke. "Whatever force he used in there was absolutely necessary."

Jack felt something work at his chest as he listened to her angry, impassioned speech to the police officer. Taylor didn't realize that he was only doing the hard, dirty job he was trained to do, and Jack couldn't enlighten her.

She strode closer, blocking their way. "I'm prepared to offer a statement if necessary."

"I'll be sure to note your observations." The officer nodded at Jack, and they resumed walking.

"You'd better," Taylor called. "Otherwise, I'll be calling the mayor tonight. The newspapers, too." Jack could feel her eyes burning on his back as they passed Harris Rains, who was giving a wild and entirely fictional account of his "ordeal" to a female officer.

"Hey, Broussard. I'm going to thank you somehow," Taylor called loudly.

Jack raised a hand and gave a two-finger wave, while the officer beside him smiled. "Now that might be seriously worth seeing."

Jack was pretty sure it might be worth seeing, too.

Ten minutes later Taylor was sitting in the back of a cruiser with an attractive female police lieutenant, repeating that she was fine and didn't need to go to the hospital.

But her hands were trembling, and both of them knew she wasn't as cool as she seemed, which only made Taylor more tense.

"The clerk told us this was yours." The lieutenant held out Taylor's purse.

"It's mine. I threw it at one of those men." Taylor gripped the purse tensely, feeling sick.

"Look, you've been through a life-threatening experience, Ms. O'Toole. You also took quite a fall. You should be seen by a doctor."

"I just want to go home." A few feet away, two medics were lifting a body bag. Taylor swallowed hard and looked away. "Did you see the store? Those bodies?" She shook her head. "We all could have died. I've seen it in my mind a hundred times. I've written hostage scenes without a second thought."

"You're a writer, Ms. O'Toole?"

Taylor nodded and ran a hand through her hair. "*The Forever Code*. Someone got tossed off a roof in that one. But I didn't get it right at all. I never knew how it feels from the inside." *Or how it hurts.*

"It's not neat and pretty." The officer frowned. "Sometimes the crimes we see don't even make sense. Books are supposed to make sense, but life often doesn't, I'm afraid, and the random crimes can be the hardest to accept. Now about that medical attention?"

But Taylor wasn't really listening. She was remembering how Jack had looked when he'd come after her, his eyes calm and cold.

What a story, she thought.

What a man.

Across the parking lot, Harris Rains was talking with a perky reporter who anchored the local evening news. Rains was describing how he'd helped subdue one of the wounded suspects while Jack was out in the back corridor.

Like hell he had. Rains had been petrified when she'd last seen him. The man couldn't have subdued a hamster. "Rains is lying," she said. "He did nothing."

The policewoman smiled grimly, as if this was no surprise. "In the heat of the moment, people often get carried away with their stories."

"Jack Broussard saved those people. He saved me, too. If he hadn't come after me, I wouldn't have escaped." Taylor took an angry breath, feeling sick as she listened to Rains' outpouring of lies.

"We'll check it out, Ms. O'Toole. Now I suggest that —"

"Forget about the hospital."

"I strongly recommend —"

"Thank you for your help, Lieutenant." Taylor didn't look back, didn't watch the black body bag being loaded into the ambulance.

She'd seen enough blood and death for one day. Suddenly, being alive was a very precious thing indeed.

Chapter Seven

The phone was ringing when Taylor opened her front door. *What now?*

She grabbed the receiver, smiling when she heard her brother-in-law's deep voice. "Taylor, we just saw you on the news. Annie's approaching hysteria. What's going on up there?"

"I'm fine, Sam. It's all over."

He didn't sound at all convinced. "You sure about that? Annie's got the car packed. She's ready to leave."

"Keep her there." Taylor frowned. "She's okay, isn't she? I mean — with the baby and everything?"

The truth was, Taylor still wasn't used to her baby sister being happily married and very pregnant. A longtime workaholic, Annie O'Toole had managed their family's resort on the rugged California coast near Carmel for years. Always a workaholic perfectionist, she was superb at nurturing strangers but slow to take time for herself.

A hunky Navy SEAL named Sam McKade had changed all that.

Another woman might have succumbed to serious jealousy. But when Taylor saw the two together, hopelessly in love despite Sam's frequent absences, Taylor knew she couldn't begrudge them one second of happiness. Especially since she was one of the few people who knew that the two of them had nearly died several months before at the hands of a deranged killer.

"Here she is, Taylor." Taylor heard muttered voices as the phone changed hands.

"Taylor, what's happening?"

"Don't worry, Annie. I'm fine."

"Don't *worry?*" Her sister's voice spiked. "You're abducted at gunpoint, thrown from a window, nearly shot — and you tell me *not to worry?* Are we sisters or aren't we?"

Taylor rubbed her shoulder, which was still aching from her fall. "Of course we are. I meant that you should think about the baby, not me. Go pamper yourself with a salt-glow rub." She smiled wickedly. "Better yet, have that sexy man with the cute butt who called me give you a long, steamy massage."

Annie chuckled. "Sam, Taylor says you've got a cute butt. How does she know *that?*"

Taylor heard Sam bend close to the receiver. "Tell Taylor that her imagination is just as fertile as ever."

"Very diplomatic. I always said your husband would go far, Annie. I can see him heading the Joint Chiefs in a few years."

"Why stop there?" her sister said proudly. "I can see him as president."

Taylor heard Sam's strangled protest. "You couldn't say anything that would frighten him more, Annie. I think you two definitely need to go relax in the hot tub. I remember reading somewhere that pregnant women have heightened libidos."

"No more hot tub visits until after the baby's born. No more long runs on the beach, either," Annie added grumpily. "Sam and that doctor he found are driving me nuts. Next thing you know, they'll tell me I can't work."

Sam muttered something in the background that made Annie sniff.

"They only want you to take it easy. You push things too hard." Taylor felt a pang of guilt. For the last few years since their parents' deaths, she had been only too glad to leave the day-to-day resort operations to Annie. "Look, do you want me to come down and fill in for several weeks while you two take a vacation? If you want me, I'll be there."

"You'd do that? With a book in the works?"

Taylor took a deep breath, recalling how much she hated handing out spa recipes and aromatherapy wraps to the well-heeled clientele of Summerwind Resort. "If you need me, I'll come. Of course, it *may* require heavy animal tranquilizers to get me in the door, but I'll do whatever it takes to help you. Just say the word."

"Idiot. You can forget the animal tranquilizers." Annie's voice softened. "I'll manage. I've got a great staff — and *they* don't need tranquilizers to greet our clients. But thanks anyway." She sighed. "I don't even mind cutting back to half-days now. My back hurts sometimes, and it's a relief to get off my feet."

Now it was Taylor's turn to imagine the worst. "What do you mean?" She gripped the phone. "When did your back start hurting? Is something wrong? Is the baby —"

Annie gave a soft laugh. "The baby is fine. We had an ultrasound last week, and everything's just where it's supposed to be." She sighed. "Ignore me, please. I'm an irritable old cow these days. I *hate* being a blimp and I hate not being able to wear anything that isn't Lycra or a size 16 wide. I hate not being able to run, and I know it's wrong, since I have everything in the world to be thankful for — Sam, you, my work. Oh, hell." She made a watery sound that wrenched Taylor's heart. "Pay no attention. It's just the hormones at work."

"Take some time off." Taylor said quietly. "Rest and enjoy the attention. I can't imagine a more beautiful, glowing mother-to-be."

"You really *do* have a fabulous imagination." Annie cleared her throat. "Except for my bouts of temporary insanity, I'm fine, Taylor. Sam's been wonderful. The whole staff has been great. Even Izzy called last week."

Taylor grinned at the thought of the big, hunky Denzel Washington look-alike who had worked on a recent government mission with Annie's husband. "How's our electronics genius doing?"

"You know Izzy, off on something hush-hush and gravely important. But stop trying to distract me. You're sure you weren't hurt in that robbery?"

"All my fingers and toes are in working order, I promise." They hurt, but they worked, Taylor thought.

"Did you see a doctor?"

"Of course," she lied. "Now go rest, the way Sam and your doctor have been telling you. I want to be an aunt before I'm too senile to enjoy the experience." Taylor smiled. "By the way, watch out for runaway golf carts."

"They only go runaway when *you're* driving them."

Taylor was laughing when her eyes fell on the big gray envelope forgotten on her desk. The sight was like cold water tossed in her face. Gone was the easy teasing, the gentle rivalry. Taylor knew that Annie had no inkling of the revelations contained in that envelope, and Taylor wasn't sure she'd ever tell her. Meanwhile, the awareness of her parents' lie haunted Taylor, driving a subtle wedge between her and the sister she adored. Fair or not, the fragile, wounded part of Taylor's mind kept asking why *Annie* couldn't have been the adopted one. *Why me?*

And the question sickened her.

She leaned against the wall, hit by the same churning emotions that came hourly since she'd found out the truth about her birth.

"Hey — are you sure you're okay?"

Taylor took a jerky breath. "Sure, I — I'm strong as a horse, you know that." As she spoke, the phone clattered to the floor. One minute her fingers worked, the next minute they simply gave way.

"That does it," Annie snapped when Taylor recovered the receiver. "We're leaving this second."

"No." Taylor couldn't see her sister now. She'd never be able to hide her emotions. "Look, I'll admit it. I'm behind on my writing and it's got me all worked up. I love you both to death, but if you appear on my doorstep while I'm trying to get caught up, I'll just let the bell go on ringing."

Taylor held her breath, hoping Annie bought the story.

"You know, if you weren't my sister, I'd probably hate you for a comment like that."

Taylor closed her eyes. They *weren't* sisters by blood. With the news of her birth, that part of her identity had shifted, too. Until Taylor came to grips with how much had changed — and how much she would allow it to change *her* — seeing Annie was impossible.

With tears in her eyes, she picked up a smiling photo of Annie and her handsome SEAL husband at their wedding. Annie looked radiant and Sam looked exactly like the hero he was. Taylor remembered the bumpy times with Annie, their years of competition as teenagers followed by years of drifting apart. Annie had been the rock, and Taylor had been the screwup, and each had secretly envied the other. All that had ended one night when Taylor and Annie had gotten seriously drunk, then dredged up the past. It hadn't helped that Taylor had crashed a golf cart in the process, but at least the outcome had been good. For the first time in years, the two sisters had really talked about holding back, keeping grudges, and all their secret, deepest hurts.

Since then, they had never been closer. It was almost as if Taylor had been given a new sister — and the chance to correct some of the mistakes she had made when young and irresponsible. But the big envelope on her desk challenged that closeness.

Taylor shoved down her hurt, fully aware that Annie wasn't to blame for the recent revelations. In fact, her sister would be devastated by the news, primarily out of concern for Taylor. That was one of the reasons Taylor was determined to keep the details secret until she could sort through her feelings of loss and betrayal. She knew that Annie, softhearted and gentle, would instantly want to comfort her and pull her close to stanch the pain.

For Taylor, comfort would be too close to pity, and pity was the last thing she wanted.

So she put a smile on her face and laughter in her voice, even as tears coasted down her cheeks. "Get off the phone, Annie. Go give that man with a cute butt a kiss and let me work."

She hung up while her sister was still laughing. For long moments she stood by the desk, pulling herself together piece by piece, memory by memory. She'd make her choice soon, and then she'd decide what to tell her sister. Sam would help her make that decision.

Meanwhile, one demon at a time.

She stripped off her ruined clothes and padded into her bedroom, pulling on her oldest sweatpants. Eating was out. Her stomach was still too queasy for anything solid. Nursing a cup of tea, she flipped on the evening news, only to feel her nausea grow worse.

Every channel focused on the afternoon's robbery, featuring interviews with the angry store clerk and the shaken woman in the last month of pregnancy. Next came an outraged Harris Rains demanding to know why law-abiding citizens couldn't be safe on the streets of San Francisco. The way Rains told it, he had risked his life by shielding the pregnant woman and attempting to grapple with one of the wounded assailants, which was almost funny considering that when Taylor had seen him last, he'd been rigid with terror.

If anyone had saved those customers, it was Jack Broussard.

So why hadn't he taken any credit? The man deserved a medal, but no one on television had even mentioned his name. Meanwhile, Rains was setting himself up to be *Time*'s next Man of the Year.

When her own picture appeared, pale and frightened, Taylor switched off the television. She was suddenly aware that her apartment seemed too big and too quiet. She crossed to the big picture window, watching traffic flow east in a noisy rush. As Taylor stared at the blur of cars, buses, and cabs, she found herself remembering the reassurance in Jack's eyes as he'd come after her. For some reason, it didn't matter that he was a stranger. She'd felt safer with him than any man she knew.

She closed her eyes, wanting to feel his strong arms around her in the silence of her lonely apartment.

Not to be touched sexually, but held quietly, calmly, while she fought her way through this suffocating fear.

Which was crazy, considering she barely knew the man.

So she'd forget about Mr. Jack Broussard with the sexy smile and get back to work. He probably wasn't even home. There were no sounds next door, no wonderful cooking smells. No doubt he'd gone to the nearest bar to get smashed with friends after his ordeal. Getting smashed sounded like a good idea to her, but for some reason Taylor couldn't move, a soft, desperate sob spilling from her throat.

She felt stripped and violated, marked by a stranger's casual violence. No matter what she did, the violation wouldn't go away. She rubbed her face with her sleeve, but the tears didn't stop. As she stared out her window, she kept seeing tear gas, blood, and a black body bag.

Taylor closed her eyes and sank into a chair by the window, wondering when she would start to feel normal again. She was pretty sure it wouldn't be anytime soon.

Another set of demons to add to her collection.

When the doorbell rang, she ignored it.

Outside in the hallway, Jack pushed Taylor's buzzer again. Maybe she was in the shower or talking on the phone. Maybe she was listening to music with her headphones on. He knew she was home because the doorman had told him she'd come in and hadn't gone out.

He'd heard her door open, followed by the conversation he'd picked up with her sister, including Sam McKade's tense questions.

Jack frowned. Why didn't she answer his ring?

He pressed an ear to the door, heard nothing, and rang again, feeling uneasy. Somewhere, a chair fell over.

This time Jack knocked on the door hard. "Taylor, are you okay? It's Jack. I need to talk with you."

He heard a brushing sound that might have been bare feet, and then the door opened. She'd been crying — face pale, eyes puffy.

"Sorry to bother you."

She rubbed her cheek awkwardly with one sleeve. "No problem."

"You okay?"

She rubbed a bare foot against her calf and didn't meet his eyes. "Why wouldn't I be?"

She was wearing old navy sweatpants and a blue T-shirt just tight enough to show the smooth curve of her breasts. Puffy eyes or not, she had the kind of glow that didn't come from rouge or any of the things that most women felt they needed to be beautiful.

Jack wanted to pull her into his arms. He realized suddenly that he wanted to make love to her for seven or eight hours, until all the pain left her face. In fact, the urge was so strong it shocked him.

"You're sure that you're okay?"

Taylor looked down at her locked fingers. "Of course."

"I'm glad to hear it." Did she think he was a *complete* fool? He propped one hand against the wall. "In that case, I need to borrow some sugar."

She blinked. "Sugar?"

He held out an empty measuring cup. "That's right. I'm all out."

Taylor's mouth curved in the hint of a smile. "Is this one of your less inventive lines, Mr. Broussard?"

"Call me Jack. And it's no line. Scout's honor."

"Somehow I can't picture you as a Boy Scout."

"Now that's downright cruel. At last count, I had forty-three merit badges." He smiled lazily. "You want to hear the oath?"

"Forget the oath. Come on, I'll get you some sugar." She gave a shaky laugh. "It's the least I can do after — well, everything." She turned, wiping her face surreptitiously. "Ignore my raccoon eyes."

"Your eyes look fine." He waited until she looked at him. "And you don't owe me anything, Taylor. Let's get that straight." There was an edge to his voice that surprised him.

After a long time she nodded. "Okay. I don't owe you." She motioned him inside, opened a drawer, and began filling his cup with sugar. "Tell me why you didn't take credit for saving those people."

Jack shrugged. "Doing the thing is what counts — not talking about it afterward."

"Most men I know would be getting drunk right now — and bragging at the top of their lungs."

Jack didn't answer.

"Damn it, you're so calm, so controlled. Who *are* you?"

"Just a friend."

She bent over suddenly, her body tense. "Give me a minute here."

Jack saw her shiver. "Take all the time you need. It's normal to feel shaky after a thing like this."

Sugar spilled, dusting the counter. "I'll be fine. I can take the heat." Her hand trembled and sugar drifted down onto the wooden floor.

Very gently Jack pulled the cup out of her hand and turned her around to face him. "No one said you couldn't. But sometimes it's better if you don't have to take the heat alone."

She didn't move. "I *never* do this."

"Spill sugar?"

"No, fall apart. Cry at shadows. I can't stop seeing the body bag." She took a jerky breath. "The blood at the back of the store."

Blood wasn't something you forgot easily, Jack thought.

"Doesn't it bother you?" Her eyes were dark, like North Sea breakers he'd seen churning near the big oil rigs in a winter squall. They weren't beautiful, but they were unforgettable.

"Yeah, it bothers me. I shot a man a few hours ago, and his face is the last thing I'll see tonight. Probably the first thing I'll see when I wake up. Right now, all I want to do is go home, strip, and wash until I start feeling clean again." His voice was harsh, and he shook his head. "Yes, it bothers me. But letting him kill an innocent man or woman would bother me a hell of a lot more." He stared at the sugar scattered over the counter. "Tonight, that old clerk is going home to his family. He's going to kiss his wife and hug his grandkids and be glad to be alive. That's good enough for me, Taylor. It should be good enough for you, too."

"It should be." She closed her eyes. "I'm having some trouble with this." She pressed her hands flat against the sugar-covered counter. "My apartment feels too quiet. I can still feel his hands on my throat when he shoved me down that corridor. I expect to turn around and see him here, waiting for me."

"You want me to look in the other room?"

She stared at him as if checking to see if this was a bad attempt at humor, but Jack's face was serious.

"No, I know he's not here. At least the logical part of my mind knows."

"Look, I'd be happy to walk through with you."

Shuddering, she put one hand out to steady herself. Somehow her hand found its way to his chest. It seemed an eternity that she stared at him, then slowly pulled away. "I'm sorry," she said softly. "You're being very nice."

"No need to be sorry. Lean away."

She pulled away slowly. "I'm not a leaner."

Jack had already figured out that much about her. From her file he knew Taylor O'Toole valued her independence, even if it occasionally got her into trouble. "Everybody leans sometime."

"I can't imagine you leaning." Her eyes roamed his face. "Your cheek's cut."

"It's nothing."

Taylor swallowed. "Nothing? I saw the store. I heard the shots." Her voice fell. "I've seen it in my mind dozens of times. I've written the scene without blinking an eye. But I've never . . . lived it. I — I owe you a lot."

He started to protest, but she cut him off. "*I do.* We both know that. At the time it was a blur, but now things are clearing. I can hear his voice and feel him twitch behind me. He smelled like old beer and garlic." She ran a hand through her hair, trembling. "I don't think I can ever smell garlic again without re-membering."

"Maybe not now, but you'll forget. That's the way we're made." Jack had a hard time staying still, keeping his distance. He reminded himself that this was a mission and she was his assign-ment.

It almost worked.

"I hope you're right." Her hand shook. "Oh, no. I think I'm going to —"

She clutched her stomach, and Jack turned her gently, bracing her head over the sink, sup-porting her shoulders with one arm. He went on holding her that way while she retched vio-lently.

Chapter Eight

Jack's hands tightened. "Go on and let it out."

"Sick," she rasped, between hacking breaths.

"Only normal." Jack steadied her with one hand at her shoulders while she spilled out her guts.

When the spasms finally stopped, her legs simply gave way, and he caught her, bracing her against his chest. "Deep breaths. Come on now."

Taylor shuddered. "Why do I keep seeing him? Seeing the blood?"

"It's called being alive. You see it until it starts making some kind of sense."

"There isn't any sense. It was violence — random and brutal."

That kind was the worst, Jack knew. You wondered if you could have done anything different to change the outcome. The answer was usually no.

He brushed a hand over her hair. "I'm sorry it happened, Taylor. I'm sorry you're hurting."

"I don't want to remember."

He didn't bother lying, telling her she'd forget. The hard truth was that she wouldn't.

The violence would always be with her, every time she went into a crowded store or looked down a dark street.

"So what do I do?"

Instead of empty promises, he focused on practical advice. "Take a deep breath."

"I can't. It makes me dizzy."

"Do it anyway."

He felt her body shift. She dragged in air and her breasts brushed his chest. He ignored the instant swell of heat stirred by that brief touch.

"Any better?"

"Some," she said weakly. "I'll probably be fine in a minute. You can let me go. I'm sure you've got places to go, people to see. Women to seduce."

He smiled at her. "I'm in no particular rush."

"I didn't mean — about that last part. About the women." She cleared her throat. "Who you seduce is none of my business."

He kept a straight face. "Damned right."

"I mean, I hardly know you."

"Not much," he agreed.

"Two strangers." She took a breath. "They met over lasagna." She made a watery sound that might have been a step toward a laugh. "Of course, right now one of them looks like an anemic raccoon. Clothes torn. Hair a wreck. Tossing her cookies. How much would it take for you to forget this ever happened?"

Jack frowned and thought about pulling her closer. Darker images came to mind as he brushed his hand lightly over her cheek.

"What's to forget?" He eased away, suddenly aware of grave temptation. "Your body's simply reacting to the shock, trying to force it out of your system."

She looked up, frowning. "So this is a good thing, being gut-wrenchingly sick in front of a complete stranger who happens to be sexy as hell?"

"Absolutely." His brow rose. "Sexy as hell?"

She flushed. "Definitely hot. So how did you get to be so smart, Mr. Jack Broussard?"

Once again she caught him by surprise. Since the urge to pull her close was greater than ever, he did exactly the opposite, stepping back, forcing a mental distance. But their eyes held, framing silent questions, measuring subtle possibilities. Strangers — but not quite strangers.

She wouldn't hide her emotions, not this woman. She'd bite him one minute and screw his brains out the next. She'd be absolutely unforgettable, in bed and out of it.

And any man would be lucky to have her for even one night.

Bed?

Jack gave himself a mental shake.

"Now that you're done being sick, I should get moving." He reached for his cup. "Thanks for the sugar."

Watching her reaction was fascinating. He could see her take a breath, compose herself, working hard at control. "I dropped most of it."

Her cheeks were still flushed, and her voice was husky.

Not that Jack was about to read anything into her reaction. Being touched by violence shook people up and made them react unpredictably. He wouldn't take advantage of that vulnerability — especially not with a mission in progress. Besides, he liked soft, easygoing women who didn't argue so much. Getting involved with Taylor O'Toole would be like getting tossed naked from a chopper with no parachute.

"Hey, don't let me keep you from your work. Studs and planks." She carefully brushed the spilled sugar into the garbage. Only when that was done did she turn, and by then her face was neutral. "I guess I should thank you for the counseling session. But who the heck are you? Don't tell me you're a simple, ordinary carpenter or I might throw up again."

"I'm a great carpenter," Jack protested.

"You may be, but it's not who you are — or what you really do. Are you an undercover cop? CIA?"

Hell. These were the questions he'd hoped to avoid. "I'm not a Fed."

"A cop?"

He shook his head. "I'm a P.I., okay? As it happens, Harris Rains' wife is putting together a file as part of her divorce proceedings. She hired me to fill in some of the details."

She stopped brushing the sugar. "You appeared today because you were following Rains?"

"Afraid so. But that's got to remain absolutely confidential or it will blow my case."

"He deserves to lose his shirt. The man gives protozoa a bad name."

"What makes you say that?"

She started to answer, then shrugged. "Let's just say I have my reasons."

So she wasn't going to tell him about the climbing bolt that pulled free or the funeral wreath she'd received in a box. Clearly, trust didn't come easy to Taylor O'Toole. He wondered briefly what had hurt her, making her lose her trust. "Want to share those reasons?"

"Not particularly. So what kind of investigation work do you handle?"

"The usual mix. Runaways, shoplifting rings, cheating spouses. Amazing, but there are just as many women to follow as men these days. It appears that infidelity has become an equal opportunity vice. I also have an occasional adoption case."

Taylor looked down, one hand tensed on the counter. "I don't understand. Why would someone dump a baby, then want to know what happened ten years later?"

"Lives change. People change their minds."

"Maybe." She crossed her arms, staring at a bar of sunlight that fell on a corner of her desk. "Not that I know anything about the subject."

Neither of them moved. The apartment was

very quiet, and Jack was uncomfortably aware of her T-shirt hugging the curves of what were clearly very nice breasts.

Not that he was ranking them.

Not that he'd even meant to look closely.

Hell.

"Uh, I'd better —"

"Well, maybe you should —"

They spoke at the same moment, then stopped, suddenly awkward. Jack started for the door, sugar in hand. Outside in the hall, the elevator chimed. Slippers crossed the tile floor, and Taylor's doorbell rang in three quick bursts.

"Taylor, is that you? Are you all right?"

"That's Mrs. Pulaski, my oldest neighbor." Taylor ran a hand through her hair. "Her husband died last year and she worries about people." She moved past Jack to the door. Once again, he had the sense she was reining in deep emotions, constructing a layer of composure she didn't really feel.

When Taylor opened the door, a tiny woman with snapping eyes and ramrod-straight posture was pacing outside. She was dressed in a black exercise leotard and what, to Jack's uneducated eye, looked like about twelve layers of parrot feathers at her neck. She immediately gripped Taylor in a tight hug. "You must be frightened to death."

"I'm fine, Bella. Just a little shaky."

"I saw it on the news. I was so worried about

you." She studied Taylor anxiously. "Maybe you should go take a nice long bath. I've got a bottle of vodka in case you'd like to get drunk." She smiled at Jack. "Maybe your friend wants to join you."

Taylor smiled wanly. "I doubt that alcohol would agree with me right now."

"Sick, were you? Maybe tomorrow, then." Taylor's neighbor glanced up at Jack, her eyes narrowed. "I don't believe I've met your friend."

"This is Mr. Broussard. He was there, too."

Bella Pulaski shook Jack's hand, her grip surprisingly hard. "Are you the one that shot Taylor's kidnapper?"

Jack nodded.

"What do you carry?"

He blinked. "Excuse me?"

"For firepower. I favor a Smith and Wesson myself, but my late husband always swore by his Beretta. I keep telling Taylor she should get a gun for safety, with her being a young, pretty woman. Single, you know, out at night doing research in all kinds of seedy places. This city's not what it used to be," she said pensively. "Well, young man, I hope they give you a medal."

"No need for that, ma'am. I only did what anyone would do."

The elderly woman snorted. "Most men would have run in the opposite direction. No guts, not like my Ben." She continued to study

Jack. "Are you in the military? I can usually spot the carriage since my grandson just finished at Camp Pendleton. A jarhead," she added proudly.

"A what?" Taylor asked.

"Marine. A true credit to his family," Bella said crisply. "Are you in the Marines, Mr. Broussard?"

"I'm not a Marine, ma'am." *No lie there.*

"Too bad. Taylor could use someone to keep her safe. Can you imagine being pushed from a window by that lunatic? Oh, dear, she's looking white again. I think she's about to —"

As Mrs. Pulaski spoke, Taylor spun around and disappeared into the bathroom.

Bella shook her head. "She's a writer, you know. Creative — doesn't sleep well. I hear her at night, pacing the floor. My apartment's one floor down. Not that I listen," she added quickly.

"Of course not."

She leaned toward Jack, her voice low. "Taylor doesn't see many men. Mainly she works. Wonderful stories with great characters, but no time for herself. Oh, she goes climbing on occasion — and look what happens. The last time she went on a date, she complained for a week. And there's no one special," she added helpfully. "None of them stay overnight."

As Taylor went on making sounds of distress in the bathroom, Bella sized up Jack slowly.

"It's about time she had a real man in her life." She gave him another sharp look. "Navy?"

Jack sidestepped the question. "I think she's about done in there."

"She shouldn't be alone right now."

"No, she shouldn't," Jack agreed. "But I'd have to work to convince her of that."

Just then Taylor appeared, her face whiter than ever. "Are you two talking about me?"

"I thought Mr. Broussard should know the lay of the land."

Taylor ran a hand across her face. "I think he knows the lay of the land better than we ever will. He has that kind of face."

"Exactly what I thought." The tiny woman frowned at Jack. "Air Force?"

"Not a chance," Jack said with complete candor. He held out a crumpled tissue to Taylor. "I'd love to stay and talk, but I think Taylor needs some rest. She should go to bed before another bout starts."

"You think there'll be more?" Taylor asked weakly.

"It's a definite possibility." He nodded politely at Bella Pulaski. "Don't worry, I'll keep an eye on her."

"I'll hold you to that." The tiny woman left in a flurry of quivering feathers.

Taylor was still pale when Jack closed the door, but her voice was firm. "I'll be fine. You really don't need to stick around."

"No trouble. Where's your bedroom?"

She crossed her arms. Something stirred between them in the silence. "I'm not sure I want to answer that."

"Stop glaring at me. This is strictly one neighbor helping another. Let's go."

"You like giving orders, don't you?"

"Only when they're necessary." Before she could argue further, he headed down the hall past a sunny room lined with bookshelves and a huge picture of cliffs above a windswept beach. In the last room, soft curtains framed a view of city hills and distant water. Her bed was near the window, buried beneath pillows in a dozen shades of blue.

Jack turned down the comforter. "Hit the sack, O'Toole."

"More orders?" Taylor sighed and sat down. She took a deep breath and toyed with one of the blue pillows. "This feels extremely . . . odd."

"Tough." Jack peeled the comforter all the way back. "Lie down."

After a moment, Taylor sank backward, the pillow clutched to her chest. "You're a hard man to refuse."

"So I've heard." He slid the comforter up around her. "Get some sleep. If you need me, just bang on the wall."

Taylor was very still beneath the blanket. "You don't have to do all this."

"True. And you don't have to argue so much."

"I've always been good at arguing."

Jack didn't move, just watched her. He felt his breath go raw and heavy with lust — and something more elusive. "Is it true what Mrs. Pulaski said? Only an occasional date?" His voice tightened. "And none of them spend the night?"

"I'm not sure that's any of your business."

"Probably not. So is it true?"

She studied him warily. "That's still none of your business."

He shrugged, all too aware that he was far too curious about her private life. "You're right. Sorry."

But Taylor's voice caught him at the door. "Thanks for — everything. I'm glad you told me the truth about why you were following Rains."

Jack winced inwardly. "Just keep it quiet."

"Of course. Remember, I owe you coffee."

He turned out the light. "It's a deal."

Jack didn't look back, even though he wanted to. Near the front door he spotted a bag filled with ropes and climbing gear. He hesitated, but decided that taking the bag would raise too many questions. Taylor would never buy a simple explanation that he was having the things repaired as a gesture of his neighborliness.

That meant his inspection would have to wait.

He let himself out, closing her front door

quietly. He could have used the key he'd been given to throw her bolt, but that would have been another dead giveaway to Taylor. *By the book,* he told himself sternly.

But somehow he couldn't shake the memory of her staring up at him from that blue sea of pillows on her bed. *She's getting to you,* a voice warned. Big mouth, big attitude and all.

Like *hell* she was.

The woman was major trouble, and nothing was going on here, even if she *did* have gorgeous legs and more courage than most men.

Back in his apartment, he set his unneeded sugar on the nearest counter. Now that he'd checked on Taylor, he had to shower, then phone in a report to Izzy. After that —

His cell phone vibrated in silent mode. "Broussard."

"My office. Twenty minutes." The voice was tight, just on the edge of anger.

Jack cursed silently as the line went dead.

Apparently his commanding officer had just seen the latest news footage about the convenience store robbery.

"I expect an explanation, Commander."

Here it comes, Jack thought. *Right between the eyes.*

His gaze didn't stray from a spot on the opposite wall. "I was handling surveillance on Taylor O'Toole, sir. I saw Harris Rains enter a convenience store on Market Street without any

Federal presence visible. When Rains and Ms. O'Toole didn't come out, I became suspicious."

Admiral Reed Braden steepled his big fingers. Forty years of active duty had taught him how to make a man sweat by the simple force of silence. He tried to do it now, but Jack wasn't sweating.

After what seemed like a century, the admiral glanced down at the file on his desk. "What made you assume there was trouble inside, Commander?"

"I realized no one was moving around."

"Did you see any actual signs of threat?"

Jack reviewed the afternoon's events to that point. "No, sir."

"Were weapons drawn?"

"None in evidence, sir."

"So you had no concrete proof that the men in the store were planning violence?"

"No, sir."

"And yet you made that vast leap of intuition. Do you have mental skills you haven't told the Navy about, Commander?"

"No, sir." Jack stood stiffly, controlling his anger. He'd used deadly force in a civilian situation. One man was dead, and the mission could have been seriously jeopardized, so his c.o. had every reason to ream him out.

"I see. What exactly *was* your mission, Commander Broussard?"

"To stand surveillance on Taylor O'Toole, noting all contacts and establishing a pattern of

108

movement, sir. Especially in regard to Harris Rains and Candace Jensen, who is a friend of Ms. O'Toole."

"I see. So you weren't assigned to go kill civilians in the middle of San Francisco?" The admiral's voice could have scored marble.

"No, sir."

A chair squeaked. Admiral Braden tossed a photo across the table. "What do you have to say about *this?*"

Jack glanced down, wincing at his face caught in a grainy shot that appeared to be pulled from an amateur's video footage. Hell, he hadn't appeared on the six o'clock news, had he? There had been no TV vans in sight when he'd left the scene. "Nothing, sir."

"No? In that case, let me fill in the words for you. *This* is a material breach of orders." He jabbed at the photo on his desk. "*This* is grounds for pulling you off this mission and sending you up to Alaska to count Russian trawlers for the next eight years. If you were photographed on television, your usefulness would be nil. Is that clear enough, sailor?"

Jack didn't move. "Yes, sir."

"It had better be. You won't get a second chance." The file closed with a snap. "Dismissed. Report to the lab for a toxicology briefing. We just got data on a newly weaponized form of ricin hitting the streets."

"Air or water dispersed, sir?"

"Air."

Inhalant; the worst kind. A thousand times more deadly than botulin toxin.

"Aye, aye, sir."

Jack saluted and strode out, fighting to hold his anger in check. If he hadn't gone in, Rains would be in a black body bag right now, their one and only existing trail of evidence destroyed irrevocably. Admiral Braden knew that as well as everyone else on this mission. The only thing that kept Jack quiet was the knowledge that Rains' two Federal handlers had already received far more serious reprimands, followed by immediate transfer.

Not to Alaska, but somewhere damned close.

A body loomed up before him. Jack snarled when broad shoulders blocked his way. He started to shove past, but a hand gripped his shoulder. "You have a reception problem, Broussard?"

Jack relaxed slightly. "Sorry, Izzy. I didn't see you."

"You didn't see anyone, ace. Was Braden that bad?"

Jack gave a dry laugh. "You don't want to know."

Izzy's dark features tightened in annoyance. He dropped some coins into the coffee machine and watched a cup fill with tepid liquid. "I suppose he'd prefer that you let Rains take a bullet?"

"The alternatives didn't come up. But there was some discussion as to whether I had psychic abilities for predicting the robbery when it hadn't happened yet."

"Ouch." Izzy passed Jack the cup of coffee. From experience, they both knew the drink would resemble dishwater.

Jack studied the cup, frowning. "I shouldn't have gone in, not without clear sign of danger."

Izzy said nothing.

"I could have blown the whole mission."

Izzy stared back, still silent.

"Mission directives," Jack said tightly. "Discretion. By the book."

Izzy crossed his arms. "Discretion, hell. You exercised the judgment you've trained night and day to develop and you made a hard call. It's what they *pay* you to do, damn it." He bought a cup for himself and then stood, coffee forgotten, glaring down the corridor. "You want to know about the first man you took down? According to my search, he had priors in six other states, three of them for armed robbery. Currently he has outstanding warrants in California and Arizona. The man you shot at the window? His specialty happens to be late-night assaults and taking hostages. He's been locked up four times before, but this time some lunatic let him out on parole. The fact is, all of those guys were highly dangerous, Broussard. You and I know that. So does Admiral Stiff-Ass Braden."

Jack gave a crooked grin. "Anytime you want to argue my case, I'll sign you on." He stared at the coffee, his smile fading. "But this time Braden's right. I should have found some other way."

"Sometimes there *isn't* another way. Let me tell you about a man I used to know." Izzy moved to the only window, framing flat fields and cold sky. "He was doing his job, minding his own business when he saw a truck pass. He followed because something about that truck didn't feel right, and a few miles down the road he saw a man being dragged out of the back." A muscle moved at Izzy's jaw. "Then five other men appeared. They took out ropes. They were getting ready to nail the man to a wooden wall, and no one who saw them was going to lift a hand to stop it."

Jack felt something twist at his gut. He'd seen the scars on Izzy's wrists, the old slashes of knives and deep rope burns. Izzy never explained, and after one look at Izzy's face, no one dared to ask. Was this his story? "Sounds like unfair numbers to me."

"Not when the man I'm telling you about was done. He hosed down the scene by himself." Izzy's voice hardened. "But they got to him later. He was minding his business then, too. But he ended up buried in a box cut into a hill somewhere in Thailand, and he stayed there for months while they tortured him."

Jack felt the stab again. So this is what made Ishmael Teague hard and calm and the most dangerous civilian operative in the field, bar none. "A friend of yours?"

Both of them knew the question wasn't casual. Izzy looked at his coffee for a long time, as if remembering things he'd rather not. "Yeah. The best. He did the right thing, too, and it got him four years in hell. Sometimes it works out that way." He drained his cup. "From where I'm standing, you did the right thing."

"Thanks." The anger in Jack's stomach slowly began to uncoil. "But if I say I'm going into a convenience store anytime soon, do me a favor. Just shoot me."

Izzy smiled faintly. "My pleasure. Right now, you're wanted at the lab for a ricin briefing. And I just heard that Rains is on the move again." He looked as if he were going to say more.

"Something else on your mind?"

"What about Taylor O'Toole? How is she taking all this?"

Jack shrugged. "Badly, the way any civilian would. I'll say this, she was one amazing sight, even in torn leather. Hell, *especially* in torn leather." Jack shook his head. "One of the SWAT officers told me she picked up a brick and sucker-punched the driver. He was flat on the ground by the time the cops got to him. She even kicked his gun across the parking lot so he couldn't reach it. San Francisco's finest didn't have to waste a single bullet."

Izzy didn't smile back. "The woman has a definite talent for trouble."

"You know her pretty well?"

"Let's say we have mutual friends." Izzy pulled out his cell phone, his face unreadable. "See you after you finish up in Toxicology." He was already dialing as he started down the hall.

Jack wondered about those mutual friends, but when he took another look at Izzy's shuttered face, he knew there was no point in asking for details.

Chapter Nine

Harris Rains needed a drink bad.

He rubbed his jaw, staring at the pink phone messages on his desk. More reporters asking for interviews. What had possessed him to shoot off his mouth after the robbery? Why hadn't he just walked away, merging into the crowd? Publicity was the last thing he needed, especially now.

Two more stations were pleading for interviews. At any other time he would have wallowed in his new hero status — even though it seemed odd that the reporters hadn't gone after the hotshot with the gun instead of him.

And right now he needed to lie low, with interviews the lowest thing on his agenda.

His story to the press hadn't been a complete fabrication. He'd come close to protecting that woman from one of the thugs. At least he'd *thought* about protecting her. If it had been necessary, he probably would have intervened. That still made him a hero of sorts, even if the hothead had acted first.

Frowning, Rains glanced through the lab

results on his desk. Right now he had more important things to worry about than news interviews. He pulled out the file that had arrived only ten minutes before. His eyes narrowed as he skimmed the lines of batch numbers.

When he was done, he skimmed the numbers again, then checked them against a different file.

The last lab results checked out perfectly. No loose ends. He'd planned damned carefully this time.

Too bad he couldn't tell anyone the details.

He walked to the door and locked it, then carefully drew a small silver cylinder from the heel of his right shoe. This was his future, his ticket to a new life. All he had to do was stay calm and hold off his new purchaser until the rest of the production was completed.

He relaxed slightly, sitting back in the big leather chair behind his expensive mahogany desk. Outside his door, visible through a small peephole, a dozen drones in white coats hunched over microscopes. Rains knew exactly what each one was working on, and he liked them to know that he was watching them.

One more week of this and he'd be ready to retire for undisclosed health reasons. Assuming he finished his work in time and turned over his sample product.

And assuming the buyers accepted it.

He looked down at his hands. They were shaking.

Danger was good, he told himself. Fear made you sharp.

But he didn't quite believe it. There had been one delay too many, one argument too many. Lately he'd even begun to suspect Candace, which was about as crazy an idea as they came. Hell, he'd produced in spades, but it wasn't enough for his Argentinean associates. They'd warned him that his time was up. If his friend from the mayor's office hadn't arrived, he'd be writhing under a knife somewhere in a deserted warehouse now.

Then had come the holdup this afternoon. The crazy, blinding panic. All that blood.

Rains looked at the photo on his desk. A smiling brunette with straight teeth stared back at him. They'd had some nice times, and he looked at her photo for a long time, trying to feel some emotion. His wife was pleasant, but she wasn't half as inventive as Candace. It was getting harder and harder for him to stay away.

His pager began to vibrate. Looking down, he read the number that no one else used. Another summons, he thought. This time they wouldn't waste time talking.

Maybe it was time to disappear.

He cleared his throat, wanting a drink. Instead, he closed his eyes, feeling sweat run down the back of his shirt. He realized he'd been a fool not to build more layers of protection for himself from the beginning. It was going to be hard now, when they had people following him everywhere.

They thought they were brilliant. They thought they had calculated all his moves. But maybe they were about to get a big surprise.

He jumped when his door popped open. His colleague, overweight and frowning in an unattractive Ann Taylor suit, strode inside with a sheaf of papers under her arm. "Something wrong, Martha?" With Martha, there was *always* something wrong.

"It's your corporate credit card, Harris. You've exceeded your account limit." Her lips tightened. "Again."

Stuff it, Rains wanted to say. But not to Martha Sorensen, who ran the bookkeeping department with an iron hand. No point in raising any eyebrows when his work was within a few days of completion. The access to materials was damned useful, after all.

He sat back in his chair, making his face contrite. "Gee, I'm sorry about that, Martha. I can't imagine how it got past me. Of course I'll make up the difference with a personal check." He treated her to his most boyish smile. "By the way, that's a great outfit you're wearing. Have you lost a few pounds?"

Her face filled with color. "Not really. But — thank you." She gave him a tentative smile. "I know you've been busy with overtime, so I'll take care of this for you. Just leave me a personal check for $423.72 and we'll call it even."

"No problem. You'll have a check on your

desk first thing tomorrow." His pager hummed for a second time and Harris shook his head. "Gotta go, Martha. It's the patent office again. Those guys in D.C. really know how to bust my chops. The paperwork never ends." He waited politely. "Are we all done here?"

"I believe so." She smoothed her suit jacket and shifted the papers under her arm. "By the way, I saw you on the news. You were very . . . heroic. How did it feel?"

"How did what feel?"

"To face down a killer that way. Weren't you frightened? I mean, the report told all about what happened, Harris."

"Well, a man's gotta do what a man's gotta do, Martha." Harris looked at his beeper and sighed. "Now if you'll excuse me, *this* man's gotta go five rounds with the midget bureaucratic minds in D.C."

"Of course. Good luck, Harris." Martha smiled shyly and closed the door, and he sat back, laughing softly. Being a hero definitely had its charms. Women could be so gullible, especially when you knew what buttons to push.

As he stared at the screen of his pager, he smiled. He needed to complete the batch of vaccine he'd been working on down in his secret lab in Mexico. Once that was done he could make the transfer, collect his money, then blow this job without a second thought.

But they wouldn't make it easy for him. He'd

stalled them once too often. So now they were going to hurt him.

Unless he was smarter than they were.

And he was.

Because the best protection was the kind they'd never suspect.

Chapter Ten

FROM TAYLOR'S BOOK OF RULES:
Whoever said surveillance is fun should try peeing into an empty Starbucks cup at midnight from the front seat of a freezing Wrangler.

Did the man *ever* sleep?

Taylor watched the deserted corner, fighting to keep her eyes open. It had been no fun rolling out of bed in the dark, especially when she still had bruises from her fall, but she couldn't relax. She wanted answers about Rains and why he had sent her that sick funeral arrangement. Even her writing was suffering now, and she had to resolve Candace's questions before she could get back to work.

Hence her current position in a cold, cramped car at the bottom of a trendy street in Nob Hill. Rains would have an incredible view of the bay from his tenth-floor terrace. Taylor wondered what kind of lab job paid for such a swank apartment.

Springsteen started to sing a raw, smoky lament. Her fingers tapped in time to "Hearts on Fire" as a car passed, all hip-hop bass drilling her eardrums. She shook her head. People today didn't recognize decent music.

Springsteen would always be the king in her book.

She pushed away a wrinkled copy of *Premiere*, which landed on an empty container of yogurt and a giant bag of M&M's with peanuts, the remains of her on-the-job dinner. Much more of this surveillance business, and she'd gain twenty pounds along with a severe insulin imbalance. Then she'd have to go back to rock climbing for exercise.

Taylor almost choked on an M&M at the mere thought.

Candace had called her late the prior night. Like almost every other resident of greater San Francisco, she had seen the news broadcasts about the convenience store robbery. When she was finally convinced that Taylor was fine, Candace confided that Harris had called her to recount the story of his bravery.

"Here's the weird part," Candace had explained. "Harris asked me what I'd done with our climbing equipment. When I lied and told him I'd thrown everything away, he blew up. He seemed so emotional about it that I hardly recognized him."

Candace had pleaded with Taylor to help her for two more days. If Taylor found out that Rains was involved with another woman or committing a crime, Candace reluctantly agreed to break off all ties with him.

Yet it was clear from her voice that she hoped Taylor would fail.

Which was why Taylor was sitting in her car staring at Rains' apartment and wishing she hadn't drunk quite so much coffee.

Up on the tenth floor the lights went off.

Hel-lo.

Taylor's hands tightened on the wheel of her Wrangler as Harris Rains sailed out the front door three minutes later. Keys in hand, he crossed the street and slid into a shiny white BMW.

Taylor followed half a block back. At midnight, there wasn't much traffic, and she kept her distance as Rains cruised along the edge of Chinatown, then pulled onto a side street and parked in front of a building with a flickering sign that read TONY'S LITTLE SHANGHAI. A big man with a gold earring opened the heavy brass door, releasing waves of loud bass music, and Taylor caught a glimpse of Rains greeting a blonde with very big hair. The two made a big deal of kissing, then Rains put a hand on her rump and said something that made her laugh.

Clearly the two were more than lab buddies.

Rains and his companion went at it a little longer, then Rains said something to the man with the earring and money changed hands. With the woman still plastered to his arm, Rains vanished inside the club.

Taylor was trying to decide how to break the news to Candace when the door closed.

Sighing, she wrote down the time and address in her notebook and sat back to wait.

Taylor sat up, blinking. Rain streaked the glass, and her shoulder was completely soaked. Water traced a dirty path onto the floor.

Damn. She must have fallen asleep with the window open.

She pulled out a pile of napkins and went to work on her shoulder, then mopped up the floor. Peering through the cold gray light, she started the car and flipped on her wipers. Down the street, the man with the earring was sitting on an overturned crate, listening to a portable radio. Yawning, he watched a torn newspaper skitter up the street, carried on the wind. Rains' car was still parked where he'd left it.

5:20.

Harris Rains was a regular party animal, Taylor thought grimly. And she felt like the *Titanic* had just rammed her.

She was dreaming about coffee — black with lots of sugar — when she heard a tap at her window.

"You okay in there, lady?" A gray form appeared in the darkness, rain sheeting off a plastic parka.

Taylor saw the gun and the uniform beneath the poncho as she rolled down the window. "Just fine, Officer."

Hard eyes swept her face. "Lost?"

"Not exactly."

"Waiting for someone?"

"Er . . . sort of."

The beat officer glanced at the seat beside Taylor, taking in the open magazine and the general litter. "Had a fight with your husband and decided to teach him a lesson, right?"

"Uh . . . yeah. That's it exactly."

"Better go home. This isn't the best place to sleep." He glanced up the street. "Some of these clubs can get pretty rough."

"I guess you're right." Taylor reached for the ignition.

"Wait a minute."

She swallowed. Had Rains called in a complaint? Was she going to get arrested as a stalker?

Could her life get any worse?

The policeman stared at her. "You were at that robbery, weren't you?"

Taylor nodded, wondering where the question was headed.

"You're the one that blasted the perp with a brick, then kicked his gun across the parking lot."

"That would be me."

The officer shook his head, grinning. "Wish I coulda seen that, especially the part with the brick. If your husband gives you hell after an afternoon like you had, get rid of the bum. He's not half-good enough for you."

Taylor smiled. "Can I tell him you said that?"

"Damned straight. Better yet, send him down to the precinct if he gives you any lip."

"I'll remember. One question, Officer. How did you know I was here?"

He gave a shrug. "Got an anonymous complaint. Person thought you might be dealing drugs from your car."

Dealing drugs? Taylor felt a stab of anger. "I can assure you, the report was wrong. I don't even have any Tylenol handy, and believe me, with the day I've had, I could use a few dozen."

"Probably just some kook with nothing better to do." He tipped his hat. "Have a nice day."

Taylor rolled up her window and stared out at the rain. Had someone in the area seen her and phoned in the complaint? She glanced up at the surrounding buildings. No lights were on. No one was peeking through a curtain, staring down at the street.

Had Rains phoned in the complaint?

The officer was waiting for her to leave, so she started her car and pulled out. At the door of the club, old newspapers littered the front step. The man with the earring was asleep on a box, snoring.

Harris Rains was nowhere to be seen.

So much for Taylor's crack surveillance.

Jack Broussard sat in his dusty, government-issue van as the yellow Wrangler raced past him. He had to admit, the woman was stubborn. She'd been sitting out there waiting for Rains for hours. Finally, he'd asked Izzy to call in an anonymous police complaint to roust her.

126

Given the high priority of this mission, everyone with even a remote connection with the Navy's vaccine research program was being watched, and Rains had met the Navy's missing vaccine scientist twice last year. Until the link between Taylor, Candace, and Rains was clear, Jack's orders were to watch Taylor 24/7.

To watch *over* her, too, if necessary. Her brother-in-law had pulled strings to see to that.

The SEAL cursed, remembering his recent reprimand. No way was he going to stick out his neck again. If Taylor O'Toole insisted on stalking Rains, he'd be right behind her, short-circuiting her every step of the way.

As Jack studied the private club, the front door opened, and Harris Rains appeared, all smiles, a woman on both arms. To his left was a blonde with a dress that stopped just short of being indecent. To the right was a high-maintenance brunette who could have eaten a dozen Harris Rains for breakfast.

Jack swept up a camera and fired off a dozen shots with his long-range lens, then climbed out quietly and framed a shot of Rains enjoying a wet good-bye kiss with the blonde. With a Federal team assigned to handle Rains, this material would be used strictly for backup, but Izzy had asked for anything Jack could collect. The Feds were being tight-assed with their information, releasing only what they had to, which left Izzy busy filling in the gaps. Thanks to Izzy's resources, Jack now had some new toys. He shifted the long-range microphone and triggered his recorder. Even if the talk was gibberish, Izzy and his team back at the lab would tweak it until every syllable rang out, loud and clear.

Moments later, Rains' car was brought around by a sleepy attendant and Jack watched the white BMW angle off into traffic. The BMW was followed by Taylor's yellow Wrangler, slow and steady, four cars back.

Jack muttered a long, graphic curse. What did it take to scare the crazy woman off?

Scowling, he eased into traffic a little behind Taylor and headed south toward San Jose.

Jack punched in Izzy's number forty minutes later, stiff, tired, and grouchy as hell. "Rains is inside a warehouse facility near San Jose and he hasn't come out. Taylor's parked outside."

"She's *still* on him?"

"Like a nasty tick on a dirty dog. You want me to go sniff around the warehouse?"

"Negative. The Feds have warned us off, so you stick with Taylor. What we need are contacts and a pattern of activity. We'll send someone in later to check the facility." Izzy made an irritated sound. "Doesn't the man ever sleep?"

"Maybe he got a little mind candy at the club. No one coming out seemed to be feeling any pain."

"We'll check the club out, too," Izzy said tightly.

"I got photos of the women he was with. I also recorded their conversation, but the tape may need some enhancement."

"Enhancement is my specialty," Izzy said. "Follow Taylor back to her place, then bring everything here. After that you might need a few hours sleep."

Sleep? What was that? Jack thought cynically. He cleared his throat. "You know, Taylor could be involved." The possibility had to be faced.

"Taylor O'Toole wouldn't know a weaponized biohazard from a golf cart." There was a long silence. "Trust me, she isn't involved with Rains or the missing scientist."

"You're absolutely certain? If so, you must know her pretty well."

"It doesn't take a genius to see she's not the type to fall for Rains or his promises — even if *some* people here insist that she is." A muffled voice interrupted him. "Hold on, Broussard." When Izzy returned, he sounded rushed. "Someone should be there to relieve you shortly. He'll follow Taylor back to her place. I need you back here."

Jack felt a sudden kick of adrenaline. "Why?"

"We just got word on a possible biohazard threat near Nogales. A border guard was running a standard crossing check and when he went in for a closer look, the dogs picked up something in a produce truck inbound from Mexico City."

"Plague? Anthrax?"

"Ricin. The company usually sends several workers along inside the compartment with the produce. When the guard opened the back, both men were dead. We have a team prepping the bodies for autopsy right now."

Jack frowned at the quiet warehouse. If he hadn't been pulled away for this surveillance, he would have been part of the team working with the biohazard unit. He felt a stab of anger at being reassigned to a lightweight assignment, baby-sitting a lunatic female with more energy than sense. "I belong with the biohazard team, Izzy. Not carrying out surveillance on a secondary suspect."

"Point noted, Broussard, but I'm not handing down the orders."

A car pulled up, and Jack recognized the driver. "We're ahead of schedule. Your man just arrived." He gave a two-finger wave to the driver.

"Good. Get back here pronto. Is she still parked outside the warehouse?"

"Can't miss her."

Izzy's voice hardened. "In that case, I need you to do one more thing before you leave."

Rains still hadn't reappeared.

Taylor finished the last of a warm soda and tossed the empty can in the backseat with two others, then sat glaring at the gray sky. Jeeps were great cars, totally cool cars, but they simply weren't made for cold weather and

130

large quantities of rain.

A stream of water trickled past the window frame and pooled up on the floor mat near her foot. Okay, so surveillance wasn't as easy as she'd thought. But how hard could it be to follow a person from point A to point B and not get arrested? All she had to do was stay awake and avoid getting hypothermia.

She looked up as a car drove through the intersection behind her. Just a grimy gray van. No police cruiser sent to arrest a crazy female stalker.

Yawning, she sat back and watched the gate at the front of the warehouse compound, praying for Rains to reappear.

But there was no hint of his sleek white BMW — only rain, pounding on and on, making her whole body numb. She shoved her heater to high, but nothing seemed to cut the damp chill. When her eyelids drooped, she sat up with a sigh.

Her watch said 6:40.

What was Rains *doing* inside the warehouse?

Suddenly her Wrangler jerked to the left. Taylor heard a faint hissing and grabbed the door, bracing for an earthquake.

But an earthquake would have made the whole car shake, along with the street. Was something wedged beneath the car?

Grimacing, she opened her door and stood in the rain, studying the quiet street. No trucks passing. No noise. No nothing. Water dripped beneath her collar and trickled between her shoulder blades. Shivering harder, she looked down. Her left rear tire was almost as flat as Kansas.

Wind slapped at her face and she kicked her tire hard.

She was searching for her tire iron when she saw a flash of white at the gate. In disbelief and fury, she watched Rains shoot past the guarded entrance and sail west toward the freeway. Taylor yelled as he passed, ready to run after him. Then sanity returned.

This was crazy. She couldn't run after a *car*. Besides, she had a flat tire. If Rains didn't have her arrested, she'd probably die of pneumonia.

Finesse, she told herself grimly. Cleverness.

Her eyes narrowed.

Uncle Vinnie.

Chapter Eleven

Taylor stepped out of a hot shower, fighting a sneeze. No way was she getting sick now. It would take more than a floral death threat and a rotten flat tire to throw her out of the game. Failure was making her mad, and as any of her friends knew, Taylor O'Toole got dangerous when she was mad.

Her fury had struck the boiling point when the helpful man from the auto assistance service examined her tire and told her it had been slashed.

Not blown. Not a nail puncture. *Slashed.* As in slashed by a slimeball with revenge on his mind. No way was Harris Rains getting away with slashing her tire. Not in *this* lifetime.

While she was waiting for a call back from Uncle Vinnie, Taylor punched in Candace's number and sat through twenty rings until her friend answered, sounding exhausted. "What's wrong, Taylor? I just got to sleep."

"At eight o'clock?"

"I had a rock-climbing class until ten last night. After that, some of us went out to celebrate the launch of a new set of ropes from Black Diamond."

Celebrate new climbing ropes? Suddenly Taylor felt old.

"I just wanted to know if you'd heard anything from Rains. Has he bothered you again?"

"He called once last night but he sounded rushed. Nothing since then. Have you had the climbing gear inspected yet?" The sleep was fading and Candace was starting to sound tense. "Is that why you called?"

"Not yet. I wanted to ask if you'd heard of a nightclub in Chinatown called Tony's Little Shanghai."

Candace repeated the name slowly. "I don't think so. Is it a good scene?"

"The scene doesn't exactly matter." Taylor gave up trying to find a gentle way to break the bad news to her friend. "I followed Harris there last night and saw him getting very chummy with a blonde with big hair."

"A woman? You're sure Harris was — was *with* her, not just talking to her?"

Taylor reined in her impatience. "They weren't discussing mortgage rates, Candace. Harris had his hands all over her."

"Oh." Candace sounded shattered. "You're positive it was Harris you saw?"

Talk about denial. "I'm sure, Candace. Did he ever mention that club to you?"

"It doesn't ring a bell. Of course, we didn't go out on real dates that often. Mostly a movie or sometimes a workout at my health club."

"One more question. When did Harris get his white BMW?"

"He used to drive a red Honda Civic, but

about two months ago he got the Beemer. He said he needed it for his new image."

So Harris was making money and spending it fast. Doing what? Taylor wondered. "Did he ever tell you why he was getting a stock bonus?"

"He never talked about his work with me. Why do you ask?"

"I'm just wondering how a lab job buys you a brand-new BMW."

"Harris runs the lab, I think. He's really a brilliant scientist, you know, and his work is completely cutting edge."

"What kind of work?"

"Something with vaccines, I think. Or maybe that genetic stuff. I heard him once or twice on the phone to his boss, but I didn't really understand."

That genetic stuff, as in recombinant DNA technology? Was Rains involved in designing some sort of new vaccine?

Taylor chose her next words carefully. "Do you remember if he mentioned any details, Candace? You know, possibly a vaccine for Lyme disease or AIDS? Maybe hantavirus?"

"No, he never talked about stuff like that with me. He even kept his papers locked in his briefcase. He told me never to touch it because he'd rigged the thing to explode if anyone tried to open it." Candace hesitated. "Do you think that was a lie?"

Taylor made a mental note to avoid any briefcases Rains might be carrying. "I hope we never find out."

"It was really Harris you saw?" Candace went on doggedly. "I mean, maybe it was just a man who looked like him. I'm sure that's the answer. In fact, I'm going to call him right now and ask him —"

"*No.* Don't talk to him, don't meet him, don't even think about him. The man is *poison.*"

"I just can't believe this, Taylor. It's like a bad dream, and I keep thinking it will go away if I ignore it." Candace sighed. "I'm so sorry to get you involved. I mean, you're my friend, with no connection to Harris, and now someone . . ." Her voice trailed away. "First our equipment, then that horrible flower arrangement. What will happen next?"

"Nothing, as long as you steer clear of him. Promise?"

"I — I'll think about it."

"But, Candace, he's seeing other women."

"I said I'd think about it, Taylor." She seemed to be fighting tears. "Now I'm sorry but I have to go."

After she hung up, Taylor sat for a long time looking at the phone, trying to understand Candace's attraction to Rains. But who knew how anyone behaved behind closed doors? Maybe Harris Rains was a gentle, caring friend with Candace when they were alone.

Somehow Taylor couldn't picture it.

After a quick shower, she calculated her next step in protecting Candace — and herself. She hadn't come to any noteworthy conclusions ten minutes later, when she checked her phone and found two new messages waiting. Cradling a cup of coffee, she hit the PLAY button.

"Taylor, this is Annie. I'm worried, so call me soon." Her sister's voice was anxious. "That means right now, not after you finish another chapter."

Taking another gulp of coffee, Taylor hit the button for the next message.

"Ms. O'Toole, this is Andrew Sturgess calling about the adoption inquiry you requested. I have an investigator ready to begin work, but we'll need your particulars, as well as legal consent to request that the sealed files from California be opened for medical purposes. I'd appreciate hearing from you as soon as possible so we can begin the process. As you know, it may be very lengthy."

Taylor sank down at her desk as the lawyer repeated his office number and two cell numbers. He was impatient, as if he had other clients who would pay well and he didn't need this aggravation. She took a deep breath, looked at the phone, took another deep breath. She wanted to return the call, but something held her frozen. *Do it. Call him. What are you so afraid of?*

Afraid? Actually, she was terrified, gripped by panic at what she might learn. What if the trail led to lost dreams, shattered hopes, ruined lives? All of these would change her forever.

Now at least she had the comfort of her illusions.

Taylor stared at the envelope on her desk. *Take control. Make the damned call.*

But she couldn't.

Her favorite photo of her parents stared back at her from a nearby shelf, a cipher she couldn't penetrate. Day after day she tried, but nothing came through. They had told her nothing — and now it was too late.

With a broken sound, Taylor caught the picture frame and slammed it down on the desk. She shivered when she saw that the glass had cracked. A broken line now ran through her parents' faces, making their smiles look grim and inhuman.

They looked back at her, two strangers witness to the unraveling of her life, and she had the sick certainty that there was worse yet to come.

Standing next to the wall, Jack turned off his audio equipment and removed his earphones. He closed his eyes, rubbing his neck slowly.

Hell, she was *adopted?*

A bad thing to find out on short notice, especially when you had no parents around to explain what had happened — and why.

He frowned at his surveillance equipment for a long time. Then he sighed, hit a few buttons, listened, and hit another button.

Erasing the call.

Taylor's birth parents weren't part of the mission objectives — and that meant she was entitled to some kind of privacy. If anyone asked, he'd say a line pulled free. No big deal.

Except to Taylor.

He was resetting his equipment when the phone rang. He listened in silence, his face growing darker. "You've got to be kidding."

"Afraid not," Izzy said. "Rains is gone. All hell is about to break loose."

It was almost noon when Taylor pushed away from her desk and stretched slowly. Her neck and shoulders were aching, but she'd racked up twelve pages, which was almost respectable. Maybe the characters from hell were finally starting to shape up and remember who was boss.

She finished the last dregs of her coffee and decided she needed a break, something to take her mind off her book completely.

Five minutes later, she was dressed in spandex leggings and an oversized Lakers T-shirt, locking her door and adjusting her Walkman. She was preparing for a nice, long run when something gripped her shoulder. She whirled around — and felt her hand slam against Jack's right arm as he dodged her blow.

She yanked off her headphones. "What do you mean sneaking up like that?"

"No need to scream. I called your name twice, but your music was too loud."

"I *like* loud music, Broussard. If you want quiet, go find a nice retirement home."

"Had a lot of caffeine today, have you?"

"None of your business." Six cups, but who was counting.

Without waiting for her approval, he tugged off her earphones and was instantly enveloped in churning rock and roll. "Springsteen?"

"Who else? Only the classics for me."

He handed back the headphones. "Bach would turn over in his grave."

"Who?" She grinned. "A little joke."

"Where are you headed?"

"Off for some exercise. I'm in grave need of fresh air and sunshine."

He seemed to be studying her closely. "Anything wrong?"

Only everything in her life. When he didn't move, Taylor had an odd feeling he was trying to read her thoughts, but that was crazy. "I'm just restless. So if there is nothing else . . ."

"Spend the day with me."

"I beg your pardon?"

"Spend the day with me," he repeated. "You know — talk, laugh, have fun."

Taylor fidgeted with her Walkman. "Are we talking about a *date* here?"

"Would that be a problem? Bella says you haven't been on a real date in six months." His eyes narrowed. "And he didn't stay overnight."

Taylor felt her face fill with heat. "Bella talks way too much," she snapped. "And I'm out of here." She dug two hand weights out of her pocket and headed for the elevator.

Jack cut her off with an ease that left alarm bells ringing.

"Where did you learn to be fast and sneaky like that?"

"Here and there."

"Well, *that's* a conclusive answer." Without warning, she swung low and stepped in behind him, her left leg sliding behind his right leg in a classic aikido attack posture. But somehow Jack was two seconds in front of her, hands moving to block her while he spun back out of reach of her destabilizing move.

"Pretty slick, Broussard." Taylor's hands fell. "Don't tell me you learned that in carpentry school."

"Aikido is wonderful exercise, as well as a powerful mental discipline."

Taylor kept staring at him.

Slowly, carefully, Jack brushed a strand of hair from her cheek, his callused fingers lingering until she felt the touch race all the way to her toes.

She closed her eyes, shook her head. "No. Sorry. I'm too busy." *Too off balance when you're around.* "Besides, I have to buy food."

"I'll feed you."

"I also need to exercise."

"Then we'll exercise together."

141

She snapped open her eyes. If this was a sexual innuendo, he was a dead man.

But his face was perfectly serious. "I know a great place to run. There's also a wonderful spot where we can eat afterward."

Taylor wanted to cut him off, but there was immense appeal in the idea of spending the rest of the day in sheer relaxation. "I shouldn't. I've got way too much to do. Besides, I barely know you."

"Then start learning."

Stubble darkened his face, making him look dangerous. So did his clipped intensity. Taylor realized she was already too attracted to this man she knew nearly nothing about. Spending more time with him could be a bad idea. "Jack, I don't think —"

Inside her apartment the phone rang and she dug wildly for her key — dropping a hand weight on Jack's foot in the process.

He grunted, but didn't say a word.

"Nice restraint." Taylor swung open her door and ran to the phone. "Hello?"

"Taylor, it's Sunny. I've got someone who wants to speak with you."

"Who —"

"Taylor, this is Vinnie de Vito." The voice was low and accented, each word spoken with authority. "I'm calling about the item you received in the basket. You remember the one?"

The floral display from hell.

Taylor swallowed. "I remember."

"I've checked and it came through Flowers 'R Us. I asked a friend to trace the order, and it appears to have been purchased with cash at a participating florist in the Mission District."

"Did they have a name?"

"None that will help you," he said dryly. "The man signed the order form as John Smith."

"Cute. What about an address?"

"He listed the same location as the downtown YMCA. As you probably have guessed, they have no John Smith on their residents' list." His voice tightened with frustration, and Taylor had a clear sense that she wouldn't *ever* want to be on this man's bad side. "I'll keep trying, of course, but the chances of finding anything more are very slim."

"Could they give any description of the man who placed the order?"

Uncle Vinnie laughed coldly. "Average height, average build, average weight. Dark hair, dark eyes. Age anywhere from twenty-five to forty. With that description, I could rule out maybe two people."

Taylor frowned. "Didn't they wonder about the order? I can't believe many people send black flowers as gifts."

"It seems that they are a known gag item." He sighed. "We live in troubled times."

No kidding.

Taylor rolled her shoulders, trying to work out the tension that was suddenly digging deep.

"Well, it was a good try. Thanks again for all the help. Give my love to Sunny, will you?"

"Of course. Call me if you need any more help, my dear."

Taylor responded in a daze, then disconnected.

"What's going on?" Jack took her arm. "You look pale."

Floral death threats did that to a person.

Taylor took a sharp breath. "I just need some fresh air. I think I'll go with you after all. But I have to do one thing before I leave," she said tightly.

Jack followed her to the door, frowning, "Where are you going?"

"Downstairs to see a friend."

Candace answered her bell on the third ring, dressed in climbing pants and a tank top that showed off perfect shoulders. A bracelet with black cats gleamed on one wrist, her only jewelry.

She gave Taylor a warm hug, then pulled her inside. "Hey, I'm just heading up north for a climb. You want to come?"

"No, I'll pass on the climbing. I need to talk to you about something. It's about your boyfriend." *Your lunatic boyfriend.*

Candace closed the door and leaned against it, looking anxious. "What did Harris do now?"

"That floral arrangement I received was ordered by someone named John Smith, which is a little strange, I'd say." Taylor paced the small apartment angrily. There was a bag of climbing equipment in one corner next to an expensive digital camera. "I didn't know you liked photography."

"Oh, I'm not very good at it yet, but there should be some great shots today." Candace rubbed her neck. "But I don't see the connection." She stared at Taylor. "You think the man was Harris?"

Earth to Mars. "Who else do we know who is acting deranged?" Taylor stopped pacing, trying to control her anger at Candace's continued denial. "I came to warn you not to see him. The man is seriously unhinged, Candace. Promise me you won't have anything to do with him. You could be in danger."

"Harris wouldn't hurt me."

"He already *did.* He hit you when you asked about the men following him, remember?"

Candace shifted her eyes as if the memory hurt. "I don't think he knew what he was doing that day. He was afraid, confused."

"You've got to see him for what he is, Candace. Not for what you want him to be."

Candace stared down at her hands. The bracelet tinkled, tiny cats dancing in a row. "I bought this the very first day we met at the lab where he worked. He was so helpful then, so charming." She moved her hand slowly, watching the cats sway and spin. "I suppose I should throw it away, but I love watching these cats — maybe because they're so alive, so happy." Her voice turned wistful. "Or do they only look happy?"

"Candace, *promise* me you won't see him. You've got to accept that the relationship is over."

"If it's over, why does it still hurt?"

"Candace, please —"

"Look, I'd better go. Someone is picking me up and I don't want to be late." She didn't meet Taylor's eyes as she grabbed her climbing bag and camera. "Finding things to distract me is a good idea, isn't it?"

Taylor forced a smile. "You bet. Ignore Harris Rains and get on with your life."

Candace nodded slowly as they walked out to the elevator. "Sure you don't want to come today? We're going to practice bridging and stemming."

No way was she dangling on another wall of rock. "Gee, I can't. Not today," Taylor lied, trying to sound regretful. As she spoke, the elevator doors opened.

Jack was waiting inside, fingers on the HOLD button. His keen eyes raked Taylor's face, then checked both corridors leading away from the elevator. "I got tired of waiting. Care for a ride, ladies?"

Candace locked her door and hefted her gear, assessing the look that passed between Taylor and Jack. "A friend of yours?"

"Sort of."

Candace held out her hand. "Candace Jensen. Do you do any climbing?"

He shook her hand. "Jack Broussard. And I've done a little, here and there."

Candace tilted her head. "Anyplace locally? Joshua Tree? Yosemite?"

"Nothing around here. Sorry."

The elevator chimed, stopping at the ground floor. Candace leaned closer to Taylor. "Are you two involved?"

Taylor felt her face growing hot. "No."

"Not even loosely?"

"Not loosely or any other way."

A speculative gleam flared in Candace's eyes. Then she giggled, sounding very young. "Just as well. I doubt there's *anything* loose about that man."

Chapter Twelve

"What was that about?" Jack rode back upstairs with Taylor after Candace got off in the lobby.

"It doesn't matter."

Jack took her arm and pulled her around to face him. "Stop brushing me off. You were scared, Taylor. I saw it on your face. Who called you?"

An aging mafioso with information about anonymous death threats. "Look, forget it, will you?"

"Like hell I will."

There was fury in his eyes, and the sight fascinated her. Coupled with the sexy stubble, it made him look very dangerous.

"I don't want to think about it now. I want to go outside and clear my head."

"Was it about Rains?" Jack gripped her shoulder. "Trust me, you're getting nowhere _near_ him."

When Jack continued to glare at her, Taylor touched his cheek. "Hey — no amount of inducement would get me close to that psycho. No one's fighting you here."

Jack let out a hard breath. "Good. You saw

148

him after the robbery, sucking up to the press. He's not the kind of person you want to be involved with, trust me. I've seen it — working on this divorce case, you know?"

"I know, but I think that you're beating yourself up over what happened in that robbery. You look like you haven't slept for a month." Taylor frowned. "It's because of the man you shot."

Jack leaned closer, trapping her against the wall. "Maybe I'm worried about *you,* damn it. Maybe I can't stop thinking about Rains and what he'll do if you get too close to him."

"That sounds personal." Taylor was intensely aware of his hard thighs locked against hers.

"Like hell it is. I'm just a man doing a job. There's not a hint of anything personal going on here. Got that?"

"Sure." Taylor shifted slightly and her eyebrow rose. "And maybe that's the outline of your gun I'm feeling right now."

"My Beretta's in a holster under my left shoulder." Jack's voice was harsh.

"Which means this is getting personal." Taylor met his angry look without flinching. "Should that frighten me, Jack?"

He pulled away, cursing. "If you knew what I was thinking, you'd be frightened as hell."

"Why? Maybe I'm thinking the same thing," Taylor whispered. "Ever since you barreled down that corridor and saved my life in that robbery, I can't get you out of my mind." The words spilled out, almost against her will. "Things don't get any more personal than that."

"Could you stop being so honest? It can be damned unnerving — especially when I'm trying to be calm and rational for both of us."

"Does honesty frighten you?"

Jack crossed his arms. "Honey, *everything* about you frightens me."

"Well, in that case, you can just haul yourself out of my way and out of my life." She tried to push past, only to find herself captured against the wall, pinned in place by his powerful body.

"Let me rephrase that. You shake me up bad. You make me want to have you about twenty different ways, okay? The hell of it is, the thought's becoming something of an obsession, which means I can't do my job."

"Oh."

Jack shook his head. "That's *all* you've got to say? I'm spilling out my guts here, and you say *oh?*"

Taylor gave a crooked smile. "I have one other thing to say."

"It better be good."

She touched Jack's cheek, fascinated by this hard, cool side of him. She was beginning to realize that this kind of curiosity could become very dangerous. "I was just going to point out that you're sweating, Broussard. And I believe the gun is back."

He stared at her for what felt like an eternity,

then shook his head, breaking into reluctant laughter. "You're over the top, you know that?"

"Being over the top is a special skill of mine. So what are we going to do about this little obsession thing we have going?"

"It's mutual?"

She nodded. This time her eyes were serious.

Jack's hands moved to her shoulders, then eased through her hair as if he was fascinated by all its wild colors. "We could pretend we never met." Something about his tone told Taylor the idea was only half in jest.

"It would never work. I'm under your skin, and you know it."

He stared back at her, mesmerized by her laugh. The woman was trouble, but he couldn't control the direction his thoughts were taking. "Then we could go back to your place," he said tightly. "In a couple of hours, we could work this out of our systems for good."

Part of him prayed she'd say yes.

Part of him was terrified that touching her would drag him under worse than ever.

"Oh, I think *that* would be a little excessive," she said sweetly. "Any other options?"

"Try this one." His mouth moved over hers, tested, skimmed, then locked hard. Heat shimmered as the kiss grew more intimate and their tongues met. Taylor's hands slid to his shoulders, trembling, and that small betraying movement made Jack curse, wanting her fiercely. Even though this was a mission and he *never* should have been thinking the things he was.

Then his hands were on her hips, dragging her closer, shaping her to the hard need neither of them could ignore, while a ragged little moan escaped her lips.

Behind them the elevator chimed. The doorman looked out and chuckled. "Sorry about that, folks. Don't let me interrupt you."

The door closed and the elevator whisked away.

"Great." Taylor dragged in a breath. "That kiss will be all over the building in an hour. Taylor and the new tenant all but stripping each other in the corridor."

"Do you mind?" Jack frowned. These were her friends and her life, after all. He would be walking out of that life as soon as his mission was finished.

"I should mind. Besides, you're *definitely* not my type."

"Hallelujah for that," Jack said grimly.

"See? I should punch you for that comment — but I don't. I'm still trying to figure out why."

Jack couldn't resist sliding one last kiss across those warm, sleek lips. "Must be because I'm under your skin, O'Toole. *Seriously* under your skin."

"Dream on, hard case."

"Oh, I'm dreaming, all right. They're definitely X-rated. Now let's go."

"Where?"

"Wherever I want. You agreed to spend the day with me, remember?"

Taylor crossed her arms. "Tell me again why I agreed to do that."

"Because we're both saying to hell with Harris Rains for one day. I'll feed you. We'll talk. We'll relax. Nothing serious, so let's not analyze it to death." He waited impatiently. "Get your purse, and we'll hit the road. Remember to ditch those hand weights or I may end up crippled."

Taylor sighed. "Are you *always* this alpha?"

"Pretty much, yeah. Now do you move or do I have to kiss you again until you shiver and make that sexy little moan?"

"I do nothing of the sort."

His grin was dark and confident. "Sexy moan. No mistake about it."

"You must be hallucinating." Color drifted over Taylor's cheeks while she locked her door.

"Why don't we take your car? Mine's been acting up." Jack's orders had been to arrange for Taylor to drive, making it clear to anyone watching that she was out of the action for the day. Meanwhile, her absence would create one less problem for the federal team scrambling to locate Rains.

If anyone followed Taylor, Jack would nail them.

"Fine with me." Taylor watched him as he headed for her passenger door. "You're not demanding to drive?"

"Your car. You get to drive it."

Taylor stared. "Most men chew their knuckles when a woman takes the wheel."

Jack considered chewing his knuckles when she shoved in the gearshift and shot into traffic. He managed a cool smile. "As far as I know, sex never affects driving ability."

"That depends on how much, where, and with whom." Taylor's throaty laugh made Jack swallow a curse. She turned to look at him. "*You* could definitely affect my road handling."

"Drive," he said in a rough voice. "Stop giving me bad ideas."

"Where *am* I driving to?"

"Monterey," Jack said casually as she merged into the flow of traffic. "When did you last eat?"

Taylor frowned. "This morning. A handful of M&M's around ten."

Jack shook his head. "For a smart person, you are seriously disturbed." He reached over and dug in her purse.

"Hey, what are you —"

"Here." He held up a smashed protein bar. "Eat it. Cars can't run on air, and neither can people."

"You're doing that alpha thing again, Broussard."

"You haven't seen anything yet. Now stop arguing and eat."

"But —"

"Now. You know I'm right."

Muttering, Taylor grabbed the bar and started eating, ignoring Jack's raised eyebrow when her stomach growled loudly.

He shook his head. "*Seriously* disturbed."

But Taylor was enjoying the beautiful drive, and by the time they parked near the beach at the Monterey wharf, she realized she was ravenous.

"I insist that we split all costs right down the middle today. Fair is fair." Taylor grabbed his arm and pulled him toward an old man selling Belgian waffles dusted with cinnamon and sugar. "I'll have one of these for starters. With chocolate syrup." Before they reached the water's edge, Taylor had finished off a bag of popcorn, a hot dog with chili, and half of a chocolate chip cone with everything on it.

Hidden in the shadows, someone watched her every step of the way.

"Do you *always* eat like this?"

Wind ruffled the water. At the far end of the beach kayakers tested the broad, sheltered waters of Monterey Bay.

Taylor gave Jack's question serious consideration. "It's nerves. Sometimes I lose my appetite, and other times I can't turn it off." She stopped to lick a trail of ice cream from her finger.

"Why the nerves?"

155

"Let's just say that my life has become a general mess."

Jack handed her a napkin as a second ice cream trail ran down another finger. "What kind of mess?"

Taylor dangled her shoes in one hand and ate her ice cream cone with the other. "Things. You know. Problems."

"Like?"

"Work. Friends. Family stuff." She stared down the beach at a little girl tugging a red balloon over her head. "I also found out I was adopted." She stopped walking, her face going pale. "I can't believe I told you that. I haven't told *anyone* that."

He studied her gravely. "When did you find out?"

"A few weeks ago."

"Did you discuss it with your parents?" Jack asked carefully.

"They're dead." Taylor looked down, watching water skim over her bare feet. Ice cream trickled down her cone, but she didn't seem to notice. "They're gone, and I have no one else to ask. My sister doesn't even know."

"How did you find out?"

"A letter from the law firm that took over after our family lawyer died." Her voice tightened. "I found some papers stuffed in the middle of the file."

"*That's* how you found out?"

Taylor nodded stiffly.

"It seems I have a brand-new reason to hate lawyers." Jack stared at a spot out in the bay. "They ought to be sued for incompetence."

"Maybe. But if they hadn't been sloppy, I'd never have learned the truth. I would have just gone on the way I had — oblivious, living a happy little lie." She frowned at her hand as if she'd just realized it was covered with melting ice cream. "I think I've lost my appetite."

Without a word, Jack took the cone and tossed it in a nearby garbage can. After scanning the beach around them, he walked back to Taylor. She hadn't moved, staring down at the tide that rose up to lap at her feet. "You okay?"

"Probably. But I'm going to stay here for a while."

"Take your time."

"Funny, when we were little, my sister and I used to stand like this for hours, talking about everything, arguing about nothing. We were filled with more dreams than two hearts could hold." She took a breath. "But Annie stayed behind. All those years she was the rock, always and ever, while I . . . ran. And I ran. I visited all the places we'd dreamed about and put those old, half-forgotten dreams into words, then I built books trying to figure out what they meant. But I'll never know, because I'm not who I *thought* I was. I'm not really Taylor O'Toole, older sister of Annie O'Toole. I'm nameless, uprooted, and I hate that almost as much as I hate myself for believing it matters."

She scooped up a handful of sand and watched it hiss through her wet fingers. "You grow up taking so many things for granted. Day after day you think you know yourself and how the world works, but you don't," she whispered. "Then everything falls away and no matter how you try, you can't hold it because you can barely even see it." She sank onto the sand, her eyes closed. "I hate what I'm saying. I hate *caring* so much. And it's not even your problem — it's got nothing at *all* to do with you, so why don't you go on walking while I stay here for a few minutes and remember how to be a sane, mature adult who doesn't embarrass *both* of us." She frowned when she realized he was bending down beside her on the wet sand. "Why haven't you gone away?"

"Hell if I know." He took her sandy hand between his. "You're right, it's none of my business, but here's what I think. Mothers don't give away their children easily or without reasons. The problem is, you may never know those reasons. That's going to be hard to live with."

She swallowed as he traced a line through the sand on her palm. "I feel so . . . stupid about this. So childish. It happened years ago."

"You *are* a child, at least where your parents are concerned. Maybe you need to listen to what that child is telling you right now."

She managed a faint smile. "What, no brisk orders? No snappy value judgments? Just gentle advice?"

Jack pulled her to her feet. "Stick around. The day's not over yet."

Taylor rose onto her toes and kissed him. "That was rude of me. I apologize."

"Never apologize for telling the truth." Jack looked over her shoulder, frowning. "Did you have any particular plans for those red sneakers of yours?"

"Why?"

"Because at the moment they're floating away into the surf."

Taylor spun around, soaking them both as she lunged after her shoes and caught them just before the tide swept them out of reach. She laughed when she saw the water on the front of his shirt. Without a pause, she splashed him again, then darted away over the sand.

Jack watched her clutch her wet sneakers, laughing breathlessly, her hair a dozen bright colors in the sunlight, her laugh reckless and far too infectious for the hardened, by-the-book professional he always had been and always would be. "Let's go."

She stopped running and frowned at him. "What's wrong? There was something in your face just now — something hard."

"Must be your overdeveloped writer's imagination at work." Jack cursed the ease with which she drew out emotions he wasn't supposed to feel. He grabbed her arm, tugging her up the beach, but he hadn't taken two steps when the fine hairs rose on the back of his neck.

She pulled against his grip, her body tense. "Jack, what is it?"

To lie or not to lie? "I'm not sure," he said quietly. "But I think we're being watched."

She moved closer. Her hand found its way into his. "Where?"

"No, don't look. Just put your arms around me. Do it right now." He felt her slim, strong body pressed against his and scowled at the instant stab of desire. As he drew her closer, he scanned the beach, looking for any faces seen too often or too close.

Nothing. Everything seemed normal. But the prickle of warning didn't leave as they jogged over the sand back to the car.

"What now?" Taylor stared at him.

"We're going for a drive — and I'll take the wheel."

She nodded slowly and handed him the keys. "So you can watch for pursuit cars. In that case, take Sunset Drive to Pebble Beach."

Jack's eyes narrowed. "17 Mile Drive? Good idea. The route's narrow and winding. We can slip off and see who's behind us."

Fifteen minutes later they were looping through some of the most beautiful real estate in the country, while the Pacific bubbled and surged just beneath them. Jack kept glancing into the rearview mirror, where a fury of sea spray and whitecaps churned behind them.

"There's the picnic turnoff near Cypress

Point." Taylor pointed along the rugged road in front of them. "Pull over there and you can see for several miles."

Jack took the turn, nosed in next to a camper, and motioned Taylor to a table while they watched the traffic behind them.

A minivan sped by, followed by a pool maintenance truck. Neither turned off, nor did the dusty black sedan that followed. Jack kept his vigil for ten minutes, then stood up. "That should be long enough. Now let's see who comes after us."

As they wound along the wave-swept headlands, a dusty sedan turned out of the visitors' parking area at one of the pricey golf resorts.

"Isn't that interesting?" Jack nudged the Wrangler faster.

The sedan speeded up, too.

Taylor already had pen and paper in hand. "I've got his plate number. A friend at the DMV can run a name check for me."

"Let's be sure he's really on us first."

Ten more minutes of leisurely stops and winding detours proved what he had suspected: their unknown friend in the dusty Lincoln Town Car wasn't going away.

Taylor was looking a little pale when they exited the drive near Carmel Gate. "Aren't you going to stop him?"

Jack shook his head. Keeping a low profile was a mission priority. Like it or not, he had to leave the rest to Izzy and his team. "I want to see how persistent our friend is."

"Try Pacific Grove. We can do some window shopping and see if he tags along."

Since her plan was as good as any he had, they parked, and then strolled past antique dealers, bookstores, and a crowded farmers' market. Despite constant checking, Jack saw no suspicious lurkers or familiar faces. But Taylor was looking strained, so he pulled her onto a bench angled toward the route they had just walked along.

"Why are we stopping?"

"Because you need a break."

Taylor frowned. "And because you need to check the street behind us."

"That, too. After a few more minutes, I'll make some calls."

She didn't look completely convinced, but she pulled off one sneaker and brushed sand from her foot, then closed her eyes, soaking up the sunlight.

When Jack finished checking the street, he turned back.

Taylor was staring at the traffic, one hand shading her eyes. "I don't believe it. What are they doing here?"

"Who?"

Taylor's eyes were locked on the slow-moving traffic. "Sam is with her, too. I'm not ready for this."

Jack studied the nearby pedestrians. "Ready for what?"

A woman called out, and he stood up, automatically shielding Taylor. Two people hurried toward them, waving their hands. Abruptly, the details from his mission briefing kicked in.

The pregnant, smiling woman was Taylor's sister. The big man beside her, sizing Jack up carefully, was her husband, a highly decorated Navy SEAL named Sam McKade.

Chapter Thirteen

FROM TAYLOR'S BOOK OF RULES:
Remember who brought you.

Hell.
Could the day possibly get any worse?

Jack schooled his face to amiable surprise as he watched Taylor wrapped in her sister's excited hug. After several rapid-fire questions, Taylor gave her brother-in-law a quick kiss, then turned to make introductions. Jack knew that this was a meeting she dreaded, and he saw hints of awkwardness in her eyes. The meeting left him edgy, too, since the real reason for his involvement with Taylor had to remain a secret.

But Sam McKade didn't look like the sort of man you could fool for long, especially since he was the one who had wrangled Navy protection for his sister-in-law — until Rains was in jail or cleared.

As Jack waited politely for Taylor to finish her introductions, he knew he was being sized up. Sam McKade's intense stare also told him that he was going to be grilled thoroughly before the afternoon was over.

Jack gave a casual glance down the busy street, then gestured toward a nearby restaurant. "Why don't we adjourn inside?"

"Sounds good to me." Annie McKade winced as she rubbed her stomach, full and rounded in her eighth month of pregnancy. "I'd enjoy getting off my feet for a few minutes."

Instantly Sam had an arm around her waist, steadying her. "Is your back bothering you again? Should I call the doctor?"

"I'll be fine, Sam. I need a little break, not a wheelchair to the delivery room. I've got a month to go, remember?"

"You're sure? *Really* sure?"

"Relax, big guy." Annie gave her husband a loving pat on the cheek. "I won't go into labor while your back is turned, okay?"

Sam McKade took a deep breath and managed to smile. "You just keep promising, honey, and I'll keep trying to believe it." He smoothed her hair, then shot a glance at Taylor. "She insisted on coming. It's her volunteer day."

"Don't tell me. The Butterfly Sanctuary."

"Hey, it's an important job," Annie protested. "Somebody's got to see that those beautiful creatures have a safe refuge after flying two thousand miles in four weeks. There are only a few microclimates in North America that will support them. If those habitats are lost, we'll lose their beauty forever."

"Whoa," Taylor cut in. "Nobody's going to attack your monarchs, Annie. We just want to be sure *you're* in good shape, too."

"I'm fine," Annie said firmly, smiling at Jack as he held open the door to the restaurant. "I'd

165

love some hot and sour soup. Maybe some sesame noodles. One or two fried dumplings, too." Before the men could sit down, she took Taylor's arm. "But first things first." The two headed off toward the bathroom, leaving Jack and Sam to stare warily at each other.

"So, have you known Taylor long, Mr. Broussard?"

"About a week. And call me Jack."

"Fair enough. The name's Sam. Are you a writer, too?"

"Not me. You'd have to shoot me to squeeze out a page of text. I do investigations in the Bay area."

"Private work?"

Jack nodded, glad to be interrupted by the arrival of a waiter with tea. Where were the women anyway? Couldn't they gossip some other time?

"What kind of investigations do you handle?"

"You name it," Jack lied. "Asset searches, missing persons, background checks. Also a little corporate work now and again because the pay is good."

Sam leaned back and gave him a hard stare. "We both know that's a crock. You're the man Izzy told me about."

"That's right." Jack decided it was time to take the offensive. "Is there a problem with that?"

Sam met his gaze squarely. "There could be if you make one."

"This is strictly a friendly outing. We're not reenacting *Romeo and Juliet* as far as I know."

For long moments, Sam McKade didn't answer. He turned his teacup thoughtfully. "Taylor's had some trouble recently. Did you know about that?"

"I know she had a climbing fall and was damned lucky to escape with stitches."

Sam met him with a cool stare. "I don't want anything to happen to her."

"Neither do I." Jack looked up, relieved to feel a hand on his shoulder.

Taylor was frowning at him. "Why are you two glaring at each other like hungry pit bulls?"

"Just having a little chat, weren't we, Jack?" Sam's smile didn't quite reach his eyes.

No wonder the man had a reputation as a tough operator.

Jack smiled back. "That's right. Nothing special. What do you want to eat, Taylor?"

She glanced from one man to the other, then sighed. "Gee, I could have sworn I smelled testosterone burning over here. Must have been my imagination." She glanced at the menu. "I'll go with Annie. Soup and noodles." The waiter had returned, and Taylor smiled at him. "No, wait, let me see if I can do this." She delivered a phrase of halting Cantonese, then waited for a response from the astonished waiter.

Jack cleared his throat and murmured a few phrases that made the waiter laugh and trot toward the kitchen.

"What's wrong?" Taylor demanded. "I told him it was a special occasion and I wanted to celebrate with my sister."

"Actually, you just told the waiter that he was a drunken pig and his children's children would be born without noses."

Taylor winced. "I studied some Cantonese while I was in Hong Kong researching a book. Funny, I never could get the tones right."

"It's okay. I told him you picked up your Cantonese in Shanghai. Everyone knows they can't speak Cantonese worth a damn up there."

"Spent some time in Asia, have you?" The wariness was back in Sam McKade's face.

"Off and on. My father was stationed in Asia in the Navy. I get back for an occasional visit." Calmly, Jack poured tea for Taylor. "I ordered a few other things, in case you want to be a little adventurous."

Annie studied him as she sipped her tea. "Let's definitely be adventurous. Don't you agree, Sam?"

"You bet." But his voice was stiff.

The meal was fraught with tension. Only Annie seemed to enjoy her food, grilling Jack about how long he'd known Taylor and whether he liked her books, then complimenting his choice of dishes, including prawns dipped in sugar and a vegetarian wonder with black bean sauce.

Finally, Annie sat back with a sigh, put down

her napkin, and eyed the two men. "If you two are done playing cat and mouse, maybe we can show Jack the butterfly trees. But I'm going nowhere if you're at his throat, my love."

So she hadn't missed a thing. Smart lady, Jack thought. He realized that Taylor was laughing behind her napkin. Eventually even Sam joined in.

"Okay, no more interrogation. Let's go take that walk, as long as you really feel up to it."

Annie gave him a slow, tender kiss. "I'm pregnant, not housebound, remember?"

Sam followed her outside, grinning ruefully, leaving Taylor to study Jack with cool curiosity. "Were you in Asia long?"

"Off and on, just the way I told McKade."

"Right." Taylor stuck her tongue in her cheek. "Next you'll be trying to sell me some nice, quiet property near Groom Lake, Nevada."

Jack frowned. "Groom Lake, as in Area 51? You don't believe those lunatic stories, do you?"

"Don't get me started, ace." Taylor took Jack's arm. "By the way, I apologize for Sam. He can be a little overprotective."

Before or after he tore my head off? Jack thought irritably. Though the prospect of a hike down to the Monarch Sanctuary near the beach left him uneasy, he had no plausible reason to object, so he followed Taylor outside, scanning people, traffic, and any construction barriers that could pose hazards. Annie was obviously in excellent shape and kept a brisk pace despite her advanced pregnancy, running through a string of different topics with Taylor. Jack listened idly, tensing when he heard a familiar name.

"Any news from Izzy?" Taylor asked. "Or is he still in the middle of some hush-hush project?"

"He must be, because we haven't heard a word." Annie frowned. "I hope nothing's wrong."

"Don't worry about Izzy. The man has got to be the king of survivors. We'll hear from him when he's ready, not a second before," Sam said dryly.

Suddenly Annie gripped her husband's arm. "Look — there they *are*."

They stood unmoving, arrested by the sight of thousands of orange-and-black wings fluttering on the trees. It was almost impossible to imagine that these fragile creatures covered a hundred miles a day, reaching heights of ten thousand feet. Jack could see why Annie called them small miracles.

Annie called out to a docent shepherding a group of European visitors along a shady path. When she and Sam wandered over for a chat, Jack took the opportunity for another covert surveillance of the grove and its surrounding walkways.

Down the street, a garbage truck took on a

load. Two bicyclists stopped to enjoy the view. Mothers strolled with children, while teenagers maneuvered skateboards along the adjacent sidewalk. There were too many ways in and out, Jack thought tensely.

The garbage truck lumbered away and silence returned, sunlight filtering rich and green through the canopy. He tried to relax, but the little warning prickle was back, sharper than ever.

Taylor walked over to Sam and gestured at a cloud of butterflies drifting over the flowering bushes. Jack edged in closer, one eye on the German tourists scattered along the path. When a new group of tourists headed up the sidewalk, he decided it was time to pull Taylor away. The place was too crowded. Once they were in the car, he'd make up some story about a forgotten appointment and apologize.

Sam and Taylor turned to stare at a butterfly that fluttered down and settled on Annie's shoulder, vivid in a bar of afternoon sunlight. The image was so arresting that neither one heard the low *whirring* from a shadowed walkway as a riderless skateboard rumbled over the sidewalk, heading straight toward Annie.

With a shout, Jack sprinted forward, jumping a wrought-iron fence. He heard Sam shout a belated warning to his wife, but in the next second the big board struck Annie hard at the ankles and she cried out, swaying sideways with arms outstretched.

Jack kicked hard and dove.

Chapter Fourteen

In an instant the grove was a blur of movement.

One moment a butterfly had fluttered down in orange splendor, settling on Annie's shoulder, and then the peace was shattered by noise — Jack's shout, Sam's instant reaction, the hammering of metal wheels on concrete as an out-of-control skateboard raced out of the shadows.

Taylor heard her own cry, but she couldn't move fast enough. There was more shouting and she raced after Sam as Annie fell sideways toward the sidewalk, her hands instinctively cradling her stomach.

At the same moment Jack dove through a bar of sunlight, arms outstretched like a first baseman. When his shoulder bumped Annie's shoulder, he twisted, putting his body beneath hers. They landed in a sprawl on the cement.

Annie blinked as Taylor and Sam knelt, gripping her hands.

"Hey, I'm fine, you two," she said shakily. "It was just a tumble, nothing serious — thanks to Jack. Sorry I weigh as much as a horse these days."

Jack eased back to make room for Sam, who cradled Annie's face in trembling hands. "Is there any pain? Do you hurt anywhere, honey?"

"Just my elbow. Otherwise I'm —" She gasped and her body went stiff.

"Annie, what's wrong?" Sam stroked her hair, his face lined with strain.

"It was just a pain. Probably nothing." Annie's smile was forced. "Help me stand up and —"

Her eyes closed tight and she locked her arms over her stomach.

Taylor watched anxiously, dimly aware of a group of tourists milling in the periphery.

"I called the ambulance." The docent's voice was unsteady. "They're only two blocks away, so —"

The rest of her words were drowned out by a burst of noise. An ambulance angled to a halt a few feet away. Two paramedics sprinted up with a stretcher, lifted Annie in place, and carried her to the ambulance.

"Jack, I'm going. I can't —" Taylor clutched his hand tightly, trying to make sense. "Thank you," she gasped, "but I've got to be with her."

She scrambled up onto the seat beside Sam, the doors closed, and the big ambulance swayed out into the street, lights blazing.

Jack ignored his throbbing arm. "Where's the hospital?"

The worried docent gave quick instructions. "Young man, I don't know if you're a baseball player or something else entirely, but thank you for what you just did."

Jack managed a grim smile. He was punching

numbers as he sprinted back to the Wrangler.

Izzy answered on the first ring. "What's up?"

"It's Jack. I'm in Monterey, but you're not going to like what's happened."

"Taylor?"

"She's fine — except for the fact that someone's been trailing us all day. But something has happened to Taylor's sister, Annie McKade."

"Annie? But how did —" Izzy bit back a curse. "Give me an update. Where are you now?"

"On the way to the hospital." Before Jack unlocked the Wrangler, he turned to survey the street behind him. The prickling at his neck was still there, in full force. "Check on a Lincoln Town Car, California license 71 G94. Someone's out there, Izzy. The bastard's watching everything we do."

Viktor Lemka was not a patient man under the best of circumstances, but today all shreds of patience were gone, overwhelmed by icy fury. The stupid American woman had eluded him again, and Viktor was not in the habit of being bested by women.

He sat on a bench across from the entrance to the butterfly sanctuary — such a singularly pathetic American concept — his face shielded by the most recent *San Francisco Chronicle*, cursing the ambulance that raced up the street. He had meant his little diversion to occur later, when Taylor O'Toole was separated from the others, but the whining teenager had noticed that his skateboard was gone and summoned his noisy friends from the beach. Then more tourists had arrived, blocking his way.

That left Viktor with no time for the careful planning that was his trademark, so he had been forced to improvise. As a result, the diversion had come too soon, and the wrong woman was targeted. Worse yet, the nosy tourists had pulled out their cameras and begun shooting nonstop. He couldn't afford to have his face connected with the scene, not even on the amateur photos of a group of visiting German tourists, so he had had no choice but to pull back, melting into the crowd while the ambulance raced closer.

Yet again he cursed the stupid American woman. What had possessed Harris Rains to hide his lab samples in such a ridiculous place?

But furious as he was, Lemka realized the scientist had been clever, outmaneuvering them with his neat little plan. Now that they had Rains in a boat offshore, the scientist was talking as fast as the words could spill out. It had taken Lemka only two bouts with a knife to free the man's speech.

Now it was up to Lemka to get the lab samples back. Unfortunately, that had been harder than he'd expected. Hidden behind his paper, he cursed the man with hard gray eyes who seemed to follow the O'Toole woman everywhere. There was little information to be found about this man Broussard, not even by Viktor's well-paid and extensive network of contacts, which was most disturbing.

He peered over the paper, watching Broussard sprint up the street, all too aware that his employers were unforgiving men. Continued mistakes would most certainly bring lethal consequences.

Unthinkable, after fighting his way out of the slime of Albania's worst slum. Unthinkable, with five million U.S. dollars nearly at his fingertips. The imbeciles he had hired to kidnap Rains in the convenience store would soon be silenced, suitable repayment for their bungling. With Rains in his grasp, his goal was also in sight. All he needed was the woman's cursed purse.

Viktor watched the big American sprint toward the yellow car, an expensive cell phone at his ear. It was a conversation the Albanian would have paid dearly to overhear, but for some reason, none of his usual surveillance equipment penetrated the static of those calls.

Another disturbing factor.

Lemka smiled thinly, feeling the edge of the surgical knife hidden in his boot. There would be ample time for him to practice his craft during the days to come. First on Rains, then the woman. He knew how to sever nerves, shatter bones, and flay tendons with medical precision, courtesy of an overworked British doctor who had plucked him frightened and stinking from a rat-infested slum. Viktor had repaid his mentor with two years of uncomplaining labor, the full attention of a cunning young mind.

And a quick, relatively painless death via a scalpel implanted directly in the lower brain stem.

It had been Viktor's first step toward greatness, but many more had followed. There was no possibility that he would fail.

The yellow Wrangler raced past.

He closed his paper, folded it neatly, then tossed it in the trashcan. One plan had failed.

He was already moving on to the next one.

Jack had gotten through most of his report by the time he pulled up at the hospital. He angled into a parking space as an ambulance raced by. "I'm at the hospital now. I'll call as soon as I have any news. Better use the pager if you need me."

"Can do."

"One other thing. Have you gotten word on the plate number I gave you a few minutes ago?"

Izzy's voice tightened. "The Lincoln is registered to a corporate fleet in Huntington Beach. The company is called Homeland Technologies — some kind of home-monitoring service. I'll check it, but I've got a hunch the car will come up stolen."

"Which means we've got nothing." Jack studied the E.R. entrance. "What about our pals from the convenience store?"

"They're not talking. Sounds to me like they're more scared of their people than of us, but we'll keep working on it."

Jack switched off the motor, frowning. "Anything from the Feds? Like how they happened to lose Rains at the warehouse?"

"They say that the man who left Chinatown wasn't Rains after all. Those photos you took outside the club prove it, though the hair and makeup were good enough to pass a rough inspection. And all of us took the bait — the Feds, you, even Taylor. Meanwhile, the real Rains was no doubt being hustled away."

"By his plan or against his will?" Jack wondered out loud.

"Hard to say. The Feds are telling me nothing. Interagency competition sucks."

"Tell me about it. See what you can find, and I'll call in twenty minutes."

"Copy that. Meanwhile, watch your six o'clock."

Jack scanned the parking lot. "I always do."

Taylor paced a crowded hospital corridor next to two homeless men, a woman with a hacking cough, and a girl with a broken arm. Annie was nowhere in sight.

"How is she?" Jack cornered her in midstride.

"I'm glad you're here. Annie's being evaluated down the hall by an obstetrician. We haven't heard anything yet, and Sam's about to explode." Taylor took a sharp breath. "So am I."

"Let the doctor do his job."

"*Her* job," Taylor said. "And I'm trying, but it's hell to wait, not knowing what's going on. Not knowing if —"

"Why don't you sit down. I'll go talk to Sam about an update."

After a moment Taylor nodded, her hands clenched. "Okay, I'll sit. You go — just hurry, please."

She watched him stride through the crowded lobby, his calm presence making her feel safer. But after the string of bad things that had happened to her in the last few days, she had to face the fact that she probably *wasn't* safe, and the accident today could have been part of that pattern. If so, she had endangered her sister. . . .

If Annie lost the baby, Taylor didn't know how she could forgive herself.

She didn't realize she was trembling until she looked up and saw the little girl staring at her with big, curious eyes.

Suck it in, O'Toole. Falling apart now won't help anyone. She leaned back against the ugly green wall and closed her eyes, telling herself it would be okay because Annie was strong, Annie was tough, please God, nothing could happen to Annie.

Someone bumped her shoulder. Taylor frowned, opening her eyes to the same ugly green walls and the same crowded lobby.

She saw Jack standing beside Sam, listening intently, nodding a few times as if he really cared, even though these people were strangers he'd met just an hour before. Taylor tried not to worry as he came toward her, but it was impossible to do anything else.

"What did Sam say?"

"Take a walk with me and I'll fill you in."

"But Annie —"

"They've taken her upstairs for more tests."

Taylor felt her body go cold. Her knees buckled. "It's bad; I knew it."

"She's doing fine, Taylor." Jack pulled her close, steadying her. "It's protocol, they told Sam, something they do with any trauma in the last trimester of pregnancy. Also, her blood pressure's a little high, so they want to be sure that's not causing any fetal distress."

"Fetal distress?" Taylor closed her eyes. "Dear God, I knew it. She's in trouble — she could lose the baby."

Jack cradled her face, his hands rough and warm against her skin. "Your sister's *not* going to lose the baby. She's doing fine. They just want to keep her overnight for observation as a precaution."

"The baby's fine? Really?"

"All the vital signs are strong and absolutely healthy. Now let's go get some coffee in the cafeteria. Sam will come find us as soon as he has any news."

The baby was strong.

Annie was going to be okay.

Taylor let out a long breath. She wasn't sure when her hand found its way to his, but she didn't let go, not when they sat down at a chipped Formica table, not when he pulled her head down on his shoulder and she gave up trying to hold back tears.

It took two hours for Annie to finish all her tests, and another hour to complete the paperwork so that she could be admitted to a room on the obstetrics floor. Taylor was carrying a bouquet of daffodils from the gift shop when she pushed open the door.

Sam got up from the bed and waved them in. "Welcome to the Ritz," he said. "Ms. Hard Case here is complaining because she only gets gelatin and soup to eat. She's trying to bribe me to bring her some Godiva chocolate ice cream."

"Just a little," Annie said guiltily. She reached out and hugged Taylor. "I guess that proves I'm feeling fine, so you can stop looking panicky."

"Me, panicky?" Taylor set the flowers on Annie's table. "Don't think these flowers mean anything special. I just found them in the lobby, so I figured I'd bring them up."

Jack hid a smile at this banter, knowing it had taken Taylor five agonizing minutes to decide which flowers her sister would like best. "Why don't I go find a vase?" he murmured.

"Good idea." Sam gave his wife a kiss, then followed Jack to the door. "I'll come with you so these two can talk." But his smile faded as soon as they were outside. "I owe you, Broussard. Whoever you are, whatever you are — I owe you," he said harshly.

"Forget it. I just happened to be looking the right way at the right time."

"Luck? Is that all it was?"

Jack shrugged. "She's going to be fine. That's what matters."

The two men walked to the nursing station, oblivious to the stares of more than one woman around them. Sam borrowed a vase from one of the attendants, and then the two headed back down the hall.

"I saw the way you reacted, Broussard. Nice moves. But you'd better be as good as Izzy says."

Jack kept walking.

Sam moved in front of him. "No answers?"

"Nope."

Sam followed, scowling. "I may owe you for what you did, but if you screw up with Taylor, I'm going to kick your sorry butt from here to San Diego."

"There's no need to shout," Jack said quietly.

"Who's *shouting?*"

"You are. I'm pretty sure that would upset Annie."

"I want answers, Broussard." Sam moved closer, his face hard.

Hell.

Jack checked the hall, then lowered his voice. "If you've got questions, ask Izzy."

"That's exactly what I'll do. Meanwhile, you'd better hope that nothing strange happens around here. Otherwise, I'll do a hell of a lot more than shouting."

Jack resisted the instinct to salute as the SEAL strode off.

Chapter Fifteen

"You're *sure* you're okay?" Taylor asked anxiously. "You're not just saying that to placate me?"

"Healthy as a horse. And hungry, too." Annie laid one hand gently on her stomach. "We're *both* fine. I can feel it. Now stop worrying and tell me about that gorgeous man who can't take his eyes off you."

In a second, the interrogator became the interrogated. Taylor shrugged defensively. "You mean Jack? I told you, he's just a neighbor."

"Good try, Taylor. Except I've seen how he looks at you — amused and amazed. The man is battling a serious case of lust."

Taylor looked away, drumming her fingers on the rolling table beside Annie's bed. "What on earth are you talking about? Jack shows as much emotion as a fire hydrant. And if there's serious lust involved, I'm not seeing it."

"Odd, it's not like you to miss anything concerning sex."

"I should take offense at that comment. If you weren't my favorite sister —"

"Only sister."

"Whatever," Taylor snapped. "And I'm not getting into this now. There will be no poking,

184

no prying, no infuriatingly personal questions, is that clear?"

Annie sniffed. "As I recall, your performance in the personal interrogation department could have received an Oscar. When I met Sam, no detail was too small, no question too irritating. You wanted dates and places. And we won't even *start* on the red lace."

"You loved the red lace," Taylor countered. "So did Sam." She was suddenly aware that Annie looked tired. "What am I doing? You're in the hospital, under observation, and I'm arguing." She smacked a hand to her forehead. "At least when I'm stupid, I'm world-class stupid."

"And when you're wonderful, you're world-class wonderful. In my book, that's always."

"None of that nice talk or you'll make my mascara run."

"As if that mattered. You've probably got three tubes in your purse right now."

Taylor sniffed. "Four actually. It pays to be prepared."

"For what, a cosmetologists' convention?" But Annie was laughing as she patted the bed beside her. "Sit here for a moment. I have to ask you a question."

Taylor had the sudden instinct that this was serious. Had Annie found out about the adoption? Did some detail reach her by mistake?

Taylor sat down, hiding her worry.

"There's no need to look so anxious. I'm not

going to ask you to renounce dermabrasion or imported chocolate."

"I'm glad we got *that* cleared up." Taylor's voice fell. "I was worried — so worried. We all were."

Annie just nodded. Her eyes were bright with moisture as she cleared her throat. "So here it is, the thing I need to ask you." Her eyes locked on Taylor. "If anything . . . happens, I want you to take care of Sam. He's tough, we both know that. The things he has to do keep him tough. But he's got one weakness." She smiled crookedly. "Me. If something should happen to me, it would be that much harder for him because he's never known how it feels to be weak. He'd hide it, deny it — and the denial would destroy him. That's why I need you to promise that you'd take care of him, make him face things and work through them."

"Annie, Sam isn't —"

"Please, Taylor."

"But I can't —"

"Promise."

"Annie, this is *nuts*. Nothing is going to happen to you." Taylor's voice was shrill. *"Nothing."*

"I happen to agree. But I still want your promise. You'll take care of Sam — and the baby, if it should come to that."

"It *won't*," Taylor said hoarsely. "And of course I'd help, in any way possible." Her eyes narrowed. "You're not asking me to marry him,

186

are you? One of those wife-dies-so-take-the-sister things? I mean, Sam's a hunk, but I just couldn't do it. Sorry, but it would be too *completely* weird."

Annie was laughing now, which left Taylor somewhat relieved. "I wouldn't carry sisterly devotion that far."

"Thank God. I mean, the man has a seriously cute butt, but I have to draw the line somewhere. Even for my favorite sister."

"Only sister," Annie murmured. "Now that that's settled, tell me about Jack. You can't go wrong with a man who has great hands."

Taylor frowned. "How do you know that he —"

"When he caught me. One minute I was headed down, out of control, with the ground spinning, and the next minute he was just *there,* gentle even as he dove to catch me. I felt his hands go around my back and I knew he was trying to take the fall for me." Her voice wavered. "A pretty special thing to do." She looked at Taylor. "So are you two sleeping together yet?"

Heat filled Taylor's face. "*Yet?* Excuse me, I didn't know I was dealing with the Sisters' Psychic Network here."

"Knows all, sees all. And don't you forget it." Annie waited patiently. "So are you?"

"The answer, since you persist, is no. Not yet. Possibly not ever. I am a very busy woman and he is . . ." Taylor's voice trailed off.

"Wildly sexy?" Annie suggested. "Gloriously uninhibited. Please don't tell me he's married?"

"Of course he's not married. Not that the subject ever came up."

"Does he have one of those Hemingwayesque war wounds that make him forever only half a man?"

"We never got around to discussing his war wounds," Taylor said dryly.

"Excellent." Annie sat back with a contented smile. "Then you will be sleeping with him — and soon. He can't keep his hands off you now. Nice haircut, by the way. Did Sunny do it?"

"Who else? She'd have her uncle take out a hit if anyone else touched my hair. And don't think you're changing the subject," Taylor snapped. "Just because I enjoy being with Jack *doesn't* mean that we're going to tumble into —"

The door opened. Sam was carrying a vase, and Jack was a few steps behind him. Neither was smiling. In fact, the silence between them was loud enough to trigger an avalanche.

Uh-oh, Taylor thought.

Annie looked from one man to the other. "Any problem getting a vase?"

"No problem." Sam put down the vase with a snap. "Feeling okay?"

"Wonderful. But I'd feel better if I knew what you two were discussing out there."

"Us?" Sam rubbed his neck. "Football. Wide receivers. That kind of stuff."

Annie crossed her arms. "You two were arguing about something and it wasn't *tight ends*. Spill, Sam."

"I think you're getting tired, Annie. When you get tired, you worry."

There was a knock at the door. Everyone turned as a nurse peered in. "Time to hook you up for another hour of monitoring, Mrs. McKade."

Annie sighed. "I'm ready." She squeezed Taylor's hand. "You two get out of here. Go have a fabulous dinner somewhere. Drink champagne, then dance barefoot on the beach." She pulled Taylor closer. "I'll want a complete report in the morning, of course."

"She's right," Sam said gruffly. "Go have some fun."

Taylor frowned. "But —"

"I'll call you if anything comes up," Sam said firmly. "That's a promise."

Taylor could have sworn he shot a look at Jack when he mentioned the part about the promise.

The sun was a dying glimmer in the west when they parked at a hotel overlooking Monterey's wave-swept beach.

"We could get a suite." Jack looked at her, holding out her keys. "With all the crazy things that are happening, it might be a good idea."

"We could also eat worms and die," Taylor said sweetly, pocketing her keys. "But let me make this very clear. We'll be getting two rooms. One for me, and one for you and your big ego." She tugged her purse over her shoulder, glaring at him.

"The suggestion was for security, not for sex, Taylor."

Taylor rubbed her forehead as if it hurt. "Look, let's drop the negotiations, shall we? It's been a long day and I —"

"I don't think you should be alone tonight. You've had one hell of a day, and if there are any complications, I'd like to be around."

"What complications could there be? I'll go into my room, lock my door, and throw the bolt. End of scene, end of chapter."

"Just in case. No groping. No questions. I promise."

Staring into his eyes, Taylor could almost believe he was sincere. "Why are you looking at me that way?"

Jack sighed. He was trying damned hard to keep this strictly business, but Taylor made it impossible. She was too alive, too irritating, too honest — and she made Jack feel totally alive whenever he was around her. Through the open window he could smell the tang of pine trees and ocean winds; both told him how long it had been since he'd sat in the darkness with a woman. Arguing. Laughing.

Wanting.

"We should go in." His voice was harder than he'd intended. "Forget what I said about the suite." He'd just have to rig an alarm to go off if her door opened. It wouldn't take him long.

"You're giving up, just like that?"

Jack shrugged. "It was only a suggestion. If it complicates things, forget it."

"Maybe things already are complicated." Taylor looked down at her hands. "I was rude before, and I'm sorry. I thought you expected . . ."

Sex? Because he'd done her a few favors? What kind of men had there been in her life? "I'm expecting nothing beyond a good night's sleep, but I like your sister. If something comes up, I'd like to tag along."

"Okay, fine. You win." Taylor took a sharp breath. "We'll get a suite. It's probably more practical." She watched him closely.

Warily, Jack realized. As if she expected him to make some kind of move on her.

He simply walked around and opened her door. "Okay."

"No argument? No celebration. That's it?" Taylor sounded bemused.

"That's it."

"Are you at least going to tell me what you and Sam were *really* discussing at the hospital?"

"Football."

Her face was touched by the glow of the rising moon. "Football? Right. And that's why you were glaring at each other."

"It's a guy thing. Something about those Y chromosomes. Medically speaking, it means you have thick skulls and take football very seriously."

Taylor crossed her arms. "Medically speaking." Her expression told him she knew she was being conned but she wasn't sure what to do about it. "I'll just get the details from Annie, after she works the truth out of Sam."

Not this time she won't, Jack thought grimly. "Can we check in now or do you want to waste more time looking for an argument?" He didn't like their position, a target for anyone who might be lurking in a dark corner of the parking lot — not that he was going to tell Taylor that.

She straightened her shoulders, shifted her purse. "Are you suggesting that I am a person who takes pleasure in arguing?"

"Honey, it's one of your major traits."

Taylor snorted, walking toward the hotel, her body very stiff.

Jack followed, scanning the darkness around them for any sign of sudden movement. The woman had the temper of a pit bull and no mistake. The truly sick thing was that he was actually starting to enjoy it.

The hospital orderly had a friendly smile for everyone.

He made sure of that as he wheeled his gurney into the main basement service elevator. It was one of the busiest times at the hospital; when the evening shift changed, no one paid any attention to one more gurney or white uniform.

When the elevator doors opened at the

fourth floor, the orderly wheeled his gurney off with quiet efficiency, not rushing, but not dallying either. Later, two people in the elevator would comment that he seemed like your normal, average Joe. Not too smart, but no basket case either.

Just a regular guy doing his job.

The orderly stopped at a storage room outside one of the hospital's subsidiary power stations. He fished a key from a big ring, unlocked the door, and wheeled his gurney inside, whistling a Frank Sinatra tune. Once inside, the smile dropped away.

He checked his watch. Twelve minutes until a call would summon Sam McKade to the business office for an important insurance matter. When he got there, he would find out the call was a mistake. After a few more questions, and several apologies, he'd head back upstairs to the obstetrics floor.

By that time, his wife would be gone. Annie McKade would be all he needed to reel in her sister.

Viktor Lemka checked the syringe under the pillow, straightened the sheet and blanket on the gurney, and then wheeled back into the hallway, just an average face going about an average job. He would have preferred targeting Taylor O'Toole, but when he found that she'd checked into a suite with the man named Broussard, Lemka scratched his plan to snatch her from the hotel. His instincts told him there were too many risks with Broussard so close.

So he'd take her sister instead. His syringe would have her under in ten seconds, and no one would notice a sleeping patient headed to surgery. Lemka even had a fake medical chart with him in case anyone showed some interest.

He locked the storage room behind him, straightened the fresh pillow, then steered his way toward the elevator, whistling softly all the while, a man with no cares. He was going to enjoy his time with Taylor's sister. The fact that she was carrying a baby would make her far more excitable when she recovered from the drug. She'd be more inclined to negotiate, to cry, and finally, to beg hysterically.

Not that her tears would make the slightest difference to Viktor. She'd do whatever he told her to, whatever he needed. And when he had one sister, it was only a matter of hours until he had the second sister begging, too.

He looked at his watch and smiled.

Six more minutes . . .

Jack closed the door and slid the safety chain in place.

He felt a momentary twinge at sticking Uncle Sam with the bill for the lavish suite, but orders were orders.

Taylor was outside enjoying the last touch of twilight from a magnificent terrace. "What do you think?"

"Hell of a view." He moved beside her,

watching the lights of fishing trawlers, yachts, and oil tankers rocking against the dark blue line of the Pacific.

"For once, I agree with you." Taylor rubbed her neck restlessly, then kicked off her shoes. "I feel like I could sleep for about a century. Must be all the exercise and fresh air."

"Don't stay up on my account." He needed to check in with Izzy and get an update on the Lincoln Town Car that had been following them. He also had several security precautions to be implemented, in case Izzy hadn't already thought of them.

A wall of fog was moving in from the west. Taylor watched it, shivering.

"Cold?"

"I was just thinking about Annie." She frowned. "How fast things happened today."

"Stop worrying." Jack leaned against the terrace rail, studying her in the moonlight. "Go take a long bath and crawl into bed. You should sleep like a baby."

She rubbed her arms, frowning. "You really aren't going to put on any moves, are you?"

"Sex is always fun and often amazing, but I figure we both could use some sleep tonight."

She stared at him. "Which category would you put me in, fun or amazing?"

"Why do I get the feeling this is a trick question?"

"No tricks. Consider it a scientific survey.

195

You know, like the judges with the scorecards: 9.5. 9.6. 9.8."

Just when he thought he had her pegged, she'd ask a question like this. Jack took his time considering his options while the sky darkened to obsidian above them.

"Well? Fun or amazing?" Taylor tilted her head. "Or neither?"

"Both. Depending on your mood. I have the feeling you can be as outrageous as they come."

"Very diplomatic." Taylor pushed away from the rail and picked up her shoes. "So you're not going to be a cliché and suggest sex to take my mind off my problems?"

"Sex wouldn't be my first drug of choice, no." Jack's eyes narrowed. "Imported chocolate, maybe."

Taylor's soft laugh spilled through the night. "I can see that you are a *dangerous* man. On that note, I believe I'll head for my bath — which should be fun, but not amazing. If I appear to be babbling, please ignore me. I'll make sense again in the morning." She swung her shoes from her fingers. "Probably."

Jack waited until she had crossed the living room. As soon as the bathroom door closed, he pulled out his secure cell phone and dialed Izzy.

"Teague here."

"We're in the hotel, Izzy. Room 1404. Have you got anything else on that car plate from Carmel?"

196

"You'll love this. The car was found abandoned an hour ago, next to U.S. 1."

"So our guy is fast and takes no chances," Jack said. "Not the kind to make careless mistakes. And he was involved in Annie's accident?"

"In my experience, the frequency of coincidence is highly exaggerated."

Spoken like Izzy, Jack thought. "What about security at the hospital?"

"All taken care of. Sam hasn't called me yet, but I'm sure he will. No doubt he'll be spitting nails. I'll tell him what I can and leave the rest for him to ferret out. With his contacts, I give him about twenty-four hours before he has your file accessed. After he saved that busload of kids last year, a lot of people in Washington owe him favors."

According to the grapevine, Sam McKade had saved more than a bus full of schoolkids, but the details remained hazy, even to a fellow SEAL. "You worked with him on that?"

"On what?" Izzy's tone was calm but final.

Jack realized the subject was closed. "He looks like a good man to have guarding your back in a firefight."

"None better." Izzy's chair creaked. "What's the plan for tomorrow?"

"If Taylor's sister is doing okay, we'll head back about midday. I'll fill in the details when we leave."

"Copy." Izzy seemed to choose his next

words carefully. "So, you got that suite."

"Safer that way."

"I agree. Just remember to keep your ammunition dry."

Jack stared at the bathroom door. Running water didn't quite cover Taylor's off-key rendition of Springsteen's "Hungry Heart." The woman had great taste in music, he had to admit.

"Yeah," he muttered. "That and everything else."

Chapter Sixteen

Even after half an hour in a tub full of bubbles, Taylor felt restless. She scooped up the hotel's terry cloth robe hanging on the bathroom door.

The hotel rates were stiff, so she'd insist on paying the bill. Considering the way Jack had helped Annie, it was the least Taylor could do.

Not that Mr. Macho would let her pay.

She ran a brush through her hair, whisked on some moisturizing cream, and stepped outside. "All yours, Jack."

There was no answer. The lights were dim in the main room, and Taylor realized that a gas fire was burning while Jack made popcorn in the microwave.

Dangerously competent, she thought, watching him joggle a bowl, toss in the finished popcorn, and mix the kernels with a few deft motions.

He braced a shoulder on the wall, taking in the sight of her. "You look relaxed."

"Blissfully. Are you going to share that popcorn before I whimper?"

"Dig in."

Taylor closed her eyes, savoring her first warm, buttery mouthful. "Popcorn might just be my new drug of choice." She took another bite, then handed the bowl back to Jack.

"Thanks for everything you did today."

Jack shrugged. "Glad I happened to be around. You and your sister seem pretty close."

"Off and on. A serious case of sibling rivalry, you understand." And now the business with her adoption, Taylor thought grimly.

One demon at a time.

"Something tells me you two were a handful growing up. Probably gave your parents gray hairs."

Taylor gave a dry laugh. "The gray hairs came strictly from me. Annie was the rock, the one everyone could count on. She still is."

"What about you?"

She rolled her shoulders, wandering through the room. Silently, she straightened a picture, shifted a vase of flowers. "I was the one caught smoking cigarettes behind the library in third grade." She smiled faintly at some private memory. "The one who dyed her hair green for senior prom and came dressed in a miniskirt made out of duct tape. Call me the screwup."

Jack grimaced. "How'd you get the tape off?"

"Scissors." Taylor wandered the room again, touching and straightening, touching and straightening. "Cut it in seven different places. Hurt like hell even then — and no, don't ask for details." She rubbed her shoulder restlessly. "Through it all, Annie was the rock. For years she held things together, being a saint. I wonder if my parents were ever sorry . . ." Her voice trailed away and she stared down at the fire.

Jack moved behind her. *"Don't."*

She didn't turn. "Don't what, itemize my many and various indiscretions?"

"Don't question your parents' choices or their happiness." Jack saw something cross her face. He realized it was regret. "You can go back or you can go forward, not both. Don't waste time trying."

"Wise counsel. Except sometimes late at night, when my demons are howling louder than usual, it's hard to believe in wise counsel." Her voice fell. "Or anything else."

Because he wanted to touch her, Jack took a step back. The room was already too warm, the fire too intimate. Besides, he had a gut instinct that if he touched her even once, he'd be gone. They both would. "Yeah, the late hours when the demons are out — those can be a bitch." He'd had his share, usually after a mission. He carried a lot of angry faces in his memory, and they were always waiting, ready to haunt him.

"So what do you do?" Taylor turned slowly, firelight in her hair.

She was a hundred shades of gold, Jack thought, and he yearned to see how her skin glowed beneath that heavy robe.

Forget your fantasies, he told himself grimly. "It's getting late."

"No, please." She touched his arm. "What do you do? Seriously."

He looked down at her fingers resting gently on his arm. He felt the heat of her skin reach down through his shirt — then race through the rest of his body. "You let them howl," he said harshly. "Sometimes you may even learn something. Either way, you'll find they get tired fast. Then you go on with your life."

She nodded slowly. "Let them howl. Pretty good advice."

Their eyes met. Neither moved.

Jack stepped away, not because he wanted to, but because he had to. "Anytime."

"It's getting late," she said, as if unaware he'd just said that. "But I'm still worried about Annie. I can't put my finger on it."

"Call her. Then you'll feel better."

She took the phone and dialed the number Sam had given her earlier. Even from several feet away, Jack could see the tension in her shoulders.

"Sam, it's Taylor. I — I just wanted to know how she's doing. For some reason, I can't stop worrying." She listened tensely, nodding once. "You're sure?"

More silence. Then she took a deep breath and smiled. "I'm glad, Sam. Be sure to give her a kiss for me." There was more silence. Then her face flushed. "Yes, he's here. You want to talk with him? Sure." She turned, phone in hand, color in her cheeks. Jack realized he'd never seen anyone more beautiful.

"Sam wants to speak with you, but Annie's fine. All the tests came out normal. She's checking out in the morning."

"Great." Jack took the phone, frowning. No conversation with Sam McKade could be pleasant right now. "Yeah, Broussard here."

"You're sharing a room with Taylor?"

"A suite."

Silence.

"Your business, buddy. As long as she's not hurt."

"Understood."

"By the way," Sam continued tightly, "Izzy said to give his regards."

"Glad to hear it."

"You're still telling me nothing?"

Taylor wandered closer, studying Jack.

"I figure you'll get whatever you need."

"In other words, buzz off." Sam muttered a soft curse. "My wife is sleeping and I don't want to wake her or I'd say a whole lot more, Broussard. But I'll tell you this: If Taylor has walked into the middle of something, get her out of it fast."

Taylor moved closer, holding out the bowl of popcorn.

Jack smiled and shook his head. "No, my vote goes to the 49ers. No contest."

"What? Is Taylor there? She's listening?"

"No way," Jack countered. "Definitely the 49ers."

"Okay, I read you. Just remember this." Sam's voice was low and lethal. "She doesn't get hurt, Broussard. Neither does my wife. Otherwise, you answer to me."

"That's a bet," Jack said calmly, then hung up.

Sam held the phone, listening to the dial tone.

Annie stirred in the big white hospital bed, reaching out a hand. "Sam?" she asked sleepily. "Are you there?"

"Right here, babe. Go back to sleep. Everything's fine."

"I had a bad dream. There was a big man in a white hat. He was singing and then the butterflies came, all around him like a cloud of orange." Annie's fingers tightened. "He had a knife, Sam. He was slashing at the air, at the butterflies, saying something I couldn't understand." She took a sharp breath. "It seemed so *real*."

"Just a dream, Annie. I'm right here. Trust me, no one is getting near you." He'd lay down his life first, Sam promised silently.

Annie's breath eased out slowly and her fingers relaxed in his. "Just . . . don't go. Hospitals give me goose bumps." She smiled. "Too many sick people."

Sam bent and kissed her as her eyes closed. She was asleep again in seconds.

He moved his chair so it faced the door, then poured himself a cup of fresh coffee from the thermos on the table.

It was going to be a long night.

Two floors down, the elevator doors opened.

Three nurses got out, followed by a big gurney. The orderly turned down the hall, smiling pleasantly at a white-haired patient in a wheelchair.

Four more minutes, Viktor thought.

The night's pleasures were about to begin.

"You're *hurt.*"

"What do you mean?"

Taylor glared at him. "Hurt. H-u-r-t. I've been watching how you move your right shoulder. You wince when you think I'm not looking."

"It's a little stiff, that's all." Jack feigned a yawn. "Why don't you get some sleep?"

Taylor put down the bowl of popcorn. "Sure. Good idea." Instead of moving toward the bedroom, she reached past him and shoved open the top button of his shirt.

"Hey."

"Shut up, ace." The second button slid free. "I've always wanted to play nurse."

"Taylor, stop." Jack blocked her hand, then sidestepped.

She moved behind him, pulled the tails of his shirt free, and ran her palms up his back.

This time Jack had to grit his teeth to keep from cursing. He was relieved he'd already removed his shoulder holster.

Taylor tugged the shirt away, and her eyes widened. "My God. Your back is one big bruise."

Jack shrugged. "By tomorrow it will be fine."

"When were you going to say something?" Her face was pale. "You let me moan and groan about shadows and you said nothing."

His shoulder throbbed, but it was nothing he couldn't handle. "A little ice and I'll be fine. Get some rest."

"No, I'm getting the ice for you. Then I'm cleaning up those cuts on your wrist."

"Forget it."

Taylor turned over his hand. "See these? You still have a few pieces of gravel in here, too. You idiot." She strode toward the door. "I'm going for that ice."

"You're going nowhere." Jack gripped her hand. "I'll go, damn it."

"You really are worried, aren't you? That's what this is about — you think someone could still be following me." She stood unmoving, emotions churning across her face. "What happened today with Annie wasn't an accident, was it?"

"We don't know that."

Her hands locked, shaking badly. "I've got to call Sam. To warn him, in case someone goes after Annie."

"Annie's fine. Sam's with her, remember? He won't let anything happen."

"You *told* him about me?"

"Only that there have been some problems. He promised he'd keep an eye on Annie, just in case."

"So that's why he looked so angry at the hospital?"

"He loves his wife very much. He's worried about you, too."

Taylor looked down at her hands. "Go get the ice. It will give me something to do, and I need a major distraction right now."

"Taylor —"

She looked up, her eyes resolute. "Either you go or I go."

"Hell." Jack grabbed an ice bucket from the table. "Lock the door behind me. Don't open it for anyone."

After a moment, she nodded. "It's bad, isn't it?" she whispered.

Jack didn't want to lie to her, not after all the lies that had come and were yet to come. "It could be. Let me do my job and we'll make it through fine."

He opened the door, waited until she threw the bolt, then headed for the ice machine.

When the phone rang beside Annie's bed, Sam grabbed it before it could wake her. "Hello?"

"Mr. McKade?"

"That's right."

"This is Mrs. Quinn in patient billing. I'm sorry to bother you at this late hour, but we have a problem with your insurance. I need further information in order to complete the billing for your wife's stay." The woman's voice

207

was brisk but polite. "It should only take a minute."

"You want me to come down now?"

"That would be a help, Mr. McKade. In the morning, Mrs. McKade will be checking out and things could be too rushed."

Sam frowned. "Can't you send someone up here with the papers?"

"I'm afraid not. Privacy issues are involved, you understand. For legal reasons, I have to witness your signature."

"Where are you?"

"The second floor. Patient billing. We're right next to medical records."

"I'll be there shortly." Sam put down the phone, staring at his wife. He didn't like the uneasiness nudging at his neck.

He opened the door and motioned to the man sitting in a wheelchair just outside the next room. Without a word, the man wheeled forward, his IV swaying.

"Someone just called me from the billing department," Sam said softly. "Watch her, will you?"

"No problem." The man was big and looked surprisingly healthy for someone with an IV. "Izzy said to stay as long as you need me, Commander McKade."

"Something feels off," Sam said quietly. "Maybe it's me, but — keep an eye on my wife. I won't be long."

"You got it, Commander."

An orderly was just stepping off the elevator as Sam came out. The man seemed to be in no particular rush and gave Sam a pleasant smile, whistling as he wheeled his big gurney down the corridor.

Chapter Seventeen

Taylor tensed as she heard a tap at the door. "Who is it?"

"It's Jack."

She checked the view hole, then slid open the bolt. "Let me have the ice. Go lie down on the bed."

In another time and place, Jack would have taken great pleasure in those words. But not now. "I can handle this, Taylor."

"Shut up and lie down." She locked the door and threw the bolt. "Get moving. I can be as alpha as you are, and I only give orders when I have to."

Irritated, Jack sat on the bed. "Then get it over with so we can sleep."

"Hold out your hand." Taylor drew in a sharp breath as she saw his wrist and the underside of his arm. "This could hurt. There's alcohol in the travel-size mouthwash, which is the only antiseptic I have."

"Honey, it will take more than mouthwash to bring me to my knees," Jack muttered.

"No need to sound so smug about it." Taylor poured on some of the red liquid, then brushed Jack's wrist with a clean washcloth. "There's some gravel here. Are you okay?"

"I think I can stop myself from begging for

mercy." But not, Jack decided, if her legs kept pressing against his thigh and her breast teased his back as she explored his arm.

Then she put the ice bucket between his legs. "Does that hurt?"

He gritted his teeth. Maybe the ice between his legs was a good idea, considering the way her robe gaped open above her breasts.

"Look, are we about done here?"

"There's more ground-in dirt and gravel." Her robe gaped open again, granting him an unforgettable view of shadowed cleavage and one perfect pink nipple.

"Finish it." His voice was hoarse. He was pretty sure he was sweating. "Just do it."

Taylor stared at him. "You're sweating. It really must hurt. I'm so sorry, Jack."

She started to take the ice bucket, but he held it in place with one hand. "I'll keep it here."

"I found a plastic bag. We can fill it with ice, then tie it off to use on your back." She bent over, scooping up ice by the handful.

As she did, Jack had a circuit-sizzling view of her other breast. He closed his eyes, definitely feeling sweat on his forehead. When the ice bag pressed against his back, he heaved a silent prayer of thanks for the distraction.

"You're a mess, you know that, Broussard?"

No mistake about it. And if her hips kept grinding against his back, he was going to turn around, yank off her robe, and see how she

looked wearing nothing but firelight and promises.

Taylor bent closer. "Are you listening to anything I've said?"

He turned his head.

Big mistake. That one simple movement offered an excellent view down the front of her
robe. The woman was built, he thought grimly.

And he was the dumb side of a jackass.

"I'm going to sleep." He brushed past her as
he stood up. "You've done enough fussing for
one night."

"I'm sorry if I hurt you." Her voice was
ragged.

"Hell, Taylor. It's not that." He tried to rub a
knot out of his neck, keeping his eyes focused
anywhere but on her amazing body. "It's not
my shoulder that hurts right now. The fact is, I
don't want things to slip out of control."

She gripped the ice bag, frowning. "Is there a
chance of that happening?"

"Speaking for myself, there's a definite
chance."

"Because you're thinking about me. About
us." Her voice fell. "About how that bed might
feel."

"Damn it, yes."

She swallowed hard. "So was I." She frowned
down at her robe, which had slid open a few
inches. "But that would be a stupid thing to do,
because we barely know each other and we're
both busy people, with busy lives that will

probably take us in completely different directions. Which means tonight will end up as merely a short and rather pleasant memory. A few months from now we might even pass on the street without any sign of recognition."

The hell he would. He'd recognize those legs anywhere. "Probably."

"My ice bag is leaking." She took a hard breath. "Why do you make me babble this way? I never babble."

Jack could think of too many things he wanted to do besides talk, and the bed seemed too close, so he grabbed the dripping ice bag and strode into the living room. "Get some rest. Tomorrow this will be a bad dream. You'll forget all about me and the bed and this conversation."

"Probably."

Jack grimaced when he heard her robe hit the floor, but he managed not to turn around. "Night."

The lights went off in the bedroom. "Night, Jack." The sheets rustled softly. She released a sigh. "It would have been fun, just the same. Maybe even amazing."

Jack felt his body tighten. He ordered himself not to move, not to look. Not to think about her body under those soft white sheets.

When the wave of lust finally passed, he looked down and saw that the ice was melting on his shoes, which were now soaked.

A fitting end to the day from hell.

The corridor was quiet as the man in the white uniform tapped at the door. "Orderly. May I come in, Mrs. McKade?"

Hearing no answer, he pushed his gurney up to the door.

The woman was asleep. Her husband was off on his little errand, exactly as planned. It was almost too easy, the Albanian thought.

Sam watched the floors slip past with growing impatience. When the elevator reached the second floor, he looked out, scanning both corridors.

It took him only a second to register the nursing station and the low *whir* of monitoring equipment. He was in the Cardiac Care Unit.

There was no billing department anywhere in sight, only patient rooms that stretched in both directions.

Cursing, he grabbed a passing doctor. "Get hospital security up to room 9010."

"Why? Who are —"

"Do it now." Sam shot out a hand just before the elevator doors snapped shut and prayed he wasn't too late.

Noise echoed across the hall behind Viktor. A man rolled closer, seated in a wheelchair. "Who are you?"

"Orderly." Viktor shoved his syringe out of sight beneath a pillow. "I was told to transfer

214

this patient to the I.C.U."

"On orders from who?" The man wheeled closer, frowning. One hand slipped to his pocket.

"Feel free to check her medical chart." Viktor spoke with casual confidence. "The call came in five minutes ago." He was smiling as he moved to the head of the gurney and pushed open the door to the room. "Nobody tells me anything, of course. Just 'Henry, go here, Henry, go there. Orderly, take this patient and go get that one.' Never ends."

"Stop." The man in the wheelchair shot to his feet. Viktor saw the outline of a gun inside his pocket. A trick. But how?

"Step away from the patient."

Viktor made a careful movement backward, his hands still on the gurney. "But I'm supposed to take her down to I.C.U. Stat." Viktor had heard that on a medical show on TV. He liked how the letters rolled off his tongue.

I.C.U. Stat. It sounded so American.

"I said step away. Now."

"Okay, sure. No problem." Viktor was busy running through risks and possibilities.

On the bed, the woman made a low sound and sat up sleepily. "What's wrong?"

He saw his moment, driving the gurney into the side of the wheelchair so that the man was knocked off balance. Before his target could twist around and level his gun, Viktor pulled his own weapon from beneath his loose white

215

uniform and shot the man twice in the chest.

On the bed, the woman started to scream. She threw the vase of flowers, soaking him, but doing no damage.

Down the hall he heard the crackle of a walkie-talkie. Calmly he shoved the patient with the IV onto the floor and sat down in his chair, wheeling through the door with his weapon beneath a towel on his lap.

He heard footsteps near the elevator. Urgent voices rumbled down the corridor as he rolled toward the service stairs at the far end of the hall, then walked into the stairwell, calmly stripping off the white uniform to reveal a conservative business suit underneath. A pair of wire-rimmed glasses and a stethoscope looped casually around his neck completed the transformation. Anyone looking at him now would see a tired and slightly distracted physician on his way home after final rounds and a long day.

Viktor even had a fake hospital ID in his pocket. Nothing left to chance.

But his hands were shaking and he shoved down a wail of rage as he tossed his white uniform into the first garbage can he passed. Next time would be different, he swore.

Icily calm, he made his way to the car he had stolen an hour earlier. No more errors would be permitted. The people he worked for had zero tolerance for failure. Viktor knew that well, because he was the person they usually called to deal with any failures.

He was stepping into a shiny black Audi with new plates when a police car shot to a halt outside the hospital entrance, sirens flashing.

Too late.

Viktor smiled as he drove away.

Chapter Eighteen

"What the *hell* went on here?" Sam paced angrily as Izzy's wounded agent was lifted onto a gurney by two orderlies and a nurse.

The hospital security officer beside Sam shook his head, looking baffled. "Shots were heard, and a nurse saw a man heading down the hall in a wheelchair, but she didn't pay much attention at the time." He gestured at the bleeding man on the gurney. "We can't find any information about him. He's not wearing a patient ID."

Izzy's man opened his eyes, searching the room until he saw Sam, who bent beside him, touching his shoulder.

"Take it easy," Sam said, even as fury boiled through him. At least Annie was safe. A nurse was helping her dress right now, and Sam was dead set on having her out of the hospital immediately. But he wanted some questions answered first, by God. "What happened in here?" he asked the man on the gurney.

"One man. White — uniform." He swallowed as if his throat hurt. "Hit me with the cart. Too slow." He turned his head, his eyes anxious. "Your wife — Is she —"

"Annie's fine. We got to her in time."

The agent closed his eyes, his breath a sharp

rush. "Thank . . . God."

Sam looked up as the attendant interrupted. "No more, sir. We have to get him to surgery."

Sam nodded and stepped back. He had no doubt that someone had come here for his wife. The only question was why — and how soon they would pay for the attempt.

Jack shot awake on the couch. The room was dark and there was no noise from the bedroom. He padded across the floor, cracked open the door, and checked on Taylor.

She had one foot dangling over the edge of the bed and a pillow across her head.

Jack closed the door and moved outside. The bolt on the outside door was thrown, the chain securely in place. No sounds came through from the hallway.

But something bothered him, making his shoulders tense as he checked the doors to the terrace. All quiet, all secure. Even then, the cold tension remained.

His pager vibrated. Jack scanned the number. *Izzy.*

Something told him the news wouldn't be good.

He dialed Izzy's secure line, trying to rein in his tension. "Broussard here," he said tensely.

"Report." Izzy's voice was low and hard.

"Nothing to report. Taylor's asleep, the room's secure. No developments of any sort."

"Someone went after Annie McKade in the

hospital. I just got off the phone with the local police, who were helpful but completely out of their depths."

"Didn't you have a man in place?"

"Two shots to the chest. He's in surgery right now."

Jack cursed softly. "And Annie?" He was almost afraid to ask. Unbearable to think that all her light and laughter could be lost.

"She's safe. Sam got to her in time. He had a call to sign some important insurance forms and told my man to keep an eye on Annie. When the office location was wrong, he charged back upstairs and found Annie awake, frightened, but trying to help my agent, who was on the floor, bleeding badly. Needless to say, Sam is furious and he's taking this all the way to the top. Given his heroism with those kids last year, people are going to listen."

"What about video surveillance at the hospital?" Jack frowned. "Most hospitals have some security at their main entrance."

"I'm checking on that as we speak. One thing is certain. We're all going to get our asses chewed," Izzy growled. "And maybe we should. The attack on Annie was too damned close. I wasn't prepared for that." His voice hardened. "But I will be next time."

They both would be.

"I'm getting Taylor out of here." Jack was already reaching for his shirt. "She's going to want to see Annie before she goes."

"Negative. Sam wants her kept away from Annie, and he's right. Taylor will be furious, but she's no fool. When she starts throwing things, call me and put her on the phone."

When, not if, Jack thought. Clearly, Izzy knew Taylor pretty damn well. "Where do I take her?"

"I'll let you know. Right now we've got another problem."

Jack checked his Beretta and holstered it. "I'm not sure I want to hear this."

"Remember the bozo in the denim jacket from the convenience store robbery?"

"I remember. He's being held in solitary confinement pending further questioning."

"*Was*," Izzy said angrily. "He bought it last night. A razor in the neck. It happened right after shift change."

"The security cameras didn't catch anything?"

"Inoperative. Unspecified malfunction."

"What about his colleagues?"

"One suffocated with a prison towel. Very messy. The driver has been incoherent after the head wounds he suffered at the robbery."

"How convenient." Jack frowned at the door to the bedroom. "I'm getting Taylor out of here now. We could be on the move for a while, so I'll check back in several hours."

"What do you have planned?"

"A little car-switching. I want to find out who's been shadowing us around Monterey."

"No direct encounters. Get a plate number and contact me. I'll handle the takedown."

Jack didn't answer. His mind was too busy screaming for the hunt and the raw pleasure of jerking someone out of a car and tossing him around until he shook loose some answers.

"Broussard?"

"Copy. No direct encounters. But if he makes one move against Taylor, I'm going after the bastard, and you can key *that* into your mission update in big black letters."

Taylor blinked. "What's wrong?"

"Time to go."

She rubbed her eyes, trying to focus. "Go where?"

Jack was sitting beside her in the darkness. "I thought we should see the moon going down over the bay. After that, I know an all-night seafood place with shrimp to make you weep."

"Rather sleep." She burrowed into her pillow, then froze. "Wait." She shot upright. "Annie. Is she okay? Has something —"

"Annie's fine."

Taylor just stared at him. Something was definitely wrong. "If she's fine, why are you here frowning and trying not to?"

"Taylor, we need to go. We'll discuss *why* once we're on the way."

"I'd rather know now." Her lungs were working but she couldn't seem to get enough air.

"In the car." Jack softened the order. "Please."

"I want to call Annie at the hospital."

Jack was already picking up her clothes, a neat pile on a nearby chair. "She's not there," he said tightly. "She and Sam left an hour ago."

"Why? Damn it, Jack, what's happened?"

"In the car," he repeated. "You've got three minutes." He tossed over her clothes. The bedroom door shut before she could finish her next question.

Taylor was frowning when she walked into the living room, fully dressed, her purse on her arm. "We both know this has nothing to do with moonlight over the bay."

"It was worth a shot," Jack said grimly. He checked the view hole, then freed the security chain. "Stay behind me. Do what I say, and no questions."

"But —"

"*No* questions."

Taylor didn't like the possibilities playing through her head, but Jack's face told her this was *real*, no tricks and no test, so she nodded impatiently.

Jack opened the door, scanned the hall, and motioned her out after him. Neither spoke until they were in the elevator, headed down.

"When we get to the lobby, lean in close to me and walk slow. Pretend you've had too much to drink."

She started to speak, then bit off the question, realizing it was a waste of time. When they hit the lobby, Jack scanned every corner with calm thoroughness, moved closer, and guided her toward the front door.

Always keeping to her right, Taylor realized. So his shooting hand was free.

"Bend over a little," he said quietly. They were approaching the front entrance. "Hold your stomach as if it hurts."

Taylor did just as he asked. They were rewarded when the doorman approached at a trot, looking concerned.

"Can I help you?"

"My wife's not well. I wonder if you could bring around our car. It's the yellow Wrangler under the second light." Jack smiled, holding out Taylor's keys.

"Of course, sir. I won't be a moment."

He strode off, his red uniform jacket the only color in the shadowed parking lot. As the motor turned over and lights cut through the darkness, Taylor felt the tension in Jack's body. He turned casually, looking from one end of the lot to the other, then out to the adjoining street.

Nothing else moved.

When the Wrangler pulled up, Jack helped Taylor into the passenger seat and handed the attendant twenty dollars.

Taylor gripped her knees, trying to stay calm. "Why the masquerade?"

"I wanted to watch for any reaction. Lights

on the street or movement at the back of the parking lot, things like that."

"Did you see any?"

"Nothing." He didn't sound relieved, so Taylor decided they weren't out of trouble yet. "Now you can answer my question. Why are we here?"

Jack took his time adjusting the rearview mirror. He scanned the area one more time, then revved the Wrangler into gear and headed toward the main access road. "Something happened at the hospital tonight."

Taylor felt all the blood drain out of her body. *"What?"*

"Someone was shot. The authorities won't release that information to the public, but that's what happened."

"Not Annie or Sam?" Her voice was strangled.

"No. But the man was in Annie's room when it happened."

"My God." Taylor stared out the front of the Wrangler, breathing hard, trying to figure out how far she could trust this man she barely knew. "None of this was coincidence." When Jack didn't answer, she took that for a *yes.* "Why go after Annie? It all has something to do with me." She rubbed her face, trying to wake up fast. Trying vainly to make this nightmare go away. "Because you were with me? Because we had a suite?"

"That appears likely."

"I don't understand any of this."

Jack reached into his pocket and pulled out a cell phone. "Take the phone. Hit number two."

"Why should I do that?"

"Because you want answers." Jack continued to hold out the phone. "Call the number. You'll get your answers."

"I don't want to talk to a stranger. I want to hear it from *you.*"

"Not even if it's Izzy?"

She stared at him for long moments in silence. "You know Izzy?" she said slowly.

Jack nodded.

"You *work* with Izzy Teague?"

"Our paths cross from time to time."

"How close do they cross?"

"Ask Izzy."

"Are you a Fed or a freelancer?"

"Ask Izzy," Jack repeated.

"Great." She took the phone carefully. "If you're lying to me about this —"

"Dial the number, Taylor."

She hit the button, then waited tensely.

"Teague here."

Taylor felt her breath catch. "Izzy? Is that really you?"

"In the flesh. Beautiful and pure of heart, as always."

There was no doubt about that rich, gravelly voice. "Fine, so talk to me. What's going on and how do you know Jack Broussard?"

"How doesn't matter. What matters is that

you can trust him, Taylor."

"Yeah, right," she snapped. "Especially when he tells me nothing."

"He's just doing his job."

"*What* job is that? Running a divorce investigation for Rains' wife? Since when do routine divorces involve armed assaults in public places?"

"Calm down. I know you're angry, so I'll try to fill in the blanks. I pulled Jack in to help me with some surveillance. In case you don't know it, Rains is playing with some nasty people. We think he owes money to the wrong crowd — the kind who collect by taking out a few family members."

Taylor had a sudden memory of Annie's tense face as the ambulance raced her to the hospital. "It doesn't fit. I've got nothing to do with Rains."

"You've been following him. And you were in the convenience store." Izzy's voice was flat, cold. He was in his professional mode, the way he'd been when Taylor had first met him. "When you started staking out Rains, that tossed you into the mix. We think the robbery might have been meant to cover up an attack on Rains. Whether to frighten him or abduct him, we aren't sure."

"But they went after me in that store, not Rains." Taylor turned away, aware of Jack's eyes on her.

"We're dealing with hired muscle, not

Fulbright scholars here. When Jack showed up like their worst nightmare, they probably panicked. Given the circumstances, you looked like their best ticket out."

Taylor closed her eyes while her mind worked furiously. "So Rains is in real trouble. What happens now?"

"Jack stays with you." A chair creaked. "When you go out, he goes out, too. No excuses."

"Like some kind of bodyguard?"

"You're in danger, Taylor. Until we know why, Jack stays close." Izzy paused. "That means everywhere, night and day. We're assigning people to the spa, too. Now would you put Jack on again, please?"

She stared at Jack. "He wants to talk with you."

She handed over the phone and shivered as wind cut through the open window. Why was someone targeting *her?* So what if she had followed Rains around town? She knew next to nothing about the man or the details of his shady activities.

She heard Jack hang up, but she didn't take her eyes from the headlights cutting over the road. She kept hoping she would wake up and the night would be gone and this would be no more than a bad memory.

But the road continued to flash in front of her, all darkness and fog.

"We're almost there."

"The place with the shrimp to make me weep? Funny, but I just lost my appetite."

Jack put on his blinker. "We're going for information, not food — even though the shrimp really will make you weep." A few minutes later, their headlights flashed off a glass-and-stone structure rising from a low hill overlooking the coast.

"How well do you know these people?"

"Well enough to trust them with my life — and yours. We won't be here long anyway."

Taylor wasn't convinced, but Jack was already parking and pocketing the keys. *Her* keys, if she'd had the energy to argue, which she didn't. By recklessness and sheer rotten luck, she had stumbled into real danger, and obstinacy had driven her in deeper. Now it was time to wise up and get clear, even if it meant swallowing her pride and taking orders.

She followed Jack into a large room with a stone fireplace that covered one whole wall. A fire blazed, casting a golden glow over empty tables covered by spotless white tablecloths.

"Jack, is that really you? Hell, it's gotta be, what, six years?" A big man in a white apron barreled out of the kitchen, arms outstretched.

"Seven, but who's counting. Dad sends his love, Rock."

The two men hugged, then stood back for some hard backslapping. The man named Rock seemed to give as hard as he got. "How is the old pit bull?"

"Doesn't look a day over forty." Jack smiled. "As he tells anyone who will listen. You're looking pretty solid, too. Cooking must agree with you, Rock."

"It has its moments." Their host wiped his hands on his apron, shaking his head. Taylor pegged him as somewhere between fifty and sixty, but he could have been a few years older. The hand he held out to her was heavily callused, and his smile infectious.

"So this is your important package. Glad to see you're finally showing some taste, Jack, my boy. This one's a looker."

Taylor flushed as she shook hands with the older man.

"Taylor, meet Bo Rockney, alias Rock — and a few less polite names. Just remember, do not ever play cards with this man and don't believe a word he says."

The older man laughed as he drew Taylor closer to the fire. "Have a seat and warm up. Any friend of Jack and his daddy is a friend of mine." Rock glanced at Jack. "How about some wine?"

"Not tonight. Coffee would be great though." Jack glanced at Taylor. "We've got some driving ahead of us."

"Two espressos coming right up."

"Did you get those things I called about?"

"Right over here." Rock tossed a cardboard box to Jack. "I figure you'll tell me in good time why you need a scarf and two sun hats in the middle of the night. Now, I'll get that coffee and call my son."

Jack stiffened. "Your son? You're not handling this personally?"

Their host sighed. "Damned arthritis in the right knee, Jack. I don't do the heavy driving I used to. But my son is better than I ever was, so you'll have no complaints."

"Your call," Jack said, but he was frowning as his friend left the room.

"What's going on? I don't understand any of this," Taylor said uneasily.

"You will. Put these on." He tossed her a floppy sun hat and a long red scarf. "There's one more thing I need you to wear, too."

It took them twenty minutes to run through Jack's route, finish two espressos, and get suited up.

"The car's outside. Good luck, you two." Rock shook hands with Jack, then Taylor, and checked his watch. "My son's got your cell numbers if anything turns up."

By now Taylor had a few thousand questions, but she held them, aware that these two men were pros — even if she wasn't sure at what.

She tugged at the black Kevlar vest Jack had made her put on. It felt like a gorilla draped over her chest.

The weight reminded her this wasn't book research. The danger had somehow become her life.

Chapter Nineteen

"Keep your eyes on the side roads. Watch for lights or movement of any sort. And if I say *down,* get your head between your knees and stay that way." They were driving inland toward the freeway, and Jack never stopped checking the rearview mirror. The ease with which he'd strapped on his Kevlar told Taylor he wore it often. She yearned to ask *where* and *when,* but now was clearly not the time for distractions. "You think someone followed us from the hotel?"

"It's possible."

"And if we do find someone?"

"I'll call Izzy. He'll handle the rest."

He frowned when he said it, and Taylor realized he wasn't happy about the idea.

For ten minutes they followed U.S. 1 toward Castroville, looping back often, then slowing and turning as if in search of a particular address. Finally, they pulled off at a service station, where Jack pulled out a map, pretending to study it.

He didn't look up as Taylor's cell phone rang. "Take it. Rock's son should be calling with an update."

"Hello?"

"Hey, there. This is Rock's son. Tell Jack that

I picked up a car two miles back. Blue Volvo sedan. Give me a few minutes and I'll have the plate number."

"I'll tell him." Taylor relayed the information to Jack, who folded up the map and headed back to the highway. She tried to contain her uneasiness. "You don't look surprised."

"I'm not. I made the Volvo right after we left the restaurant, but he's a pro, keeping the rhythm and holding back, so I needed to be sure." He made a sharp turn down a side street, then a quick U-turn.

No blue Volvo raced past.

"Damned good," Jack muttered.

He pulled back onto the highway.

"What happened to the Lincoln from this morning?"

"They're taking no chances we'll spot them."

"What do they *want?*" Taylor had gone over the last week backward and forward, but the most crucial piece of the puzzle still eluded her.

Jack glanced over, unsmiling. "You tell me."

"I don't know, damn it. Or do you think I'm hiding something on purpose? Maybe you think I planned this all so my sister would be attacked."

"No, I don't think either of those things." Jack's hand covered her knee.

"Maybe Sam does," she whispered. "Maybe Annie does, too. I'm the screwup O'Toole sister, after all. It looks like I'm *really* living up to my reputation this time."

"No one's saying anything close to that." His voice hardened as he glanced into the mirror.

"He's there, isn't he?"

Jack didn't answer.

They shot into Rock's parking lot a few minutes later, but this time Jack parked closer to the front, just at the edge of the big overhead lights. "Take everything you need," he said quietly. "We're switching cars."

Two people bustled out the restaurant's front door several minutes later. The woman stopped at the edge of the shadows, adjusting her red scarf carefully. The man held open her door, gave her a quick kiss, then slid behind the wheel of the Wrangler. Together they headed back to downtown Monterey.

Jack and Taylor watched from the darkened kitchen.

When the Wrangler disappeared, Jack turned to his father's friend and gripped his hand. "Thanks, Rock. I owe you big for this."

"Hell, forget it. I owe your old man a dozen favors. Jamie will see you home safe and sound in Frisco. Just remember to come see me when you've got time for some serious eating. Tell the old man I said hello, too."

"Will do."

They left via a back door from the kitchen, where a big Audi waited with a driver at the wheel. Rock's son happened to be two hundred and fifty pounds of solid muscle, Taylor saw as they slid into the backseat.

"Make yourselves comfortable, folks. You might want to stay down while I loop around a few times to be sure you've lost your tail."

When he was finally satisfied they were clear, Jack sat up. "Good work, Jamie. Any news from your brother in the other car?"

"Yeah, he picked up your friend right outside the lot. Blue Volvo. Plate number 76 Bravo Foxtrot 5. He'll be hitting most of Monterey and Carmel for the next two hours, so the Volvo will be nice and busy."

"Thanks, Jamie. Tell them to be careful. If anyone approaches, they are to evade immediately. No macho stuff."

"Don't worry. My brother's done a lot of stunt-driving. They'll be fine."

Jack's tense expression told Taylor that he wasn't close to relaxing. After the news that came in a few minutes later, Taylor understood why.

Jamie glanced back as he cut off from his brother's call. "You've got a second car in place. Gray Acura, plate number 22 Alpha Charlie 9." His eyes met Jack's in the rearview mirror. "You two must be pretty special."

Taylor was caught somewhere between tension and exhaustion. "Jack?"

"Later," he muttered. "Get some rest." He pulled her head down against his shoulder. "The night isn't over yet."

★ ★ ★

They were ten minutes south of Redwood City when Jack eased away from Taylor and tapped Jamie on the shoulder. "Pull off at the next exit."

"You got it."

Jack had seen no other tails, but he was taking no chances. He'd relayed the two plate numbers to Izzy for a trace, but both men knew that the presence of a second car indicated serious players who were highly paid and highly trained.

And Jack wanted them bad.

Chapter Twenty

It was almost five a.m. when Jamie angled against the curb in front of Taylor's apartment building. After a little banter and quick handshakes, his two passengers headed in past the yawning doorman. Maybe it was exhaustion that left Taylor with the uncomfortable feeling she was being herded along, given orders rather than explanations at every turn.

Or maybe it was fear.

She watched Jack as they waited for the elevator. "Do you work for Izzy or for the government?"

"I work *with* Izzy, off and on."

"I don't understand why he's so interested in Rains." She frowned. "Unless Rains has government connections. Does he?"

Jack said nothing, his face tense.

"Hello? I believe I just asked a question."

"Look, we're tired right now. I've got to call Izzy and we both need to grab some sleep." The elevator door opened. "In the meantime, here are the ground rules. I'll be right next door. Call me before you open your door to anyone. That means the doorman or a deliveryman. It means Candace and anyone else in the building. Call me before you go out — and that means *anywhere*. We'll review all the other precautions tomorrow."

"*Other?* Wait a minute —"

The elevator opened at their floor. Jack squeezed her shoulder. "Trust me, Taylor. This is the only way." He handed her a piece of paper. "Here's my number. Remember to use it."

He looked almost as tired as she was, standing in the dim light outside the elevator. Only that knowledge kept Taylor from demanding more answers before she agreed to these ground rules — or any others.

He pulled out her key, taken from her key ring before they'd left Monterey. "I'll go in and take a look. Just in case."

Taylor took a sharp breath. "Fine. But tomorrow I want answers, Jack."

"Sure. Tomorrow." He motioned her behind him as he opened the door, one hand slipping under his jacket near his holstered Beretta. Once inside, he made a quick loop through the apartment, checked the windows and her small terrace, then nodded. "All clear. Lock up and be sure to put on the chain."

"You're *certain* you got those numbers right?" Izzy sounded edgy. Hardly surprising at 5 a.m., Jack thought grimly.

"Absolutely."

"Hell. That makes it official. The two cars following you in Monterey are leased under contract to the federal government."

"That was *our* people out there?" Jack worked hard to rein in his fury. "You want to tell me what's going on?"

"I would if I knew. Believe me, I'm going to hold a few feet to the fire until I find out. Meanwhile, we have a new development."

"Rains has reappeared?"

"So to speak. He's still underground, but he made a call from a pay phone to the San Francisco D.A. He asked to go WITSEC."

"Witness protection? With what?"

"According to Rains, he's got names, dates, and numbered accounts, but he won't give any details until his security can be guaranteed. No safety guarantee, no deals. Believe me, he sounds pretty damned scared."

Jack blew out a breath. "This makes him a federal concern. The U.S. Marshals will handle his protection."

"Until Rains gives us some answers, you're still on the job. I'm faxing through a photograph now. Memorize it, then destroy it."

Jack heard his fax machine beep. "Anyone I should know?"

"Viktor Lemka — at least that's his current alias. An enforcer who used to work out of Chechnya. These days, he deals from a cesspit in Paraguay called Ciudad del Este. You want a top-notch hitman, Ciudad is the place to go.

You want to get fake passports or broker a big arms deal, that's the place — and Lemka is considered the best."

"Why is he still walking around?"

"Because he's only been in the U.S. officially once. Any other visits were made under a phony passport. His file's sketchy, and he changes his appearance frequently. We've only got one photo of him, and it's grainy. Take a look."

The fax spewed out a sheet, which Jack studied carefully. The man had cold eyes and a narrow forehead. Jack couldn't pick up too many other details. "I may have seen him somewhere. Is he Russian?"

"Albanian national."

"Just like the bozos in the convenience store holdup," Jack mused.

"You got it, and I doubt it's a coincidence. Lemka appears to specialize in torture and extortion using surgical techniques. Possibly he trained as a doctor somewhere along the line, but you don't want this joker changing your IV, trust me. A waitress at a Chinatown nightclub says she saw him arguing with Rains and two other men. The Albanian thought she was getting too close, so he roughed her up. Since her brother is a cop, she was suspicious and clued him in, so now the Feds have people watching the club in case he returns. They've also got feelers out among the Albanian community."

Jack was quiet, thinking. "Lemka was the

man who went after Annie in the hospital, wasn't he?"

"It's possible. My agent just came out of surgery, so he hasn't given much of a description. Because Annie was half asleep, she didn't see much, either, but a nurse was coming up the stairs when she saw a man pass. She noticed an orderly's uniform discarded in a garbage can one floor away. She's fairly sure this is the man, though now he has a moustache."

Jack studied the grainy photo. The eyes turned even colder and the mouth looked too thin to smile. It was a face that wouldn't stand out or be easily remembered.

When he had committed the features to memory, he reached for a lighter. "Shouldn't I show this to Taylor? He could go after her next."

"Negative. I've been told to keep her out of the loop on this. I fought it hard, but I lost." Izzy didn't sound happy about the outcome.

Jack touched his lighter to the corner of the sheet and watched the thin lips glow, curling into a sneer. "What about Rains' girlfriend? Has she been seen with Lemka?"

"No, but we're checking Candace Jensen out thoroughly. She met Rains a year ago while she was doing temp work at his lab. She quit a few months later to work at a local gym. We have no real proof that she's involved — except I had an expert climber check Taylor's gear while you were gone. He tells me the equipment was in perfect shape, as was the part of the bolt still attached to the rope. On a hunch, I sent him out to check the other half of the expansion bolt still on the rocks."

This was Izzy, Jack thought. The man was nothing if not fanatically thorough. "What did he find?"

"That particular bolt was brand-new, for one thing, which was interesting since all the others on that rock were worn. When he took a closer look, he saw the broken bolt was twisted, showing tension fractures that couldn't come from normal climbing stress. In short, someone meant to guarantee that the bolt would blow."

Jack rubbed his neck, frowning. "Candace?"

"She was there. She had the skill."

"But why? What could she gain from hurting Taylor?"

"Beats me. Until we know more, I suggest you keep this from Taylor."

"Are we going to tell her *anything?*" Jack asked grimly. "After all, Candace is her friend. Both their lives may be in danger."

"As soon as we know what we're dealing with, we'll make that decision. We can't risk Taylor letting something slip to Candace. For now, this stays under wraps. Orders, Jack."

"Some orders suck."

"I happen to agree." Izzy's chair creaked. "What does Taylor have on the agenda today?"

"Nothing much. She mentioned she was

staying in so she could work. Book deadline or something."

"Good. Grab some sleep." Izzy sighed. "Let's pray that her writing deadline will keep her out of trouble for a while."

At ten o'clock Taylor rolled out of a sound sleep. When she opened her eyes, she was instantly flooded by bad memories. How had her life gone straight to hell in only forty-eight hours?

She tried calling Annie at home, but the message machine clicked in. After leaving a message, Taylor listened to her own messages. Candace had phoned twice, sounding worried and asking Taylor to call her soon. But when Taylor tried phoning, she reached Candace's message machine. Was *everyone* in the world out? she wondered irritably.

Wandering into the kitchen, she surveyed her food options. They included two jars of olives and a discolored orange that appeared to be growing white hair.

Wincing, Taylor closed the refrigerator and decided coffee would have to do. With a cup of steaming espresso straight from her machine, she headed off to work.

After half a dozen false starts, she finally got into the pace of her story. She kicked off her slippers and settled in, halfway through a hair-raising pursuit when her doorbell rang. She looked up, frowning, trying to place the sound.

With the words flowing, the last thing she needed was an interruption.

She closed her eyes, hunched over her laptop as she let the scene replay in her mind. She heard the lap of water in the distance. Somewhere, dogs were barking in frantic excitement. A red Toyota spun around a corner, fishtailing crazily —

The doorbell sounded again, cutting off her concentration, and Chinatown fell away.

Taylor shot to her feet. "Fine, fine, I'm coming, but this better be damned important." After straightening the old sweatshirt she always wore when writing, she glanced in the view hole and flung open the door. "*What?*"

Jack raised an eyebrow. "Good morning to you, too."

"Yeah, it might be, but I'm working and I don't want to be interrupted."

"Not even for fresh sourdough bread and French onion soup?" Jack held out two big paper bags. "I had it sent over from the restaurant on the corner."

Taylor's irritation wavered when she smelled the rich aroma of melted cheese and perfectly caramelized onions, but she still had a scene to finish. "That's — that's nice of you, Jack. I'll take a break soon." She frowned. "Unless there's something important you need to tell me?"

He looked long and lean in blue jeans and a gray T-shirt that hugged muscular shoulders.

Don't drool, Taylor told herself firmly.

"Nothing urgent. Just checking to be sure you eat. Annie warned me that you forget everything when you're writing."

"You've heard from Annie?"

"Not today. She told me yesterday, at the restaurant."

"I called, but she wasn't in." Taylor rubbed her neck, which was starting to ache. "I just want to find out how she's feeling."

"I'm sure she'll call." He held up the bags. "Can I put these down?"

"Oh — sure. And thanks. But I really do —" She frowned as he opened cabinets and took out a pot. "What are you doing?"

"Heating the soup. Once you're eating, I'll leave. Annie made me promise."

Taylor bit back a complaint and tried to hold the scene in her head. *Dogs barking. Red Toyota.*

Jack paid no attention, turning on the oven and sliding the bread in to warm. "So you don't go out and you don't eat when you're writing?"

"Not much. Not when I've got a deadline closing in."

"How close?"

Taylor sighed, trying to be patient. "Six weeks."

"So what does that mean?"

"It means I'm up at night, pacing the floor. It means I eat on the run or not at all, and that you may hear occasional banging sounds on the wall. Don't worry, it's only my head. There may be some cursing, too."

"All this just to write a book?

She crossed her arms. "*Just?* Have you ever tried it?"

"No way. Not me. Still, it seems an uncomfortable way to make a living."

"You don't write to be *comfortable*." The scene was slipping away now, and Taylor realized that in a few moments it would be gone forever. "Look, why don't you —"

Jack turned off the burner and poured soup into a bowl. "Almost done here. I'll cut you some bread, then hit the road."

Red Toyota, two men on foot. Taylor closed her eyes, repeating the image like a mantra, trying not to smell the warm bread.

"All done." He set a plate with bread on her kitchen table and gestured at the last bag. "Wine's in there, too, if you feel like it. I wasn't sure if you gave that up when you were writing, too."

"Not wine, only sex." She saw his face and shrugged. "Just a joke. I'll have the wine later, thanks. But right now I really need to —"

"So you're not going out at all today?"

"No way. Too much work."

"And you'll call me if your plans change."

"Sure."

"Okay, I'm out of here. Good luck with the writing." Jack's eyes narrowed, and he ran his thumb gently over her cheek. "You've got some ink here." He traced her lip. "Here, too."

Taylor tried to ignore an instant kick of desire at his touch. "Occupational hazard."

"I could get rid of it for you." His eyes glinted.

Taylor took a jerky breath. "Out, Broussard." It was only as she was closing the door that she realized Jack had told her nothing about the cars that had followed them the night before. Nor had he given her any more information about the attack in Annie's hospital room.

After a mental head slap, she headed back to her computer. Food could wait. Right now she had a hot date.

Two men and a red Toyota.

Jack picked up the banging about twenty minutes later. He shot out of his chair and scanned the hall.

Nothing.

Frowning, he checked the elevator. No sounds there, either. On the way back inside, he passed Taylor's door and heard muffled noises. He pressed one ear to the door, trying to pick out the source of the noise, but it stopped abruptly, replaced by footsteps and low muttering. After that came a thud, like a pillow hitting the wall, followed by more muttering.

Jack was starting to worry when he heard footsteps drum past the door. This time he made out Taylor's voice, lowered in a silky drawl.

"Touch me like that *again,* and I'll have to call the police." With a throaty laugh, she continued in a deeper voice. "Honey, I *am* the police."

He heard a ripple of laughter, and then the footsteps moved to the back of her apartment.

The crazy female was writing. Apparently that meant walking, talking, cursing, and banging on walls. Jack shook his head. Who knew that making up stories could be so much work?

Judging by the sounds from her apartment, this writing stuff made a person completely crazy. And if you were Taylor O'Toole, who was already more than a little crazy to start with . . .

For no particular reason, Jack found himself smiling. The lady was a kook all right.

The window opened inside and cool air spilled beneath her door. A chair creaked, and he heard the tap of computer keys, fast and steady.

She was finally in her zone.

Jack walked back into his apartment, frowning as his cell phone vibrated.

"What's Taylor doing?" As usual, Izzy wasted no time on preliminaries.

"She's writing. If you call pillows flying and general cursing behind closed doors writing."

"Hey, if it was easy, we'd all be doing it. Of course no one would *believe* our stories," Izzy mused.

The sound of steady typing continued from

Taylor's office as Jack opened the briefing file he'd been given the week before. Inside, he found half a dozen photographs.

Taylor in a firing stance beside a police officer in full SWAT gear.

Taylor in a wet suit standing on a beach north of Malibu with an L.A.P.D. rescue team.

He shook his head. "What's with the woman? She sky-dives, she trains with SWAT officers. These people are picky about who they train with. I know that from personal experience."

"Taylor's not just anyone." Izzy's chair creaked. "But I think you already noticed that, too."

"Understatement of this or any other century." Jack picked up a picture of Taylor with a class of junior high students who appeared to be doing the conga while dressed in Roman togas. "Sometimes I think she's nuts. And others . . ." He cleared his throat. "She gets to you. Somewhere deep."

"Welcome to the club." Izzy cleared his throat. "You okay with this assignment? If it's getting too personal —"

"I can deal with my feelings, Teague." Jack spoke more sharply than he planned. "So can Taylor."

"We're counting on that," Izzy said calmly, then disconnected.

Jack picked up another photo with Taylor standing next to her sister. Behind them, a cedar-and-glass building rose over a pristine beach below the cliffs of Big Sur.

This must be the family resort south of Carmel.

The sisters were laughing, caught in the intimacy of some private joke, and Jack could almost feel the force of their connection. He had been relieved when Izzy reported the government had assigned two men to the spa to protect Annie from any future attacks.

He picked up a photo of Taylor in goggles, hunched over a skeleton on an examining table. A sign in the background read SMITHSONIAN LABS — AUTHORIZED PERSONNEL ONLY.

It was clear that something drove her. Who else would go to these lengths to get every detail right? Jack could understand that kind of determination, since it carried him through every mission, but he still couldn't get a handle on this writing thing. How did you pull people and conversations out of thin air? Where did you get your ideas? None of it made sense to him.

He heard another *thump* as something struck the adjoining wall. After more muttering noises, the keyboard clicked away in high gear again.

Jack shook his head. As far as he could see, there were easier ways to make a living.

Like raising the *Titanic*.

Chapter Twenty-one

At first, Taylor didn't hear her phone. It wasn't only because she was in the middle of a tense confrontation between her heroine, the cop she'd fallen for, and two Triad hit men. The earphones helped, too.

Frowning, she slipped off the regulation airline safety coverings that were her favorite writing accessory. With the big orange ear covers off, she heard ringing, checked her caller ID, then lunged for the phone.

"Annie, is that you?"

"No, Taylor. It's Sam."

There was something impersonal about his voice that made Taylor frown. "Is everything okay with Annie?"

"She's fine. Just a little tired." He seemed to hesitate.

"What is it?" Taylor gripped the phone. "Not the baby . . ."

"No, not that."

Taylor heard a muffled voice in the background. "Is someone there?"

"Izzy sent some men down." Sam's voice hardened. "I can't be here all the time, and I want Annie protected."

Taylor stared at the phone, feeling sick.

"What happened in the hospital, Sam? No one will tell me."

"Annie was attacked last night. Izzy had an undercover agent in place, but someone got past him. One more minute and I could have been too late."

Taylor flinched at the anger in his voice. "Sam, I'm so sorry. I never saw any of this coming. One minute I was doing a favor for a friend, and the next I was being followed."

Receiving funeral wreaths.

Taken hostage in a robbery gone wrong.

She took a sharp breath. "Sam?"

"I'm here, Taylor." He didn't sound particularly happy about it, either.

"I didn't think there was any real danger. Definitely not for anyone else. I'm so —" Her voice broke, but she recovered. "So damned sorry."

The silence stretched out, worse than a slap on the face.

"I'd like to speak to Annie." Her voice sounded stiff and awkward. "I need to apologize."

"She's sleeping right now."

"Then I'll drive down. I can be there in two hours. She'll be awake by then."

"*No.*" Sam bit back a low curse. "This is hard for me to say, but —"

Taylor's fingers were ice cold where they gripped the phone. "You don't want me there, do you? You think it could put Annie at risk."

"I think it's possible, and I can't take that chance, Taylor. Do you understand?"

She stared at the framed photographs on her desk.

Annie holding a handful of wildflowers from the garden. Annie and Sam with a class of schoolchildren in D.C. Annie and Sam getting married, their faces filled with a glow that radiated right off the paper.

Taylor had threatened all that. She closed her eyes, squeezed back the bite of tears. "I . . . understand. I won't see her. I won't call. Not until all this is over. Just tell her . . ."

Tell her what?

That she was sorry she had always been a screwup? That she was sorry she had endangered the one person she loved most?

So empty. So pointless.

"Tell her hello. That's all."

Taylor hung up quickly. The windows blurred as she stared out toward the bay, blue and gold in the afternoon sun.

The alarm screamed, and Taylor shot upright, clutching her pillow.

3:30 a.m.

Normal people hadn't even gone to bed yet.

Sighing, she stumbled toward the closet. At least her clothes were hung where she could find them. Otherwise she'd be throwing on red leather with purple plaid.

She'd have worn her favorite black leather

jacket except it was history, thanks to the thugs who'd tried to kidnap her at the convenience store. Instead, she held up a pair of nicely fitted black jeans. Okay, so they were nicely *tight,* thanks to all her surveillance snacking.

She tossed the clothes over her shoulder with a sigh. The next time her publisher asked her to do a warehouse signing, she'd take out a gun and shoot herself.

"She did *what?*" Izzy sounded exhausted.

Jack knew exactly how he felt. He was tugging on his shoes and grabbing his jacket as he talked. "She ducked out at 3:45. Lucky I have a silent alarm to alert me when her front door opens." Jack holstered his gun, sprinted for the door. "She's already in the elevator, damn it. I'll have to call the doorman and ask him to hold her."

"Good luck."

Jack rang off, then punched the intercom.

"Yes, Mr. Broussard?"

"Ms. O'Toole is on her way down, and I need to talk to her. Can you tell her to wait for me in the lobby?"

"Happy to, sir. Hold on, please." There was some bustling, then the sound of footsteps. "Sorry, Mr. Broussard. She says a limousine is waiting. She'd prefer to speak to you later."

Like hell she would. "Tell her to wait. There's a fifty-dollar tip in it for you."

"Yes, *sir.*"

Jack fumed as he waited for the elevator, then jumped on and pounded the button for the lobby. The doors had barely opened when he shot out after Taylor.

The doorman was on the front steps, looking anxious. "Sorry, Mr. Broussard. I tried to stop her, but —"

"*Which car?*"

"Over there. The black limo. Her publisher always uses the same company."

Jack didn't hear anything else because he was sprinting along the sidewalk, reaching the limousine just as the driver started out into traffic.

Jack cut him off, standing in the street and blocking his way.

The driver frowned. "Sorry, Ms. O'Toole, but there's some nut out there waving his arms. You know him?"

Taylor stared into the beam of the headlights, then sighed. The nut was her neighbor. "I'll talk to him, Curtis." She rolled down her window and leaned out. "I'm late, Jack. Could you please move?"

"Get out of the car." He was dressed all in black, and his eyes could have scored diamonds as he strode around to her window.

"I beg your pardon."

"*Out.* Now." When she didn't move fast enough, he slid a hand inside, unlocked her door, and yanked it open.

The driver spun his head. "Hey, buddy, you can't —"

"I just did," Jack snapped, pulling Taylor outside.

"Ms. O'Toole?"

Taylor crossed her arms as fury tore through her. "Wait a moment, Curtis. I'm certain this is all a mistake."

"Like hell it is." Jack scanned the dark street, then motioned to the driver. "You can clear out now. The lady won't need your services. I'll be driving her wherever she needs to go."

"No way. I can't just drive off."

"Sure you can." Jack pulled out a leather wallet with a picture ID. "S.F.P.D. The lady and I have business to finish." He stared at Taylor. "Don't we, Ms. O'Toole?"

Taylor pulled at his hand, but it was like trying to move a tank. "Jack, this is ridiculous," she hissed.

"Send the driver away. You won't be needing him."

"But —"

"Don't waste any more of his time."

Taylor bit back an angry answer and dredged up a smile. "Thanks, Curtis. I'll get to the signing myself. It will be fine."

"But, Ms. O'Toole —"

Jack shoved a card at the limo driver. "You heard the lady. If there's a problem about your bill, send it there." He pulled Taylor back into the building. "It's the least Izzy can do."

"I still don't see the problem."

Taylor was fuming as she followed Jack through the parking garage. "I was on company business and I have a company-arranged driver. Why are you getting so worked up about this?"

"Why? Because we had an agreement. You gave me your promise."

"Of course I did. But I didn't think —"

Jack yanked open her door. "Yeah, you don't think. This is real, Taylor. If something goes wrong here, people *bleed,* and the red stuff isn't in your imagination. Maybe you can manage to remember that."

She stood by the car, livid, her hands opening and closing. "Are you saying I'm irresponsible as well as stupid?"

"I'm saying that there are rules, Taylor. We discussed them, and you agreed. I expect you to abide by them, whether they're convenient, whether you like them, or even whether they make sense. You just follow them."

She glared at him. "Rules are a big thing with you, Broussard. Do you want me to click my heels and salute now?"

His eyes didn't waver. "No, I want you to get in the damned car. I won't be pulled into an argument or a discussion, even if it will make you feel better."

She tried for a snappy, biting answer, but all her words were gone, swept away by the nagging thought that he could be right. "Fine. You can drive me." She slid into the seat, her body stiff. "We're going to Oakland, with one stop on the way."

"Where in Oakland?"

Taylor rattled off an address, then pointed across the street. "Stop over there first."

She expected a protest.

She got only cool reserve.

The man had ice in his veins. She *hated* people who evaded her questions — especially when she was in the mood for a nice, full-decibel argument.

Bavarian cream.

Vanilla cream.

Chocolate cream.

Muttering, Taylor mulled over the merits of raspberry filling versus marble ribbon frosting. In the end she took a dozen of both, for a grand total of twelve dozen.

To say nothing of five gallons of iced cappuccino.

The flustered young woman rang up what was probably her biggest order ever and laboriously made change. While she boxed the doughnuts, Taylor rubbed her neck and forced herself to relax. She wasn't wrong and she *wasn't* going to apologize. No way. How was she to know that Jack meant she couldn't go *anywhere*, even with a trustworthy driver? She rode with Curtis every time she went to Oakland, for heaven's sake.

And she *wasn't* argumentative.

Jack was waiting at the door when she stepped outside, nearly hidden behind a tower of cardboard boxes.

She made a point of not looking at him.

"I'll take those."

"I can manage," Taylor said tightly, hefting the boxes and trying not to drop the large thermos filled with coffee.

She positioned her assorted treasures in Jack's car without a word, and the silence held for almost twenty minutes, until they turned into a huge warehouse parking lot surrounded by floodlights. Even at this early hour, vans and tractor-trailers were revved up beside brawny men who rolled boxes from truck to truck.

Two raised their hands and called out a greeting.

In answer, Taylor held up a doughnut box like a battle prize. By the time he had parked in a space near the front door, there were four men waiting to help her unload.

Jack didn't look happy at her audience. "Friends?"

"The best. They're the ones that keep the books moving — any day and every day. See you later, Broussard."

She figured the doughnuts would last maybe fifteen minutes, given these guys' appetites. And that was a *generous* estimate.

Experience had taught her that book merchandisers were a hungry lot.

Jack watched, frowning. What in the hell was she doing *now?* Hauling a thousand doughnuts into the middle of an Oakland warehouse an hour before dawn?

The front door opened. More people spilled out. They were calling her Ms. Taylor. Jack scratched his head and then the image clicked in.

M.M. Taylor was her pseudonym.

Okay, so it was something to do with her books, but why here? Hotshot writers went to fancy galas at big, glittering hotels, didn't they?

Taylor gave a warm hug to a woman with a long apron and a pencil shoved above her ear. They walked inside together arm in arm.

As the door closed, Jack moved in closer, studying a big poster by the front entrance. Taylor's picture and three book covers were fanned out over white cardboard.

She was signing *here?*

Thoroughly confused, Jack pulled out his phone. If he had to be up at this miserable hour, Izzy might as well be, too.

But Izzy sounded fit and chipper, Jack noted sourly. "Okay, I give up. What's she doing in a warehouse in south Oakland at 5 a.m.?"

"Coffee and doughnuts with the drivers and merchandisers."

"Merchandisers?"

"The most important people in the literary food chain, buddy. They're the ones who re-stock the books in grocery stores, pharmacies, discount stores. Everywhere books are sold that isn't a bookstore."

The picture began to dawn. "Authors do this a lot?"

"Some. Taylor's got a knack for making readers where you wouldn't always expect them."

Jack watched two big men in flannel shirts stride inside, pointing at the sign. "No kidding." He sat down on a bench where he could see the front door and most of the parking lot. "With this kind of audience, I guess she'll be safe." He sighed. "Of course, I'd give my right arm for a fresh doughnut and a cup of that coffee."

"No one said surveillance was fun."

Jack watched Taylor handing off boxes to several new arrivals who were wearing long aprons with big pockets. "Looks like she enjoys this kind of stuff."

"That's why she's so good at it."

"So this is what — some kind of goodwill visit?"

"Not exactly. They've been after her to come for several months. They're all trying to find out what happens in her next book."

Jack shook his head. Books were okay, but he couldn't see what all the excitement was about. Sure, he read Clancy and Patterson, but he wouldn't die if he had to do without. "What's the big deal? Some things happen, some people talk a lot, the book ends."

Izzy chuckled. "Read the book, Jack. See for yourself."

The line clicked off.

Chapter Twenty-two

Trucks were coming and going and the parking lot was filling up, but Taylor still hadn't reappeared.

Twenty minutes had passed and Jack was getting edgy. Not that he thought she was in danger, but mission rules specified keeping the subject in visual range, and he didn't like violating procedure, no matter how strange the location or the assignment.

He walked into the front lobby, thinking how good a doughnut would taste, not to mention a hot cup of coffee. Frowning, he studied the hand-lettered sign on the poster. *Will she or won't she?* was written across the top in big red letters.

What was that all about?

Beneath the lettering, Taylor's picture held an air of mystery, but the effect was offset by her jaunty black beret and the little Jack Russell terrier she held in her arms.

It was a knockout all right. Jack felt his mouth easing into a grin without conscious effort.

"If you're here to meet Ms. Taylor, you'd better hurry. She's running out of books back there." A big man with a blue tattoo was waving to Jack from the inner doorway.

Through the swinging doors behind him, laughter drifted out.

Okay, Broussard. Think fast. "Uh, actually, I —"

"Go on. No need to be shy. She's great."

Jack cleared his throat. "Well, I don't really need to —"

"Hang on." The man crossed his big arms, studying Jack. "You a friend of hers?"

Jack nodded.

The man held out a callused hand, studying Jack hard. "Name's O'Reilly. You in the Marines?"

"No."

"Something close. You got the look. Rangers?"

Jack shifted uncomfortably. "Navy."

The man didn't look convinced. "Regular Navy?"

"This and that," Jack muttered.

"How long you been out?"

"Sometimes it seems like forever," Jack said dryly.

"I hear you there. So what are you doing with Ms. Taylor?"

"I'm here because —" Jack cleared his throat, racking his brain. "Because I'm Ms. Taylor's —"

Brother?

Boyfriend?

Agent?

"Driver," he finished briskly. "Shuttling her around. Keeping an eye on things. You understand."

The big man nodded. "Well, why didn't you *say* so? Important lady like her needs a driver." He kept on nodding. "You take care of her, okay? Meanwhile, we're taking bets on what happens in the next book. I got a hundred dollars riding on the little lady."

Jack tried not to look blank.

"Don't tell me you haven't read *The Forever Code*?"

"No."

"*The Seventh Circle*?"

Jack shook his head.

"Hell, you don't know what you're missing. Hang on." The driver vanished into a nearby office and returned with three thick books. "On the house. Read them in order. I'd get you a doughnut, but they were picked clean fifteen minutes ago. The boxes might be gone soon." He smiled happily. "Some of those guys are animals."

"How about some coffee instead?" Jack took the books, but caffeine was what he really wanted. He had no intention of reading Taylor's stories, but he didn't want to be rude. As soon as he got outside, he'd dump them and no one would be the wiser.

He sipped the coffee O'Reilly had given him. "Thanks. So you're telling me a lot of guys read her stuff?"

"Hell, yes. After a few books, you get to know the characters. Like one big crazy family, except someone's always killing someone else.

And that Lola. You gotta love her."

Jack raised one brow. "Lola is the heroine?"

"Nah." O'Reilly tapped the photograph on the poster. "Lola's the *dog*. The name's a mistake, because she's really a *he,* only the previous owner was too nearsighted to notice. Only cross-dressing Jack Russell terrier I ever heard about." The big driver shook his head. "That little mutt gets into more trouble than all the other characters combined. Wears a little red tartan coat, sharp as anything. Worth the cost of the book just to see what she — I mean *he* — is gonna do next."

A cross-dressing Jack Russell terrier?

"And that P.I. of hers. Hell of an ending to a book."

"How's that?"

O'Reilly snorted. "No way, pal. You wanna find out, read the book. Then you'll be in misery waiting for the next one along with the rest of us."

Jack smiled politely, but he couldn't imagine any book bothering him after the last page. After all, it was just someone's imagination. What was the big deal about made-up people and made-up conversations?

He was all set to ask O'Reilly how much longer the signing would last when he heard a low trill of laughter behind him. The sound did something odd to his muscles.

So what if she had a great laugh? Stow it, idiot.

The door swung open. "What are you doing

in here?" Taylor stood holding a company apron and hat.

"Ready to take you to your next signing, Ms. Taylor." Jack tried to sound cool and professional. "The car's outside. Anything you need me to carry for you?"

"I'll tell you what you can carry —"

Jack cleared his throat. "We don't want to be late."

She put one hand on her hip and stared at him some more. "Is that a fact? Well, if you think I'm going to —"

Jack cut her off, taking the briefcase she was carrying, along with the hat and apron. "Almost seven. Freeway's going to be a nightmare." He nodded at O'Reilly. "Thanks for the coffee, but we'd better get moving."

"No problem. See you next year, Ms. Taylor. Just get that new book finished, okay. We're dying here."

Taylor looked distracted as she smiled at the big Irishman. "I'm working on it, Thomas. You just keep those books moving while I do that, okay?"

"You got yourself a deal."

Taylor frowned as Jack hustled her toward the entrance. "Hey, what are you —"

"Time is money, Ms. Taylor. Remember what your agent told you."

"My agent never —"

Jack pushed her through the door and let it swing closed behind him. "Can't you do *any-*

thing without an argument?" He shook his head, striding down the closest row of cars. "I'm parked over here."

"Good for you. Have a nice trip back." Taylor grabbed her briefcase and pulled, but Jack didn't let go.

"Not without you." He studied her stonily. "You're in danger and my job is to keep you safe."

She stood stiffly. "I don't need a babysitter. I'm all grown up, Broussard, in case you didn't notice."

Oh, he'd noticed.

Footsteps crunched on gravel and O'Reilly appeared behind them, looking uneasy. "Everything okay out here?"

"Sure," Jack said calmly. "Everything's fine, O'Reilly. Just a little discussion about the fastest way back to Russian Hill."

The Irishman didn't move, looking from one to the other.

Jack was ready to dish up another lie when his cell phone rang. Aware that only one person had the number, he answered tensely. "Hold on." He covered the phone and nodded at O'Reilly. "Looks like a change of plans. Now we'll really be late." He pointed toward his sedan. "Why don't you get in, Ms. Taylor?"

She didn't move.

Jack wondered if he was going to have to knock her out and carry her to the car. That meant fighting the big Irishman, of course.

Probably half the drivers in the building would join in the melee, and wouldn't *that* make one hell of a headline.

"Fine." Taylor gave O'Reilly a forced smile and a thumbs-up signal, then strode toward Jack's sedan. When O'Reilly was out of earshot, she spun around. "I want to talk to Izzy."

Jack held out the phone. "Talk away."

Taylor glared at Jack, then grabbed the phone. Could her life get any worse? "I want to know what's going on, Izzy. I don't need a baby-sitter tagging along."

"Don't give him a hard time, Taylor. The man's just doing his job."

"And what job is that? Wasting taxpayer's money?" She blew out an angry breath. "Look, Izzy, I'll help all I can, but the fact is, I know nothing." Jack opened her door and Taylor slid into the passenger seat, frowning. "Of course, if Rains actually came *after* me, things would be different."

"Rains has disappeared." Izzy's voice was flat.

Professional mode, Taylor thought.

"So what? He probably took a trip to Aruba with one of his girlfriends. That has nothing to do with *me*."

Izzy's chair creaked. "For starters, Rains is involved with your friend Candace. You and Candace had a climbing accident last week for no clear reason. Except, of course, that the bolt was tampered with."

Taylor swallowed hard. "How do you know that?"

"Because I sent an expert up on that cliff to check it out. He said there was no question. That break didn't come from normal climbing usage, Taylor. Someone had damaged the bolt."

"You think Rains set that up?" she whispered.

"Very probable. I'm going to need everything you know about him."

"There isn't much. He's Candace's friend, not mine. I've never spoken to him." Taylor frowned. "And I still don't understand why —"

"No details," Izzy said. "I'll meet you. Jack knows where."

When Taylor glanced over, Jack was scanning the nearby traffic, his eyes hard.

Looking the way Izzy had looked.

Looking the way her sister's wounded SEAL, Sam McKade, had looked.

"Is he a Fed, Izzy?"

"He's the man I've assigned to keep you safe, Taylor. The rest is irrelevant."

She took a deep breath, trying to digest this new information. "What happens now?"

"Jack stays with you. That means everywhere. Rains may decide to contact you."

"But he has no *reason* to contact me."

"None that we know of. That doesn't mean none exists."

"Don't get philosophical with me, Izzy. What

about my television interview tomorrow?"

"Canceled."

"Are you crazy? The publicity department has been working on this for six months!"

"We're not going to make you an easy target, Taylor. Not for Rains or anyone else. For the moment, you can keep your regular appointments, anything low profile."

"But anything *really* good, like television, gets canned, is that it?"

"I'm afraid so." Izzy covered the phone and Taylor heard muffled voices. "Gotta go, Taylor. Put Jack on, will you?"

She held out the phone. "Here," she said. But her hand was shaking as Izzy's words hit her.

Not for Rains or anyone else.

Dear Lord, how many people were watching her right now?

Chapter Twenty-three

They argued for fifteen minutes before they decided to stop for breakfast. Then they argued for ten more minutes about *where* to stop. Taylor's stomach was growling when they finally agreed on a Denny's near Union Square.

Jack glanced around a room filled with upwardly mobile young professionals rushing through high-fiber muffins with ersatz butter. "If they offer me an egg substitute omelet, I'm going to shoot someone," he muttered. When the waitress came, he scowled and ordered two eggs over easy, a big stack of pancakes, and sausage on the side.

Taylor snapped her menu shut and said she'd have the same.

Lacing her fingers, she watched him tensely. "Maybe it's time you told me what you really do."

"I already told you."

"Oh, please. If you work this closely with Izzy, you're probably with one of those three-letter agencies. Which is it, the CIA or NSA?"

The waitress returned, giving Jack an interested smile as she filled his coffee. He took a drink and watched her retreating back. "Neither."

"FBI?"

He turned his coffee cup slowly. "Wrong again."

"Izzy's a pro. That means you're a pro." She drummed her fingers lightly. "Marines?"

He snorted.

Taylor sat back, her eyes narrowed. "Is this one of those macho, interforce rivalry things?"

"I don't know what you're talking about."

"You're not going to tell me anything, are you? Not how long Rains has been gone. Not even why he's gone."

Jack drank some coffee, saying nothing. Taylor realized that answered her question. She doodled on her napkin, feeling the first stab of a headache. "Just so you know, I've got a charity event tomorrow night. There's no way I'm canceling that."

"Take it up with Izzy. I'm just the hired help," Jack said dryly.

The waitress returned, balancing a tray with half a dozen plates. After filling the table with eggs, pancakes, and sausages, the woman slanted Jack another interested look and swiveled away.

Taylor noticed that he took his time watching her progress back to the kitchen. "Do women always look at you that way?"

He put an arm over the top of the seat. "What way?"

"Like they could eat you for breakfast."

Jack shrugged. "Doesn't mean anything. She was just being friendly."

Sure. And I'm Agatha Christie. Taylor frowned, struck by just how attractive he was, something that went far beyond bone structure and jacket size.

Because the thought irritated her, she set down her coffee cup with a snap. "I expected her to slip you her phone number." Taylor realized she was being catty and took a deep breath. "Sorry. Not my business." She raised a hand. "Even if I'm on edge, there's no reason to take it out on you."

"There's no reason for you to be edgy." A muscle moved at Jack's jaw. "Not yet, anyway."

"Meaning what?"

"Meaning when it's time to worry, I'll tell you."

Taylor stared at her plate of pancakes, her appetite fading fast. "So you're telling me that things are going to get worse?"

"I'm saying it's likely."

Taylor was working on a curt answer when her cell phone rang. She glanced at the screen but didn't recognize the number. "Hello?"

"Taylor, where are you? I've left three message already." It was Candace, sounding out of breath.

"I'm eating breakfast near Union Square." Taylor pushed away her plate. "What's wrong?"

Her friend sounded very worried. "Harris just called. He said he needed to borrow my climbing equipment to give to a friend. I remembered just in time that I had said I'd thrown everything away after our accident. Do you think he believed me?"

"It doesn't matter. Just don't let him in and you'll be fine."

"But what do I say if he shows up?"

"*Nothing*. Don't open the door. Don't answer the bell."

Jack slid a napkin in front of her and wrote *Who?* in big letters. *Candace,* Taylor wrote back. *Harris just called her,* she added.

"Candace, are you listening?"

Her friend dragged in a tense breath. "He also asked about you, Taylor. He wanted to know where you are and who your friend was." Candace hesitated. "I think he's been watching you."

"Rains asked about me?" Taylor stared down at the pool of butter melting on her untouched pancakes. "What else did he want to know?"

"If you had received something in the mail recently. He sounded upset, and he wasn't making a lot of sense. I heard car horns, so I think he was calling from a pay phone, maybe near Fisherman's Wharf."

Taylor wrote *Fisherman's Wharf* on the napkin and pushed it toward Jack, who turned and spoke quietly on his cell phone.

To Izzy, no doubt.

"Listen, Candace, everything will be fine. Just do what I told you and stay away from Rains."

"I understand, Taylor. But I'm scared, really

scared. I think I'm going to leave for a few weeks. Maybe I'll go down to Cancún for a while. I've got some climbing buddies down there. Could I see you before I go? You know, just to say good-bye?"

"Of course, Candace. Where do you want to meet?"

Taylor was listening to her friend's directions when Jack pushed another napkin in front of her.

No meeting, it said.

"Hold on a minute, Candace." Taylor covered the phone and glared at Jack. "Why can't I meet my friend?"

"No meeting," he said flatly. "Now you'd better hang up. The call could be traced."

"This is *crazy.* I'm not listening." She lifted the phone. "Candace, I'll meet you at the —"

The line went dead, thanks to the finger Jack jabbed against the POWER button.

"Now I *know* you're a lunatic. That was the most rude, the most —"

"How do you know she was alone?" Jack said quietly. "How do you know Rains or one of his nasty buddies wasn't right beside her with a gun to her head?"

Taylor sat back slowly, feeling a little sick. "But you don't *know* that."

"I don't know he wasn't, Taylor, and I'm not about to risk your life on the possibility."

She looked down, fidgeting. "Candace wasn't calling from her home phone," she said slowly.

"And it wasn't her cell phone or I'd have recognized the number."

Jack frowned. "We'll check it out."

"But you don't really believe that Candace —"

Jack rubbed his neck, frowning at the restaurant's front window. "I believe that someone wants Rains, and now they might want you." His eyes narrowed on the passing traffic. "I'd say the people Rains was doing business with are trying to recoup their losses. If they can't get what they want from Rains, they'll move to the next choice. Candace may even have agreed to help them."

"Impossible. It's just that she still cares about the jerk. Don't ask me why." Taylor's appetite was definitely gone. In fact, she might never eat again as long as she lived. Under the circumstances, that might *not* be a very long time.

"Scoot over."

When Taylor looked up, her eyes widened. He was as handsome as ever, his dark features too intelligent for the linebacker's shoulders and torso. "Izzy?"

"In the flesh." His lips twitched. "Scoot over before we make a scene here."

Taylor shifted over to make room, all the while taking in the sight of his familiar features. A year earlier, Ishmael Teague had worked with Sam McKade on a secret operation involving a traitor inside the Navy, and Sam had said there was no one finer. Taylor still didn't know exactly what Izzy did, which was proof of how good Izzy was.

"Candace called you just now?"

Taylor looked at Jack, frowning. "Yes, it was Candace."

"This is important, Taylor. What did she want?"

"She wanted to see me, that's all. Rains had called her, asking about me, and she was worried."

Izzy said nothing.

"You don't believe her?"

"Did Rains ever give you anything?"

Taylor shook her head impatiently. "Nothing. I've seen him once or twice in the building, but we've never talked. And you're wrong about Candace," she said sharply. "She doesn't understand any of this."

"Maybe. Maybe not." Izzy stared at his hands, open on the table. "I had that climbing gear checked while you were in Monterey. The bolt could never have blown from normal climbing stress. Someone gave it a good workout before they took it up on the rock."

Taylor tried to keep calm. "Who?"

"Rains could have paid someone. Or Candace may have done it."

"That's ridiculous. Candace got hurt in that fall, too."

"I'm simply outlining the possibilities, Taylor. We need to work from facts, not emotions." He drummed his fingers on the table. "I want you to go over every detail of the last few months. Think about when and where you've seen Candace and Harris Rains. Think of anything that changed hands between them. Think of anyone else you saw with them. Every detail is crucial."

"But —"

"Just do it. The transfer may not have been obvious, so think hard." His eyes narrowed. "A lot is riding on this, Taylor. We've got a missing Navy scientist, a possible connection with highly toxic materials, and we need to know how Rains fits in."

"Toxic as in smallpox?"

"Toxic as in ricin," Izzy said quietly.

Chapter Twenty-four

Ricin.

The most lethal natural biological toxin in existence, seven times more deadly than cobra venom. Less than two grams could kill hundreds of people, if dispersed as an inhalant.

Taylor shuddered. Research like *that* you didn't soon forget. "You're frightening me."

"Good." Izzy's eyes were hard. "Maybe now you'll stop being so thickheaded."

"Why can't you find Rains and the rest of these people? I want my life back, Izzy."

"We're working on it. For now, you're on a short leash. No more sneaking off without Jack."

Taylor looked away, remembering what had happened in Annie's hospital room. "Fine, even if I don't like it." She crossed her arms. "By the way, I have a big charity function tomorrow night. I'm raffling off a set of my books."

"I'll need to get approval on that."

Taylor's eyes narrowed. "As it happens, a lot of Navy brass from Monterey and San Diego are scheduled to be there. I'm supposed to be escorted by an Admiral Bader or Baden."

"Braden," Izzy muttered. "Just great."

"You know him?"

"Vaguely. Look, Taylor, I need to go through

channels on this. Since the Feds are involved, I want everyone on the same page."

Taylor looked from one man to the other. "The Feds?"

"Don't ask." Izzy was standing by the table when the waitress returned.

She gave him a long, assessing glance. "Can I get something for you, honey?"

"No thanks, ma'am. Just leaving."

"Now that's a *real* shame." The waitress raised on eyebrow at Jack. "Anything for you two?"

"All taken care of."

"Too bad." Her hips took on a definite sway as she headed back to the kitchen.

"You ruined her day," Taylor murmured. "She was definitely interested, Izzy."

"I don't want to know. As for you, listen to Jack. These people are a walking disaster area, and I don't want you becoming their next victim."

He gave her a hard look, then strode out.

Taylor stood up. "I'm ready to go." She grabbed her purse, watching Jack impatiently. "I have to get back to work." She frowned as her cell phone rang again.

"What?" she snarled.

"In a bad mood again or is it just that time of the month?"

Taylor sighed as she recognized Sunny de Vito's voice. "I'm a little tied up right now, Sunny."

"I hope he's built. If so, save some rope for me."

"Very funny."

"So, what time do you need me tomorrow?"

"Need you to do what?"

"Well, I *could* do a stand-up routine, but I figure doing your hair and makeup might be more useful for the charity gala tomorrow night. Your sister called me last week to arrange it. Didn't she tell you?"

A surprise from Annie?

Unfortunately, Annie had been a little busy lately and she hadn't had a chance to tell her sister.

Taylor swallowed hard. "You two are something else. Six o'clock would be good, but I don't know if I'm still going."

"You, turn down a charity event that involves shopping? Do you have a fever or what?"

"Something's . . . come up. Can I get back to you later?"

"Listen, are you okay? You sound upset, Taylor. I mean, extremely upset."

Taylor managed a laugh. "Just a little stressed. Book deadlines and all that. I'll call you tonight."

After she rang off, she stared at Jack. "So I can't go *anywhere* alone?"

"Afraid not. It's for your own good, Taylor."

"Somehow, people always say that just before they do something that really sucks." She wasn't taking this lying down, Taylor thought.

"I'll be back in a minute. I have to go to the bathroom."

"Why?" Jack scowled at her. "You barely ate or drank."

She gave him a withering look. "Harassing me already?" As soon as she walked past the table, Taylor had her cell phone out, dialing. "Sunny?"

"Yeah, and you'd better be Publishers Clearinghouse or Brad Pitt."

"Be serious for a minute, Sunny. I need your uncle Vinnie's number."

Silence. "I knew something was wrong. What did that guy Rains do now?"

"Trust me, you don't want to know."

"Hold on." There was a lot of laughing, then the sound of papers rustling. "Okay, here's his newest number."

Taylor wrote it down, frowning. "Why new?"

"He changes it a lot. He has to be careful. People watch him."

Great, Taylor thought. Talking to the King of Wiseguys might get her onto some top-secret government list. Of course, thanks to Rains, she was probably on the list already.

She sighed with relief as she saw the ladies' room was empty. Tossing down her purse, she sat on the nearest sink and jotted down Uncle Vinnie's number. "Thanks for your help, Sunny." Taylor needed a second opinion from an informed resource, and outside J. Edgar Hoover, no one was as informed as Vinnie de Vito.

"You haven't received any more Goth flower arrangements via messenger, have you?"

"No, all quiet." *Except for an attack on my sister and vehicular pursuit.* "I'll let you know about the time for tomorrow. Thanks for . . . you know." Taylor smiled into the phone. "Everything. You're pretty great, Sunny."

"Stow it, kid. You'll have me blubbering and I've got clients stacked up wall to wall here." Sunny's voice fell. "And for the record, so are you. Just remember, Green Goddess drinks for a month."

After making a gagging sound, much to Sunny's delight, Taylor hung up and dialed again. This time a woman with a cultured European voice answered. "Weston Financial."

Wrong number?

But the woman put Taylor through immediately, and then Uncle Vinnie was on the line.

"Taylor, how are you? Sunny says you're close to finishing your next book. I hope she's right."

Not exactly. She had to stay alive long enough. But Taylor managed a laugh. "It's coming along fine."

"Really." That dry, canny voice was strangely relaxing. "Then why do you sound so nervous?"

Taylor glanced at her face in the nearest mirror. White cheeks. Tired eyes. Who was she kidding?

She took a deep breath. "Deadlines are never

fun. But I'm calling to ask a favor."

"Ah." Silence fell.

"Nothing — physical," Taylor said quickly. *Not a hit.* "Just some information."

"I imagine that can be arranged. Are we talking about Harris Rains?"

"I'm impressed."

"Don't be." Vinnie gave a dry laugh. "Not yet, at least. My niece has a large mouth and she mentioned your problems. I don't like the fact that your friend Rains has vanished."

"Where did you hear *that?*"

"People owe me favors. Sometimes I collect in information. But I'm not getting much about Rains. When no one gives details, it's always a bad sign. I suggest that you be careful."

"What about Rains?" Taylor lowered her voice. "Any idea where he went?"

"Nothing solid. But a number of people seem to be looking for him. Most of them appear to be from South America." His voice was grim. "And now they also appear to be following you."

Did the man know *everything?*

"Any names?"

"I'll work on it. But if this is research for a book you've been engaged in, I suggest you put it aside. No book is worth dying over."

"This isn't about my book, Uncle Vinnie. It's about my *life.*"

"Did you know that the government's involved?"

"I did, but how do you know that?"

He made a noncommittal sound. "This man Broussard has a solid reputation. Stay close to him, Taylor."

"But —"

"Take my advice. Leave this to Broussard and his people. This is not a good time for taking chances. Too many people are already involved." Somewhere on his end of the phone a car horn blared. "Now I'd better go. *Ciao,* Taylor." The line went dead.

For a long time she didn't move. When she realized she was still holding the cell phone, she shoved it back into her purse, then stared bleakly into the mirror.

She looked as if she hadn't slept for a month. She was pretty sure she looked scared, too, except she was working hard to hide it. Maybe Uncle Vinnie was exaggerating about the danger. But maybe not.

She clutched her purse to her chest. She didn't know *anything* about Rains, but the guys who were after him didn't appear to know that. What was she supposed to do, wear a sign? Something like DON'T SHOOT ME, BECAUSE I DON'T KNOW ANYTHING.

Taylor closed her eyes. Someone was following her. Someone had attacked her sister. She had to deal with the cold reality of these two facts.

She slammed on the water, washed her hands, then added a quick swipe of lipstick, just so she wasn't mistaken for Lady Dracula when she went back outside.

As she finished, the outer door opened, booming eerily in the empty room. With Uncle Vinnie's warning still fresh in her eyes, Taylor backed into a corner and took off her shoe, gripping it like a weapon.

Her waitress sauntered in, eyes narrowed as she took in Taylor's bare foot. "You Taylor?"

"That's right."

The waitress gestured over her shoulder toward the door. "Your boyfriend is out there worried something might have happened to you." She pursed her lips. "Don't see what could happen in a bathroom, but what do I know?" She smiled dreamily. "Of course, if a man as fine as *that* was worrying about me, I wouldn't be hiding in here. I'd be in the backseat of a car giving him *whatever* he wanted." She angled Taylor another curious look.

Taylor straightened her clothes and dropped her shoe. "We're not — involved. Not that way."

"Are you kidding? That man is prime. Did you check out his butt?"

"Not actually," Taylor lied.

The waitress gave Taylor a look that questioned her sanity. "You telling the truth? He's not yours?"

Taylor slid on her shoe, frowning. "Consider him free territory."

"Territory?" The waitress frowned for a moment. "Oh — you mean no claims. Like that."

Taylor nodded. "Like that."

"Thanks for the tip." The waitress went out whistling, digging in her pocket for a pen.

Taylor emerged to find Jack outside, drumming his fingers on the wall, looking downright surly.

"I thought you came down with an intestinal disorder. Considering you barely ate, that seemed unlikely."

"So you sent in your crack interrogation person."

Jack smiled faintly. "She was more than willing to help."

"I'll bet she was." Taylor sniffed as she walked past him.

"Your food's cold. I asked her to put the pancakes in a take-out container, along with the sausages and syrup."

Taylor stopped. "Being nice, Broussard?"

"Don't take it personally. It's called being practical. You can't think on an empty tank."

"I'll be sure to remember that nutritional gem." Actually, Taylor did feel a little wobbly, but her discussion with Uncle Vinnie had killed all remains of her appetite.

"Were you talking to someone in there?" Jack asked suspiciously.

"My friend Sunny called back about makeup for tomorrow." As Taylor hoped, the talk of makeup stopped Jack cold.

He shrugged and scooped up the check. "Let's go."

"Only if we split half."

"Forget being politically correct. Uncle Sam is paying. As long as you're an official target, I'm picking up the tab."

"Just because I've accepted protection doesn't mean I'm giving up economic control over my life."

His eyes narrowed. "So this is about control?"

"Probably."

"You *want* to pay? You're getting a meal ticket and you're turning it down?"

"Not that I expect *you* to understand," she added tightly.

Jack turned away. Taylor was pretty sure he muttered something rude as he pulled out his wallet. "Fine. I'll pay half. Now can we go?"

"Not quite." Taylor pointed across the table. "I think you've forgotten something."

"What? I've got the check and your food." He turned as Taylor pulled a folded piece of paper from underneath his napkin, dangling it in the air.

A phone number was scrawled in big bold strokes. Taylor read the words underneath. " 'Call me if you want some major action.' " She raised an eyebrow and sighed. "I just love it when a woman gets sexual with a man she barely knows. It's such — gender equality." To her surprise, Taylor could have sworn he flushed. "I suppose women try to pick you up for sex all the time."

Jack grabbed the paper and shoved it deep into his pocket, scowling. "Forget about it. Let's get moving."

Taylor ran a finger across his leather jacket and flipped up his collar. "What, you aren't going to leave her an answer?"

Jack caught her hand. Something flashed through his eyes as he stood beside her, his body tense, their thighs brushing. Taylor felt a sudden jolt of awareness in the pit of her stomach. To her shock, his fingers slid down, curling around her palm.

Suddenly, inexplicably, she wanted to feel his hand on her cheek. On her skin.

Everywhere.

His face was unreadable. "Just for the record, I don't jump strangers."

"No?" Taylor's mouth got even drier as he stepped her back against the booth until they were chest to chest, glare to glare. *What a body,* she thought dimly. "Who *do* you jump?" she asked breathlessly.

Their eyes locked. Taylor had an odd sense of weightlessness, of utter buoyancy as their bodies slid together. The waitress was right. The man had one prime body, and everything was in perfect working order, as far as Taylor could tell. The fit was almost enough to give her an orgasm right there, surrounded by people eating oatmeal, muffins, and tofu-burgers.

And he was definitely having a reaction, judging by the feel of his thighs pressed against her. What if he kissed her right here?

Worse yet, what if she closed her eyes and kissed him right back, letting her fingers slide through that thick hair while their tongues did a slow, shameless dance of discovery?

Her heart was slamming when he moved away, scooping up her napkin. "Can't forget this."

"Why not?" Taylor blinked at the crumpled paper.

"Because you were doodling. This is government evidence."

"Of what?"

"Beats me, but someone might decide it meant something. Izzy can probably make out your life story from those scrawls." His brow rose. "Something wrong? You're breathing a little too hard."

Taylor took an angry step back and smoothed her sweater. "Jerk," she muttered.

"At your service." He smiled coolly. "And I'm *always* ready for major action."

"Tell it to someone who cares."

Not a great answer, but it was the best Taylor could manage with her knees shaking and her heart lurching around in her chest while images of hot, impersonal sex shot through her brain.

Why now? And why, God help her, with *him?*

"What do you mean, he blew up the lab?" Viktor Lemka strode onboard the yacht *Andromeda,* moored a mile out beyond the Oregon coast. He'd been gone for barely twenty-four hours and these dog-faced fools destroyed everything. *"Where is he?"*

The nearest man, a pockmarked Albanian hired three weeks earlier in a bar in Los Angeles, took a step away from Lemka. "There is another problem, sir. You see, after the explosion burned the galley, the American —"

Lemka backhanded the frightened man, sending him right off the deck, down into the cold, choppy waves.

No one went to his aid.

"I want no problems. I want only solutions. *You.*" He jabbed a finger at the nearest man, who went pale. "Take me to Rains."

"Of course, Mr. Lemka." The man gestured hopefully toward the companionway.

Lemka frowned as he saw the black marks streaking the wall. Rains would howl with pain for this, he swore. He'd choke on his own sobs while he lost his fingers one by one. "Show me." Lemka swung down the steps, blind with his anger and a vast need for revenge.

When he saw the devastated room covered in ash, he screamed in fury.

Because the galley was gutted, empty. His precious captive was gone.

Chapter Twenty-five

Taylor turned at her door, keys in hand. "You can go now."

Jack didn't move.

"Did you want something else?"

"I'd like to look around."

"You want to go through my desk, dig in my drawers? The answer is no."

"I need to get a sense of possibilities. I can't help feeling there's something we overlooked. I want this thing finished as much as you do."

Taylor sighed, then held open the door. "All right. But you call me before you dig in anything . . . personal."

"Promise."

She watched him roam past the big bookcase, running his fingers over the book covers. "I'll be in my office if you need me."

Jack waved a hand, studying the room. "Don't let me keep you."

Jack knew he was about to rip up at her for things that weren't her fault, like this whole misbegotten assignment. To avoid that, he'd been purposefully rude. He was relieved when she vanished and her keyboard began clicking. Slowly he wandered through the room, past the bookcases, past two framed prints of sea otters in a churning sea, wondering how she and

Rains were connected.

He picked up a photo of Taylor and Annie bodysurfing in Big Sur as teenagers. Next to it was a photo of Sam and Annie McKade at their wedding, both looking happy as hell. He prowled some more, searching for anything out of place.

A scrap of paper.

A postage stamp printed wrong.

A package with no labels.

Was there something shoved into a corner or stacked out of sight where Taylor might have missed it? Slowly, methodically, he went from one bookshelf to the next, scanning every title, checking above and behind. Next he lifted all the art on the wall, looking for envelopes or papers tacked out of sight on the back of the frame.

After that, he checked under the chairs, desk, and couch, then lifted the rug.

Nothing again.

Hell, what did he expect, a capsule of toxic white powder hidden inside a flowerpot? A piece of paper with scrawled lab notes shoved beneath the blotter on her desk? Rains was immoral and unstable, but he was no fool. He'd won awards for fast-track research in plant lectins and he had a reputation for getting results when no one else could. The thing that bothered Jack was, why Taylor? She wasn't part of the scientific circles Rains moved in. She probably wouldn't have recognized the lethal yet beautifully decorative castor bean, even if she was about to bite into one.

Maybe *that* was part of the attraction. As an outsider, Taylor wouldn't realize what she had. Assuming she found it, she wouldn't even know whom to contact for answers. In a strange way, she would be the safest haven, a place where Rains could park something out of sight indefinitely — something to use as a bargaining chip if his business buddies got impatient and decided to rearrange his face.

There was a strange logic in its illogic. With Taylor and Candace friends, Rains could easily track Taylor down and reclaim whatever he'd left with her, if and when he needed it. But if this was Rains' plan, why would he threaten Taylor with the funeral flowers? And above all, why the tampering with the bolt, causing the climbing accident?

More questions Jack couldn't answer.

He gave the room another thorough sweep. Book by book, he riffled pages, then checked the window frames and blinds. He opened drawers and ran his hand inside and underneath every corner. He even checked the wallboards.

No folded papers. No computer disks taped just out of reach. Hell, in the movies, James Bond always found the hidden microchip just about now.

In the next room, the typing continued. At least someone was being productive, Jack thought grimly. On impulse, he pulled out Taylor's latest book and flipped to chapter one.

What the hell? If you wanted to understand a writer's life, maybe you had to start with what they had written. Not that Jack meant to read for long. Most stories left him cold, and he gave this one about two minutes to do the same thing. He was only searching for an angle they'd overlooked.

He listened to see if the typing continued.

It did.

Feeling uncomfortable, almost like a voyeur, he sank onto the sofa, propped her book stiffly on his chest, and began to read. After a while he put up his feet, settled back, and read some more.

After that, he kept on reading, chuckling once or twice.

Outside, clouds gathered above Russian Hill, and the sky slid from azure into lavender. Lights shimmered to life atop the Golden Gate Bridge, while out in the bay freighters from Shanghai and Singapore steamed through the first indigo mist of evening.

Book in hand, Jack didn't notice.

Harris Rains was frightened.

He hunched away from the light, dialing quickly inside the grimy phone booth. Every movement made him wince, and fresh blood spilled from the piece of gauze he'd wrapped around his throbbing wrist.

The explosion in the galley had been a gamble, but it had worked. Fortunately, when he'd used the distraction to slip on deck and jump into the water, he'd been only a quarter-mile from shore.

Instead of heading inland from there, he'd climbed a wall and taken cover inside a Coast Guard supply depot. Lemka's goons hadn't dared check the area closely and had lumbered off, arguing noisily.

Standing in the darkness, Harris listened to the phone ringing. He counted thirty rings before he finally hung up. Where was Candace? She hadn't said anything about leaving for a vacation or a climbing trip, damn it. Not that she and her straggly friends ever planned anything in advance.

A cold drizzle began to fall.

Down the street, a dog barked restlessly, and Rains stiffened as a police car rounded the corner. Dropping the phone, he plunged blindly into the gloom.

When the patrol car came to a stop, its lights picked up only a phone swinging by its cord and a wall of damp, forgotten garbage that had long since stopped mattering to anyone.

Taylor noticed the silence first. She'd expected to find Jack either gone or stretched out with the TV roaring, engrossed in a Lakers game. When she walked into the hallway, his feet were the first thing she saw, perched on the edge of her coffee table. Then she saw his long legs and his body slanted comfortably against her couch.

She went dead-still when she saw that he was reading.

And chuckling.

Holding her latest book.

Her breath skated hard and she felt a little electric jolt of desire for that long, lean body stretched out in front of her. She closed her eyes.

This was not good. Not good at all.

She started to walk quietly away, but something held her. She'd done the research, knew all the patterns. When two people were cooped up together, they got close fast, and their loyalties could shift drastically, like Patty Hearst and her bodyguard. Princess Diana and her security officer.

Taylor took a quiet step back. Out of sight, she leaned against the wall and closed her eyes, trying not to hear Jack's steady breathing and low laughter. Trying not to feel warm, insidious fingers of pleasure at the thought of him immersed in her book.

A curse word came to mind.

She mouthed it silently, her hands pressed against the wall, while her heart beat loudly, almost painfully. What was happening here? She had always been the cool one, the aloof, amused, experienced one. Her sister, Annie, kept telling her she made cynicism an art form.

So how had this one man gotten through all her defenses, making her mind fumble like a football throw gone bad?

Even with her eyes closed, she could see his strong hand curled around the cover of her book. She could see the careful way he turned the pages, the way he nodded. The way his eyes squinted into laugh lines as he read.

How could a man seduce you just by the way he held a *book?*

It wasn't happening to *her,* thank you very much. Not to Taylor O'Toole, who had tangled with more men than she liked to remember. Jack Broussard would vanish the second his work was done, and he wasn't leaving her heart in shreds when he did.

Taylor straightened her shoulders. *Forget the sadness in his eyes. Forget the way he makes your body come alive.*

She wasn't looking for a prince — charming or any other sort. She knew the rules. Men didn't commit, and women didn't stop hoping they would.

She cleared her throat loudly and closed the door of her office with a loud snap, alerting Jack that she was coming. When she got to the living room, he was reading a magazine, her book nowhere to be seen.

She started to speak, then stopped. She was used to people reading her books and denying it. But this time it hurt her.

Jack looked up, frowning. He gave her a thorough scrutiny, one brow raised. "What are you, five months or six?"

Taylor straightened the loose sweater and elastic-front skirt she'd forgotten completely. "Probably about seven, but I had to take out the pillow. It made me feel like a blimp."

"Is there a reason you're wearing maternity clothes?" he asked grimly.

"Calm down, Broussard. It's research, pure and simple. I need to know how a character thinks, how she moves."

"So you're thinking about having someone get pregnant?"

"Possibly. When I get blocked, I spend some time doing exactly what my character would do."

"That's got to be craziest thing I've ever heard."

"Now you're a literary expert?"

He looked her up and down, then shook his head again. "My sister says you get used to it."

"What?"

"Feeling like a blimp. She's on her fourth. Loves kids." Jack tossed down the magazine and stood up. "How about some coffee?"

Taylor sighed. "Is the Pope Catholic?"

Jack headed for the kitchen. "Seems I read somewhere that caffeine was out for pregnant women."

Taylor closed her eyes, rubbing the sore muscles in her neck, and sat down. "Stuff it, Broussard."

China clattered. A moment later she smelled the intoxicating fragrance of fresh Kona blend.

She didn't open her eyes. "Did you enjoy the magazine?"

"Not really. Nothing good on television, either."

"Yeah, I know how that goes." For some reason, his smooth lie hurt far more than it should have. *Distance,* she reminded herself. "Being pregnant is hard work."

"That's another thing my sister says." Taylor heard him move behind her. "Lean back."

"Why?"

"Just do it." His fingers slid into her hair.

Taylor frowned as he smoothed her shoulders, kneading steadily. Her breath skimmed out in a sigh. "I'll pay you a hundred dollars an hour if you never stop."

He did more of the same slow magic, working out every line of bad dialogue and flawed characterization that had found its way deep into her knotted muscles.

Taylor took a slow breath. Not quite a moan, but close. "Make that a million dollars."

"You always get this tense when you work?"

"Usually. If the words come, you forget everything else. When you stand up a few hours later, the feeling is roughly like a hundred little men driving bamboo stakes into your back."

Jack didn't answer.

She turned, one eye cracked open. "A problem?"

"Yeah." He massaged her neck. "I lied."

"You did?"

"About the magazine. The truth is, I was reading your book."

Taylor opened her other eye, wary now. "Yeah?"

He rolled his shoulders. "It was pretty damned good."

She couldn't help but smile. "Am I supposed to sing the Hallelujah Chorus now?"

"No." He touched her cheek. "You're supposed to shut up and let me apologize. I liked the book, but I didn't want you to know. All of which puts me roughly on a par with the other unicellular organisms living in the sewer."

Taylor laughed, oddly moved by his gruff confession. "No problem. I'm used to it."

"It was still a slimy thing to do." His voice was tight. "I'm sorry."

"Forget it."

He walked around her slowly. "I'm not sure I can. Being low and mean isn't usually my style. I'm asking myself, why now? Why with you?"

"And?" Her voice was a whisper.

"I go by the book, Taylor. Always have. But now I keep wondering what if I didn't, just once." He caught her palm, turned it slowly. "The whole idea has got me a little frightened. A little angry."

She heard the edge in his voice, the confusion. The need. "Throwing away the rule book can be nerve-wracking." She managed a smile.

"Which is why I try to do it at least once a week."

He turned her other palm, his eyes hard. "I can't be what I'm not. I'd try and it would make us both unhappy." His fingers tightened. "But you make me wish I could."

He pulled her to her feet, his face unreadable. "I liked your damned book. I liked your damned characters. I even liked the damned dog."

"Don't make it sound so painful."

"Oh, it *was* painful. I hate being proved wrong. Besides, you're nowhere near my type. You're reckless and snappy and a complete irritation." His fingers moved around her waist and he pulled her against him — not gently but with anger, as if compelled, and hating every second.

He shifted to be sure she felt the raw need she was kindling. "And it doesn't make any difference."

"Hardly a compliment, Jack."

"It's not meant to be a damned compliment. I'm changing and that makes me mad as hell. I don't like change." He cupped her hips and drove their bodies together, closing his eyes. "Sex with you should be the last thing on my list, but I can't seem to think of anything else."

"Who says I'd even *consider* having sex with you?" Her eyes narrowed. "You have the emotional range of a reptile and your literary knowledge stinks."

"Thank God for it, too." His fingers tangled in her hair. "You'd drive a man to drink in twenty-four hours." His jaw hardened. "So, your place or mine? I'm going to die if I don't have you in the next fifteen minutes."

Though her throat was dry, Taylor managed a laugh. "Is this your idea of foreplay?"

He pulled her head back slowly, every muscle taut. "No, *this* is."

Chapter Twenty-six

He backed her against the bookshelf, catching her wrists in his hands — not hard, but not letting her go, either. Taylor realized he hadn't even kissed her yet and she was more aroused than she'd been in months.

Alarm bells went off.

She ignored them. "Do you do this often?"

"Not nearly often enough, I'm thinking." Her blouse traveled up beneath his slow hands. He watched her as he flicked open the clasp of her bra.

"Are we about to do something amazingly stupid, Jack?"

"Sure as hell looks that way." He shifted his legs, moving in closer, and her blouse slid from her shoulders.

Taylor's heart slammed hard. It was impossible to breathe, much less stay rational, with his hand exploring her breast and his lips cruising over her neck, then lower, nudging hollows, finding the exact spots that made her body tighten in a rush of liquid sensation until all she could think was *more more right now.*

Which was completely crazy.

She pulled away, dragging in a deep breath. "Maybe we should pretend this never happened."

"That would be stupid. Besides, it wouldn't work."

"Why not?"

"Because we're both too smart for that. We both know what's happening here."

"*I* don't."

"The hell you don't. And neither of us is going to walk away from this easily."

Taylor closed her eyes, struck by the same awful certainty. "We haven't done anything yet."

"We're thinking about it," he said hoarsely. "Speaking for myself, I've been thinking about it nearly every waking moment."

Taylor sighed. "We're probably making a big deal out of nothing."

His eyes narrowed. His long fingers moved, stroking her tight nipples until the remaining air slammed out of her lungs.

"Or not," she whispered.

"Damned right." His lips closed over hers with slow, sensual friction, and then he added his tongue until Taylor struggled to be closer, to be hotter, to be *part* of him.

Now, right now.

Her hands went to his belt. Panting, she yanked his shirt free, sighing when she felt the planes of his chest against her fingers. He shoved away her hands, tugged off his shirt, then slanted her head back. His eyes were restless, greedy.

"Where *do* you get your ideas?"

"Now? You're asking me that now?"

"It's fascinating. Frightening in a way, too." He kissed the hollow beneath her cheekbone, while his hands closed over her breasts, stroking, teasing.

Taylor could have sworn her head exploded.

"What, no answer?"

She closed her eyes and shook her head and then he sank in front of her, his lips covering her as his hands had done. He worked his way over the dark, aroused tips of her breasts with focused intensity, as if they were the only thing left in the universe and he meant to take his time so he missed no detail about them.

Which was fine with Taylor, since her blood was slow and heavy and her whole body was hot and getting hotter, especially between her legs when he trailed a hand up her thighs until he couldn't go any higher.

He hooked one finger. Her silk bikini panties took a quick descent and her skirt was bunched in his hand.

"Yes," Taylor said, and he answered with something low and inaudible and Taylor pushed against his hand so that he found his way up and inside her. She lost herself in the pleasure of every hot, wet touch, surprising both of them when she said his name and dug her hands into his shoulders, moaning while something grew and grew until it dragged away her breath. Shuddering blindly, she swayed, grabbing the bookshelf and Jack's shoulders, only half aware she was falling. Lost completely, she slid along the row of books, their spines digging into her back while her knees gave way and Jack shot one arm around her waist. But they kept going and ended up on the floor.

She opened one eye.

She was sprawled on the Oriental rug, with her skirt bunched high and his leg wedged underneath her. "Did I break anything?"

"A few speed records," he said hoarsely. "Otherwise, no." He tried to hold her up, but she slid bonelessly down until her head rested on his bare chest.

He smelled wonderful, like doughnuts and aftershave and clean clothes. She felt his muscles bunch and shift beneath her, heard the steady pump of his heart just beneath her head. "God," she whispered. "If I wasn't so amazed, I'd be embarrassed." She wriggled closer against his chest. "Can we do that again sometime?"

She was pretty sure he chuckled, but it might have been a curse. She didn't wait to find out, because some instinct made her turn her head and slide her lips along his chest, then lower, until she felt the tight ridge of his zipper over the truly impressive erection straining beneath. Smiling, she explored those hard inches separated by taut denim. *Definitely built,* she thought, framing him with her fingers.

"This zipper has to go," she whispered,

suiting actions to words, with hands that were shaky.

"I doubt this is anywhere in my mission assignment," Jack said harshly.

Taylor turned her head. "Complaints?"

"Hardly." His jaw was locked, his eyes very dark. "But some other time."

"*Now*, Jack. I want to feel you."

He closed his eyes on a curse, then caught her body and hauled her up until she was propped against his chest. "Not now." He brushed a strand of hair off her face. "Izzy's expecting a report in five minutes."

She scowled. "So, I could be fast."

Jack couldn't help it; he laughed. She was sulking — a beautiful, unbelievably sexual sulk, considering what she had in mind, and he gave a gritty gut-laugh that shook them both.

"You think this is *funny?*" she snapped.

"Honey, if I don't laugh right now, I'm going to be buried inside you so fast that your heart's going to stop."

"Which would be wrong because . . . ?"

He traced her breasts, awed at her beauty and instant, responsive shudder. "Because when I'm finally inside you, I don't plan on rushing through the job."

"When — not *if?*"

So she'd noticed that, had she? "That's right. Any complaints?"

She sat back, still frowning, then stretched slowly. Considering she was more naked than dressed, the sight made him grow ever harder, which he wouldn't have thought was physically possible.

"About a hundred." She shoved back her hair and came shakily to her feet. In the process her skirt fell off, leaving her absolutely naked.

Jack closed his eyes on a groan.

"I didn't say I'd make it easy, Broussard. Just so you know."

"Message received," he said thickly. "Now would you please get some clothes on?"

"Maybe." She picked up her skirt and tossed it over her shoulder "Maybe not. By the way," she added in a voice like silk, "I sure do like your idea of foreplay."

The woman was as dangerous as they came.

Jack let out a slow breath as she sauntered down the hall, long legs gleaming beneath the skirt tossed over her shoulder.

For some bizarre reason he was grinning, which was strange because the rest of his body was so hard that even thought required a major force of will.

A good thing that SEALs are expert at pain and suffering, he thought grimly. Something told him that being around Taylor O'Toole was going to occasion both.

He glanced at his watch, then pulled out his cell phone with a sigh. Time for Izzy's report.

"Yeah, it's me," he said. "Any sign of Rains?"

"No luck — not that the Feds are saying

much." Izzy sounded disgusted. "Looks like he's still underground, and he's trusting no one."

"What about the man who went after Taylor's sister? What about the hospital's video surveillance?"

"He used the service entrance off the doctors' lounge. No cameras there. He's good." Izzy's voice hardened. "But we're still going to get him. I've got a new composite sketch based on descriptions from the witness at Tony's Little Shanghai and the nurse at the hospital in Monterey. I'll fax it through along with the building blueprints for the gala tomorrow."

"So they're letting Taylor go after all?"

"Afraid so. The good news is, she'll only need to be there for about forty-five minutes, just to take part in the auction."

"A lot can happen in forty-five minutes," Jack said grimly. "I want a complete guest list, along with the store's security plan."

"On its way. I'll try to get you one other person for the evening. Meanwhile, S.F.P.D. will be around since the mayor will be there, and I hear he's a big fan of Taylor's books. He's making some kind of speech."

Jack moved restlessly through the room, listening to water run in the bathroom. "Any updates on the missing Navy bioweapons expert?"

"Maybe. It seems a yacht ran aground off the Oregon coast last night. When the Coast Guard boarded, they said it had been completely trashed. Fires in both staterooms, furniture gone. Even the fixtures were ripped out."

"You don't think it's that simple."

"I asked them to send me pictures and there was a lot of burned and broken glass, so I sent in a forensics team to pull some blood samples. Our Navy scientist had definitely been onboard."

Jack frowned. "The glass was from broken lab equipment?"

"Bingo. We found traces of assay material and chemicals consistent with recombinant DNA work in progress."

"So he's alive, at least. Anyone see the crew?"

"We're working on it. Preliminary inquiry suggests most of the hired help were illegals."

"Let me guess," Jack said grimly. "South American."

"Right again. But we found other blood, too. This time it belonged to Rains. He may have escaped in the explosion."

Jack gave a soundless whistle. "Any samples from the broken glass to suggest what they were making?"

"Plant lectins. Dangerous stuff. Genetically modified to enhance its toxic capability."

"Ricin."

"No question about it." Izzy made a sound as if shuffling papers. "And this stuff is a variety more lethal than anything we've ever seen. Right now, we don't have a hint of an antidote."

"That's what Rains was up to." Jack stared at the traffic racing along the street. "I should have shot him inside that convenience store."

"My sentiments exactly. I know you're going to be busy prepping for security at that charity event, but I need you to run some possible scenarios. Airborne or waterborne targets are both possible. They would probably go after something accessible, a civilian venue with the highest casualty option."

"Like a stadium." Jack bit back a curse. "Or a music event."

"Give me whatever you can come up with. I'm running some computer simulations so we aren't sitting on our asses if these wackos get serious."

"It would help if your tech people could determine means of transmission. The recombinant form ought to show some evidence of that."

"I'll get them on it," Izzy muttered. "How's Taylor?"

"Crazy as ever. Of course, she'll be thrilled about tomorrow's event." Jack picked up a framed photo of Taylor with a tall man seated at an impressive desk. His eyes narrowed. "Is it true that the vice president is a fan of hers?"

"That's what I hear. The word is, he passes on the books to the man in charge, but that's never been confirmed. By the way, one more thing. You'll be getting a visit tomorrow morning from a tailor with your tux."

"The hell I will," Jack growled.

"Orders, my friend. You have to look presentable for the press."

"*I* won't be seeing any press. Besides, I've got a perfectly decent suit hanging in the closet."

"Black-tie, remember? I told the tailor to factor in room for your shoulder holster. I've worked with him before, so he knows the drill."

Jack thought of an evening of aggressive interviewers, crowded bodies, and the security nightmare both presented. "Do me a favor. The next time I accept a mission away from the water, just shoot me."

Izzy was chuckling as he hung up.

The charity gala was bound to be chaos. Anyone with half a brain would have nixed Taylor's appearance at a sensitive time like this, but the presence of half a dozen Navy bigwigs put a different spin on things. In these days of budget reviews and Senate Oversight Committee investigations, the Navy needed all the good publicity it could get. Canceling a major event at the last minute, with no reasonable explanation, would have resulted in a shipload of bad press. So the plans stayed, and since Taylor was part of the publicity, *she* stayed.

Jack would need blueprints of the building, a detailed guest list with photos, and all the security arrangements — which were bound to be next to nil. If he knew Izzy, the material should be arriving next door any second for Jack's review. With a bit of luck, he could persuade

Taylor to stay in for dinner, giving him more time to work.

He heard a *beep* behind him and turned to see her cell phone chirping on the kitchen counter. Jack scanned the screen. The number was the one Izzy had traced to a second cell phone belonging to Candace. They were still wondering why Candace needed two cell phones.

He knocked at the bathroom door, cutting off Taylor's energetic rendition of "What's Love Got to Do with It." When she opened the door, her hair was in some kind of curlers. She was wearing tight blue jeans and holding a fuzzy pink sweater against her amazing breasts.

Would the pain never end?

Jack held out the ringing phone. With luck, she might drop the sweater.

But she worked one hand free and grabbed the phone. "Thanks." She glanced at the screen, then punched a button. "Hello?" She moved the phone away from her ear. *"Hello?"* She waited, then shook her head, terminating the call. "Another hang-up. Probably a wrong number."

Jack frowned. "Does that happen to you often?"

"Once yesterday." She shrugged. "No big deal." She tossed the phone on the vanity, between an eyelash curler and a manicure file.

Time for the truth, Jack decided. "Taylor, the call was from Candace. Izzy traced the number."

Taylor stiffened. "You must be mistaken. I'm going to finish dressing now." The pink sweater started to slide down over her breasts, and she made a low sound, her face pale. "You really think it was Candace? That she is definitely involved in this?"

"Let's leave that to Izzy and his people to determine. Why don't you get dressed?"

Taylor frowned at the sweater scrunched in her fingers. She took a breath, visibly fighting for control, all her normal humor and banter gone. Jack wanted to pull her into his arms and tell her not to worry. He wanted to touch her slowly, assuring her everything would be smooth sailing from now on.

But he didn't, because she needed to know this was serious, with real bullets involved and people's lives at stake.

Especially her own.

Without a word she began pulling rollers from her hair, each curl spilling down in a tumbled mass.

Her eyes met his in the mirror. "This has gone too deep for me to get out, hasn't it?" Her face was pale, her eyes wary. There was a fragility about her that hit him in the chest like a fall from a train.

"I'm here, and Izzy's on backup. No one will get past us, Taylor. That's a promise."

She nodded, rubbing at her eyes.

Oh, hell, not tears. *Anything* but tears.

Jack started to reach for her, but she shook

her head, one hand raised. "No, I'm f-fine here. But if I keep seeing a broad chest near me, I'm going to start leaning on it sooner or later. Possibly a lot of tears may be involved, which neither of us wants." She turned, her chin rising. "Get out of here, Broussard. Go plan a takedown or fieldstrip your gun or whatever you muscle types do on your time off."

What time off? Jack thought irritably.

"I'll be fine," Taylor repeated mechanically. "I've got a load of work. With any luck, in a few minutes I'll have forgotten all about this, being fully occupied by a car chase through downtown Honolulu at rush hour."

"At rush hour?" His voice was gruff with tenderness. Jack couldn't help it.

"Yeah. You got a problem with that?"

"Not me." He kissed her carefully, slowly. He couldn't help *that*, either. Then he took a step back. "Aloha. Enjoy Honolulu." When he left, he had her cell phone in his pocket.

Chapter Twenty-seven

"You can't be *serious*."

Jack glared at Izzy, who was carrying a garment bag and two boxes. Izzy smiled as he dumped everything on Jack's couch. All other available space was occupied by building plans, evacuation diagrams, and printouts with guest lists and photos.

"Been a busy guy, haven't you?" Izzy gestured at Jack's diagram of the kitchen service entrance, accompanied by his handwritten notes.

"Not busy enough. It would take three men to guarantee complete safety in a public venue like this one tonight. I finished my walk-through this morning and the layout is enough to give me gray hair. On the other hand, we're not dealing with a sniper threat or explosive devices, as far as I can see. The most likely goal would be kidnapping, which would take place in or near the restroom, based on my assessment."

Izzy tried to hide a grin. "No problem there. Just tell Taylor she can't use the facilities after she leaves her apartment."

Jack rubbed his neck. "I considered it, I mean, *seriously.* You don't happen to have a female agent we could borrow for a couple of hours, do you?"

Izzy shook his head. "I've wrangled myself

free of HQ. Afraid that's all they'll give."

"Fine. Taylor can loan you a dress. You'll look great in drag."

Izzy's only answer was to throw the garment bag at Jack. "I'll be wearing a waiter's uniform, thank you very much. *You'll* be wearing the tux with full accessories."

Jack opened the nearest box and made a choking sound. "Why don't you take Taylor? I *hate* tuxes."

Izzy glanced at his watch. "A job's a job — wet suit or black-tie. And you'd better shake the lead out. The limo will be here at 1745 hours." He glanced at his watch. "Which is twenty-five minutes from now."

"Did you take care of her cell phone?"

"All set."

The SEAL scowled down at the items piled on his couch. "How am I supposed to run in a pair of damn monkey shoes like these?"

"Specially made, my friend. Composition rubber soles. You could finish a marathon in these babies."

Jack muttered something under his breath and headed for the bathroom. "I hope I'm getting hazardous duty pay for this."

"Dream on. I know a lot of people who consider a formal evening to be fun."

"You must know a lot of seriously disturbed individuals," Jack muttered.

"One comment and you're a dead man,

Teague." Jack snapped a cuff link in place, scowling. "I'll never get past the metal detector."

"Don't worry. You have clearance. Everything's been arranged."

Jack holstered his gun. "It better be. If I smell anything off, I'm pulling Taylor out, publicity be damned." He snapped his other cuff link in place, caught a glance at himself in the mirror, and winced. "A monkey in a monkey suit."

"Don't be so touchy. Taylor's going to love it." Izzy grinned. "She's got a thing for Armani."

Jack was ready to tell him what he could do with the Armani, when they heard banging in the hall, followed by a woman's voice. Instantly, the two men sprinted to the door, Jack in front, surveying the hall.

A woman with purple silk pants, a pink silk blouse, and purple hair was hammering on Taylor's door. Two large bags stood on the floor beside her.

"Can I help you, ma'am?"

The woman gave Jack an anxious look. "I'm trying to reach my friend, but she doesn't answer her phone or the door."

Jack frowned. "Taylor O'Toole?"

She nodded. "I'm supposed to help her get ready for a charity event tonight." She studied Jack's tux. "Are you Jack?"

"That's me." He pulled out his cell phone,

punching in Taylor's number while he knocked on her door.

Her phone shot right to the recorded message.

"Something's wrong." Taylor's friend paced nervously, a burst of color in the dark hallway. "This isn't like her. She *loves* dressing up and she'd never miss an event like this. I think we should call the police."

Behind Taylor's friend, Izzy held up a key. Jack grabbed it and went for the door, only to be halted by the security chain. She hadn't left the apartment or his monitoring equipment would have alerted him. What in the hell was wrong?

He nodded at Izzy. "Left drawer by the kitchen sink."

Izzy vanished into Jack's apartment.

"Maybe you should stand back, ma'am." His voice was grim, and Taylor's friend was looking more and more worried.

"What are you going to do?"

Izzy appeared carrying a small pair of wire cutters. The chain gave way after two cuts and Jack raised a finger to his lips, then drew his gun.

The apartment was quiet as he moved inside, with gun in low, ready position. There was no sign of Taylor in the living room or kitchen, and he took the corridor slowly, alert for any sounds of struggle or an intruder. Hearing nothing, he nudged open the door to her office.

Relief kicked in hard when he saw her asleep on top of her laptop, one arm dangling from the corner of her desk, the other wedged inside a forensics textbook.

No blood. No assault.

Jack holstered his gun, bringing himself out of attack-readiness mode as he listened to her faint snoring.

No doubt she'd gotten caught up in her work and forgotten the time, then dozed off. She'd probably turned off the ringer on her home phone so she could concentrate.

For a second, anger shot through him. She was blissfully asleep, oblivious to the worry she had caused her friends. She was irresponsible, undependable, and irritating as hell — and *he* was stuck with her.

Jack shook his head and moved to the hall, giving a silent thumbs-up to Izzy. As he turned around, Taylor shifted on the desk, her eyes blinking open.

She frowned in confusion, then shot upright in her chair. *"What?"*

"Your friend was ready to break down your door and call the police."

"Friend?" She rubbed her neck, wincing. "I fell asleep. Obviously." She peered at Jack through narrowed eyes. "You're all dressed up."

"Yeah, I got the monkey suit on. I'm all ready — except for my date, who's still dressed in a baggy Lakers T-shirt, as far as I can see. Maybe you want to do something about that."

Taylor shot to her feet with a gasp. "What time is it?"

Jack eased up his cuff. "17:34."

"No, no, *regular* time. I'm still half asleep." There was a look of panic on her face.

"Five thirty-four."

With a low cry, she headed for the door. "Where's Sunny? I'll never make it, not a chance. Full dress in less than fifteen minutes?" When she saw Sunny pacing in the living room, she gave her a quick hug. "Sorry, I was working."

"What else is new? No, forget the explanations. There's no time. Your friend here tells me you have to be in the car in —" She looked at Izzy.

"In eleven minutes," Izzy said.

Taylor grabbed Sunny's arm and charged toward the bedroom. "Thank you, Izzy. Sorry, good-bye, get lost. Sunny and I have work to do."

The two vanished down the hall, and the bedroom door slammed.

"Women," Jack muttered.

Taylor appeared from a two-minute shower, hair drier in hand.

Sunny took one look and glanced heavenward. "Formal dress? Full makeup? Tell me you're joking."

"Do I look like I'm laughing?" Taylor snapped. "And I said I was sorry." She blasted her hair with the drier, waving her arms wildly.

Sunny rolled her eyes. "Even *I* have my limits."

Taylor vanished into the bathroom and reemerged in a sleek black lace bodysuit. "I don't have time for hysterics, Sunny. Believe me, I considered it." She applied an eyelash curler and squeezed hard.

As a result, she nearly tore out all her eyelashes.

"Give me that before you do permanent damage. Then shut up and let me get organized." Sunny frowned, lining up eyebrow pencils, mascara, brow wax, and three shades of eye shadow on the nearby dresser. Satisfied, she opened the inside pocket of her travel case and started arranging lotions and creams. "No more chatter." She tossed Taylor a kitchen timer. "Read me the time in three-minute intervals."

"You've done this before?"

"Only once. It was during a shoot with Cindy Crawford. She had to go from swimsuit to full ball gown in nineteen minutes. Everything worked fine, except . . ." Sunny shook her head. "On second thought, you don't want to know. Close your eyes so I can cleanse, exfoliate, and moisturize. And *don't* interrupt me."

Taylor tried to glance over her shoulder at the mirror, but Sunny kept blocking her. Her friend was in full diva mode, dropping tissues right and left, using a beauty product, then tossing it into her bag without a second glance. She hadn't said a word in seven minutes.

But with two minutes left, Taylor's eyes were untouched and her hair was still up in hot rollers.

"What about my hair?"

"The hair can wait. And stop trying to see the clock," Sunny snapped.

"I wasn't trying to —"

"Of course you were, and it won't help. What are you going to wear?"

Taylor pointed to her bed. "Black satin bustier dress on the right."

Sunny shook her head. "Too Pamela Anderson. Next?"

"Beaded silk chiffon halter. Matching silk skirt."

Sunny shoved aside the pale peach outfit. "Too blah. It doesn't go with your sexy new hair."

Taylor tried vainly to see the mirror. "*What* sexy new hair?"

"You'll see. Next."

"Black leather skirt. Bruno Magli slingbacks. Black off-the-shoulder evening sweater."

"Too Goth." Sunny rummaged through Taylor's closet, then reappeared holding a short, very fitted black dress with a plunging neckline. "Bingo."

Taylor was already pulling on black panty hose. "Not bad."

"Not *bad?* Honey, you'll have every man in the room panting in seconds." Sunny smiled faintly. "Although the only man worth having will be the one who let me in to your apartment. Close your eyes while I add a coat of mascara."

Taylor stopped talking, knowing better than to disturb her friend at work. Heated eyelash curlers sailed past. Lipstick tubes were chosen, then rejected. Sponge wedges squished against the wall, suddenly airborne, as Sunny whisked Taylor's eyes, added lip balm, lip pencil, and a rich coat of peachy-gold gloss, every movement deft.

Taylor thought of the launch scene in *Apollo 13.*

Mascara?

Go, Houston.

Foundation?

Good to go.

Lips?

We are go, Houston.

Taylor was wise enough not to ruffle Sunny with the image.

Finally her friend stood back, hands on hips. "Not half bad." She stripped the rollers from Taylor's hair, combed her fingers through quickly. "Head down."

When Taylor complied, Sunny sprayed the roots. "Stay down. Count to twenty."

Taylor was slightly dizzy when she sat up. She blinked, grabbing the sheer black scarf

Sunny tossed onto her lap.

"Try this while I find you an evening bag."

"But —"

"Don't argue. You've got thirty seconds left."

Taylor shut up and draped the scarf around her shoulders, then stepped into her favorite evening shoes. She shook her head when Sunny held up a tiny, jeweled bag. "Too small."

Sunny dug some more. "How about this one?"

"Just right." Smooth and curved, the bag sported a row of glittering rhinestones and a beaten silver clasp. Best of all, it was big enough for Taylor's favorite pen, a small notebook, and her cell phone.

Taylor tried to look over Sunny's shoulder at the mirror, but her friend cut her off. "No time. Izzy said the limo was already waiting. By the way, your friend Jack looks buff in that tux. It's Armani or I'm not Italian. Hand-tailored, too." She made a fanning motion with her hand. "When he pulled out his gun, I almost wet myself. It was *too* James Bond. The eyes alone could kill you." She sprayed Taylor lightly with perfume, then took a step back. "You're done. Now get out of here. You've got ten seconds to spare."

Taylor took time for a quick hug. "You're amazing, Sunny."

"Damned right I am. Don't you ever forget it."

"I can't thank you enough."

"Remember that tomorrow when your Green Goddess arrives in a freezer pack. You're on record. Every day for a month."

Taylor made a strangled sound, then went out to meet Jack and Izzy, who stopped pacing when she appeared.

"Time to spare," she announced, twirling slowly.

"Hell," Jack whispered.

"Good God," Izzy muttered.

Sunny crossed her arms. "Am I a genius or what?" She frowned when neither man spoke. "Well, what are you two waiting for? Cinderella has a pumpkin to catch."

Chapter Twenty-eight

"Nice dress." Jack held open the door to the limousine, frowning. "What there *is* of it."

"It's perfectly decent." Taylor fought an urge to tug down the short, drifty skirt. "Don't be so medieval, Broussard."

"Honey, in the Middle Ages, you would have been burned at the nearest stake for wearing something that shows half what that dress shows." He sat back, his face unreadable. "I'm told this Admiral Braden is meeting you at the store."

"That's what the event people said. Mostly just a p.r. moment, I guess. Of course, it's a nice one."

Jack's eyes flickered to her lap. "Let me see your purse."

"Why?"

"This isn't a mascara check, okay." He slid her cell phone across the big leather seat. "Keep this with you, and make sure it's on."

Taylor examined the phone carefully. "You took my phone?"

"Izzy had to make some modifications. There's a direct line to me as soon as you press the star key. You've also got a personal radio beacon installed, in case you get lost."

"At a shopping gala?"

"In case you lose your head somewhere in the shoe section," Jack said grimly. "Here are the rules. One, you stay with me every second after we leave this car. No charging off to greet the mayor or haggle for perfume."

Taylor waved a hand in bored assent.

"Two, no restroom breaks. I couldn't check out the bathrooms this morning, and I won't be able to see them tonight, so that's out."

Taylor stared at him. "You visited the store this morning?"

"Of course. Walking the floor foot by foot is the only way to plan for all contingencies. The bathrooms are a definite point of vulnerability because they're on a lower level and off a long corridor."

"But what if I have to —"

"You tell me, and I'll escort you to a unisex bathroom near the kitchen. I'll be at the door when you go in and there when you come out."

"Is this really necessary?" Exasperated, Taylor glared at him from the opposite side of the seat. "What could possibly happen at an event like this?"

"I'm not paid to play guessing games, Taylor. I'll keep you safe, but only if you follow orders."

"Never one of my strong points," she muttered.

"None of this is open for discussion." Jack crossed his arms.

"Fine." She shifted restlessly, giving him a view of an endless expanse of legs. "Anything else for me to remember? Special passwords or handshakes? Maybe you have a mini spy camera for me to carry, along with a vial of poison, in case I'm captured?"

Jack's face was hard. "Just this." He leaned across the seat and pinned a small gold brooch with three diamonds to the bodice of her dress.

Taylor ignored the instant stir of heat where his fingers brushed the top of her breasts. "Diamonds on our first date? How romantic."

"I hope you won't have to use them. There's a knife behind the fake stones. Twist the circle, and the blade advances." Jack sat back. "Try it."

"This is ridiculous."

"*Try* it, Taylor."

She felt cold suddenly, staring at the simple ornament. He was so serious, so *hard*. She took an irritated breath, twisted the circle, and gasped when a tiny blade appeared behind the rhinestones. "Don't ask to dance with me tonight or I may give you a tracheotomy. How do I get rid of the blade?"

"Push the clip at the back of the pin. That retracts everything. Try it again until it feels natural."

Taylor repressed a shudder. "Trust me, it's never going to feel natural." She looked up as the driver slowed. "What's wrong?"

"The street's clogged up ahead. We'll have to walk from here."

They walked the last block, Jack scanning the throng around them, while diamonds glittered and expensive perfume drifted on the cool night air.

"I feel like I'm caught in a Lexus commercial," Taylor muttered.

Jack wasn't looking at her, and she still hadn't had a chance to see Sunny's handiwork. She hoped she didn't have huge hair or jet-black eyebrows. Sunny had been known to go overboard on occasion.

As they turned the corner, Taylor heard a low whistle. A cab driver raced past, giving her a big grin and a thumbs-up.

"Keep up." Jack turned to glare at her. "And you know you're dressed to kill, so stop trawling for compliments."

"I was doing no such thing."

His eyes narrowed. "Tell it to someone who cares," he growled, pulling her into the line of people running up the steps to the newly re-modeled store.

"Do tuxedoes always bring out the worst in you?"

"As far as I'm concerned, they should be outlawed." He pulled her into a shorter line, his eyes constantly scanning the crowd around them.

Taylor gave a little wiggle and managed to work her skirt down another inch, wondering whether she should have worn something a little longer.

"Stop tugging at your dress." Jack's eyes never left the crowd. "It's not going to do a bit of good."

Taylor ignored him, flouncing up the steps behind a bored-looking couple. The woman was carrying a little jeweled evening bag that probably cost enough to feed a Russian tank division for a month.

She stopped tugging at her skirt and forced herself to stand tall. She was going to have fun, not an attack of nerves. Eyes forward, she didn't see her reflection in the nearby window, a tall woman, sleekly elegant, with long legs and a vibrant face. She didn't see the soft hair that caught sparks of gold, red, and copper in the light as she was carried forward with the flow into a huge open foyer lit with hundreds of candles.

Taylor peered through the golden light and potted orchids, seeing no one she knew.

But someone saw *her*.

"Broussard, are you in place?"

Jack nudged his tiny earphone. "Right inside the foyer, Izzy. How's your sound?"

"Coming in loud and clear. Any action your way?"

"No sign of anyone on our surveillance list."

"It's still early. Just keep moving and cover Taylor."

"I'm trying, but it's packed in here. And if I smell any more designer perfume, I may pass out." Jack decided not to mention the two women who had tried to grope him.

"Complaints, complaints. You *could* be out testing depth charges in icy water."

"I'd be more comfortable in the water, believe me." The line broke into hissing for a moment, and Jack touched his earphone carefully. "What was that all about?"

"Feedback static. I'm recalibrating. How's that?"

The hiss disappeared. "Much better."

A woman in a backless dress shimmied past, her eyes dark with invitation.

Jack didn't return her smile, only finished his scan of the crowd and turned back to Taylor, who was about three feet away. "Damn, what *now?*"

"What's wrong, Broussard?"

"You're not going to believe this, Izzy." Taylor was surrounded by two dozen Japanese businessmen. "Check out my three o'clock."

"I see them. That's the Kobe contingent. They're one of the event sponsors."

"They certainly seem to recognize Taylor. I'm signing off now." As he moved in closer, Jack scanned the excited group, but sensed no threat. They were too busy bowing formally and holding out books to be autographed.

Apparently, Lola was *very* popular in Japan, too.

"What's going on?" Jack took his position to Taylor's right.

She looked up, pen in hand. "Some visiting fans."

"They're too damned close."

"Look again," Taylor murmured sweetly. "They're holding pens, not knives, Broussard." She took another book, signed it with a flourish, and returned it with a high-voltage smile.

Jack stayed right beside her, watching the hands, always the hands. That was where the threat came first, not in the face or the eyes or the body.

The hands did the work.

Two more men offered books. Then a reporter spotted Taylor and shoved in closer, pumping Taylor's hand and grilling her about a canine partner for Lola and the date of her next release. Jack cut in as the woman gestured across the room.

"I'm afraid I have to borrow Ms. Taylor," he said flatly. "There's a benefit meeting upstairs before the presentation."

"Oh, but can't she —"

"I'm afraid not." He was already pulling Taylor up the stairs. "Maybe later."

"Well, that was rude." Taylor blew out a little breath. "And thank you very much for it. She wanted to interview me about the store robbery

— and how it felt to be taken hostage. Yech."

"The glamour of the writing life." At the top of the stairs, Jack guided her into a recess and glanced at his watch. "I make it thirty-two minutes until they auction off your books. That gives us about twenty-five minutes to kill. I know a quiet spot —"

Taylor crossed her arms and glared at him.

"What now?"

"Forget the quiet spot. This is a shopping event to make money for charity. The store is open tonight so people can buy, not find a quiet corner and meditate."

"Damn it, Taylor —"

"I want to shop. I've done nothing but work and throw up and get followed. After the week from hell, I'm *entitled* to shop." Her voice turned shrill.

"Shopping as the new therapy?"

Her eyes were slits.

"You've got ten minutes."

"Dream on, pal."

"Okay, fifteen."

She continued to glare at him, unmoving.

"Take it or leave it."

Taylor checked the delicate face of her evening watch. "Synchronize times. I'm not losing a single minute." She pointed to a waterfall of color under a silk canopy. "First stop, evening shoes. And don't get too close. I hear they have the new Jimmy Choo samples, and these things tend to get a bit uncivilized."

"I'm feeling sick already," Jack muttered.

He watched her stride into the fray, where half a dozen women were manhandling satin mules and stiletto heels. She had one hell of a pair of legs, Jack thought. And tonight her hair was different — soft and full. It made a man itch to get his fingers into it.

The dress? Hell, it made him itch to get her out of it, especially since he figured she wasn't wearing too much underneath.

He reined in his imagination.

Work was work. Thinking about Taylor naked was bound to land them both in serious trouble.

So far so good.

Taylor had finally managed to forget about the length of her skirt. Since no one could see anything in the crush, a few inches more or less would hardly matter. Thanks to a passing waiter, she nursed a champagne cocktail as she studied a pair of stunning snakeskin evening sandals.

To her left, a woman fainted at the news she'd won an instant $1,000 shopping spree, courtesy of the store. Not far away, a man in a designer tux was giving away imported chocolate and mini-samples of the newest scent from Versace.

Taylor took another sip of her cocktail and glanced around the room. Candles flickered and laughter filled the air. Behind her there was more clapping as a lucky guest won a year's supply of Godiva chocolate. By supreme force of will, Taylor decided to forgo the evening sandals, which were immediately snapped up by a woman in a red silk tunic.

As music drifted, slow and romantic, Taylor wondered how long it had been since she'd danced slow and sexy with a man. Six months?

Closer to a year, probably.

She frowned.

As long as she could remember, she'd been far too busy to get tied down in a serious relationship. The last thing she needed was a man to clip her wings. So what if her sister had found someone who made her delirious? Sam McKade was probably the last good man left. It was just Taylor's luck that her sister had found him first.

She saw Jack two feet away, fighting off the advances of a woman in skintight black satin. The attack wasn't surprising, since he looked absolutely edible in a tux that fit him without a single gap or wrinkle. But despite all his polish and formality, one look said that the man was built for danger and probably enjoyed it.

Too bad being around him made her nuts. Even if he did have an *outstanding* way with his hands.

Don't go there.

Taylor pushed those particular memories out of her mind and tried to concentrate on shopping.

"You really don't want these?" The woman in the red tunic was staring at her in disbelief. "At half off?"

"Too small. If your shoes hurt, you can't be comfortable." Taylor smiled wryly. "So my mother always said. Although the pain would *almost* be worth it for those."

The woman shook her head. "They're too small for me, too, but I'll find a way to stretch them. These shoes are so hot I'll feel like Nicole Kidman at the Academy Awards." Her eyes narrowed. "You look familiar. It was some-thing recent. Wait, you were in that convenience store robbery. The woman that was taken hostage." She fumbled with the snakeskin shoes, then held out a hand. "Martha Sorensen. You were *amazing*."

"Taylor O'Toole, and I was scared spitless."

"Scared or not, you taught those gorillas not to mess with a woman in black leather."

"I had a little help from the San Francisco SWAT team." Taylor looked down, not wanting to remember that time of panic and confusion. She picked up a pair of Bruno Magli evening pumps with heavy rhinestone ankle straps, then shook her head. "A little too S&M for me."

Her new friend held up a pair of velvet shoes with sculpted heels. "These are more your style. Elegant, classic, but a whole lot of *zing*."

Taylor chuckled. The velvet slides were hard to resist. She checked the size, then slid on one shoe and studied it gravely. "Not bad."

"Honey, those are fabulous." Her new friend scanned a display for nearby purses and returned with a tiny beaded bag. "What do you think?"

"That you ought to be working on commission."

"Don't bring up work. It will ruin my night. Things have gone straight to hell this week since one of our people left without notice." She frowned at Taylor. "He was there, too, you know. Harris Rains."

"You work with Rains?" Taylor's mouth suddenly felt dry.

The woman sniffed. "Not to hear *him* tell it. He's Einstein and everyone else is mere slave labor. But someone has to keep the books balanced and the equipment paid for." She studied a pair of red cowboy boots. "Life would be a lot simpler if I didn't have a shoe obsession." She glanced at Taylor. "Are you going to take those velvet slides? If not, they're mine. The purse, too." She smiled a little ruefully. "Not that they'll look half as good on me."

Taylor examined the velvet shoes, keeping her voice casual. "By the way, what happened to Harris Rains? I haven't seen him since the robbery."

Martha Sorensen dug through a display of Jimmy Choo slingbacks and gasped when she found a knockout pair in red leather with contrasting white piping. "Excuse me while I faint." She slid on the shoes and studied the result carefully. "Rains? I still can't forget the nightmare that crumb left at the lab. I mean, what was he *thinking?* We're in the middle of two projects, and he's supposed to be finishing a new R & D proposal." A waiter passed with a tray, and she snagged a glass of champagne. "Thank God for champagne." She took a healthy sip, then sighed. "My job is going to kill me."

"What kind of work does your company do?" Taylor decided a little pumping was in order.

"Recombinant DNA work. Mostly pharmaceuticals."

"So Rains just vanished one day? Isn't that odd?"

Martha Sorensen put down her champagne and studied the milling crowd. "You bet. He really seemed to lose it about a month ago, always calling in sick, missing lab meetings. If he hadn't been so smart, he would have been fired right then. But results count," she said grimly. "The man always managed to produce at the last minute." She stared off into space. "I sometimes wonder if something happened to him during that robbery."

"Like what?"

The woman shrugged. "I don't know. Maybe the whole experience unhinged him. Blood and death up close, you know what I mean?"

Unfortunately, Taylor knew exactly what she meant, and the memory was not making her feel good. *No more champagne cocktails,* she told herself sternly. "Didn't he call or leave any messages before he left?"

"One day his desk was full, the next day it was stripped bare. Bizarre." Martha lunged for a pair of silver lamé pumps. "But he'll manage. Harris Rains is like a cat — he'll always land on his feet."

Taylor frowned. "Why do you say that?"

"Trust me, he could be late for a budget review or behind on quarterly lab assessments, but he'd put the squeeze on his staff until the job got done. He knew things about everyone, and I heard he wasn't afraid to indulge in a little blackmail when he needed it." She grimaced at the price tag on the silver lamé pumps, then reluctantly put them back. "The one I really feel sorry for is that young girl he was boffing." Her lips tightened. "Never mind that he's married."

"He was seeing someone?" Taylor asked, carefully casual.

"She was a temp at the lab. It took him all of a week to reel her in." Martha was reaching for a purse when she froze, her breath catching audibly. "Hel-lo. I think I'm having my first hot flash."

Taylor followed the direction of her gaze.

Jack was standing by a potted palm tree. Next to him was a waiter carrying a tray with champagne. Even from behind, Taylor recognized the waiter as Izzy. "You mean those two men?"

"Who else? I'll take one of each — and I don't mean the champagne."

"I suppose I should tell you that the one in the tux is with me."

Martha turned, nearly dropping her shoes, and gave a low whistle. "So what are you wasting time on shoes for? Honey, the women here are *sharks*. Leave him alone and he's going to get eaten." Even as she spoke, a model-thin blonde in a plunging red halter top wiggled up to Jack and offered him a glass of champagne, which he politely refused.

"You've got him well trained, I see."

"No. He just likes to do the hunting." Taylor wasn't sure why her voice sounded wistful.

"Most men do." Martha continued to stare. "He looks like someone who can be dangerous when he has to." Her brow rose. "Military? No, don't tell me. Marines?"

"Maybe. He doesn't talk about it much." Taylor was embarrassed to admit that she knew next to nothing about Jack's background. As she stared at him, he turned, gesturing at his watch.

Her new friend sighed. "In that case, I'll go flirt with that lovely waiter." She smiled conspiratorially at Taylor. "Shoes are good, but they aren't everything." She held out a hand. "Nice to meet you, Ms. O'Toole."

"Same here. Good luck with your shopping."

With a flutter of red silk, Martha Sorensen gave a tiny wave, then bore down on Izzy, shoes and empty glass in hand.

"You go, girl," Taylor murmured, wishing she could see Izzy's face.

Chapter Twenty-nine

The evening should have been fun, with Taylor pushing through the crowd in search of exciting booty. Shopping did that to her.

At least it always had before tonight.

Now the possibility of danger hidden amid the laughter and noisy celebration couldn't be discounted. But there was something else. She watched Jack prowl, checking the crowd, making a small hand gesture to Izzy near the bar.

For some reason, watching Jack at work seemed infinitely more interesting than haggling over slingbacks or evening bags. He was so competent, so cool, so intense that Taylor couldn't take her eyes off him.

She let a pair of satin Manolo Blahniks get past her — at twenty percent off, no less. Was she *crazy? Nothing* put her off shopping. Searching for the perfect gift or an unusual trinket was one of her unswerving joys in life.

Up until now.

She felt an odd flutter in her chest. Dear God, she wasn't getting serious about the man, was she? Okay, he was great to look at — in a rough sort of way — and occasionally he charmed her by doing something unexpected, like reading her book. But she was on one life trajectory, and he was on another. Sometime soon, in a week or a month, this mess with Rains would be resolved and Jack Broussard would be no more than a shadow on her doorstep, on his way to becoming a vague, rather pleasant memory. Even a fool could see they were oil to water, fire to ice.

And Taylor was no fool.

But she couldn't resist a long fantasy of ten or twenty years spent fighting and arguing, then making up with wild laughter and mind-blowing sex. From what she'd seen so far, the real thing, when they actually got around to it, was bound to shatter a few records. But it wouldn't last, that was equally obvious. Was a brief pleasure worth the deep pain of splitting up when Jack hit the road, as he certainly would?

The pain of that vision made Taylor's heart skip painfully. She pressed a hand against her chest, trying to catch her breath, trying to stay calm.

"Hey."

She looked up, startled, as Jack took her arm. "You look pale. Everything okay?"

"Everything's wonderful," she lied frantically. *No, it's horrible. How did I let this happen?* "Just a little case of nerves."

He smoothed a curl from her cheek. "There's

nothing to be nervous about. All you have to do is smile, pick a number, and break a few hundred male hearts. Then I'll get you out of here." He looked at the slinky shoes tucked under her arm. "You seemed to be doing some serious bonding with your friend in the red silk."

"Jostling for shoes can do that." Taylor tried to keep her eyes off those amazing shoulders, that hard mouth. *Forget about him. He's leaving, remember? He comes in the box marked do not touch.*

Jack was staring at her oddly. "What's wrong?" Taylor demanded. *Dear God, don't let him know.*

"I'm surprised, that's all. I've never seen you with nerves before."

"Who's nervous?" She forced a laugh. "I'll just catch my breath, then we'll go find the organizers so I can get ready for the auction."

"No more shopping?" Jack's mouth twitched. "You still have four full minutes left."

"Don't push your luck, Broussard." Their bodies touched in the crowd, and Taylor's heart did another slow cartwheel. *Get a grip. The man's history, great body or not.* She took an irritated breath as she spotted a waiter. "I need champagne."

"Later. Right now you need to have a clear head."

"That's ridiculous. I don't —"

Jack blocked her path. "That's nonnegotiable." His voice was like steel. "You're a walking target, and I expect you to remember that."

"No alcohol?"

He shook his head, already turning so his eyes could skim the nearby crowd, especially their hands.

"You watch their hands, not their faces," she said quietly. "Why?"

"Because that's where they make their move. Eyes can conceal. Faces can lie. But the hands will always show first, going for the gun or flashing the knife."

Taylor nodded slowly. "I'll remember that." Their bodies bumped again, caught in the press of the crowd, and she felt the contact whip all the way to her toes. Forget champagne, what she needed was an animal tranquilizer.

She took a sharp breath and stepped away.

As she did, a big man with a broken nose lumbered in front of her. "Ms. O'Toole?"

Taylor studied him warily. He had a heavy Italian accent and shoulders the size of Tuscany. She felt Jack move to her right, his body tense.

"Mr. de Vito asked me to find you," the giant continued.

"Uncle Vinnie?" She turned, looking around the crowd. She could always count on Sunny's uncle to make a show of support for her book events, bless his Wiseguy heart.

Jack took her arm, keeping her beside him.

"You're going nowhere."

"It's all right. He's Sunny's uncle."

Jack's face was unreadable. "Introduce me."

The giant frowned at Jack, who was standing very close to Taylor. "Is this guy bothering you, Miz O'Toole? You want I should deal with him?"

Jack's eyes narrowed. "In your dreams, Goliath."

"No, he's a friend," Taylor said quickly. "It's not a problem, okay?"

She heard her name spoken, the vowels precise, with a hint of an accent.

"Taylor, beautiful as always." He was a tall man with a creased face and wavy white hair. Taylor noticed some of the women stare as he took her hand, then kissed it with European flair.

So did some of the men.

Probably assuming she was the new mistress. All things considered, being mistress to an aging mobster was probably safer than the general direction her life was headed at the moment. "You look wonderful, Uncle Vinnie." By tacit consent, she had always referred to him the same way Sunny did.

"Not so bad for an old man." His brow rose as he saw Jack, whose body language was now set to hostile mode. "Perhaps you'll introduce me to your friend, my dear."

"Of course." Taylor took Jack's arm, smiling stiffly while she made the introductions.

"So you are a writer, too, Mr. Broussard?"

"Not in a thousand years."

"Something more physical, I'd guess." The old man made a slow assessment. After a long time he nodded. "This is good. Taylor needs a man in her life. Especially now."

Jack stared at him tensely. "Now?"

"Because of these . . . problems she's been having. My niece is very talkative, you understand. She told me about the slashed tire, the phone calls." His voice hardened. "The funeral arrangement."

Jack shot a glance at Taylor. "What was that?"

"We'll discuss it later." Taylor felt a wave of relief when she spotted one of the benefit sponsors headed their way. "I think the auction is about to begin."

"Don't let me keep you." Vinnie patted her hand. "I want to find a good spot, because I plan to go home with that set of your books."

"I'll be rooting for you." Taylor was painfully aware of Jack's silence. "It's always wonderful to see you."

"The pleasure is mine. You make an old man's heart glow." He delivered the courtly praise with a slight smile that said he was being outrageous and he didn't care a bit. When he strolled off, he was promptly hailed by the mayor's chief aide.

"You make an old man's heart glow?" Jack repeated dryly. "He probably got that from a 1940s' movie."

"Don't start with me. He's a nice man."

"Except when he's laundering money or running numbers."

"Just because he's Italian doesn't mean he's a criminal," Taylor snapped.

"It doesn't mean he isn't, either." Jack shook his head as the mayor introduced Sunny's uncle to a starlet who had been making the rounds of the television talk shows. "Gee, he's already found someone younger."

"It's not like that."

"No? How is it?"

"He's just a fan, just a nice old man who happens to be my friend's uncle."

"And a lot of other people's godfather," Jack muttered. "In case you haven't noticed, normal people don't travel with a gorilla for a bodyguard."

Taylor glared at him. "*I* do."

Jack's mouth lifted in a faint smile. "Who said you were normal?"

Before Taylor could answer, the charity sponsor moved in for air kisses and quick chatter about how wonderful Taylor looked. Then Taylor was whisked off toward the garland-covered dais, where she was introduced to two local television hosts and a nasty drive-time radio personality with bad breath. Jack stayed less than five feet away, at the side of the dais steps, where he'd positioned himself after a brief conversation with one of the uniformed security personnel. Taylor noticed he kept his position while she was introduced to the two admirals who were fellow presenters for the auction. The first, a man named Braden, seemed to enjoy the glitter and applause, but for some reason, his eyes kept wandering toward Jack.

In a blur of applause, she was called onstage and the bidding began. The prize was a signed set of all her books, along with one of Lola's canine berets, especially made for the event.

Taylor was stunned when the bids jumped right to $5,000, guided resolutely by Uncle Vinnie. To her surprise, her new friend in the red silk tunic kicked in another two hundred, followed by a bookseller from Santa Cruz and several of the visiting Japanese businessmen. Five minutes later, she was clapping for the winner, who had just forked over $20,000 for charity.

The winner was Uncle Vinnie, looking calmly triumphant and very much like Caesar Romero. On her cue, Taylor took the mike and offered thanks from Lola for this wonderful generosity on behalf of charity. She was ready to escort Uncle Vinnie from the dais when someone called up from the crowd, asking when her next book would be published.

Taylor smiled calmly. "Ask Lola," she said. "She makes all the business decisions."

A photographer was waiting to capture the winner with his prize. As the photographer arranged them in position, framed by the starlet and the chain's CEO, Taylor looked up toward the balcony, blinking to avoid the bright lights. Upstairs waiters were carrying champagne bottles and trays of drinks. Remembering Jack's comment, Taylor watched their hands while she waited for the photographer to complete his preparations.

Abruptly she noticed that two of the waiters were talking heatedly near the side staircase, paying no attention to the other staff working around them. Oddly, one had nothing in his hands, while the shorter one carried a small black bowling bag.

A waiter with a bowling bag?

Taylor frowned against the lights, trying to get a better view. She watched the taller man touch his ear, then look down, nodding at someone on the crowded main floor. At the same time, the man with the black bag paced restlessly, then checked his watch and shook his head. Brushing away the other man's hand, he drew the bowling bag to his chest and started for the stairs.

Taylor leaned to one side, trying to see as the two men continued to argue. The shorter man ducked to one side, then turned directly into the glare of the lights, and Taylor realized she was looking up at Harris Rains.

"What's wrong with Taylor? She keeps twitching up there." Izzy's voice snapped through Jack's earphone as the group posed for a photograph.

"I'm not sure. She keeps looking up at the balcony, making little hand gestures. I'd break it up if Admiral Braden weren't standing next to her. You see anything odd upstairs?"

"I can't see the balcony at all down here, but I'm circling back as we speak. Funny thing, though. I keep seeing familiar faces in the crowd."

"Familiar how?"

"Government types. And they're not here guarding your Navy VIPs, either."

Jack felt a little jab of apprehension. "What's going on?"

"No one's talking." Izzy's voice crackled for a moment. "Okay, I'm at the side staircase leading up from the kitchen. Nothing so far. Maybe Taylor's had too much champagne."

"She's dead sober. I made sure of that." Jack had to work to hold his position directly in front of the dais near Taylor. "They're almost done, Izzy. Hold on."

He pushed past the crowd of Japanese businessmen and caught Taylor's eye. "What's wrong?"

"It's Rains. He's up on the balcony," Taylor hissed. "He's dressed as a waiter."

Jack snapped into a turn. "You're *sure?*"

"I could swear it was him. He was talking with another waiter, a big man with an earphone."

"Izzy, Taylor saw Rains on the balcony. Do you copy?" Jack jostled several guests, trying to get closer to Taylor.

"Copy, Broussard. Which side?" Izzy's voice was sharp.

"Where, Taylor?"

"Right staircase. They were standing behind the big ficus tree with the miniature lights."

Jack repeated the location tensely.

"Copy. Going in."

Jack gestured to the back of the dais. "Meet me at the back steps."

Taylor nodded, but was promptly cornered by the mayor and the chain's CEO, who wanted more photographs.

Jack pushed his way forward, scowling as another set of bulbs flashed near Taylor. He was pulling her out now, and damn the consequences. At the back of the dais, he was stopped by an unfamiliar security guard with a high-tech earwire. Impatiently, Jack waved his badge while trying to keep Taylor in sight.

"Broussard, we've got trouble." Izzy's voice cut through the noise around Jack. "Get her out now."

"Copy. Heading to the secure area." Jack shot past the security guard, ignoring the man's shout. He was two feet behind Taylor when another security officer lunged in front of him, holding a Tazer stun gun and ordering him to halt.

"Security," Jack shouted. "Check the badge."

The guard scowled and kept coming.

FUBAR.

Jack snapped a karate kick to the man's knee, followed by a hard right hook that brought him down. There were too many people on the dais and too damned many next to Taylor, who was shaking hands with the mayor. Her head turned as she saw Jack. Her lips seemed to move.

And then her face went completely white.

Something was wrong, Taylor thought.

She blinked up at the balcony, but the last camera flash had left her temporarily blinded. Voices rose behind her and someone jostled her shoulder, but she paid no attention. During the last ten minutes she'd been shoved and pushed constantly by the crowd. Thank God the last photo was done.

She shook hands with the mayor, then turned anxiously to look for Jack. As the crowd parted briefly, she saw a waiter moving toward her, one hand hidden beneath a white towel. Something about his posture made her take a step back. She was jostled by someone behind her and abruptly felt a stabbing pain at her side, followed by an odd tingling. She pressed one hand to her ribs, surprised when she felt something warm and sticky on her palm.

Blood.

The voices around her seemed very loud, and the floor shifted. She tried to stand straight, but the room suddenly tilted and there was a burning pain at her side that made no sense at all.

Someone called her name. She turned, everything in slow motion, the room blurring into grays and browns while she tried to explain to Jack, who was fighting to reach her, his eyes angry, but she couldn't hear what he was saying and he was going too slowly, too slowly.

Afraid, she tried to say.

Something wrong.

Hurry.

She grabbed at the closest support, sending a display of champagne bottles crashing to the floor, but she kept falling, only now the room was dark, and for some reason she couldn't breathe and she knew she'd never get to Jack.

Not in time.

Chapter Thirty

"What the hell happened to the lights? Somebody check the damn power." The security guard was shouting, trying to be heard against the panicked voices of the guests.

In the chaos, Jack lunged sideways and groped along the location where he'd last seen Taylor. God, she'd been white. Dead white. Then she'd toppled, hitting a display of champagne bottles.

Glass crunched as he knelt, pushing away anyone who came too close in the darkness. "Taylor, where are you?"

Desperately he searched the ground, hearing a muffled sound too weak to be a groan. He tracked the noise and found her arm, then skimmed lower, looking for a pulse. "Come on, talk to me, damn it."

He found a beat, but it was fast and irregular. He touched his mike. "Izzy, she's going to need medical evaluation. Looks like some kind of poison — maybe in the champagne. Pulse is thready, skin cold to the touch. I'm leaving the dais now. If it's ricin —"

Jack didn't finish. Both of them knew what the odds were in that case.

"Copy. I'm on the way."

Jack caught Taylor against his chest and

jumped from the stage, guided by the small in-frared penlight he always carried. There was shouting all around him, women screaming, the crowd pushing blindly in search of an exit.

With the penlight for guidance, Jack headed for the rear corridor leading to the kitchen, one hand on Taylor's throat in case she stopped breathing. With ricin, labored breathing could progress swiftly into respiratory failure and there wasn't a whole lot that anyone could do to help, given the lack of a reliable antidote or inhibitor.

Ignoring the angry protests, Jack shoved people out of his way, using one hand out-stretched like a halfback plowing toward the end zone. He flashed the light again to take his bearings.

Twenty more feet.

Taylor began to cough.

"Izzy, I'm near the south entrance to the kitchen. You have any power there?"

"Negative. I'll be waiting at the secure area. How's she doing?"

"Not good. She's coughing. Get that oxygen ready."

Jack hit the swinging door to the kitchen, his penlight beam cutting through the darkness. A heartbeat later he spotted Izzy outside the locked storage room that Jack had comman-deered for use in case of problems.

He slid Taylor onto a table while Izzy relocked the door. Izzy held up a commercial flashlight that lit the small room.

"Her color's bad." Jack forced himself to focus on facts, not emotions. "No sign of cyanosis." He put an oxygen mask over Taylor's face. "Check her ribs, Izzy. She was holding her right side when she went down."

"Did you see what happened?"

"In that horde, I could have missed a tank attack," Jack said grimly. "It was a damned zoo in there. Everyone was fighting to get a photo with the mayor."

"Including Admiral Braden?"

"*Especially* him." Jack checked Taylor's pulse again. "Getting weaker. Damn it, we've got to find out what she was given."

"Whatever it was, it came via injection." Izzy pointed to the slash in Taylor's dress, now smeared with a trail of blood above her last rib.

Jack's jaw tightened. "Taylor, can you hear me?"

There was no answer.

"Hold her," Jack snapped. "I'm checking the wound." He probed her side, working along the torn skin in search of any foreign objects left behind after the attack.

"Be careful," Izzy said quietly. "Secondary dermal absorption is a possibility."

Jack gave a short, four-letter answer to the warning. There was no time to worry about finding gloves or suitable tools to protect himself. Taylor could be dead if they went by strict medical procedures.

Grimly he continued to search for foreign material. Finally he straightened. "If anything's still in there, it will take a microscope to find it." Jack put a sterile piece of gauze over the wound, frowning. "She needs an excision of the wound site, followed by local skin decontamination, but we don't have time or tools. Where's that damned ambulance?"

"On the way." Izzy touched his earphone. "Make that right outside the kitchen service entrance. Let's get moving."

Jack repositioned her oxygen mask, then lifted Taylor from the table. "How about running interference?"

"With pleasure." Izzy shoved open the door, flashlight in hand.

Neither man spoke, aware that Taylor had begun to show signs of labored breathing.

An emergency technician was waiting when they charged out of the dark kitchen. Blinking in the twin beams of an ambulance, Izzy briefed the paramedics on the attack while they loaded Taylor onto a gurney, hit the siren, and raced toward the hospital.

The paramedic shot a glance at Taylor. "Looks like an overdose, if you ask me."

"It's poison," Jack said flatly. "Possibly ricin."

"Has the wound been checked?" The EMT was already pulling on sterile gloves.

"As best I could. The conditions weren't exactly optimal." Jack tried to fight the image of

Taylor in a coma, succumbing to circulatory failure and multiple organ shutdown.

"Is she allergic to penicillin?" The paramedic probed the wound, and Taylor twisted, gasping.

"God, I don't know." Jack took her hand and brought it to his lips. "Hold on, honey," he whispered.

"Penicillin allergies?" the paramedic repeated, looking at Izzy.

"I'll check with her sister." Izzy pulled out his cell phone and dialed grimly while the siren screamed and lights flashed by in the darkness. Each burst cast Taylor's face into a waxen pallor before she faded into the darkness again.

"She's okay with penicillin," Izzy said, covering his phone.

"Any renal impairment?"

"No."

"Is she pregnant?"

There was no sound for a moment. Jack looked up, his eyes filled with furious impatience. "No, damn it. She's *not* pregnant." He forced his voice to icy control. "She'll need a chest X ray for foreign body evaluation and possible respiratory distress. You'll also need to get a direct tissue analysis."

The paramedic raised an eyebrow. "You a doctor?"

"No."

"Then you're what, some kind of expert on ricin?"

"That's exactly what he is." Izzy's voice was hard.

The paramedic stared curiously at Jack. "No shit. You with the FBI? CDC? Hey, don't tell me — you're USAMRIID." He sounded excited for the first time.

"Maybe you should concentrate on setting up that IV," Izzy said quietly, "and stop asking questions."

"I'm going to have to call her sister back." Izzy paced in front of the closed doors of the E.R. "So far there's no diagnosis, no prognosis, and no known assailant, but hey, so what?"

Jack didn't answer, staring out the door to the room where Taylor was being held.

"Not that I could give Annie any details even if I had them." Izzy put some coins in the coffee machine, then looked at Jack. "You okay?"

Jack gave a shrug, turning sharply as a doctor walked toward them, only to enter a treatment room down the hall.

Muttering, Jack pulled off his tuxedo jacket and dropped it on a battered table near the coffee machine. "I'm asking for a transfer."

Izzy took a sip of the truly awful coffee and grimaced. "I assume you're going to tell me why."

Jack could feel the tension stretch across his back and shoulders like a vice. "Because when you can't do the job, you step aside." He pulled off his bow tie and tossed it down on the jacket. "I didn't, so it's time for me to step aside."

"Was there a fumble I missed back there? I could have sworn I saw an operator who made all the right calls."

"When you can't be objective, you do no one any good. I should have pulled her out the second I saw the crowd inside that store." Jack's voice was raw. "I should also have kept her from going onto that dais, where I couldn't reach her. Then I should have paid more attention when she started making those hand gestures."

"A lot of *shoulds* there, my friend." Izzy put some more coins in the vending machine, then held out a cup to Jack.

Jack waved a hand.

Izzy just kept holding out the coffee.

Jack cursed softly, then took the white Styrofoam in callused fingers. "If she dies, it will be on me, Izzy, because I let things get personal. Because my judgment got shot to hell the first second I saw her."

"You're taking credit for the attack? For the well-planned injection of a poisonous substance? Or are you taking credit for the success of the charity event, which made access difficult and a swift exit impossible?"

"Don't split hairs, damn it. I'm at fault here."

"If there's blame to be assigned," Izzy said grimly, "you might want to start with the people who okayed Taylor's participation or the civilian security personnel who didn't put a cap on the guest list. While you're at it, you might as well blame the people who made the knife that cut her."

Jack closed his eyes and ran a hand over his face. "They didn't know what was going to happen."

"Neither did *you*. You walked the building, you made the on-site assessment, and you calculated the risks. I saw your plan, remember? It was comprehensive and it was sound."

"So why is Taylor lying on the other side of that door with a tube in her throat?"

"Because life can suck and you're not God." Izzy finished his coffee and crumpled the cup. "Live with it."

Jack glared at him. "You're saying self-blame is self-pity?"

"I'm saying the line is pretty damned fine and you just may have crossed it."

Jack took another drink of coffee. "What if she doesn't walk out of here? No more arguments. No more maternity clothes. No more irritating, harebrained schemes." His voice was harsh.

"Let them do their job," Izzy said quietly.

The double doors swung open in front of them, and a woman with tired eyes walked out holding an X ray. "Mr. Broussard? Mr. Teague?"

"Right here." Jack strode across the room, his whole body tense.

"I'm Dr. Fellows, Ms. Smith's physician." She closed the file, frowning. "Usually the next of kin are approached at a time like this, but I understand there are unusual circumstances, so I'll give you an update pending our effort to reach her family." She rubbed her neck, watching a patient wheeled past, headed for surgery. "Another drunk driver. Third one tonight."

She motioned the two men into an empty waiting area across the hall. When they were seated, she opened the file, scanning the pages. "Despite your information, the patient showed no evidence of ricin. If so, she would be facing localized necrosis and organ failure by now. Not that what we found was much better."

Jack sat forward. "What was it?"

"The wound tested positive for ketamine."

"Special K." Izzy's eyes narrowed. "A surgical anesthetic known to reverse muscular control and create dissociative experiences. It was used for battlefield surgery in Vietnam," he said grimly. "Now a drug of choice for date rape."

The doctor nodded. "Your pharmacology knowledge is impressive, Mr. Teague. Nonmedical administration of ketamine is a crime, so of course I'll have to report this."

Izzy's face was blank. "Of course."

"What about Taylor?" Jack said. "How is she doing?"

"Better than expected, considering the

364

amount of ketamine she appears to have been given. The good news is that the wound missed her rib and kidney and no foreign material was evident on the X ray. She's being monitored for suppressed breathing and possible vomiting, as well as cardiac arrest. The bad news is that the next two hours will be critical."

Jack took a hard breath. "Can I see her?"

"Not yet. She's under restraint because of possible effects of paranoia and violent behavior. Do you know if she has a history of cardiac disease?"

"I don't believe so."

"Any use of thyroid medication?"

Jack rubbed the knot of tension at his neck. "Not that she mentioned."

The doctor made a note in the chart, then tucked it under her arm. "You'll be notified when you can see the patient, gentlemen. It may be awhile."

"We'll be here. Just — do what you can for her."

The doctor raised an eyebrow. "I do what I can for *all* my patients, Mr. Broussard." She stood up, her eyes glinting with irritation, and then she sighed. "Sorry, it's been a long night. Two car accidents and a drug overdose in the last hour." She rolled her shoulders as if they hurt. "Perhaps someday you'll tell me what kind of party involved formal dress — and the injection of an intramuscular illegal anesthetic and hallucinogen. It's definitely the kind of party that I'd prefer to avoid." She didn't wait for an answer, heading back to work.

"So would I," Jack said grimly, staring at the stained gray floor.

The doctor stopped outside the E.R.'s double doors. "By the way, please tell *Ms. Smith* that I love her books." Her brows rose. "Although I don't expect to read about this in any upcoming volume."

The big doors swung closed.

"So much for using a false name," Jack muttered.

Eighty minutes later, a nurse in green scrubs motioned for them to follow her into a room filled with lights and equipment.

Taylor lay motionless, her face blank. There was an IV in her right wrist and two machines near her bed beeped loudly.

Jack fought an urge to turn and walk out again.

"I'm afraid you can only have five minutes, gentlemen. She's still hasn't come around."

"How much longer?" Jack's throat felt raw.

"Impossible to say. Maybe ten minutes. Maybe several hours. Ketamine reactions are unpredictable. Funny, but she looks familiar." The nurse shrugged, then pulled the fabric screen closed behind her.

Jack gripped the metal back of the chair beside the bed. The cross bar was cold, but not as cold as his hands. "Why doesn't she wake up?"

"You heard the nurse. These things are unpredictable. Concentrate on the fact that she's here, she's breathing, and she's in good hands."

Jack took a long, painful breath, then sank down in the chair. "I'll get whoever did this to her. That's a promise."

"We both will."

Jack took Taylor's hand carefully in his. "I still don't see why. There was never any sign that they wanted to kill her."

"Maybe they wanted to incapacitate her so they could get her outside without a fuss, but things got out of hand."

"Disorganized crime," Jack said gravely.

"Something like that."

On the bed, Taylor made a sudden movement, one hand twitching violently. Jack reached across the bed and gathered her rigid fingers gently against his palm until the tremor stopped.

"What if she doesn't come around?" His voice was a whisper. "What if it stops here, just like this? What the hell am I going to do?"

The machines kept beeping. Noises continued to drift in from the corridor, the raw evidence of life and death surging on around them.

After a long time Izzy cleared his throat. "Hell, the woman is too stubborn not to have the last word. She'll be ordering us around within the hour, trust me." He stood by the bed for a moment, then patted Taylor's hand. "Take your time. I'll be right outside."

Jack heard the footsteps cross the room, but he didn't look up. It was too hard to move. There was an emptiness around him, a cold stillness that felt as if it was about to crush him.

He shut his eyes, craving the light and movement and laughter that might never come again. There was a burning in his throat as he squeezed her hand and felt no response.

Then he sat up straighter and began to talk. In a low, calm voice, he told her exactly what had happened and how she'd come to be here and what a fool he'd been to let her go to the damned event. His voice turned raw halfway through, but he went on talking.

A nurse might have come in at some point, but Jack kept talking and she left again. He talked until he'd said everything about the night, everything about how Taylor should open her eyes and start talking or he was going to get angry.

He said everything, in fact, but what mattered most.

Which was that he didn't want to think about living if she wasn't around to irritate him, confuse him, and make his life hell.

"Can you hear me, Taylor? Can you hear any of this?"

There was no answer.

He sat beside her, watching for any movement, any hint of response. When none came, he closed his eyes, feeling as if some part of him was dying.

Annie McKade put down the telephone, her heart pounding crazily.

She looked out the big window at forty miles of rugged California coast. By day, otters dotted the kelp beds, but now all she could see was winking lights of passing trawlers.

"Hey." Her husband came to stand behind her, hands on her shoulders. "Who called?"

"It was Izzy." She swallowed. "Something's happened to Taylor."

Sam's fingers tightened. "Where is she?"

"In a hospital. Izzy wouldn't say where." Annie's voice wavered. "He said not to call, because he used a false name."

Sam said nothing, drawing her back against his chest.

"She should have told me she was in trouble. Now I don't know what's wrong or where she is, and it's serious, Sam. I heard it in Izzy's voice. I feel so *damned* useless."

"Izzy will take care of her. So will her friend Jack."

Annie shook her head, tears sliding down her face. "They're not her family. They don't care the way I do." A foghorn droned somewhere out to sea as Annie turned to look at her husband. "I understand why you told her not to come here after what happened in the hospital. I know you did it to protect me, but it was wrong."

"Annie, you don't understand."

"Maybe not." She spoke slowly, carefully. "Maybe what you and Izzy do is too far outside my world. But I understand one thing." She took a step away from Sam, one hand on the full curve of her stomach. "I understand family, and Taylor's all I have left. If she asks me to come, I will."

"No, Annie. You can't —"

She reached up, tears glistening on her face, and covered his mouth with two fingers. "I can, Sam. And I will. Because she's my sister."

She was curled up in a small place with darkness all around her.

The walls began to close, pressing in on all sides, making her smaller and smaller, swallowing her in painful pieces while she tried to scream, but nothing came out. There was no one with her in the darkness, no noise as the gray walls slowly drew shut, collapsing inward in a rush until there was nothing left of who she was but fear and darkness.

Chapter Thirty-one

"Admiral Braden called again. He wants an immediate report on Taylor's condition and a mission assessment." Izzy spoke quietly as the two men watched Taylor being moved into a private room.

"We *have* no assessment, not until Taylor wakes up. Maybe not even then, if she didn't see her attacker."

"We've got a new set of problems, too." Izzy's eyes were hard. "I finally tracked down a friend who was at the charity event. He didn't like talking to me, but I pushed him hard, and he admitted he was on assignment."

"Not for Taylor."

Izzy shook his head. "If it weren't so damned screwed up, it might almost be funny. He was there to provide backup security for a federal operation. They had a cordon in place for a key witness going into the protection program."

Jack bit off a curse. "Rains? He was going into federal custody at the gala? What genius came up with that scenario?"

"Rains did. He insisted that the crowd would make things safer for him."

"So where are they holding him now?"

"Nowhere. They lost him after the lights went out. He was snatched from the men's room."

Jack stared at Izzy in disbelief. "The Feds *had* him and they let him get away?"

"That's what they're saying. Of course, there's another possibility," Izzy said quietly.

"Somebody leaked information to the right people, who scooped Rains up under everyone's noses. After all, electricity doesn't get cut for no reason. It takes time and planning — which means a well-placed leak."

"That would be my guess."

"So what happened to Rains?"

Izzy crossed his arms tensely. "There was blood in the men's room downstairs. A section of plaster was removed from an interior wall that led to a crawl space. Beyond that, a maintenance area opened to the loading dock."

Jack shook his head. "Didn't anyone check the damned bathrooms?"

"Only once, and that was the night before."

"So Rains is snatched and no one saw anything?"

"The Feds are investigating, but most of their team was pulling inside duty. No one was watching the loading dock." Izzy sounded disgusted as he rubbed his neck. "We were outplayed, outsmarted, and outgunned, no way around it. Heads are going to roll for this."

"Maybe they should," Jack said grimly.

On the bed, Taylor's fingers moved.

Jack went very still. "Did you see that?"

"I saw it. What do you think?" Izzy said softly.

The two moved closer.

Taylor's other hand twitched.

Abruptly, her eyes opened. She stared in confusion at the white walls and the noisy machine near her bed. Her head turned and she looked at Jack.

He could almost see her fighting to piece together fragmented memories.

She raised one hand slowly. "My — my throat hurts."

Jack took a gulp of air as emotions hammered at his heart. "Okay," he said hoarsely, bending down beside her. "No problem. We'll get a nurse in here." He cleared his throat. "Do you know who I am?"

She blinked. "You?" She looked down at her fingers, gripped tightly inside his. "Broussard, Jack. I hope you have those shoes I bought." She coughed a little. "Hurts to talk."

"Then don't talk." Jack glanced at Izzy. "Maybe you should get that nurse."

"Coming right up."

Taylor watched Izzy's retreating back, frowning. "Did I have some kind of tube put in?"

"That's right. You were unconscious, Taylor. Do you remember what happened?"

She rubbed her throat. "Noise. The crowd." She closed her eyes as if remembering hurt. "I saw someone upstairs. Harris Rains. I tried to signal to you, but there were so many people."

"What happened then?"

"Pain in my side. I turned around — saw a man in a waiter's uniform coming toward me. He had a linen towel over his arm." She frowned. "I remember what you said, so I watched his hands. When the towel moved, I saw a knife."

Jack's hands tightened. "Did you see his face?"

"Too many people around us." She shook her head. "You were right. I was a walking target, and I thought you were being pigheaded and overprotective."

"Forget about that now."

"I can't forget. I remember the pain — but knowing you were fighting to get to me." She took a shaky breath. "I'm pretty sure I owe you my life."

"You don't owe me anything," he said gruffly.

Taylor looked around the room. "Do you have my purse? I need to check something."

"Right over here on the table." Jack held out the ornate evening bag.

Taylor rummaged around beneath her cell phone, then pulled out the glittering circle of rhinestones Jack had given her in the limousine. "I used your brooch on the man who attacked me. I think I had a solid hit, because he cursed for about a minute. A funny language, not quite Slavic. Not Turkish either, but something close."

"Albanian?"

"Maybe." Taylor shifted restlessly. "I'd have

to hear a sample to be sure." She handed the brooch carefully to Jack. "Better wrap that up. You might be able to get a DNA sample if there's enough blood on the blade." She tried to smile at him. "Afraid I broke it. Have the government charge me for the repairs. Not too much though." She sounded very tired. "I may not have a career left . . . if I don't finish this book on time."

She sighed. This time her eyes stayed closed.

Jack sat back, trying to take it all in.

She'd checked the hands.

She'd spotted Rains.

She'd fought back with the brooch.

"Not bad for an amateur," he said softly. He realized he was grinning, riding a strange mix of relief, irritation, and pride, along with something far deeper and more dangerous.

"Damned straight," Taylor murmured sleepily.

She left the hospital twenty-four hours later, carrying a dozen red roses, courtesy of Jack, and a box of Belgian chocolates, courtesy of Izzy. Despite her complaints, they'd insisted she use a wheelchair — and a basement exit that led directly to a waiting car.

"It's about time. I'm dying to get home," Taylor said.

Jack shot a glance at Izzy, who slid behind the wheel. "You're not going back to the apartment," Jack said. "It's too dangerous."

"What are you talking about? Of course I'm going back. All my clothes are there. All my research notes, my books, my laptop —"

"Your suitcase is in the trunk." Jack held up a nylon backpack. "I took the notes on your desk, a few books, and your laptop. Even got that big French purse you love so much. If you need anything else, we'll send someone to pick it up."

Taylor stared at him. "You're serious, aren't you?"

"As serious as it gets." He opened the door and put out a hand.

Taylor didn't take it. "I'm supposed to walk away? *Boom* — they run me out of my apartment, away from my friends?"

"It's just temporary, Taylor. Until we find these people and determine what they want." An elevator opened at the other side of the basement. "You need to get in the car," Jack said quietly, but there was steel in his voice.

"I'm tired of people telling me what I *need* to do," Taylor said. "When is this going to stop?" Her voice was angry, but a little shaky, too.

"As soon as we can make it end. You can help by getting in the car." He held out his hand a second time.

"I feel like a drowning swimmer. And the water is very cold." She sighed and took his hand. "One day I'm on dry land, the next day I'm sinking fast."

"All of us feel like that sometime or other."

Jack helped her stand up. "The trick is to ignore the cold and keep on kicking."

"You sound like maybe you've done that."

"I've done some swimming," he said calmly. "Now let's go see your new digs."

The house was a California Craftsman with a wide porch and stained-glass windows. Set on a steep slope at the top of the Berkeley Hills, it overlooked Oakland and the whole panorama of the east bay.

A black Saturn was parked in the driveway when they pulled up. Two people got out, a man with a body like a linebacker and woman with dark, cautious eyes. They nodded to Izzy, then led the way into the house, saying nothing until the door was closed.

Izzy made terse introductions. "Taylor, this is Agent Nancy Rodriguez. She'll be with you while we're here, along with Agent Davis."

Taylor shook hands.

"There will be someone outside with a dog," Izzy continued. "He'll be on the move. You may not see him, but he'll be there."

They walked through the house and ended up at a deck on the top floor, where they could see for twenty miles. Fog was creeping in, lapping at the streets below them, making them feel cut off from the rest of the world.

"Why don't you settle in and get some rest?" Jack said quietly, after Izzy and the others left.

"I'm still pretty jumpy. Maybe I'll try to

read." Taylor studied Jack's face. "You're leaving, aren't you?"

He nodded.

"Something's wrong."

Up the hill, eucalyptus trees rose in a dark, whispering line, scenting the damp air. "It's Rains. He was supposed to be taken into witness protection last night, but he vanished."

"They got him." Taylor felt icy fingers of fear slip down her spine.

"We don't know that for certain."

"But that's what happened. The man with him was a federal agent." She put the pieces together as she spoke. "Rains was arguing with him, then he held up his bag and walked away. He was at the bottom of the stairs when the electricity went off." She rubbed her neck, frowning. "Doesn't this mean that I'm finally off their radar screen? With Rains in hand, why would they bother with me?"

"They've come after you before, and they may again. Besides, we don't know *where* Rains is. He might have gotten clear in the chaos."

"You don't believe that. I can see it in your eyes."

"No, I don't." He touched her face. "Meanwhile, you are still presumed to be a target. Do exactly what Agent Rodriguez tells you, and you'll be fine. Izzy and I will be back as soon as we can."

Taylor took his hand and brought it to her lips. She bit the callused skin lightly. "You saved my life, so I guess that means you can have your way with me, Broussard. Did you have anything particular in mind — just in case you're interested?"

Jack's eyes went dark. "I'm interested. Stay out of trouble and we'll discuss the details when I get back."

Taylor forced herself to smile and not to beg him to stay, even though the thought of being alone with two strangers terrified her. "Count on it."

The mission debriefing was worse than Jack had expected. Fifteen team members were interrogated, and fifteen team members were reamed out royally for two hours. No one came out unscathed.

Which was probably fair, Jack decided. A key player had been either killed or kidnapped right under their noses, and everyone had to answer for that.

The only comfort was that the Feds had been in charge of bringing Rains in. Now they'd have to start sharing their information.

Jack was going over surveillance photographs of the gala's guests when Admiral Braden opened the door. Jack stood up immediately. "Sir?"

"New assignment, Broussard." The admiral didn't look pleased, but then he never looked pleased.

Was he being pulled off? Jack couldn't say

he'd mind. This whole op appeared to be going south fast. Hell, it was like trying to catch smoke with your hands.

But where would that leave Taylor?

Jack tried to hide his impatience as his c.o. drummed his fingers on Izzy's battered metal desk. "I'm sending you two to check the crime scene in the bathroom. See if you can find something the others missed. I've cleared it with all the other agencies involved."

He tossed a file folder onto the table beside Jack.

"Meanwhile, it appears your author friend has a lot of clout." The admiral's mouth tightened. "Mobsters. Policemen. Politicians. You know that her sister is married to a SEAL named Sam McKade, the same officer who rescued that bus full of kids in D.C. last year. Two senators had kids on that bus." Admiral Braden's voice hardened. "So did the vice president. Did you know *that?*"

"No, sir, I didn't."

"Neither did I. But I have been personally informed that we are to keep Taylor O'Toole safe at all costs, and not just because she keeps coming up ringside in this mess. Your job is to keep her quiet and keep her out of trouble. Meanwhile, I'll expect a full report on the crime scene within two hours, Teague."

"We'll get right on it, sir."

"And no more mistakes. The Navy doesn't need bad publicity. Is that understood?"

Jack bit back an angry answer. Braden's rash decision had opened Taylor to danger, but the man wouldn't admit that. She should never have been allowed to attend that gala, and everyone knew it.

Braden stared from one man to the other. "Any questions, either of you?"

"No, sir."

"Then get over to the store. After that go baby-sit your second-level mystery writer before she gets into any more trouble."

Second-level? Taylor would fry him for that particular remark.

The thought almost made Jack smile.

Chapter Thirty-two

Jack stepped over a piece of heavy tape and pushed open the door to the men's room. "How'd they get to him, Izzy? The Feds had people all over the building."

"Not in here, they didn't." Izzy gestured at the utility closet on the opposite wall. "No one was expecting *that*."

A bucket leaned against the wall, surrounded by cleaning rags and mops. Directly above, a section of plaster had been removed, leaving a three-foot hole. A rope ladder dangled inside the wall.

"Tight, but manageable. They must have gone up and crossed the corridor from inside." Izzy rubbed his neck. "A maintenance area leads to a loading dock less than eight feet from here."

"And no one saw anything?"

"Not so far."

Jack paced the room, eyes narrowed. "Heads are going to roll."

"Tell me about it. I've got people talking with the kitchen staff, even though they've been interviewed twice already, and we're checking the area around the loading docks. We've got films of all the guests present, and I'm running recognition algorithms for known criminals, but it's a long shot. At best, it's going to take hours." His face was grim. "Hours that we don't have. Any ideas?"

Jack was walking slowly through the room. "He had to be frightened. The fear would make him especially cautious. They could have taken him the same way they tried to take Taylor — knock him out with a dose of ketamine while the lights were out, haul him in here and up the ladder, then bye-bye Rains." He ran a hand along the cold tiles by the sink. "In fact, I bet if you search the women's restroom, you'll find a similar panel pre-cut but never used, because Taylor didn't go in there."

"I'll check it out."

"But something doesn't fit. You said there was blood on the floor near the wall?"

Izzy nodded. "And several broken tiles, as if there was a struggle."

"So he was still partially awake when they brought him this far. Maybe he dropped something during the struggle. I'd love to find that bag Taylor said he was clutching. Help me go over the room."

"Put these on first." Izzy pulled out rubber gloves and tossed a pair to Jack, then opened the soap dispensers and checked underneath each sink. "The Feds have sent a team through here already, you know."

"Won't hurt to look again," Jack muttered. "If Rains was carrying anything important, he'd have tossed it as soon as he got the chance." He checked the stalls one by one, then climbed up, inspecting the top of all the doors, but with no success. "Any luck out there?"

"Nothing so far." Izzy was checking the garbage can.

Jack ran a hand inside each toilet paper holder.

Nothing.

Frowning, he went out to join Izzy. "Did you try looking inside the paper towel dispenser?"

"Not yet."

Jack slid his fingers underneath the front metal plate. Then he removed the paper and checked every inch of the empty compartment inside. One by one, they covered all six.

And found nothing.

Jack stood up slowly. "Looks like that idea was a bust. Unless —"

Frowning, he bent over the first paper towel unit, which was farthest from the door. He ran his hand lower into the metal bin holding used paper towels. "This is empty. What happened to the waste paper that should have been in here?"

Izzy's eyes gleamed with excitement. "Damned good question. Let's go ask our friendly store staff."

Twenty minutes later they were staring at three neatly tied bags of garbage at the back of the kitchen, while a graying man made anxious explanations.

"It was Francisco, Mr. Teague. He was new on the custodial team. We have a clearly posted cleaning schedule, but he decided to clean up his bathrooms early so he could take a break."

Probably to go have a smoke in a quiet spot, Jack thought. "And he left all his bags here in the kitchen?"

"That's right. He's a good worker, Francisco. Sometimes forgetful, but he doesn't miss anything when he cleans."

"No one else has seen these bags or examined them?" Izzy asked quietly.

"No one, sir."

Izzy's face was blank. "Thank you. You can go now. I'll notify your supervisor that you were very helpful."

"I appreciate that, sir."

Alone in the kitchen, Izzy looked at Jack. "We could probably wait for the Feds to get a team over here," Izzy mused. "Probably take two hours, and then we'd get cut out of the loop again." He glared down at the neatly tied bags. "I don't like that scenario much, do you, Broussard?"

"Personally, I think it sucks."

Izzy pulled out clean gloves, tossed a pair to Jack, his face grim. "Be damned careful and keep contact minimal. Do not remove *anything* from your bag without my okay. Now get to work."

Jack smiled grimly. "It will be a pleasure."

They worked with infinite care, silently

sifting hundreds of crumpled paper towels. Jack was sweating when he reached the bottom of the third big.

Suddenly he stiffened. "I've got something here." He dug deeper, his eyes narrowed.

When he stood up, his gloved fingers were holding a cell phone very carefully at the top of the bag.

"Not bad, Broussard." Izzy slid the phone inside a plastic evidence bag and smiled. "Let's go see what we've got."

Three hours later Izzy was muttering over a pile of printouts. Around him, computers hummed on metal tables piled high with data disks, cords, and empty coffee cups.

"You still alive?" Jack sat down in the only empty chair.

Izzy looked up, his face lined. "Just barely. What's the news?"

"Braden wants us both upstairs."

"Works for me." Izzy pushed to his feet, smiling tightly. "It took me awhile to get Rains' battery juiced and hack his password."

Jack stared at the nearby computer screen. "Did you check his call log?"

"Not yet. He's got some kind of secondary password I'll have to break. I need another hour for that."

"Anything on his voice mail?"

"Don't know yet. When does Admiral Braden want us upstairs?"

"Yesterday," Jack said dryly.

"Then we better get moving." As Izzy pulled off his headphones, the telephone whined next to Jack. "Can you get that?" he called.

Jack started for the far wall, then realized the sound wasn't coming from the desk phone. It was Rains' cell phone, wrapped in a plastic bag on the table, which was ringing.

Izzy swung around in his chair and looked at Jack. "Does the press know about Rains yet?"

"Definitely not. Whoever's calling has to be a close contact." Jack nodded at the bag. "You want me to handle this?"

"Better let me." Izzy attached a wire to the phone, flipped a switch on his computer console, then answered. "Hello?"

His eyes widened. He pulled off the wire and cursed softly. "Please tell me this *isn't* happening."

Sitting in pajamas, Taylor frowned at the phone. Her clothes hung neatly in the closet, and her face was covered with green cucumber gel. "Hello? Is this — *Izzy?*"

"I wish it weren't."

Moonlight streamed around her. There was a long silence as Taylor stared at the phone. "Izzy, are you there?"

"Yeah. How did you get this number?"

"It was on my cell phone. According to the call log, you dialed me at 7:42 last night."

Izzy's voice was hard. "How did you know it was me?"

Uh-oh. He had his professional voice on, Taylor realized.

She sat back slowly, wincing as the movement tugged at the stitches in her side. "Nothing technical. I decided to hit the redial button."

Izzy muttered something that sounded like *why me*.

"What's going on, Izzy?"

"Believe me, you don't want to know." He took a hard breath. "I can't talk now."

"Why? Is Jack with you? Are you in some kind of trouble there?"

"Look, I can't *talk*." His voice sounded very tight. "I'll get back to you. And don't call me on this number again."

The line went dead.

Taylor stared at the moonlight dusting the Berkeley Hills and listened to her heart pounding. Something was *definitely* wrong. If Izzy hadn't placed that call to her, then who had?

She drew her knees up to her chest, shivering, suddenly very cold.

A clock ticked in the quiet office.

Jack looked at Izzy, waiting for an explanation that didn't come. "You going to tell me what that meant?"

Izzy simply stared at the cell phone.

Abruptly, he kicked a box across the room.

Jack cleared his throat. "I take that as a no."

"It meant nothing. Less than nothing. It was a wrong number," Izzy growled.

Wrong number, hell.

"Who was it, Teague?"

"Fine, it was Taylor. She had a call at 7:42 last night, and she hit the redial button."

Jack sat back, blowing out a breath. "So you're telling me that Taylor was the last person Rains called last night before he vanished?"

"I'm afraid so." Izzy put the cell phone back in its bag and sealed it tightly. "For the moment I suggest we forget this call ever happened. Otherwise, things could get very ugly for Taylor."

Jack frowned at Rains' cell phone. "I thought they already had."

"What about you?" Izzy crossed his arms. "You still going to ask Braden for reassignment?"

Jack stared at the pile of pictures of the gala. "I should, but I'm not sure I trust who Braden would replace me with."

"It's a concern," Izzy agreed. He watched Jack pull out two photos. "Something wrong?"

"Take a look at these waiters." Frowning, Jack held the photos beneath Izzy's halogen desk light. "They're definitely familiar, especially the one with the thin mouth. I think they were in the crowd after the convenience store robbery. Can you check with the television people and see if they have any B-footage from the robbery that we could borrow?"

Izzy was already lifting the phone. "Consider it done. It's about time we had another face to look for."

Viktor Lemka stared at the bound-and-gagged man lying unconscious on the grimy floor.

The cabin was surrounded by dense woods north of Lake Tahoe, and the rental records showed that it was leased by a commercial airline pilot named William Stallone.

He'd always loved the movie *Rambo*. Classic Americana. A big hit in Albania.

He nudged the man on the floor with his foot, irritated that he'd come this far, set all his traps, and now he had to wait for the drugs to wear off.

He shoved again, harder this time, and the man made a sleepy sound.

Viktor walked to the big cabinet on one wall, unlocked a drawer, and took out a new syringe. "Time to wake up, Harris. Just you and me now. No games, no more clever escapes." Whistling softly, he expressed some of the potent amphetamine he'd brought in from Mexico on his last trip. "Now you're all mine."

He sank the needle into Harris Rains' arm, then stood back, watching the pale green eyes open and flash awake with pure, terrified recognition.

"That's better. I'm glad to see you remember me."

Harris was drooling through the gag, trying to crawl away on the floor.

"I think it is time to talk, you and I." Viktor moved in closer and whispered, "Where is it? The *real* ricin we paid you to make, not the fake samples you gave me two weeks ago."

When Harris tried to wrench away, Viktor hit him hard against one cheek. "I can't hear you."

Harris whimpered through the dirty cloth at his mouth.

Kneeling, Viktor untied the gag. "Tell me again."

"Taylor O'Toole," the scientist rasped. "The writer — I gave it to her. I knew no one would think of looking there. I was about to speak with her when your people found me." Rains' voice was high, pleading. "She'll give it to me, Viktor. All I have to do is call her and say Candace is in trouble. She'll meet me wherever I say."

"But how do I know you'll give it to *me?*"

"I wouldn't lie to you," Rains whined.

Viktor sighed. "Wrong answer, my dear Harris. You always lie."

"What — do you mean?" Rains was gasping as if the fear would kill him.

"You lied every day for months. Then you took our money and lied again." Viktor's eyes

391

hardened. He refused to think about the bungled job on the American woman. "Where did you put it?"

Rains whispered painfully, clutching his side. "It was there, I swear it."

Viktor shook his head. "You were told, my friend. We paid you, and you gave us nothing. You know the consequences."

"Making recombinants is expensive. But I can make more. Ten days — a week," Rains said eagerly. "I promise. More ricin and the vaccine, too."

Viktor studied the arsenal of surgical knives on the table beside him and smiled. "Your promises no longer interest me or your employer. Besides, too many people are looking for you." He picked up a scalpel and turned it thoughtfully. "I wish I had time to take you to my little clinic in Paraguay. It is so much better equipped. But no matter. We're going to take a trip, you and I."

Harris Rains tried to scuttle away, but he was already flat against the wall. "A trip where?"

Viktor smiled slowly. "To hell, Harris. And I'm afraid that only *one* of us will be coming back."

The pain didn't stop.

He was lying in his blood, gagging. Whenever he fainted, they gave him another shot to wake him up and then they started all over again, asking questions and cutting.

He couldn't take any more pain.

The man with the cold eyes looked down at him. Whistling, always whistling. "Where are your notes? Where are your samples?"

"I didn't have time to —"

"You *did*. I know this because the manager of your lab in Mexico was very happy to tell me all the details about the one complete set of samples you finished before you left."

Rains thought frantically. He'd planned for this possibility, hiding bits and pieces here and there as protection. "Fine, I'll tell you." His throat was raw as he stared at his bandaged hand and the stumps of three fingers. "But no more cutting."

The Albanian leaned closer, turning the scalpel slowly. "Talk."

Rains blurted all the details of his careful plan.

"When did you give this to her?"

"I can't remember — a week ago, I think."

"Very stupid." The Albanian wasn't happy. His lip twitched. "And all of it is there?"

Rains nodded wildly. "Exactly where I told you. She doesn't know anything about it. No one does. It was to be my — escape route." He was starting to feel hopeful, and then something pricked just above his hairline. He fought, desperate to make Lemka listen. If they gave him a little more time, he could explain and make a new plan. With the Navy scientist they had locked up, Rains could make dozens more samples, enough to incapacitate a major city. What more did they *want*, for God's sake?

A fierce pain knocked him back. He grabbed at the air, feeling something kick deep in his chest while his heart spasmed like a fist jerking closed. Then his vision blurred and the pain tore right through his chest.

Gone, all gone.

Harris Rains felt a brief, savage moment of regret for all the things he hadn't finished, all the schemes, all the plans.

Then he was falling falling falling.

All fall down.

Chapter Thirty-three

Four days later

Taylor was on her seventh cup of coffee, watching rain streak the windows of the dingy hotel where she'd been moved. The soft patter didn't quite muffle the drone of late-night planes roaring in and out of San Jose International Airport, less than two miles away.

Her efficient female agent was sitting near the door, speaking quietly on a cell phone. Taylor knew there were two other agents outside in the parking lot, but no one had given her the reason for the escalating security — or told her where Jack had been for the last twenty-four hours.

She eyed a carton of cold Chinese rice with disgust and turned to pace some more. Since Jack and Izzy had left, she couldn't get the hum of adrenaline out of her system. Now her nerves were on overdrive and the muscles in her neck were screaming. What she needed was a hot bath and some cold champagne. Barring that, she'd settle for some answers about what had happened to Harris Rains and why *she* kept turning up in the middle of things.

She glanced at the agent near the door. Taylor had asked for news a dozen times already, and each time she was given polite smiles and cool evasions.

The agent looked up and gestured to Taylor's untouched dinner. "Would you like something else to eat, Ms. O'Toole? I can order from room service."

Taylor's stomach rebelled at the thought of greasy fries and rubber chicken. "Maybe some coffee."

"Any more coffee and you'll burn a hole right through your stomach."

"I'll risk it. But first, maybe you could check —"

Agent Nancy Rodriguez raised a brow. "The answer is no, nothing new to report. As soon as I hear anything, I'll relay it."

Muttering, Taylor hit the bathroom, settling for a shower hot enough to leave her skin raw. The pelting spray soothed some of her anxiety, allowing her to think about the days ahead.

Moving from safe house to safe house in the middle of nowhere. Round-the-clock guards and limited contact with family and friends.

And all for what? She didn't *have* anything remotely worth protecting.

She dried her hair and slipped into a pair of jeans two sizes too big, courtesy of the agent outside. When she caught a look at herself in the mirror, she rolled her eyes. Why couldn't she be *smart* about her life? A smarter person would have ignored Candace when she'd asked for help. A smarter person would have backed off and run the other way when that nasty funeral wreath had turned up with her name on it.

So why hadn't she?

Because she was stubborn and obsessive. Because she couldn't get the possibilities out of her head. It hadn't been about Candace or safety or justice. In her heart, Taylor knew it was about sheer, god-awful stubbornness.

And now that stubbornness might get her killed — taking innocent people along with her.

She yanked on a thick sweater, oversized like the jeans. Since she couldn't go back, that left going forward. For starters, she was going to demand some answers. She wasn't a casual bystander they could keep in the dark. She *deserved* an update.

She jammed a brush through her damp hair and grimaced. The fluorescent lights picked out the circles under her eyes, which Taylor knew no amount of cosmetic wizardry would hide. She dragged her hair up into a rubber band and charged outside, temper button set on high.

Before she could fire off her first question, she came to a stop, staring at the tall woman speaking quietly to Agent Rodriguez. The visitor had to be at least six feet tall, wearing a flowing southwestern skirt and cowboy boots that only enhanced her size.

Taylor frowned, unable to pick up their quiet conversation.

Shut out again.

"I want some answers," she began. "For starters, I want to know where Jack is and what happened to Rains."

The agent by the door gave a long-suffering sigh. "See what I mean. She never gives up."

"You're damned right I don't." Taylor grabbed her purse from the bed. "And unless I have answers in sixty seconds, I'll be walking right out of here."

"Ms. O'Toole, I told you —"

"That's nonnegotiable." Taylor's voice was hard.

The agent raised her hands. "Okay, pal, she's all yours. I'm going to find some gut-destroying tacos with all the works. I'll check in with the team outside in fifteen minutes." She shook her head, closing the door behind her.

What was going on? Taylor watched the woman at the window, who seemed to be moving her shoulders, as if she was shaking.

Or frightened?

Taylor started across the room. A muffled sound made her stop short.

Laughing. The woman was *laughing* at her.

"That does it. I'm out of here." Taylor headed toward the door, only to find her way blocked by two hundred pounds of male pulchritude with big feet jammed into hand-stitched size 13 cowboy boots.

Her mouth worked vainly. "I-Izzy? What are you doing like . . . like *that?*"

Ishmael Teague's broad shoulders were definitely shaking. "Trying to do my job, but hell, Taylor, you make it hard."

"I meant what I said, Izzy. No more being pushed around and lied to. I want to know what happened to Rains and who gave me that injection."

Izzy jammed a finger beneath the Day-Glo orange Afro wig he was wearing. "You have no idea how hard these wigs are to put on. I'm not even going to *start* on the whole panty hose thing."

He glanced outside, eyes narrowed, and seemed satisfied with what he saw. "Stop thrashing around and I'll fill you in. Just point me to the coffee first, will you? I've had three solicitations in the last ten minutes, and my male pride is damaged."

Taylor couldn't fight a chuckle. "I can't imagine why. You're a fine figure of a woman, and that orange number on your head is just about impossible to ignore." She glanced at his chest and ran a tongue across her teeth. "I'd love to know what they said in the lingerie store when they sold you *that* bra."

Izzy squinted down at his chest. "Too showy?"

"Not if you're center stage in Vegas. Otherwise, let's just say you're hard to overlook."

"Hell, a woman's got to make a statement on the street. Forget about a classic little black dress and pumps. This body is built for speed," he said, giving a tug at the impossibly large mounds straining beneath his tight sweater. He took a breath as Taylor handed him a steaming cup of not-quite stomach-scouring coffee from the room's pot. Izzy drank gratefully, then pulled a briefcase from the chair near the door. "Let's get to work."

"Work?" Taylor blinked. It was a little hard to hold a serious discussion with a six-foot-four-inch cross-dresser in an orange Afro, a concho belt, and a size 46D bra without putting some real effort into it. "Where's Jack?"

"Being debriefed. He'll probably be a couple more hours." Something crossed his face, but he looked away, punching in a code and shooting the locks on his briefcase. "Current security has been upgraded. I'll give you more on that in a minute." He tossed a photo on the veneer table. "First, have you seen this man before?"

Taylor stared at the grainy image. Smallish eyes. Narrow jaw. One scar beside his nose and lots of slicked-back hair. "No, definitely not."

"How about this one?" Izzy tossed down another photo.

There was something familiar about this face. "I've seen him before." Taylor rubbed her neck. "Don't ask me where."

Izzy nodded, looking pleased. "We're running his data now. Jack picked him out in the photos taken after the robbery. The man's an Albanian national with a juicy record in Europe. First time he's worked in this county, as far as we can see."

Taylor frowned. "What about the return call I made? Why did you answer?"

Izzy hesitated. "Rains had made a deal to go into witness protection, but he never got there. Jack and I found his phone, though, and *you* were the last person he called."

Taylor sat back, looking sick. "Why call me?"

"I still believe he gave you something. Can't you think of any time when you had contact with him?"

Taylor shook her head.

"What about Candace? Did she ever tell you anything?"

"She gave me some photos of my first climb at the gym, but that's all."

Izzy looked hopeful. "Tell me where and how many. I need to have them analyzed immediately."

"They're in the front of my desk. You think Rains left information on them? Something like a microdot?"

"Let's leave that to my technical team. What about that wreath you received? Where's that now?"

"With Sunny's uncle. I didn't know who else to give it to," Taylor said defensively. "I didn't know that you were involved then."

"Nice of you two to pass on this information," Izzy said irritably. He punched in numbers on his cell phone and ordered an immediate search of Taylor's desk, then had one of his team contact Vinnie de Vito for the wreath. "Anything else you need to tell me? Keep thinking about something you may have received, no matter how insignificant. The way we figure it, Rains couldn't hide anything valuable in his lab or his apartment because he was afraid those places would be searched. You were safe territory."

"Assuming I managed to stay alive."

"You're one tough customer, in case you don't know it." Izzy put a bag on the bed. "You've also got dynamite friends. Here's a change of clothes along with some comfortable shoes." He glanced at the spike heels standing neatly near the closet. "Forget the heels where you're going."

"But I have plenty of clothes back at my apartment."

Izzy shook his head. "You won't be going back there until this is settled. It's not safe."

"Are you trying to frighten me?"

"I'm *trying* to keep you alive." The orange wig started to slip and Izzy shoved it back in place with a curse. "We're starting to get leads from our South American counterparts, as well as our contacts here in the Albanian community. It's only a matter of time until we locate Rains and his pals. Whether he'll be alive or dead by then is the question. Meanwhile, you're going to be safe where no one can get at you. Jack will see to that."

Taylor stared at his hard face. "You're worried about something else."

"What makes you say that?"

"Because you're edgy, and nothing makes you edgy." Taylor sat back, watching his face. "There's a problem. Your security isn't tight enough, is it? I think you're worried you can't keep me safe. That's why you're moving me."

Izzy swept the photos back into his briefcase and locked it. "Given the situation, staying mobile is prudent."

Silence fell. "You believe that Rains was working on ricin?"

Izzy rolled his shoulders. "I can't give you details, since everything's level-two classified. But I can tell you a few things." He stared at the briefcase. "Rains was being paid a lot of money to perfect a ricin vaccine as part of the work for his company, which was a defense contractor. A year ago he had some limited contact with a Navy scientist working along similar lines. Rains asked some questions about bioengineering techniques to increase the toxicity of the basic plant lectins. If he succeeded, he'd have both a superweapon and its only available vaccine."

"Isn't ricin a vegetable poison?" In her last book Taylor had considered killing a particularly nasty villain with a ricin injection, but she'd done him in with a heart attack during three-way sex instead.

"About a thousand times more toxic than cyanide. Don't let the fact that it comes from a common bean fool you. Properly concentrated and dispersed via air, food, or water — ricin is odorless and colorless — it would kill thousands."

"And castor beans are just about everywhere."

"Impossible to lock up. Impossible to outlaw, impossible to track, since they're used for all kinds of legal purposes."

Taylor frowned. "Did Rains succeed? If so, why am I certain that he sold his research to somebody who isn't exactly concerned with truth, justice, and the American way?"

When Izzy didn't speak, Taylor realized that she had just crossed the line beyond what he was allowed to tell her. But that didn't mean she had to stop speculating.

She drummed her fingers on the tabletop. "Candace told me that he was arguing with several men who pushed him around and threatened him. Those could be the ones who wanted that research."

"I'm not corroborating any of this," Izzy cut in mildly.

"You don't have to." Taylor had become fairly good at reading Izzy's face, and his face wasn't denying anything. She stopped, hit by a sudden, arresting thought. "Jack had Rains under surveillance during that convenience store robbery, didn't he? When he realized Rains might be harmed, he was sent in as protection. You've known about Rains from the very start, haven't you?"

Again Izzy said nothing, but there was a tight set to his jaw that Taylor took for a screaming yes. "And thanks to Rains and his double cross, they're after *me*. For some reason, they believe I've got whatever Rains had. His vaccine or his notes. Something." She shot to her feet. "But I *don't*. You know that."

"Maybe you do," Izzy said quietly.

"You think I'm lying?" Taylor's voice turned shrill. "Do you think I could hide a thing like that, information that could save thousands of lives?" Shock blazed into full-blown anger. "Because if you do, Izzy Teague, you can just take that high-tech briefcase of yours and shove it right where —"

"Calm down, Taylor. I believe you don't know anything about it. But that doesn't mean Rains — or even Candace — didn't manage to pass something through. Go over every detail of every second you spent near Rains. Replay all your time with Candace, too. There's got to be something we've overlooked." Izzy leaned toward the window and eased open a slat in the blinds. "Where's Rodriguez?" he muttered. "She's taking way too long."

"She hasn't eaten for hours," Taylor said. "She needed some time off."

"Until this is done, there is no time off. Food and sleep are optional." He hiked up his skirt, fished inside his boot, and pulled out a cell phone. "She knows that. The whole team knows that. If she can't pull her weight, she's out of here."

He punched a number into his cell, eyes hard.

"Okay, now you're finally frightening me."

"Don't waste your energy. Being afraid makes you weak. Instead, start working on those things we discussed. A lot of lives depend on how much you can remember."

Talk about cold, hard pressure.

"Be prepared to move, too."

"Where are we going?"

"Not decided yet," Izzy said tersely. "Stop worrying. Some good people are working this case, Taylor. We know what we're doing."

Taylor sighed. "I'd still feel better if Jack were here."

Izzy stiffened at a soft tap at the door. When it was followed by four rapid knocks, he relaxed slightly. "About time she got back." He shot the bolts and opened the door, revealing a darkened parking lot. He let Rodriguez in and relocked the door. "Why the delay?"

"Davis had to go check on some activity near the street."

"Anything important?"

"Just some local kids who'd had too much beer. They broke a few windows, then ran off when Davis showed up."

Frown lines worked over Izzy's rouged face. "You sure that's all it was?"

Rodriguez sat down near the door and rolled her shoulders. "Relax, Teague. You're not the only one who can run a case, okay? Now get lost and let me do my work." Her head tilted. "Come to think of it, aren't you supposed to be working the street? I hear you got a pimp outside who beats his women good if they don't keep a ten-minute schedule."

Izzy put a hand on his massive chest and twitched his hips. "Sugar, don't you believe everything you hear. I got my ways, you understand?" At Taylor's stifled laughter, he turned back and grinned. "What? You got a problem with a full-figured woman? Don't you go dissing me, girl. I get bitchy when that happens."

"I wouldn't dream of it." Taylor's smile faded. "Be careful." She looked at Agent Rodriguez. "Both of you."

"We always are."

"That's right, honey," Izzy added, "this ole girl was born careful. Any man messes with *me*, he's gonna be singing with the sopranos come Sunday. You can count on that." With that, Izzy fluffed his orange wig, hitched up his concho belt, and swaggered outside.

"Who in the hell are *you* supposed to be?" Jack paced through the dark motel parking lot, matching steps with the vision in the concho belt and black cowboy boots.

"I'm the woman yo mama always warned you about, sugar." The deep voice turned sultry. "Wanna have a good time? A hundred gets you something you'll never forget."

The Day-Glo wig twitched.

Jack snorted. "Dog-ugly, that's what you are, Teague. Give a man a heart attack to get up close to you."

Izzy batted his heavily mascaraed eyelashes. "Sweet little thing like me? Surely you jest."

"Be careful, your jive accent's slipping," Jack said dryly.

Izzy gave a short but very graphic answer. Then his eyes turned serious. "What'd they throw you at HQ?"

"The local Albanians are finally talking. Looks like our man Viktor Lemka farms out to the highest bidder these days, usually in South America."

"Any news about the missing Navy scientist?"

"Zip. He had a tracking chip on him, but it's throwing out crazy readings. One minute he's in Borneo, the next minute he's in Dallas. Your guys back in the lab think there's a high-tech jamming device overriding the signals."

"Jamming devices happen to be my specialty. I'll look into it as soon as I can."

"Negative. You and I are both assigned to Taylor for the moment." Jack's eyes were hard. "That little stunt with the ketamine shook everyone up. They're sure there's a reason she's so popular, even if we don't know it yet."

The rain thinned to a cold drizzle as the two men walked on without speaking. Izzy finally said what neither wanted to believe. "There's a leak, isn't there? A damned leak somewhere in our own team."

"Looks that way," Jack said grimly. "How else did they nab our bioweapons scientist the one day he was carrying notes? How else did they know Rains was going to be at that downtown charity event? Hell, you and I didn't even find out until the last minute about what was going on that night."

"Maybe it was simple luck or good surveillance," Izzy mused. He shook his head. "Yeah, I agree. Shit happens, but it doesn't happen this often. Not without help." He stared out at the quiet parking lot. "If we have a leak, that changes everything."

They watched some more. Then Izzy sighed. "Time for you and Taylor to go solo."

"That's what I figured. Of course, I'm counting on you to be here protecting our backs and finding that damned leak." Jack smiled tightly. "While you finish hacking Rains' phone, of course."

Izzy looked resigned. "Where's your car?"

"Around by the Dumpster."

"Let's go. Suck it in, Broussard. Gotta make this look good." He made a big deal of reaching out and feeling Jack's butt, then laughing raucously.

"Damn, man. Watch where you're grabbing."

"Shut up and walk." Izzy draped an arm over Jack's shoulders, stumbling slightly. "Smiling might help. You look like you just swallowed a rat."

"That's about how I feel." Jack gave a smile that was closer to a grimace as he picked up a movement toward the street. "Who's that?"

"Relax, that's just Rodriguez's partner. Tonight he's the barrio's biggest wino."

Jack scanned the street again. "How long until we leave?"

"I'm still making the arrangements."

Jack's grimace grew more pronounced as Izzy bumped into him. "Woman who can't hold her liquor shouldn't drink," the SEAL muttered.

"I can drink *you* under the table any day, *muchacho.*"

"Just how good are these agents, Rodriguez and Davis?" Jack continued quietly.

"Solid records, both of them. Twenty years of street time and a load of citations. They'll handle things right, don't worry."

"After what's happened this week, I'll be worrying every second."

When they reached the back of the parking lot, Izzy turned as if drunk and slid into the car beside Jack. In the shadows he pulled a map from one boot. There were no markings anywhere, nor would there be. For safety, all instructions were verbal.

"This plan should keep you two alive, so pay attention." Izzy pointed to one corner of the map, slashing his finger eastward. "Here's what I have in mind."

Chapter Thirty-four

Taylor tried to sleep, but nothing was working. She closed her eyes, tossing and turning, fully aware of Agent Rodriguez's quiet breathing from the chair near the window. Jack still hadn't returned, and the weather had turned nasty, with rain hammering on and on.

Cursing, she stabbed her pillow and twisted onto her side, trying to blot out the drone of a television from a neighboring room. She was just drifting down into sleep when she heard a quick sequence of taps at the door.

One loud. Four short and fast.

She sat up stiffly, trying to see into the darkness as Rodriguez moved behind the door, her weapon raised but out of sight. "Who is it?"

A low voice answered. "Oliver Stone sent me."

Rodriguez slid the chain and opened the door. "Glad to see you. Everything's been quiet here."

"There's nothing I like to hear more." Jack put a bag on the floor near the closet and took off his jacket, shaking off rain in the process. "Pretty nasty out there."

"No problem. We have a van across the driveway. When do you want me to check back in?"

"Two hours would be good."

"You're leaving?"

"I'm still awaiting orders," Jack said quietly.

The agent pulled on her jacket and nodded. "I'll be in touch."

As soon as the door closed, Taylor was out of bed, shooting across the room. She caught Jack so hard that they both swayed.

"Steady, honey. You're safe."

Taylor hadn't realized until that moment how frightened she'd been, or how vulnerable. Only when she'd heard Jack's voice had the fear churned up from all the little spaces where she had buried it.

She leaned back, studying his face in the dim light. "I have a few million questions for you."

"I can't tell you everything. The situation's a little complicated."

Taylor moved closer. "Okay, the questions can wait."

"Just like that?"

"I've got more important things on my mind." She slid open the top button of his shirt.

"I'm pretty sure there are rules against this," Jack muttered as his shirt opened the rest of the way. "In an hour, I might even remember them."

"Forget the rules for once," Taylor said huskily, tugging his shirt free. He was hot and hard against her, the scent of rain in his damp hair, and she wanted him, wanted his body covering her until she couldn't think, only feel.

"Hold on." Jack checked the bolt and slid the chain in place. After that, he shoved a heavy chair against the door. When he turned, his face was hard. "There isn't much time. As soon as I hear from Izzy, we're moving again."

Taylor went still. "That's not what you told Agent Rodriguez."

"Pretty sharp, aren't you?"

"Forget the compliments. What's going on?"

"Everything's on a need-to-know basis starting now."

Fear blocked Taylor's throat. "Because you don't trust your own team?"

Jack cupped her face gently. "Don't read too much into this. The fewer people who know the plan, the safer you'll be."

"Don't lie to me, Jack. This is too important."

"There's nothing to worry about. Izzy and I have a plan." His voice was calm, but she felt the tension in his body as she moved into his arms. "I wish we had all night. Hell, maybe we should get some sleep before Izzy —"

Her lips cut him off, tracing a reckless path down his chest and stopping just above his belt.

"Keep it up and I won't be slow or careful," he said grimly.

But she knew him now, knew when he was trying to put distance between them because he thought that's what they needed.

Poor, misguided man.

His belt went flying. Her tongue traced wet circles over that gorgeous, rock-hard stomach. She traced the rigid muscle slowly, hungry to see all of him, and he tensed as she moved lower.

Taylor had never seen a more beautiful body. She'd never come close to *touching* one.

She wanted to see all of it right now.

She slid down his zipper, transfixed by the sight of her hands against his skin. Abruptly, the zipper caught.

Jack cursed, stopping her hands. He knew they should sleep, knew he should find the control to step back and do the right thing. But when he did, Taylor was right behind him, warm and sexy.

There in the hot darkness, with rain tapping against the window, he drank in the sight of her pale body, knowing control didn't have a chance. He opened his hands and pinned her against the wall. "Tomorrow you might see this differently," he said harshly.

"Tomorrow is another century. I want you now. I want you to make me come right here. Then I'm going to see what it takes to make a good man lose all his control. I don't want you to forget tonight. I don't want you to forget *me,* Jack."

He'd never forget her. And the big news was, his control was already gone.

Her hands moved back to his zipper, cupping him through the straining denim. If he got any harder, he wouldn't be able to walk, and damned if he'd have her rush him through something he'd dreamed about for days.

For his whole life, he realized. Only now he was able to see the face, the edgy, sassy, wonderful face that went along with all those fantasies.

He gripped her shoulders with fingers that were perilously close to trembling.

"Jack, did you hear me?" Her voice was shaky.

"I won't forget you. Not in a hundred years."

"Maybe you could prove that."

Her sweater went flying and her breasts filled his hands, warm and heavy. He shoved away her jeans.

When he was done, all she wore was a necklace with a solitaire diamond. The sight left Jack so hard he thought his zipper would split. There was a sudden pressure in his chest, as if his whole life had been leading him right to this place, this moment, this astonishing woman.

He saw her body's response to his blatant stare as dim light from the window brushed over her, with nothing barred from his hot gaze. When he didn't move, she closed her eyes and pressed against him, the hard tips of her breasts touching his chest in a slow, exotic torture.

He made a strangled sound. His fingers circled the smooth weight of each creamy breast while his thumbs found her straining nipples.

His fingers spread. She swayed as his touch

grew harder, as he pulled her breasts higher so he could see her while he gently dragged his teeth across her.

She shuddered, swallowing hard. "These walls are pretty thin. I warn you, this might get noisy. If you keep doing that thing with your mouth —"

"This thing?" His teeth gently closed over her. "Or this one?"

Taylor seemed to be having trouble breathing. She closed her eyes as if caught on some sharp edge of pleasure where release hung just out of reach.

"Let it all go, Taylor. Do it now, for me."

She was too lost to realize he was pulling her closer, his tongue tracing a hot line down to the shadow of curls that were already wet with need.

She took a broken breath. "Knock me out if I start screaming."

His chuckle was husky, possessive. Without any warning he slid lower, finding the hidden, wet cleft with his tongue and lapping at her intently. She stiffened and her body snapped back in his arms.

He didn't stop, covering her with his mouth and driving her up again as he gave the perfect rough-gentle slide of his tongue between his anchoring fingers while lightning raced out of the night, wrapped tightly around them.

The third time, Taylor closed her eyes and screamed.

Jack almost laughed.

He'd had a lot of women in thirty-five years, but none of them had trapped him between mania and delirium the way *this* woman did. None of them made him want to work his way slowly over her body, inch by inch, and see how many different kinds of pleasure there were to share.

He was hard by nature, a leader by habit. But he knew how to take time with the things that were important.

He tried to remember his patience now with Taylor standing naked, her body a lush fantasy. He didn't have to work at being generous because he was too busy enjoying the feel of her heart slamming against his hand, her hips driving up against him in restless pleasure.

He ran his tongue slowly over her again, smiling at her whimper. Even her taste was unique, salty and sweet, all sex and woman.

She was still quivering when he bent to her again, hungry for that dark taste, hungry for the way her body moved against him, slim and strong as he drove her back up into another explosive wave of pleasure.

And by God she screamed again.

He'd never felt half so much a man, and he hadn't even shucked his pants yet. But thinking was the last thing on his mind as her leg rose restlessly, wrapped around his waist, claiming them both for the taking they could no longer avoid.

Taylor closed her eyes, weightless, beyond words, yanking at his jeans to reveal the hard body she'd seen only in dreams.

His size left her awed. His need left her breathless.

Without a word she reached out to touch him reverently, and then her fingers tightened, sliding down to cup his erect tip.

She smiled as she heard him gasp. The more she touched, the more she grew dizzy with her power. She looked up at him in the darkness, saw the tension in his face. "You're not telling me to hurry?"

"Honey, take all the time you want. I'm a dead man already and I'm enjoying the ride." His constraint was palpable, his body taut beneath her slow hands.

Suddenly Taylor didn't want it slow. Her head fell and she covered him with her mouth, frowning at the bead of salty moisture that met her tongue. Touching him like this was making her own body soften and turn wet all over again.

Outside, rain tapped quietly against the window as her tongue moved delicately down his length.

"Damn it, Taylor." His fingers dug into her shoulders. "No more. I can't hold on."

"I don't want you to hold on. I want to taste you when you come inside my mouth." She'd never wanted that before, not with any other man. Only this hard man with the gentle hands.

With a curse Jack yanked her close, then followed her down and pinned her beneath him. They were both breathing hard, both trembling, caught in a game of discovery older than any words. Now it wasn't calm or civilized anymore.

She shoved at his chest. "No. I want my mouth on you. I want to feel you when —"

"Not this time." His voice was raw. "Are you protected?"

She stared at him, then shook her head. "I didn't plan —" She took a breath, and her eyes widened when he kissed her hand, then pulled away to sheathe himself. Then his hands were in her hair as he opened her legs and drove into her as his mouth covered hers. She fought him even then, wanting for him the release he'd given her three times, but she couldn't slip free of that hard, implacable body straining against hers.

By his third thrust, she no longer wanted to. Instead she wrapped her legs around him as he rose and fell, giving more of himself each time. Shuddering, Taylor dug her nails into the taut muscles of his back, her body tightening, reaching, and the sight of him was better than all her fantasies as she watched him move down against her, muttering dark, male words that made her blood hammer and her face go hot.

He said them again and she felt the first

shimmering edge of climax while she strained against him. When she looked up, there was torment in his eyes and something almost like regret. But there was no time for certainty because the shimmering exploded into a hunger that drove them together, panting, fighting their way across the jagged edge of an intolerable pleasure.

Taylor closed her eyes on a gasp. The earth dropped away and her body surged against him, convulsing.

A heartbeat later he threw his head back, his hands like a vise as he locked her body to his and hammered to a blinding release inside her.

Jack rolled weakly to one elbow and glanced at his watch. "Hell."

"Is it time to leave?" Taylor stretched carefully, pressed against his chest.

"We've got fifteen minutes yet. Better get dressed, because Izzy's running this extraction like clockwork." Already his control was returning and there was something grim in his voice.

Only later would Taylor realize its significance.

She ran a hand through the storm of her hair and hopped up, bending over in search of the suitcase that had fallen to the floor. There wasn't time for questions or promises. Maybe they both were glad for that.

Jack's eyes narrowed on her backside, then

took in her long legs. "On the other hand, don't hurry to dress on my account."

Taylor hauled the bag over her shoulder and rewarded his blatant stare with an erotic bump of her hips. "You'd better get into some clothes, too. Agent Rodriguez has an eye for a nice male body. I noticed definite interest when she checked out Izzy." Taylor cleared her throat. "Under the mascara and silicone inserts, of course."

"Of course," Jack said dryly. He swung to his feet and gave Taylor a hard kiss, his hands sliding into her hair. Then he came up for air and did it again so that they both were panting.

Her head tilted. "Are you going to tell me what that was for?"

"I would if I knew." He ran one hand down her spine, smiling when she shivered. "Can't keep away from you, I guess." He took a step back and reached for his clothes. "You take the bathroom first. I need to check in with Izzy."

"Aye, aye, sir." Taylor made a mock salute, then spoiled the military effect with an exaggerated sway of her hips when she turned away.

"Lady, you're going to be the death of me."

"But what a way to go," Taylor said huskily as the bathroom door closed.

With the lights still out, Jack eased back the curtains, staring into the darkness as he waited for his cell phone to connect.

Izzy's answer was an irritated growl. "What?"

"No more sweet talk?" Jack sniffed as he scanned the parking lot. "You almost in place out there?"

"We'll be right on schedule. You know the plan."

"Every detail." Jack tucked in his shirt with one hand, studying the far corner of the parking lot. "Looks like nothing's moving. Let's hope it stays that way."

"Amen. Hold on a minute." Izzy's voice faded as he turned away to answer a question. "Rodriguez and her partner checking in," he explained. "Okay, get your gear. We move on my signal. Five minutes."

Jack scanned the parking lot. "We'll be good to go in here."

But he continued to look into the darkness. Was it too quiet? Shouldn't a few cars be moving along the access street?

He rubbed his neck and shrugged away his uneasiness. Training had taught him to focus on facts, not shadows. "We'll be waiting."

Jack was putting away the phone when Taylor emerged, killer legs encased in snug jeans, damp hair curling around her face. Jack forced back the memories of what they'd just done, angry at his body's instant response to the sight of those soft, flaring hips.

"Put your bag over here." He tossed her the suede coat from the bed, then checked his weapon and holstered it. "Izzy will be here in four minutes."

Taylor studied his face as she pulled on her coat. "You're worried, aren't you?"

"Anytime you change locations is a time of vulnerability. Things can always go wrong." He pulled out the two oversized cowboy hats that Izzy had left him and shoved one on his head with a grimace. "Teague always did have a nasty sense of humor."

"Gee, I kinda like it, Bubba."

Jack's only answer was a snort as he tossed the other hat to Taylor. "At least this should throw off anyone looking for our faces."

Soft footsteps scuffed outside the door. Jack touched a finger to his lips, and Taylor nodded.

There was one loud tap, then four more in rapid fire. Jack pulled back the chain and opened the door.

Nancy Rodriguez frowned, her back to the parking lot. "Let's move. Our van's waiting —"

The same instant she spoke, bullets tore out of a parked car twenty feet away. Rodriguez grunted a protest, spun sideways, and fell back into Jack's arms, covering them both with blood.

"Get into the bathroom," Jack shouted to Taylor, pulling the fallen agent inside and slamming the door as a hail of bullets took out the front window. "Do it *now*." There was warm blood on his fingers as he charged for the bathroom, locked the door, and shoved Taylor into the shower.

Her face was sheet-white beneath the big hat,

but he didn't have time to comfort her. He didn't even have time to check the agent bleeding on the rug outside, though it countered all his instincts.

Because it would take every bit of his energy and focus to keep Taylor alive.

He knew the motel layout by heart and breathed a prayer of thanks for Izzy's counterplan, kept secret from the rest of the team. The small screen above the shower was unscrewed, just as Jack had left it, and it popped free into his hands. In three seconds the window was open and he was holding out his hands to Taylor.

"*Go.* A car's waiting."

She scrambled up, clutching at the window frame, asking no questions as he boosted her into the opening.

"Look down," Jack said tightly. "Can you see Izzy?"

"Right below me."

"Then get moving."

Jack watched her jump down. As prearranged in the event of an attack, Izzy had cut around to the back of the building, where he was waiting to catch Taylor, hurrying her into a green van idling on the sidewalk.

Behind him, Jack heard the front door explode with a crack. Knowing Taylor was safe with Izzy, he felt a burning urge to protect the fallen agent. He was turning back when automatic weapon fire hammered the room next door, and Jack realized it was too late to help Nancy Rodriguez. Nothing could have escaped that devastation.

He climbed into the window and dropped into the darkness, the sound of gunfire burning in his ears as he sprinted along the sidewalk. The van was already moving when he grabbed the open door and jumped inside. More gunfire exploded behind him, followed by a new burst from the back of the building.

Something stabbed at Jack's shoulder. He sighted toward the incoming burst, squeezed off four shots, and had the pleasure of an echoing scream of pain. One less bastard to hunt down later, he thought grimly.

He slammed the door while Izzy fishtailed around a line of cars. Two figures raced toward them from the back of the building, firing steadily. Izzy ran one down and careened past the other into a nearby alley, following the escape route that had been kept secret from everyone but Jack.

Now all the rules were off.

Now they could trust no one.

Chapter Thirty-five

"What the *hell* happened?" Jack braced his body against the van's metal wall as Izzy weaved into one alley and out the next.

"We were sold out, that's what."

Jack held his pistol tightly against his leg. "I want the bastard's name."

"Get in line." Izzy's fingers clenched on the wheel as he gunned along the half-empty streets. "Payback is going to be a *real* pleasure." There was raw fury in each word. "Nancy Rodriguez's niece was going to college next week. She invited me to a big send-off bash." Izzy glared out at the rainy darkness. "We can't help her now, so put it away, both of you. She was a pro, and for her, the mission came first. Taylor, are you hurt?"

"No." Her voice was a wisp of sound.

"Damn it, Jack, check her."

Jack was already stripping away her jacket and the purse she'd clutched to her chest. He searched her upper body for bullet wounds or cuts from falling glass, which she might not even feel. In a killing zone, the world flashed into a twilight rush of noise and violence, with normal sensations blurred beneath the pump of adrenaline. As a SEAL, he'd seen how serious wounds could go unnoticed until it was too late.

"She's fine. A lot of blood, but most of it's from Rodriguez," he said grimly.

"Most?" Izzy spared precious seconds to look back at Jack. "Were you hit?"

Jack grunted. "Took a round in the arm. Feels like it went right through."

"Get my medical kit from the passenger seat and take off your shirt," Izzy barked. "We've got to clean you up."

Jack shrugged off his bloody jacket and was reaching for his shirt when Taylor pushed away his hands.

Her lips were set in a hard line. "I'll do it." She flinched when she felt the blood covering his arm, then took two quick breaths. "Okay, here's what I see, Izzy. He's got an entry wound at the side of his arm, but I can't tell the exit point. There's too much blood." She took another breath, studying the jagged wound in the flicker of streetlights as the van shot onto the freeway, headed north. "What do I do next?"

"You're going to need the red box." Izzy glanced back, frowning. "Sure you can handle this?"

"I'm sure." Taylor's voice was cold. "Just tell me what to do."

They changed cars in Walnut Creek and again near Benicia, just beneath the shadow of the big bridge. Thanks to Izzy's contacts, they were met in each location, and no one asked questions or mentioned the bloody clothes

Jack had left in the van.

Two hours later they were headed toward Carson City, Nevada, eating up the miles in a big red Chrysler. Taylor had slept for a while, then taken the wheel so Izzy could check her handiwork and stitch up Jack's arm.

"Here's the bad news. No tennis for a month," Izzy muttered.

Jack stared out at the darkness. "Tell that to Nancy Rodriguez."

"Put it away, Broussard. She knew her job," Izzy said quietly. "She knew when she walked out the door each morning, it might be a one-way trip."

"Is that supposed to make her death acceptable?" Jack growled, shoving his fist against the doorframe.

"No, it's supposed to make you start being smart. Put the emotions behind you, because they can only get you killed."

After a long time Jack released an angry breath. "I know the drill, Izzy. I've lost men in firefights before, but never when my own side started the cross fire. Only a coward runs."

"Right now, only a fool would stay," Izzy said flatly. "Anyone could have set you up. I don't know who I can trust."

Jack grimaced as he tried to move his shoulder. "What story will you give Admiral Braden when you get back?"

Izzy's face was a study in quiet violence beneath the passing lights. "I'll report that you were taken by unknown assailants, and I followed you as far as the airport freight terminal, where I lost you despite my best efforts. I'll also report that you were both hit by substantial fire before you were taken. It's even possible you didn't survive."

Jack smiled for the first time since he'd heard the tap at the hotel room door. "Not bad, Teague. For a computer geek, you lie pretty good."

Izzy muttered a low answer that had Jack laughing.

In the front seat, Taylor was getting edgy. She looked back at the two men. "If this lovely moment of male bonding is done, maybe one of you could tell me where I'm supposed to turn off." Her fingers were white where they clutched the wheel.

"You're doing great." Izzy leaned forward. "The exit's about three miles ahead on the left. Watch for a gold Cadillac."

Jack raised an eyebrow. "I thought we were supposed to be inconspicuous."

"Rule number one." Izzy's voice took on the smooth rasp of his female alter ego. "Hide in plain sight, sugah. Nobody going to look for you in a big, gold Cadillac." His voice morphed back to normal. "Besides, I used up a lot of favors getting you here, so I didn't have many options left." He nodded as a green exit sign flashed in the glare of the headlights. "There it is, Taylor. Head east at the ramp. He'll be parked in an abandoned drive-in about three miles up the road." Izzy reached into his medical kit and pulled out a black zippered bag. "Suck it in, Navy." He held up a wicked-looking syringe. "Time for your yearly shots."

"Navy?" Taylor glanced back, frowning. "What does that mean?"

"I'll tell you later." Jack stared at the exit ramp as Izzy went to work with the syringe.

It was still dark when they said grim good-byes outside a run-down diner in the Sierra Nevada foothills. Izzy had done most of the driving, and after four car changes, they were nearly certain that no one had followed, especially since Izzy had been careful to toss their government pagers and cell phones into the first garbage truck they had passed rumbling out of San Jose.

Global positioning systems were standard on current tactical communications issue, and they were leaving no clues to contradict Izzy's forthcoming report. During the long ride, he and Jack had worked out a solid story about the firefight outside the hotel. Only one person would know it was a lie, and that was the insider who had betrayed them.

Izzy was determined to find out who that was.

Taylor gave Izzy a shaky kiss. "That's for saving my life. I owe you big time." She tried for a grin. "Want to be in my next book?"

430

"Only if I get to beat up the SEAL at the end."

"What SEAL?" Jack leaned against the side of the gray Explorer, scanning the highway.

"Beats me." The humor faded from Izzy's eyes. "Watch your six o'clock, Broussard. These people are damned slick. I'd come with you, but I have to stay and run damage control."

Coffee steamed in a big thermos as Jack slid behind the wheel and waited for Taylor to stow her purse. Then he reached up to shake hands with Izzy. "What Taylor said. You know." He cleared his throat. "Ditto."

Izzy cocked his head. "Don't tell me I get to be in your book, too?"

Jack slanted him an irritated look and started to speak, but Izzy cut him off. "I'll collect on any favors when I know you two are safe." He pushed away from the Explorer and swept a glance across the deserted road. "Better get moving. You should be able to make your destination in about ten hours." His eyes narrowed. "Remember the five-minute rule."

"Will do."

As the sun cleared the horizon, Jack raised a hand, and the Explorer headed east into the bloodred light of dawn.

"What did he mean by five-minute rule?"

"You know Izzy." Jack rolled his shoulders. "It's one of his jokes."

431

"I don't believe you."

Jack gave a half-grin. "You don't believe *anyone.*"

Maybe he was right. Taylor realized she was exhausted, and she wasn't thinking straight. With the adrenaline rush finally wearing off, her body had turned sluggish.

Fighting sleep, she stared into the sunrise. "Are you a SEAL?"

"Does it matter?"

"If I weren't so exhausted, it would. I don't like being lied to."

"Whatever you were told was necessary, Taylor."

"People usually say that to justify hurting someone." She watched a hawk glide through pink clouds. "So where are we headed?"

"Arizona."

"I have some friends in Tucson," she said. "We met at a great spa last year."

"There won't be any aromatherapy wraps where we're headed," Jack said grimly. "Almost is strictly a meat-and-potatoes kind of place."

"Almost what?"

"Almost, Arizona. That's where we'll be staying until we hear from Izzy."

Taylor rested her head against the seat. "Do you think he can find the leak?"

"He will." Jack's voice was grim. "Nancy Rodriguez was a good friend. He's got a personal score to settle."

Taylor frowned at him. "I thought it wasn't

supposed to be personal."

"Tell that to Izzy."

Taylor remembered Izzy's face when he'd hustled her into the van. "Good." She shuddered at the memory of the fallen agent in a pool of blood. "I only wish I could help."

"You can help by thinking about those questions Izzy asked."

"Every contact I had with Rains or Candace, you mean. Sorry, but I still don't believe that Candace is involved in anything criminal." Taylor blinked, trying to keep her eyes open, not that there was much to see on the winding road.

Jack drank some coffee, then looked across at her. "No need to stay awake. Except for necessities, we're not stopping until we get to Arizona. There's a blanket in the backseat if you want to stretch out."

"I'll stay up here." The truth was, Taylor didn't want to be out of touching range. The smell of blood and fear and gunfire overwhelmed her when she closed her eyes. Only the nearness of Jack's body held the horror at bay.

She wedged her pillow between them. He didn't speak when she ran her hand along his chest, then curled up closer.

He was too experienced with death not to know that she was fighting bad memories.

"Put it out of your mind, Taylor."

"How?" She took a raw breath. "It's one

thing to see death in your head and plot the entry wound from different angles. It's one thing to know the motive, assailant, and murder weapon." She fought a wave of pain and regret. "It's something else entirely when you watch someone fall, hear their breath cut away, and know they died for one reason — because they were protecting *you*. If I hadn't gotten involved with Rains, none of this would have happened." Her voice tightened. "If I'd been smart, Nancy Rodriguez might still be alive, too."

Jack's callused fingers gripped her shoulder. "Forget the guilt. Whoever took out Agent Rodriguez was after a lot more than you or me. The only way you'll stay focused is to remember that."

Taylor thought about his words, watching clouds boil up behind mountains that rose like dark sentinels to the south. "Does staying focused make you feel better?"

His hands clenched. "Not much."

At least he was honest.

"So what do you do?"

"You live with it. You pray that someday you won't see the image of a bloody chest or a broken body as if it had happened yesterday. And you make a vow that sometime, some way, the death will be avenged." His fingers slid into her hair and then she felt him relax. "Now go to sleep and stop asking so damned many questions."

Without looking up, Taylor found his hand. "Thanks for telling me the truth." She stifled a yawn. "I'll drive whenever you want. Your shoulder —"

Jack touched her face gently. "Is fine. Maybe you can take over in a few hours. Meanwhile, I've got about two gallons of coffee here if I need it."

"I can stay awake," she insisted.

"But you don't have to," Jack said. "Go ahead and rest while you can. Stop arguing."

"I don't." She yawned. "Argue. Not much."

"Like hell you don't. You enjoy every precious second. What's frightening is the fact that I'm starting to like it," he muttered.

No answer.

Jack looked across the seat as Taylor's purse slid off her lap onto the floor.

She was already asleep.

Lulled by the brush of Jack's warm body and the rhythm of the moving car, Taylor closed her eyes. All sound stilled; the world receded.

And instantly she was back in the killing zone.

She heard the tap at the door, saw Nancy Rodriguez step inside, smiling at Jack seconds before a hail of bullets exploded, tearing a row of crimson holes into her chest.

Taylor moaned, trying to fight her way through the dream. Blood was everywhere, carrying the cold scent of death.

"Wake up, honey. Come on, stop fighting."

Something was holding her, shaking her. The blood was thick, choking, smoke everywhere. She was falling, falling —

"Taylor, wake up. You're safe."

It was too cold, too quiet. Something was on the floor in front of her. A body that didn't move. Dark, unfocused eyes that would never see again.

Taylor flung out her arms, fighting the darkness. When her hand struck something, she opened her eyes on a sob to find Jack's arms wrapped around her. His seat belt was gone and she was curled against his chest, fighting hard, her back pressed against the wheel.

Her face was cold, slick with tears.

She took a shuddering breath. "I — was dreaming. Everything smelled like death." She pressed her face against his chest and inhaled the unforgettable scent of sweat and wind, soap and man. "I couldn't get away, Jack. I tried but they kept coming."

He pressed his lips to her hair. "Let it go, Taylor. You can't help her by replaying what happened, and you can't rewrite the lines so they come out the way you want."

Had she been doing that? Trying by sheer force of will to stop the bullets and edit away that terrible instant of spraying blood?

She made a shaky sound, pressing her cheek against the soft hair at his chest. With a sigh, she twined her arms around his neck.

The steering wheel cut into her back, and she shifted to get comfortable. As she did, her thighs pressed against his. Taylor looked up slowly. "Jack?"

"What?" His voice was husky.

Suddenly her need was immense. She wanted to hold and be held. "Do you have a pistol?"

"One in the glove compartment. One in my boot." His eyes were very dark.

She smiled faintly. "So that isn't a gun I'm feeling."

His eyes narrowed. "Bad timing."

"Oh, I don't know." Taylor slid forward, savoring the feel of him, hot and hard, thrusting against her.

He cursed as she slanted a kiss over his hard mouth, coaxing his lips open with her tongue. She was hot, but she wanted to be much hotter, and this SEAL was just the one to make it happen.

His hands tightened, gripping her arms. "Taylor, we've got a lot of driving ahead of us. It's not safe to stop here."

She bit down just hard enough to make him curse. His hands fell, cupping her hips and pulling her against him so that she felt the full outline of an amazing erection. This time he did the taking, as he caught her mouth beneath his.

When he finally pulled away, Jack's eyes held something that was one small step removed from savagery. "We'll continue this later, understand? But we'll be in a double bed with a locked door and we won't be wearing so *damned* many clothes." He deposited her back into her seat. "Buckle up," he added grimly. "I plan to skirt the edge of every speed limit between here and Arizona."

Early afternoon.
Somewhere at the edge of the Sonoran Desert.

Taylor stifled a yawn.

They'd been back and forth over every second of her few contacts with Rains and every conversation with Candace, but they'd come up with nothing new. If Rains had put any object into her apartment, it had to be invisible. The only things Candace had given her were the set of climbing photos and a dog-eared copy of *People* magazine that was two months out of date. After that, Taylor gave up.

To the south, clouds rose like rival cities in an azure sky that went on forever. The light was different here, the sense of space unnerving. On every side she saw sharp peaks and a vast, rolling desert where nothing seemed to move.

"Are we there yet?"

Jack's mouth flashed in a faint grin. "Almost."

"Very funny." She watched light play over the mountains. "We don't seem to be making any progress."

"With this kind of distances you can push all you want, but things happen in their own

438

time." He watched a hawk cut through the clear, clean air. "This isn't exactly a vacation for us, Mrs. Stone."

Taylor's brow rose. "Does this mean the honeymoon's off, Mr. Stone?"

"Ask me that in about four hours," Jack growled.

That sounded promising. Taylor sat back, enjoying the thought of Jack beside her, naked in a hot tub. Suddenly she shot upright. "Did you see *that?*"

"What?"

"Those dark things over by that spiky tree."

"They're called mesquite trees."

"Whatever." Taylor pointed to the crest of a sage-covered hill. "See, there they go again."

"The dark things are called coyotes," Jack said dryly.

"No kidding." Taylor leaned out the window, letting the warm air ruffle her hair. "There must be seven or eight of them." The small, wiry animals trotted along the rim of a wash not fifty feet away.

"They're social. Live and die as a family unit. Mate for life, too."

Taylor looked back at him, one brow rising. "How did you know that?"

"Honey, I'm a SEAL, not a hermit. Even we SEALs have been known to read a book on occasion," he said dryly.

"That's not what I meant, Jack."

"Close enough."

Taylor opened her mouth, then closed it again. "I think I deserved that."

"Probably." Jack ran a finger across her lower lip. "But I'm not keeping score. And I would have told you sooner about my background if the choice had been mine."

Taylor's answer was cut off by the wail of a siren. She was startled to see lights flashing as a police car bore up on their left. "How fast were you going?"

"Only about five miles over the speed limit."

Taylor stared back at the Blazer. "You think he's one of *them?*"

"Right now, I'm trusting no one." Jack reached into the glove compartment and set his Beretta on the floor between his feet, positioning it just out of sight. "If something goes wrong, I want you to get behind the wheel and drive like a bat out of hell. Almost is just over that rise, six miles straight east. Even with the Blazer on your tail, you should make it."

"But —"

"No questions," he growled. "Promise me you'll do it."

After a moment Taylor nodded.

"Good. Now would be a good time to put on your best smile. Praying might not be a bad idea, either. And be ready to get behind the wheel."

Nothing moved in the vast desert landscape as Jack cruised to a slow halt and the Blazer pulled around, blocking them from the front.

Chapter Thirty-six

Dust blew across the road in angry little eddies.

Neither Taylor nor Jack moved. A man in a tan uniform stepped out of the Blazer, and as he ambled toward their car, his eyes scanned back and forth. Slow moving or not, Taylor sensed he was missing nothing.

"I don't like how this feels," she whispered.

"That makes two of us."

The sheriff stopped outside Jack's window and bent his head, staring inside. "Afternoon, folks."

Taylor was mesmerized. The man in the warm sunshine was the spitting image of Mel Gibson, but somehow that didn't make her feel better.

"Afternoon, officer." Jack's feet were together, his expression calm. "Hope I wasn't speeding back there."

"Five miles over, according to my radar. Would you step out of the car, please?"

A muscle moved at Jack's jaw. "Any reason for a problem?"

The man in the uniform didn't move. "No reason at all. Are you two headed somewhere in the area?"

"My wife and I are just passing through."

"Don't suppose you're headed to a place

called Almost, are you?"

There was a tiny pause. Then Jack shook his head. "Never heard of it."

"A lot of people haven't." The officer took another long look at Taylor and adjusted his sunglasses. "That means you probably haven't heard of a fellow called Teague."

"Should I have?" Jack said pleasantly.

"Once you've met Izzy, you don't forget him" came the equally pleasant answer.

"Izzy? Odd sort of name."

The craggy face settled into a smile. "If you want to tell him that to his face, you're a better man than I am." The smile grew. "Jack Broussard, I take it?"

Jack released a tense breath. "You must be T. J. McCall."

"That would be me." The sheriff of Almost, Arizona, pushed back his brown Stetson and surveyed the two. "And you would be Mr. and Mrs. Stone?"

"If anyone asks," Jack said tightly. "Mind if I reach beneath my seat?"

"No problem. Just don't go firing that Beretta you were trying so hard to hide. Have to watch the angle of the sun this time of day, because metal tends to catch the light."

Jack's eyes narrowed. "I'll remember that."

The sheriff slipped off his mirrored sunglasses. "I expect you will." He smiled at Taylor. "I'll give you two an escort into town. Your accommodations are ready and waiting.

After that long drive, you'll probably want to shower and eat."

There in the desert stillness with sunlight playing over her shoulders, Taylor felt the tension slip out of her body. "He's the exhausted one. The big fool drove all the way and wouldn't let me help, even if he's hurting."

"Men have a way of doing that, Ms. — Mrs. Stone." T. J. McCall ran his tongue across his teeth. "My Tess would be spitting mad at me, too, truth be told. She can't wait to meet you, by the way. She's a real big fan." He rocked back on his heels. "So am I. Finished *The Forever Code* in one night."

Taylor flushed beneath those keen blue eyes. "I'm glad to hear it. We appreciate all your help."

"No need for thanks. I owed Izzy a favor. A lot of people owe Izzy favors." He shook his head. "Only problem is my wife. It took a lot of arguing to talk her out of throwing a countywide party for you two, and her parties are pretty special." His voice took on a tinge of pride. "No one ever forgets a bash at Rancho Encantador." He pointed along the brown ridge of hills to a high valley circled by mountains. "You can see the roof from here."

Taylor couldn't see much more than desert, mountains, and a hint of pink adobe walls. "It looks wonderful."

"On the big side, but Tess and I plan to fill it with kids. Already have two and another on the way. I wanted to stop at five, but she says nothing doing. Don't worry about privacy, because your casita is up the hill behind the main house. Take the dirt road north at the burned-out mesquite tree. I'll be right behind you."

As he spoke, an unearthly yowling filled the air.

Taylor blinked. "What on earth was *that?*"

"Just the song dogs talking. Funny, they usually don't get social this time of day."

Taylor looked up at the sheriff in confusion. "Song dogs?"

"Coyotes. Lots of them up here in the high desert."

The noise grew closer, an unsettling confusion of sound that made goose bumps rise on Taylor's skin. Without warning, half a dozen dark shapes flashed beneath the palo verde tree, leaving tracks across the yellow blossoms that covered the ground like snow.

T. J. McCall pushed back his hat, frowning. "I'll have to tell Miguel there was a pack up here. They don't usually come down this far to the main highway."

"Miguel?" Jack's eyes narrowed. "Is he one of your deputies?"

"No, Miguel's just a friend, but you couldn't have a better man watching your back."

"You sure you trust him?"

The sheriff crossed his arms. "With my first-born child. With my secondborn, too, come to think of it. He's taken care of them many times.

Relax, Navy. You're in good hands here."

"Don't underestimate these people, sheriff. We walked into a firefight when we left San Jose. At least one government agent was killed, and people will be trying to track us. In addition, there's a leak somewhere inside the government team. Just so you know what you're getting into," Jack added grimly.

"Izzy's already filled me in on the situation. You can rest assured we'll ride a tight herd on things here in Almost. Only my wife and Miguel know you're here, and no strangers can move anywhere in the high country without Miguel noticing."

Jack glanced at the steep mountains that ran in dark waves toward the horizon. "How can one man keep track of all this? There must be thousands of miles of open country out there."

"Most of it's too rough for anything but mountain lions and coyotes. As far as the rest, there's no better tracker than Miguel." The sheriff scratched his jaw. "Thing is, you probably won't believe what he can do. A lot of things about this beautiful country turn out to be different from what you expect."

On that obscure utterance, he headed back to his Blazer.

Casita — or little house — was definitely the wrong word for the enchanting adobe cottage nestled in the foothills above the sprawling McCall ranch. Bloodred bougainvilleas clambered over pink walls that gleamed in the afternoon sunlight as the sheriff escorted them along a flower-lined walk to the main house. Taylor couldn't take her eyes off the handmade tile and split beams, with stained-glass windows that opened to the desert.

She wanted to meet their hostess, but she sensed that Jack was dead on his feet, even though the man would never admit it.

"I expect you two want to wash up and rest, so I'll keep the welcomes brief. Unfortunately, my three girls will never forgive me if they don't get to say hello." As the sheriff opened the wooden door into the main courtyard, giggles spilled from behind a huge Mexican sage covered with purple flowers.

"Katie, you and Becca come meet our guests." When the sheriff's voice boomed through the courtyard, the thick branches parted, and two small forms shot over the ground. They both had neat braids, but their cheeks were covered with dirt, and neither could have been happier as they flung themselves into their father's strong arms. He caught them both and swung them wide, sunlight brushing two pairs of small red high-top sneakers.

"No more harum-scarum. We've got guests, remember. Say hello to Mr. and Mrs. Stone," he said gruffly.

The taller one fairly danced over the ground to shake hands with Taylor, then Jack, but her little sister held back, hugging her father's leg.

"C'mon, Becca," her sister trilled. "They're nice, can't you see? You just have to shake their hands, not *kiss* them or anything."

Becca's face filled with color. She glanced up at her father, took in his reassuring nod, then marched warily toward the new guests. She gave each hand a stiff shake and ran to the tall woman opening the French doors from the kitchen.

Sunlight played over Tess McCall's red-gold hair, and amusement touched her eyes as she squeezed her daughter's hand. Taylor noticed there was chalk dust on her nose. Becca noticed, too, whispering in her mother's ear, then reaching up to brush it off.

"This is my wife, Tess," the sheriff said proudly. "And these are my daughters. We're glad to have you here at our ranch."

There was quiet pride in his simple words, and deeper emotion in the look that passed between husband and wife as Tess guided Becca over the flagstone patio.

"I'm so happy to meet you both. I know you're both probably dead on your feet, so I'll dispense with the usual tour. There's food on warmers up in the casita, and the refrigerator's stocked. I've warmed up the hot tub, too, since it gets nippy in the evening." She reached around a magnificent rosebush to shake Taylor's hand. "I can't tell you what a pleasure it is to have you here. You, too — Mr. Stone."

"Momma, can I show them the way to the casita?"

"That would be very nice, Katie. Why don't you help her, Becca?"

Red sneakers flashed over the ground, accompanied by wild giggles. The rosebushes shook as the girls disappeared around a winding adobe fence covered with trailing morning glories.

Tess watched them with a smile. "I wish I had half their energy." She took a deep breath. "They're up at dawn and they don't stop until we tuck them in at night."

"You feeling okay?" T.J. put a hand on his wife's shoulder. "Not having any more pains, are you?"

His wife flushed. "I'm just fine."

"Are you sure?"

She nodded firmly. "A little tired, that's all. I wanted to finish that market study for Mae's new tortilla soup launch." She glanced at Taylor as they walked beneath an adobe arch fitted with an old cowbell. "We're experimenting with some local products, the hotter the better, but don't let T.J. talk you into sampling them. After my first taste, my mouth was sore for a week."

"Thanks for the warning." Taylor watched sunlight play over Tess's face and wondered if she wasn't a little pale. "Are you sure this isn't too much for you? We could stay somewhere else."

"I wouldn't hear of it. I've got months to go yet." She touched the slim curve of her stomach with a protective hand. "My husband just likes to worry. You know how men can be."

Taylor looked over at Jack, who was walking slightly ahead, talking with the sheriff. Except for her father, Jack was the only man who had ever worried about her or protected her. She had to remind herself not to get used to the experience.

"Do you know about what happened in California?" she asked quietly.

"T.J. told me. It will probably be hard for you to trust anyone now, but you can believe my husband when he tells you it's safe here. He'll see to it. The man's good at taking care of people." Her face brightened. "Whenever you feel rested, just come down to the main house. The girls and I are making biscuits today."

Taylor grimaced at her creased jeans and dusty jacket. "First I want to try out that hot tub. It sounds like heaven after driving all day. In fact, I might never come out again."

Her breath caught as she turned a corner, where a small door of teal blue opened into a courtyard filled with wildflowers. The two girls were already holding Jack's hand, tugging him inside. He reached down to grab Katie's pigtails while she danced around him, laughing.

The sight did odd things to Taylor's insides. Who knew he'd be so comfortable around children? She watched him break off a big orange hibiscus flower and tuck it into Becca's hair, smiling gravely as her face filled with color.

But she didn't pull away. Her blue eyes, so like her father's, simply gleamed. Another woman smitten by the lethal Broussard charm, Taylor thought wryly. That must make about a thousand.

A thousand and one.

She followed Tess into a room rich with the scent of piñon and cedar. Light gleamed off stained glass and hand-loomed rugs with a warmth that was nearly palpable.

"I think that's enough for now," Tess said, as Jack surreptitiously rubbed his shoulder. "Say good-bye, Katie. You, too, Becca."

There was more giggling, quiet voices, then another flash of red sneakers back out into the golden sunlight.

Taylor felt as if she'd been touched by some rare magic, a force as tangible as the clay walls that climbed the hillside. Jack's smile told her that he felt the magic, too. But he was just about to collapse.

She waved good-bye to their hosts, closed the door, and took a deep breath, savoring the warm desert air. Then she took Jack's arm and turned him toward the bedroom. "If you need help undressing, just let me know."

"I think I can manage," he said dryly.

"I'm not so sure. You look like you'll pass out any second." Taylor turned back the soft cotton sheets on the bed and mounded up the pillows.

"If so, I'll take off whatever I see fit," she said huskily.

"You're welcome to try. I might be dead-weight after all." Jack pulled her down onto his lap. "Sorry. I had other plans for how we'd spend our first few hours out of that car."

She touched his face, smoothing the lines of exhaustion. "Later, Navy. This is just a temporary reprieve. Tonight I figure we can start at the hot tub and work our way across every usable surface from there. You interested?"

Heat flared in his eyes. "Can dogs bark?"

But Taylor pushed him back onto the bed and tugged off his shoes. "Don't bother looking at me like that. When I have my way with you, I expect you to manage to be semi-conscious."

He made a muffled sound as his shoes hit the floor. After some maneuvering, Taylor pulled off his shirt, avoiding the bandage on his upper arm.

Then she went to work on his belt.

It was embarrassing to see that her hands weren't quite steady.

She blew out a breath, trying not to feel the rock-hard stomach and rigid abs, or remember how much she wanted to have him touch her in this big bed.

"I'll find something for you to eat, if you're hungry. Soup. Milk." *Stop babbling, O'Toole.* "The truth is, I can cook. An egg." *With a little luck.* "How about some iced tea?"

Jack muttered as she slid his belt free, and

Taylor swallowed in sheer lust as his pants rode low over lean, hard hips.

Sweet Mary, the man was built, no question about it.

Right now, she wanted to strip off his pants and see all the rest of that prime body. Touching him was going to take her a great deal of time.

But not now.

With a pang of regret, she shut down one of her better fantasies and went to work on his zipper, trying to keep her fingers from straying to the straining cloth on either side. She cursed as the metal stuck twice.

Sweat touched her brow. *He's just a man, damn it. It's not like you've never touched a hunk before. Rein yourself in.*

A drop of sweat fell, beading against those gorgeous stomach muscles and sliding down to the curve of his navel. Taylor wanted to moan with sheer, excruciating lust.

Forget the zipper. Forget taking off his clothes.

She shoved the snap free on his jeans and left it at that, her hands shaking when she stood up. "You're on your own from here."

There was no answer.

"Jack?"

The pillow rustled. His fingers moved, opening to encircle hers, then closing hard.

Something tightened in her throat at that one simple movement. She needed to be touched now, Taylor realized. The horror of the night before was still too close. Every time she closed her eyes she saw shadows and blood, then Agent Rodriguez's fallen body. "Aren't you ever frightened?" she whispered to Jack.

His hand moved, pinning her arm to the bed, but he didn't answer. When Taylor looked up, he was fast asleep. She tugged on his hand, trying to pull away, but his fingers only tightened. Even in sleep, he wouldn't let her go.

She sank down and curled into his hard body. At least she could feel him beside her, even if it was simply to sleep. In fact, self-restraint was probably good practice. Whatever happened, she couldn't let the magic of this high valley make her conjure up impossible dreams that had no place in the cold reality of her future.

In a few weeks Jack would be gone, vanished into a jungle in South America or a stormy sea in Asia. It was what SEALs did. And they didn't look back.

Taylor took a long breath, trying to ignore the magic scent of sage and lavender drifting through the open window. Somewhere to the south, jagged peaks shimmered like smoke above the vast green floor of the desert, and a hawk cried as it soared through the turquoise sky. The last thing she saw before her eyes closed was a dust devil churning up the valley, raising a tall brown cone of mayhem as it scattered rocks and sticks in its path.

Taylor knew exactly how those rocks felt, as Jack's hard body brushed against hers in sleep.

Chapter Thirty-seven

"They're not quite what I thought." Down in the main house, Tess McCall sipped a cup of herbal tea. "She's quiet, thoughtful. And he's . . ." Her lips curved.

"He's what?" her husband demanded.

"Most women would call him a hunk."

The sheriff snorted.

"No need to be jealous, T.J. Most women would say you're a hunk, too."

She heard another snort.

"Are they really in danger?"

T. J. McCall sat back in his chair, watching his daughters play in the courtyard. "I'm afraid so. Izzy knows when to play and when to fold. If he sent them here, the threat's real."

His wife stared thoughtfully at the casita. "I'll make them some dinner later."

T.J. shook his head. "Afraid not. You and the girls are going into town to stay with Mae until this is over."

Tess's chin rose. "We are *not*."

"Don't argue with me about this, Duchess." The gentle hand at her cheek took the sting from the order. "I won't have you in danger, and that's final. I'll handle things from here, and of course Miguel will be around."

"You expect Miguel to cook? To be a hostess?"

T.J. chuckled. "I doubt those two will be out of the casita for hours. Did you see how he looked at her when he thought she wasn't watching? The man was exhausted, but he still couldn't hide his feelings."

Tess's eyes softened. "I saw. Too bad she didn't see. Maybe I should —"

"No matchmaking. They've got enough to worry about right now."

"But I —"

He cut off her musings with a slow kiss, pulling her onto his lap and sliding his fingers through her hair.

"T.J., the girls," she rasped.

"The girls are too busy mutilating my new chile crop to notice anything." He slid one hand under her sweater and cupped the soft swell of her breast. "Your breasts are getting bigger."

"Is that a complaint?"

He shifted, bringing her into the saddle of his thighs. "Does it feel as if I'm complaining?"

Tess McCall's lips curved in a smile of sheer feminine possession. "Not where I'm sitting. So you're banishing us to town," she whispered, drawing his fingers through hers. "This calls for serious negotiation. What's in it for me if I go?"

The girls ran across the courtyard, following the flash of a hummingbird, their sneakers raising a small storm of dust in the quiet sunlight.

"I suppose I could find something." T.J. brushed aside silk and lace to find the sensitive curve of one nipple. His long fingers roamed, stroking smoothly.

"Such as?"

He bent closer, whispering huskily.

Tess took a sharp breath, shifting on his hard thighs. "That sounds illegal, Sheriff."

"Not while I'm wearing the badge, honey. If I give you the cuffs, *then* it would be illegal."

His wife tilted her head. "The last time you cuffed me, I was trying my darnedest to leave town."

"And you weren't complaining after I got you back." His eyes darkened. "Even though I didn't think we could walk for a week."

Tess drew a husky breath. "Maybe we could drop off the girls with Mae, then take the Blazer for a little drive up into the foothills. Someplace quiet, where we could try out the backseat." She smiled. "Again."

T.J. arched one dark eyebrow. "Highway safety is always a priority. I'd be remiss if I didn't check out the side roads." He found her other breast and coaxed a sigh from her parted lips. "Miguel can keep an eye on things here for an hour or so."

Tess sat up stiffly. "You wouldn't tell him that we —"

Her husband snorted. "I won't say a word, but sometimes I think that man can read minds."

Tess's cheeks went red. "You mean —"

"Let me worry about Miguel, Duchess." T.J. pulled her to her feet. "You herd the girls out to the Blazer while I get your bags."

Becca and Katie peeked around the bougain-villea vines, giggling. "Stop kissing her, Daddy. She's all red."

"Ladies get red sometimes. You two come help me find your bags while your mother stops being red."

Katie frowned at her dusty sneaker. "I don't *ever* want someone kissing me. Nobody except for you and Momma. Maybe Becca." She screwed up her perfect little cheeks. "But no *boys*."

The sheriff shoved back his Stetson and smiled. "A good thing, too, darlin'. I'd have to shoot any boy who tried."

Katie looked shocked for a moment, then saw her father's lazy smile. "You're teasing, Daddy." She took Becca's hand and danced up the walk. "Last one to the car's a stinky old crow's egg."

"As for you, ma'am, I have some thoughts in mind," T.J. murmured. "And it's not wise to argue with an officer of the law."

"Always giving orders." Tess pursed her lips. "Just remember, a woman can do a lot of damage with a pair of handcuffs."

"A man can always hope."

Tess's laugh was a smoky ripple of pleasure as she drew his arm through hers.

457

"How did they get away?" The South American voice on the cell phone rose in a crescendo of fury.

"They had a car waiting. Now they're gone and two of my men are dead." Viktor Lemka took his time before continuing. "That's going to cost you."

"You know we will pay. Just find us the compounds that the scientist promised."

"All the rest is with the damned American woman."

"Then *get* her."

"Oh, I plan to. But your contact didn't tell me the man guarding her was a Navy SEAL." Viktor's voice hardened. "Or that his friend was an ex-DEA field operative with a black belt in Tae Kwon Do."

"I will call my contact and —"

"You will call *no one*." The Albanian studied the glowing tip of his cigarette. In the darkness outside, road lights flashed past. "I'm already on my way. Get the final payment ready, because I will have the woman soon."

He cut off the call and flicked his cigarette out the window, whistling as he considered his next plan. He'd always loved American heroes.

Now he would have a chance to see just how tough these Americans really were.

Chapter Thirty-eight

FROM TAYLOR'S BOOK OF RULES:
Amor vincit omnia.
According to the Romans, anyway.

She was going to make biscuits if it *killed* her.

Taylor glared at the flour-covered cookbook on the counter. One cup of buttermilk. One-half stick of butter. A teaspoon of something else. And what in the heck was a pastry cutter?

She dropped the butter into the flour and sneezed as powder flew everywhere. Muttering, she went to work with her fingers, squeezing in the butter just the way the directions said. When things were nice and gooey, she turned the mess out on a wooden board and kneaded it hard.

With any luck, cooking would make her stop thinking about Jack, and how he'd felt before she'd finally managed to wriggle out from beneath him. She closed her eyes, feeling her brain start to short-circuit all over again. It was bad enough to smell his scent, a mix of soap and man and fresh air that drove her crazy.

Then he'd rolled over, pinning her beneath him on the bed, one thigh across her hip. That's when her circuits had really blown.

And all the time, the big, dumb man was

stretched out on top of her, sound asleep.

Taylor slammed the dough down against the board. Because it felt so good, she did it again. "What is wrong with this picture? All I want is a little uncomplicated sex. What is so damned difficult about *that?*"

She shoved a strand of hair out of her eyes, blinking as dough streaked her face. Probably Jack would have another excuse when he got up, something about mission integrity or operational preparedness. Taylor wondered how she could have convinced herself he was your ordinary, garden-variety P.I. when the man had SEAL written all over him.

Maybe she'd wanted to be deceived. If she believed he was a regular civilian, they could have a chance at a future together.

Taylor whacked the dough hard.

Not that she cared either way. Let the lug try to maneuver her into bed now and see what happened. He'd find out how it felt to be on the receiving end of a huge yawn.

Taylor shoved the dough into a circle and began cutting out biscuits with a glass. She refused to think about getting up close and personal with that amazing body stretched out in the bed next door.

Metal clattered as she shoved a row of uneven biscuits onto a tray bound for the oven. Who said baking was hard? All it took was a little organization and research, skills which any author had.

Her eyes narrowed. Too bad you couldn't conjure up stunning sex with the same ease. Not that she was going to think about sex.

She closed the cookbook with a snap, wondering what she should do next. Sleep was impossible. With all this nervous energy, writing was out of the question, too. Pacing would be downright humiliating.

She rubbed at her cheek, spreading the streak of wet dough. Probably she should go clean up. Maybe she'd try a cold shower. No, *frigid* shower.

She checked the clock, added up minutes until the biscuits would be done, and decided she had just enough time to —

Callused fingers circled her wrists. "Going somewhere?"

He turned her slowly and she nearly swallowed her tongue.

Jack's face was lined with stubble, his eyes were heavy with sleep, and he was naked except for a pair of partially unbuttoned jeans that left Taylor a mouthwatering view of great abs, sculpted shoulders, and a wedge of dark hair that tapered down and vanished beneath tight denim.

Her heart punched hard. *Don't lose it here, O'Toole. No need to get double vision over a naked male chest.*

"To shower," she snapped. "And I'd appreciate if you'd let go of my hands."

He backed her against the kitchen cabinet.

"What's the white goop on your face?"

"The white goop is buttermilk dough. I'm making biscuits," she said stonily. "And I need to clean up while they cook."

His fingers were at her belt, tugging at the knot. "You can shower later. In fact, we can shower together."

"Sorry. Not interested." *Who* wasn't interested? Why was she fighting him?

Because a woman had her pride, to say nothing of her honor and self-respect. All of these demanded she prove her control was fully operational.

"Why aren't you asleep?" she demanded.

"I slept long enough."

She stared down at his hands, locked around her wrists. "Do you mind?"

His eyes narrowed. "Definitely. And just for the record, you can forget about the shower."

Taylor realized she was caught against the kitchen cabinet. His hands snaked under her robe, hot and hard. "What are you doing?" She bit back a gasp as he caught her hips and lifted her onto the smooth counter, moving between her thighs.

Rough denim and straining muscle pressed against her sensitive skin.

No whimpering, she told herself sternly. *No begging, either. Remember your pride.* "Is there a point to this display?"

His lips curved. "I'm getting to it." He slid her robe open slowly. "I just need to have your undivided attention."

Taylor felt color shoot into her face as her body lay revealed to him, covered by the sheerest triangle of pink lace. He could see most of her, right down to the auburn curls showing through the strategically placed flower cutout.

A muscle moved at his jaw. "Nice lingerie. Mind if they get ruined?"

She couldn't manage an answer, held by the energy in his eyes. "Ruined how?"

"Any damned way I feel like." There was something in his face, in his touch, that hadn't been there before. It was primitive, unnerving.

Her breasts tightened, brushed his chest. She swallowed hard. "Jack, I don't —"

"Yeah, you do. We both do. We've waited too damned long already," he said harshly. His fingers circled her waist, drawing her forward until she rode damply against him, pressed against straining denim.

Taylor made a low sound, wanting him blindly, and to hell with pride. She speared her fingers into his hair and jerked him down. Their hungry kiss was all teeth and tongue.

She pulled away, shaking her head. "I thought we tried everything important in that motel room."

"Honey, we haven't even started. I've got things in mind they don't have names for."

"I hope that's a promise." She licked his upper lip and bit him lightly, then slid her tongue hungrily over his, wildly pleased when he ground out a graphic one-word response. The thought of his control in shreds left her grinning as she ran her hands along those hard shoulders, then worked her way beneath his snug jeans to revel in the erection straining blatantly against her.

Her legs rose, wrapped around his waist. Cursing with impatience, Jack shoved aside her robe and bent low, his mouth against her breast.

Taylor pushed down the zipper, shoving down his jeans, intent on exploring what felt like a truly awesome erection.

When he sprang free and filled her fingers, Taylor closed her eyes, instinctively lifting her body, pressing against the warm, straining tip of his penis. "Now," she rasped.

He held her hips and stroked between her thighs. One finger, then two pushed inside her.

"Jack?"

Slowly he skimmed her slick skin. "You're driving me insane."

Taylor moaned and drove against him harder.

"A body in motion is a true miracle." His voice was hoarse.

"*Jack.*" Her legs pumped. "If you don't shut up and screw my brains out, I'm going to —"

"It's always nice to see a woman who knows what she wants." In one panting thrust, he filled her deeply. Taylor felt the counter beneath her, flour slipping as he pinned her stroke by stroke while she moaned with the heat of him, with the amazing shock of being taken so completely. Around her, all sound faded and she strained upward, open to him in a way she'd never imagined possible.

He muttered her name and rocked inside her again, making her body clench until suddenly she was *there*, right at the edge, panting and straining.

Coming her brains out, digging her nails against his shoulders while he pushed inside her and she hung blindly on the wave he created, half lost, certain that the pleasure couldn't get any better. Then he pulled her closer, his fingers exploring her softness so the pleasure stabbed through her again and she rocked wildly, coming in a swift, furious rush.

Fingers in his hair. Legs against that rock-hard body, lost in the total explosion of her senses.

Amazing.

Eons later, noises drifted back and she felt the world returning.

The counter beneath her back. His hands locked on her flour-covered hips.

Something wrong.

She blinked and tried to sit up. "J-Jack?"

"What?" His voice was hoarse with strain.

Taylor knew why he sounded hoarse, because she felt the evidence sheathed inside her, as hard as ever, his desire unsated.

"Wait — what's that smell?"

With a curse he twisted, moving them as one while he grabbed the oven door. Smoke billowed out, spewing from the black remains of Taylor's biscuits, while Jack swatted vainly, trying to reach the oven controls. When nothing else worked, he lifted her and lunged, pounding the controls until the light went off. Then he shifted, their bodies as one, sliding back against the counter.

"Damned oven. Damned biscuits. Damned bad idea. This is probably going to get nasty and messy before we're done." His hands clenched on the counter. "You want out?"

"Saved by the biscuits?"

"Something like that."

Her eyes slitted. "Try it and die, sailor."

He gave a tight nod, utterly serious, utterly focused. He didn't argue, and there were no more words. Taylor realized his eyes were beyond hard, beyond control as he stared at her and began to move again, short strokes alternating with long, savage thrusts that gave her no time to prepare, no choice but to follow as he slammed her up instantly, back into the lost place where she couldn't think, couldn't breathe, her body taking over, slick with sweat and need.

Only now there was a surety to every move, a surge of muscle, a *knowing* that might have been terrifying if it hadn't felt so amazing. As Taylor watched him take her, watched him lose himself in the power of their joining, she felt an ache in her chest where her heart probably wasn't but might have been. The ache grew, shivered, opened, then climbed as his breath came in hard bursts and his eyes held her, hiding nothing, demanding her presence completely in the moment.

Claimed, she claimed back, legs locked around his back, fingers driving up, digging into his shoulders. This close, this intimate, there was no mistaking the way his hands shook as he trapped her thighs to hold her tighter, no mistaking his pleasure in every movement, no ignoring her own delight in the power of his body driving down, hot and sweet and so real inside her that she came again, his name a raw sound on her lips.

The world blurred for a moment. Taylor felt him tense, balanced just at the edge. Then he followed, gripping her with barely contained violence, spilling himself endlessly, hotly, inside her while the world burned away into nothingness.

Taylor sneezed. That was all she had the energy for.

Flour tickled her nose. Her legs were shaking, and sweat touched their sated bodies.

She took a raw breath. "Wow."

"And you, a writer."

She opened one eye. "Was that an insult?"

"I simply expected something . . . more elegant."

"Give me a few minutes and I'll sing the opening libretto from *Carmen*."

Jack grunted, tried to move, failed. "Give me a few years and I'll join you."

"Take a century. I'm not going anywhere."

He found her fingers, slid them through his, then brought them with great effort to his lips. "This is usually the part where it starts getting messy."

"Maybe we'll break the mold."

"Maybe." Using their locked hands, he brushed flour from her chin.

Taylor caught his finger and bit down gently. "Gee, I almost forgot. Want a biscuit?"

She saw the flash of a grin and it claimed her heart with stunning force. *Watch it,* sanity whispered. *This is strictly a case of nerves and hormones at work.*

"Trying to get rid of me already?"

"What, a big SEAL like you is afraid of a few charcoal briquettes for lunch? I thought you hard bodies lived on adrenaline and raw eggs."

"I've done a little of that." He eased to one elbow, surveyed their locked bodies, and took a hard breath. "If it brought me here, I'm not complaining."

She sank back with a sated smile. "It seems that cooking isn't my strong point."

He whisked flour off her nose. "You've got other skills, I'm happy to report."

"And those would be?"

"Attitude out to here." He tongued her damp

lower lip. "A really big mouth." He circled one taut nipple, then kissed it gently. "Hell-if-I-care stubbornness. Oh, did I mention you have great breasts?"

She was already melting, already damp, already wanting him again. "What's not to like?"

"Two weeks ago I would have said a great deal." His voice fell, suddenly grave. "I'm a man who goes by the book — and you just keep *rewriting* it."

He shifted and Taylor felt him grow inside her.

"Jack, this isn't —" She fought for words, furious that when she needed them most they should desert her. "You don't have to make promises. We're both adults. Eyes wide open and all that. There's no need to think this changes anything."

"Speak for yourself." The words were so low she could have imagined them. But she didn't imagine the pressure of him shifting or the first rocking thrust, hot and powerful inside her.

She took a sharp breath. The heat was already driving her crazy again. "No promises, Jack. I don't expect them. I —"

"Could you please shut up?" He was moving in lovely, controlled strokes that had her circuits frying all over again. "You're interrupting my plans."

Her legs tightened around his waist. "Such as?"

"Making you scream again."

She tried to look disappointed. "Only once?"

He slid her back against the counter, huge and hard, making her pant and clench around him. "Actually, this time I'm going for double digits."

The sun was hidden by the mountains when Taylor opened her eyes and dragged in a breath. Her knees were cellophane. If she tried to get off the counter, she'd end up kissing the floor.

Not bad for an old woman, she thought smugly.

She groped blindly around her. "You there, Broussard?"

"Let me get back to you." He was on his face, an arm outstretched on her breasts.

She slapped him on that amazing butt and smiled wickedly. "Three times. Not bad for an old man."

"Four." His pained laugh rumbled through their locked bodies. "*Who's* old?"

"We are. Sort of." She grinned up at him. "Or not."

"Not if hormones count for anything."

Boots grated on gravel. Through the open window Taylor heard the gate scrape. She was pretty sure it was Sheriff McCall.

"Hell, why can't he come back later?" Jack stretched an arm over the counter and pushed to an elbow. "We're sleeping." He groaned. "Maybe we're dead."

The bell rang above the arched adobe gate. "Hello in there?" More gravel sounds. "Mr. and Mrs. Stone?"

Taylor dug an elbow into his ribs. "It's the sheriff."

Jack stood up awkwardly. "How many laws did we break?"

"I stopped counting after the third scream."

He smiled, a dark slash of male pride that had her senses fogging again. "No kidding." Grimacing, he looked around for his jeans. "I'll go."

Taylor groped until she found her robe. "No, I'll go." She took a staggering step toward the door. "As soon as I remember how to walk. You know, there's a word for sex like that."

"Stupendous?" Jack carefully zipped up his jeans.

"I was thinking more along the lines of illegal." Taylor tugged on her robe and took a wobbling step, fighting down a giggle. Her belt was mostly knotted by the time she reached the door, where Jack stopped her.

"Let me have a look first." He moved silently around the house, pulled himself up the wall and looked over, then slid down, giving Taylor a thumbs-up. "Sheriff," he said.

She shoved aside the little wooden opening at the top of the door. "Sorry, Sheriff. We were asleep."

T. J. McCall looked anxious. "The fire alarm went off down at the main house. Is everything okay?"

Taylor flushed. "I was making some biscuits and they got a little overcooked. Completely black, actually. Sorry about that."

"That's what triggered the alarm? You're sure?"

Taylor gave an embarrassed grin. "I guess I'm not cut out to be a cook."

"So you're both okay?"

"Just great." *Sated. Dazed. Extraordinary, actually.* "We're fine. No problems here, Sheriff."

Jack moved in behind her. "Sorry about the smoke alarm, Sheriff."

He searched their faces, then shoved his Stetson back on his head and looked away. "Well then, sorry to bother you. If you need anything, let me know."

"Absolutely." Like hell. Over her dead body. Taylor wasn't leaving this casita for hours, and neither was Jack. They weren't even going to leave the kitchen until they worked this thing out of their system, no matter if it took hours.

Long, hot hours of amazing sex.

Taylor froze as muscular arms slid around her waist. Hard fingers snaked under her robe and cupped her hips.

"Fine. I'll be down at the main house if you need me." The sheriff turned with a wave.

"Thank you." Taylor swallowed as Jack's fingers slid between her thighs, stroking expertly, making her neurons sizzle. She felt the scrape of denim. "We — we'll be sure to call, Sheriff. If anything comes up."

Something came up just then, hard and heavy and male, nudging her backside. "Wow."

T.J. turned. "Did you say something?"

"Oh — I meant, will. We will call. You can count on it, Sheriff. Soon." Taylor blinked as Jack's teeth bit gently at her shoulder, just out of sight of the small window in the courtyard door.

Her fingers closed on the wooden latch. She was going to lose it any second. Right here, with Jack's fingers searching, slipping into her, hard and warm. "Thanks." She shivered against Jack's chest. "Talk to you later."

"Right." Sheriff McCall's tongue ran over his teeth. "You two enjoy your rest."

"Definitely," Taylor murmured. Boots crunched, moving away over the gravel and down the hill.

"I wouldn't exactly call it a rest," Jack murmured behind her.

Taylor shoved the window shut and arched back against Jack's hard body, hungry for his hands, wanting all of him. As the pleasure grew, she looked at his face. At the eyes that too often carried wariness and regret. At the lines carved by duty and hard responsibility.

She loved him.

Oh, God, how had this happened? How had she lost her logic and her heart without any hint of warning?

Wind blew over the adobe walls, sweet with the scent of sage, and Taylor tried to talk but it was too late. She was in that blind place again, panting, twisting, while Jack's hand touched her mouth and she bit down hard, stifling her scream as the boots moved all the way down the hill and Jack's fingers moved inside her.

With the wind brushing her shoulders, she came in a wild, truly amazing rush of pleasure.

Chapter Thirty-nine

She was panting when he flipped her back against the adobe wall and wrenched open her robe.

"How ready are you?" he asked hoarsely.

She was seeing double. Probably oxygen deprivation.

No problem. Both versions of him were naked and sexy as hell. "Is this a trick question?"

"I need you now, Taylor." He filled her, then cursed and drove into her again. *"Right — now."*

She managed a throaty sound. "Am I arguing?"

"The wall." He put up one hand, cupping her shoulders. "Your back —"

"Can't — feel a thing." She closed her eyes, lost in a blur of sensation, feeling him pant as he drove into her again. Just as lost as she was. "Whatever happens, don't stop. Even if I appear to stop breathing." She moaned as he filled her again. *"Especially* if I stop breathing."

"Hell." His forehead touched hers. "It's not supposed to do this."

"Do what?"

"Get better." His breath whispered across her cheek. "It's not supposed to feel this good."

"Good doesn't even come close. I'm a writer," she panted. "Trust me. I know about descriptions. I'm a highly trained professional who —"

He lifted her knee and made the angle even better.

"Oh, God." Her head tilted back. "*Again. Just like that.*"

She might have stopped breathing then, but his hands gripped her and sunlight touched her shoulders, and he didn't stop so it didn't matter.

Nothing mattered but what he was doing to her and what she was feeling while he did it, so that even the rough adobe scraping her shoulders didn't matter, as the world blurred hard and she collapsed against him while he shuddered and ground out her name and lost himself inside her.

So deep.

The thought came dimly, more instinct than real reflection.

This deep in a woman, this deep with *this* woman, and a man could get lost forever, never finding his way back to who he was and what really mattered.

For some reason it didn't seem important. Not with Taylor's nails digging into his back and her voice panting out his name.

Yeah, this was definitely where the messy stuff began.

Odd, but Jack couldn't summon up the energy to care.

They collapsed against the wall.

Jack's face was hard as he stroked her hair.

After several moments of labored breath, he carried her over the flagstones to the little pool beneath a cascade of boulders. Crimson petals dropped around them as they stumbled into the bubbling water. "I sure hope he doesn't come back."

"Who?"

"Sheriff. The man in the uniform. The one you were talking to before I made you come, screaming."

"Oh — him." Taylor drifted on the hot, lazy currents. "Too bad my biscuits were duly noted." She turned her head lazily. "Our Sheriff McCall is a careful man."

"He would be, if Izzy chose him." He stared down at her. "We're not out of the woods yet, you know."

"Is this the part where you get all professional and cold again?"

Jack didn't move.

"Because if it is, Commander Broussard, I don't want to hear it." Her fingers found him, cupped him, traced him slowly. "I'd rather think about what we just did. Several times, if my memory holds."

He didn't want to count. He definitely didn't want to remember. "Look, Taylor, I need to make some calls. Why don't you rest?"

She stared at him. "What's wrong?"

"Nothing that I know of, but Izzy should have some answers by now. We'll be missed, and I want to find out who's asking the most questions."

"Because that will be the person who set us up."

"That's how I figure it." He took a hard breath. "Look, I'll admit I'd rather stay out here right now. I'm not half finished with you." He frowned. "With *us*. But the responsibilities don't end until you're out of danger and all mission objectives are secured."

"Which means?"

"Which means I do the work I'm trained to do."

After what felt like a lifetime, she nodded. "Understood, Captain. Aye, aye. Over and out. Roger." She looked away, her face wreathed in drifting mist. "Just bear with me if I don't want to think about that other world yet. If I do, I'll see Nancy Rodriguez's face." Her voice tightened. "I'll see her body, twisting as she falls, and I'll feel your blood, fresh on my hands. So make your calls, Navy. I'll be here, trying to put the pieces together so I can be strong again, too."

"You are strong," Jack said quietly. "Never doubt that, Taylor."

Then why did she feel so weak? Taylor didn't watch him pull on his jeans and walk back to the casita. As the silence fell around her, she closed her eyes.

She didn't want the world to come back, and strong was the very *last* thing she felt.

Jack put away everything but the mission as he dialed the new number Izzy had left him.

As usual, Izzy answered on the first ring. "Yo. How are things in sunny Arizona?"

"Nice place. Good people. The sheriff sends his regards." Jack frowned. "What have you found?"

"The U.S. Marshals are going nuts after what happened in San Jose. They've got people looking everywhere for you and Taylor. Of course, I'm demanding answers, since this happened on my watch."

"Give 'em hell," Jack said dryly.

"Damned straight. Whoever passed the information is staying very cool. No one has given away any clue of involvement. I've planted a story that Rodriguez was worried about a possible leak, and I'm getting some interesting reactions. Pretty soon someone will make a slip, and when they do, I'll be waiting."

Jack nodded. It was a good plan, and no one could bluff like Izzy.

"Did you get anything out of Taylor? Any information she'd overlooked?"

"Nothing." Jack rubbed his neck. "But we'll go over it again."

"There's got to be something." Izzy's voice

fell. "Someone coming." His tone changed, suddenly surly. "And I don't give a damn how many people you've got working on this. Put on a dozen more. I want that van. Check all abandoned vehicle lists, and don't forget Canada and Mexico. They could be out of the country by now — assuming they're still alive."

After a moment, Izzy came back on the line. "You there?"

"Yeah. Nice misdirection."

"I do my best."

"Who was that?"

"Rodriguez's partner. This really hit him hard, and he's putting in a lot of overtime. So is her boss, though not so willingly." He ruffled some papers, and a door closed. "Listen, I've got a secret weapon headed your way. This will help facilitate your search."

He spoke tersely, and when he was done Jack nodded. "It might work. What's the E.T.A.?"

"McCall should be arranging it as we speak," Izzy said grimly. "Happy hunting."

"Count on it."

After Izzy rang off, Jack stood in the gathering twilight, studying the distant mountains and trying to juggle the bits of information they had so far. What was Taylor's real place in all this? Had they overlooked some small detail?

Or was Taylor lying to them?

He forced himself to consider the question with cold, unbiased logic. She'd been a target from the start, and there had to be a reason for it.

But no matter how he tried shifting the pieces, he came to the conclusion that Taylor wasn't hiding anything. The woman would be a terrible liar, and her fear was no act.

Remembering Izzy's plan, he picked up the phone and called Sheriff McCall, who told him their package had just arrived. Jack's eyes narrowed on the big purse next to the window. He remembered Taylor carrying it into the store where she'd been taken hostage along with Rains. She carried it just about everywhere, in fact.

He fingered his cell phone. "Izzy, I need you to go back to the convenience store. See if you can track down their security videotape from the robbery."

"Come on, Cinderella. Time to rise and shine." Jack bent over Taylor, who was drowsing in the mist-covered water.

Taylor opened one eye. "Don't tell me my coaches are turning into pumpkins already."

"I think all our coaches are turning into pumpkins," Jack said tightly as he held out a towel.

Taylor sat up straighter. "What's wrong? Has someone been hurt?"

"Not yet, but we may have a lead on what Rains gave you."

She wrapped the towel around her, frowning.

"There was nothing. Not a single thing."

"But now we're going to try it a different way. We'll go over everything again until we get it right. We can do this, Taylor. Trust me."

"I can't bear the thought of people dying." The words were a whisper.

Jack knew just how she felt, but he was trained at boxing up those emotions and putting them away until the mission was done. It was the only way you survived as a soldier.

Jack was starting to understand that a writer survived by acting just the opposite. A good story demanded opening up the box all the way. Then you got right inside with all your personal demons and explored the emotions until you came away raw and bleeding. A hell of a thing to do for a living, he thought grimly.

Sometime, he'd tell her just how brave he thought that was.

"Forget about what could go wrong, Taylor. Do the job. That's your best contribution." Jack stroked her hair, then raised her face to his. "Besides, we've got a special weapon."

"Izzy sent a team?"

"Not a team. Someone who's very good at his job." At Jack's whistle, a big brown dog trotted out of the house. "Sheriff McCall just brought him up from town. Izzy had him flown in from a special Navy program in California. Now L.Z. is going to earn his chow."

"L.Z.?" Taylor shook her head. "I don't understand."

"It stands for Landing Zone. This dog does things you wouldn't believe," Jack said tightly. "Let's go inside and I'll show you." He patted the big Belgian Malinois, who was watching him alertly. "Come on, L.Z. It's time to do a search."

At the last word, the dog barked once, ears erect.

Taylor looked confused. "But what's he going to search?"

Lightning flickered over the mountains as Jack stretched out on the rug near the big glass-and-granite coffee table, while L.Z. sat expectantly, pressed against his shoulder. "Put your purse down in front of me on the floor."

Taylor studied him warily. "I still don't understand. We've been through my purse a dozen times already."

"Not with L.Z. along, we haven't. Izzy's had someone train him to Harris Rains' scent. He can find things we'd never notice."

Taylor scratched L.Z.'s head. "Well, now, aren't you a clever fellow? Not that I think this is going to produce anything new."

"If it's there, L.Z. will tell us. He can target a scent too minuscule for any human to pick up."

"I hope you won't have to damage my purse. It always brings me good luck."

"I won't shoot it unless it talks back," Jack said dryly. "Take the contents out one by one and put them on the floor. Wait for my signal before you move to the next item. And no hair spray or perfume."

Taylor unzipped the purse and delved inside. "Any particular order?"

"You call it." Jack patted the dog on the head. "Search, L.Z."

Taylor pulled out a hairbrush and set it on the floor in front of L.Z., who sniffed delicately, then raised his head and didn't move.

"That's a no." Jack gestured to the purse. "Next."

"Travel aspirin." Taylor put the foil-wrapped square on the rug, where the dog gave it a cursory sniff, then turned away to look at Jack.

"Next, one pearl earring." When L.Z. had no response, Taylor moved on. "Mascara." The dog didn't move. "Mascara." Another no response. "Mascara."

"How much mascara does one woman need?" Jack muttered.

"Don't crowd me, pal. Getting sexy is hard work."

"You don't need mascara to be sexy," he answered gravely.

Taylor clutched the mascara. "Don't look at me that way, as if you want to start something dangerous."

"I do," Jack snapped. "Later. Keep them coming."

Taylor fished a length of shiny black fabric out of one large pocket. L.Z. showed no interest, but Jack raised an eyebrow. "Planning on attending a Hell's Angel's convention?"

"Faux leather capri pants. They're extremely comfortable and go with nearly anything."

"Sexy as hell, I bet." Jack rubbed his neck. "If I stop breathing, just keep going," he muttered.

"I'll pretend I didn't hear that." Taylor held up a pair of black lace stockings. "Gee, I thought I'd lost these." When L.Z. still showed no sign of interest, she proceeded to a heated eyelash curler, followed by a book of postage stamps and some breath mints.

Next to emerge was a lace tube top with tiny rhinestone straps.

L.Z. showed no interest.

Jack looked ready to bark. "MTV awards night?"

"In case I get a hot date," Taylor muttered. "Be nice and I'll model it later."

He took a breath. "Keep going."

Taylor groped in the bag and came up with two tubes of lipstick, a small notebook, and a plastic pen.

She frowned. "Wait a minute." She turned the red pen over. "This isn't mine."

L.Z. growled.

"Put it down slowly, then move away." Jack's voice was tight. "Give him some space."

Taylor did as directed. Immediately the dog bent low, sniffing intently. His head snapped up and he looked at Jack, raising one paw.

"Unbelievable," Taylor breathed. "He really

can tell, can't he?"

"It's not magic, just good training and a phenomenal sense of smell."

"Does this belong to Rains?"

"Too soon to say. But that paw response means he's got a solid scent connection."

L.Z. was sitting again, staring expectantly at Jack. "Okay, keep going. There may be more."

Taylor suppressed a shiver as she continued. "But how did it get in there? When —"

"Later."

"There's not much else. My notebook." Taylor frowned. "I've had this forever."

She put it on the floor and L.Z. immediately moved in for a long exploration, then sat once again.

Negative response.

"Good job, L.Z." Jack patted the dog, offering quiet encouragement.

"This is getting spooky," Taylor whispered, pulling out two pens, which the dog ignored. "There's not much left." She groped inside one compartment and shrugged. "Sundries, you know."

"Let's see."

"But —"

"We need to examine everything, Taylor. Take it out."

With a sigh, she held up a long, paper-wrapped container. "Just in case it's that time of the month. I always keep one on hand." She flushed a little. "You don't actually think —"

486

As she spoke, L.Z. snapped toward her, his body tense. Then he gave the paw signal.

"Put it with the pen," Jack said quietly.

"But it can't be."

"No? What better thing to put in a woman's purse? Odds are next to perfect that you wouldn't notice."

Taylor stared at L.Z., who was still waiting alertly, one paw raised. "I can't *believe* this. I feel so . . . violated. All this time I was carrying those things around without a single clue."

"Rains was smart. He knew he was dealing with tough people, and you were his insurance," Jack said grimly. "Dump the purse completely."

Taylor turned over the bag and shook it, but nothing appeared.

"Shake out the lining."

"There isn't anything left to —" Taylor's protest faded as L.Z. sat up suddenly. She pulled out the signature-print lining of each compartment and shook each one carefully.

As she opened the last section of lining, she frowned. There was a small hole she'd never noticed before. L.Z. shot upright, body tense. He ran to Jack, burst into wild barking, then fell flat on the floor, his whole body quivering.

Jack took a deep breath. "Bingo."

Chapter Forty

Taylor edged away from the purse. "What is he saying?"

"He's saying don't worry about the purse." Jack pulled a penknife out of his pocket. "If what I think is in there, the government will buy you a dozen new purses." He looked down. "Sit, L.Z."

When the dog was still, Jack checked the bottom of the seam, then carefully slit the lining from one end to the other. The silky material spilled open, and Jack pulled out the inside of the purse, then traced each neat leather seam, probing each corner where the stitches met.

Suddenly L.Z. growled, his whole body stiff.

Jack put the purse carefully on the floor. "Search, L.Z."

The dog moved in, sniffing furiously. At the inside top corner he stopped, paw raised. This time his body stayed rigid, not a muscle moving.

"Dog biscuits for life, pal. Keep up the good work and you may even get a medal." Jack patted the dog's rigid head and pulled a chewy treat out of his pocket. "Great work, L.Z." While the dog went to work on the treat, Jack frowned at the purse, bending closer. "Something is worked into that seam. It looks like a small chip of metal." His face was hard when he looked at Taylor. "Get my cell phone and punch in 244. When Izzy answers, tell him we've made contact. If anyone but Izzy answers, hang up immediately without a word."

Taylor nodded. "Got it. 244." As she dialed, her eyes stayed on her purse.

"Joe's pizza."

"I-Izzy?"

"Yeah." His voice tightened. "Taylor?"

"It's me. I'm trying not to be frightened here, Izzy. Jack is sitting by me with L.Z. and we were going through my purse and —" She stopped and took a breath. "Jack says to tell you we made contact. You know what that means?"

"Sweet holy God and all the angels." Izzy's voice faded, then returned. "Okay, I'm setting up a few things here as we talk. I'm assuming that Jack's near the . . . item."

"That's right." Taylor's throat was dry.

"And the item was in your purse?"

"Right."

"L.Z. found it?"

"R-right." She couldn't seem to say anything else.

"Okay, how many things did our friend find?"

"Three." Three things hidden inside her purse. Three things that made her a target and threatened her sister's life.

Three things that had gotten Agent Nancy Rodriguez killed.

"Our friend Rains was a busy man," Izzy muttered. Taylor heard his chair squeak. "Listen, I'm going to call you back shortly. I need to go to a different room. *Stay close*. And tell Jack to remember what I said about the five-minute rule."

"Right."

The phone went dead.

"What's happening?" Jack was holding the edge of the purse and watching L.Z., who was growling low in his throat.

"He said he has to go to a different room, but he'll call back shortly. He also said to remind you about the five-minute rule."

Jack's mouth thinned. "I hear you."

"What's the five-minute rule, Jack? The truth this time."

Jack cradled the pen carefully. "I can't tell you that."

"You *have* to tell me. I'm part of this, re-member? Just *tell* me, damn it." She was working hard to control her panic.

"No."

"Fine. Then I can't answer when Izzy calls back." In her hands the phone chirped, but she made no move to answer.

Jack cursed softly. "Taylor —"

"*No.*"

Jack scowled at her. "To put it simply, if this pen contains contents that are . . . damaging, I have five minutes to respond appropriately."

She considered the words. "Or else?"

"Or else I and whoever comes into contact with those materials will probably end up dead."

Taylor looked down at his hand, then back at his tense face. "Five minutes?" she repeated. The cell phone was ringing and she slammed the button to connect. *"Hello?"*

"Izzy here."

"We found a tiny metal container. Is it ricin?" Taylor demanded.

"That's my current best estimate."

She sank into the chair opposite Jack, dizzy, sick with fear. *Rains put a deadly toxin into her purse and let her walk around with it?*

"Taylor, are you okay?"

She took a deep breath. "I'm fine."

"Describe the metal object to me."

"It looks like a tiny chip, probably one quarter of an inch long."

"Intact?" Izzy's voice was stone-cold, completely professional.

"It appears to be. What do we do next?"

She heard the hum of electronics on the other end of the line. "Is Jack touching the metal?"

"No."

"Okay, open the inside pocket of his black duffel bag. You'll find rubber gloves and a small silver canister. Both of you are to put on gloves. Then open the canister and have Jack

491

slip the metal piece you found inside. Very carefully," he added.

"I'm on the way." In seconds Taylor returned with the black bag. She handed Jack the gloves. Carefully she unscrewed the lid of the metal canister, which was heavily padded with latex foam. "Izzy says to put the metal chip inside very carefully."

It seemed like a lifetime before Jack eased the little piece of metal free of the leather seam and finished the transfer.

Taylor swallowed. "Izzy, it's done."

"Excellent. Now have him screw on the lid and put the canister in a plastic specimen bag. He's to fill that with the bleach you'll find in the side pocket of the black duffel. Then have Jack stow the bagged canister in the bottom compartment of the duffel, where it won't move."

When the canister was packed and safely stowed, Taylor offered the phone to Jack, but he shook his head. "I don't want to touch anything."

Taylor nodded. "Izzy, the canister is safe. What next?"

"Tell Jack to strip and use the foam spray that I gave him. It goes everywhere, hair, feet, face. It stays on four minutes, then he takes a thorough shower. Your used gloves go in one bag. His clothes and shoes should be put in another specimen bag. He knows where they are. Your clothes go in there, too."

"I didn't touch anything."

"We're taking no chances. Tess and T.J. will find you something to wear." Taylor heard Izzy's fingers clicking at a keyboard. "Okay, it's been two minutes twenty-six seconds since you called me. Go to work. Time Jack, too. He needs the full dose of that foam, but nothing longer."

"Right."

"Tell him I'm running for a chopper now. I should be there in about an hour."

"I'll tell him." Taylor put down the phone. Fighting to stay calm, she began relaying Izzy's terse orders.

They worked together, Taylor quickly stripping off her clothes and wrapping herself in a towel, then holding a watch while Jack stripped and stuffed his clothes into one of Izzy's thick laboratory bags. Jack sprayed himself with awful-smelling foam, while Taylor guided him to spots he'd missed.

Then they waited, Taylor calling off the minutes on her watch.

As they worked, some part of Taylor's mind registered the fact that he appeared comfortable with the procedure, as if he had done this before. Her mind recoiled at the kind of work that demanded familiarity with exposure to toxins like ricin and the certainty that one slip meant sudden death.

The cold, rational part of her mind argued

that someone had to bear the risks when deadly biohazards were involved. There would be no one better equipped to do the job than Jack.

Even if the thought of his danger left her bleeding inside.

"Time," she said breathlessly. "How do you feel?"

"Like I've lost my top layer of skin." His face was hard. "Which I probably have." He stepped into the shower, which was pouring away full blast. "Why don't you get dressed, then call T.J. and fill him in while I finish here. We can plan our strategy while we wait for Izzy."

But Taylor didn't move. She felt L.Z., standing alertly beside her. "You're sure that this is safe? If there were symptoms of exposure, you'd have them by now, wouldn't you?"

"We'd both have them by now," Jack said grimly, turning so the spray cleaned his shoulders and back. "And if there were anything else toxic in your bag, L.Z. would have sniffed it out by now." He raked back his wet hair. "Try to relax, Taylor."

Fat chance.

Taylor bent to scratch the big dog's head. Just for a moment, she thought how nice it would feel to have her fingers wrapped around Harris Rains' throat.

Snow drifted silently through the pine trees. All was hushed on the mountain, and nothing moved in the little clearing.

Harris Rains was dying.

Inside the cabin, Viktor Lemka stared in disgust at the remains of the man before him. The scientist had been smarter than they'd thought. In the throes of Lemka's final round of torment, Rains had whimpered all the details of his planning: He had split the ricin lab samples into two parts. A very small part had gone to his lab manager in Mexico for safekeeping.

The other part had been turned over to a complete stranger, someone who had not the remotest idea of what she possessed.

For weeks he'd been considering a backup location. As a result, he'd been carrying the tiny chip and two other items when Lemka's men had come after him in the street. By a stroke of fate he had escaped one danger, only to find a thug confronting him with a gun in the convenience store. Suspicious of a deeper threat than mere robbery, he had acted instantly. When Taylor O'Toole's purse had dropped, he'd slid two items inside — and then he'd slit the lining and shoved in the metal chip, quickly dropping the purse back on the floor. His maneuver had worked flawlessly; given the tense scene between the thug and the store clerk, no one had guessed what he'd done, least of all the woman.

Cursing, Viktor kicked the man bleeding to death on the cabin floor. He had to find the American woman immediately. Before this she had been a backup; now she was his only chance at staying alive and salvaging this cursed operation.

Sweating, the Albanian strode to the door. "Bury him," he ordered coldly.

Two of his men moved inside. Neither paid any attention to the fact that Rains was missing all his fingers and half of one leg. Without expression, they picked up the American, who was still alive, twitching slightly.

Not that it mattered. In a few minutes he would be six feet underground.

"Sir?" One of his men was holding a cell phone.

"What is it, Jusuf?"

"I just had a call. I think it will interest you."

Viktor listened. So their government contact had news to report. Slowly his impatience faded into triumph. The news was good — beyond good. With luck, it would keep him alive. A new plan began to take shape as he watched his men drag Rains' body through the gentle snow. So much annoyance. All of this could have been avoided if his men had gotten to Rains before he could slide his precious items into the woman's purse. Later had come the two failed attacks on Taylor O'Toole and her sister in Monterey, but her cold-eyed friend had interfered, just as he had at the charity event and again at the motel in San Jose.

"Bring me the Lexus, Jusuf."

Viktor liked the words. They sounded like a rich American automobile commercial. In the hard days and cold nights of his boyhood, he had dreamed of having the exotic life he had glimpsed so briefly on the flickering television screen.

Now that it was his, nothing would take it from him.

Taylor O'Toole was going to die. But first, she would give him everything that he wanted.

Chapter Forty-one

When T. J. McCall walked into the casita, his face could have been cut from granite. "You found something, I take it?"

Jack nodded. "It's been contained. We've put L.Z through the whole building and he has indicated no sign of contamination, so I believe we're safe." Jack was wearing his last pair of blue jeans and a flannel shirt. "Izzy is on his way now, and he's carrying equipment to verify any possibility of contamination."

T.J. walked through the room, frowning. "Can you tell me the nature of the material involved?"

"I'm afraid not, Sheriff."

T.J. didn't look particularly happy, but he nodded. "What do you need from me?"

"Izzy will be landing at these coordinates."

The sheriff scanned the numbers Jack handed him. "I'll leave right now. That's about ten minutes away."

"No need. He'll be met."

The sheriff's brow rose. "In Almost?"

"The man has contacts everywhere," Jack said dryly. "But until he leaves, security will be tight. Do you have two or three extra men to guard the ranch?"

McCall scratched his jaw. "I'll make the calls

and have them here before the chopper lands." He glanced through the window toward the north. "One of them should be here before I call. I swear the man can read minds."

There was a movement behind him in the doorway. Jack went for his Beretta, but McCall stepped in front of him. "No need for a gun. This is Miguel, the man I told you about."

Jack dropped his arm, but didn't holster his gun.

The man in the doorway wore only black, broken by a heavy silver buckle at his waist. Darkness seemed to cling to his long hair as he measured the room in silence, then nodded at Sheriff McCall. "You need me."

It wasn't a question, Taylor noticed. Who was this old man who carried such an aura of power around him?

"We do, Miguel. I appreciate your coming, though how you knew is beyond me."

The old man laughed, and the sound reminded Taylor of sand spilling over dry stones. "I see what I see." He turned, his head cocked. "Lightning coming, up near the mesa." His eyes seemed to narrow as he listened to the night.

Taylor heard only the sigh of the wind through the mesquite trees.

"Chopper. Coming in from Black Mesa."

Jack looked skeptical, but a moment later they heard the distant drone of spinning blades.

"Damn," Jack muttered.

T. J. McCall was watching his friend. "Go on, Miguel. What else?"

"Trouble. You and your friends need to know this, Sheriff." He fingered the small canvas bag at his shoulder and Taylor caught the sent of sage and rosemary. "More and more trouble coming after that." Standing motionless, he seemed part of the night, an illusion created from shadows, all darkness except for the silver buckle which gleamed at his waist.

Cold as moonlight.

Taylor heard a low whine. L.Z. trotted past her, then sat at the old man's feet, waiting alertly.

Miguel spoke several soft words in a language Taylor didn't understand, and the dog barked once, his ears pricking forward. "No need to worry about others," Miguel said without looking up. "Only the chopper. No one has followed them."

McCall nodded. "I appreciate the heads-up, Miguel."

Jack was frowning when the drone of the helicopter vanished abruptly, and they heard a car from the north, coming fast.

Izzy lifted a big aluminum case and stepped out of the dusty Bronco, looking more tired than Taylor had ever seen him. He gave a quick wave to the driver, who sat back to wait without a word.

There were no preliminaries. "Where's the item we discussed?"

"Inside the house," Jack said. "Secured the way you described."

"Show me." Izzy looked at the sheriff. "I'll meet you shortly and fill you in, T.J."

Which meant that he and the others were being dismissed, Taylor realized. Higher security issues were at stake.

The sheriff nodded. He and Miguel strode back to the main house through the darkness. When Izzy called to L.Z., the dog barked excitedly, nosing against Izzy's hands.

"Hey, there, buddy. I think you just bought yourself major job security." He laughed as the big dog jumped up and tried to lick his face. "Taylor, I'll need to talk with you after Jack and I are done." He rubbed his neck. "And I've got to tell you that some coffee would be worth a million dollars about then."

"I'll get it going."

Taylor went out to the kitchen, glad for a distraction. With the coffee brewing, she sank into a chair by the window and rubbed her face.

At least now they knew why she was so popular. The man following them in Monterey had been looking for the tiny metal container Rains had hidden in her purse.

She sat up suddenly.

The convenience store. Rains had been standing a few feet away when the pregnant woman fainted, knocking down the display of soda cans. After that had come the altercation with the store clerk, and during that time Rains had been crouched behind the big plastic garbage can. He would have had time to grab her purse, insert the metal piece into one of the seams, then toss the purse across the floor before anyone noticed.

Risky, but not entirely stupid.

And in her panic, it was unlikely she would notice the ordinary paper-wrapped package or cheap plastic pen. Certainly not the piece of metal shoved deep into one of the purse's inside seams.

Low voices echoed down the hall and L.Z. barked once. Taylor prayed that the toxin was completely contained, without harm to Jack.

She glanced at the kitchen counter, remembering the stormy encounter that had taken place there only a few hours before. Events had moved too fast for her to sort through her tangled emotions, but one thing was clear. She loved this man who had touched her and given her such pleasure. She loved his quiet strength and steely determination, which at first had struck her as sheer, pigheaded arrogance. She loved the granite sense of honor he could never hide.

But love didn't make Taylor blind. They were an impossible match — by temperament, training, and profession. What kind of future could they have, assuming that Jack was even thinking of a future that involved her?

Taylor closed her eyes, stunned to realize just how much the SEAL was figuring in her own plans. He had stormed into her life, fed her world-class lasagna, sweet-talked her into trusting him, and now . . .

Now she had given him her heart.

She sighed and got up, setting out coffee cups and making sandwiches. *Don't think about tomorrow,* she told herself grimly. *Today is complicated enough.*

She smiled when L.Z. bounded into the room, looking supremely pleased with himself. "Did you do more good work?" The big dog barked once, then shot back to the door as Izzy and Jack emerged. Taylor noticed Izzy wasn't carrying the aluminum case now.

"All taken care of," Izzy said. "Everything here looks clean, I'm happy to say. Sorry that I have to take your purse, but if it passes inspection, you'll get it back."

"You're leaving again?"

"As soon as I discuss a few things with Jack and T.J."

Taylor handed coffee to both men, unsurprised by the announcement. She had expected Izzy to make a fast turnaround, given the crucial nature of the discovery. "Still no news about Rains?"

Izzy turned his cup slowly. "The man seems to have vanished. The Feds are dealing with that, since he was their primary responsibility, but I suspect when we find the Albanian we'll find Rains."

Taylor handed out the sandwiches. "So I'm still in danger."

"I'm afraid so. We'd like you to stay here for the moment. The sheriff has offered the use of his house for as long as necessary." He glanced at Jack, who nodded.

Taylor stared from one man to the other. "What's wrong?"

Izzy sat down beside her at the table. "I've got some bad news."

"Not Annie." Taylor shot to her feet. "She isn't —"

"Annie's fine." Izzy took her hand and pulled her back into her chair, frowning.

"Then *what?* Nothing's happened to Sam or Mrs. Pulaski, has it?"

"It's Candace." Jack was standing beside her, one hand on her shoulder.

Why were they so grave? Taylor wondered. Why so quiet?

"Candace was found in her apartment several hours ago," Jack said. "She was badly beaten."

Taylor closed her eyes, stricken. "How?"

"Some of her climbing friends saw her leave a bar with a stranger. When she didn't check in for a class at the gym, one of them dropped by her apartment. She was unconscious, in bad shape."

Taylor gripped the table blindly. "I have to see her. Which hospital, Jack? I need to go now."

Jack's callused hand tightened on her shoulder.

"There's more?" She stared up at him, her whole body going cold. "Oh, God, please no."

"I'm sorry, honey." Jack's voice was gentle. "She didn't make it out of surgery."

Taylor hunched over, shaking her head. It couldn't be true. Not Candace.

Dead.

"I don't believe it." Her voice shook. "It must be a mistake. She couldn't —"

"There's no mistake." Jack pulled her into his arms. "One of her friends ID'd the body."

"I don't — I have to —" Taylor swayed, forcing herself to drag in a breath. "The funeral. I have to go. She'd want that." Silence stretched out. Taylor's heart pounded as she rubbed away tears. "When is the funeral?"

"Tomorrow afternoon," Izzy said quietly.

She eased out of Jack's arms. "I have time. I can go back in the helicopter." She stopped, looking at Jack. "Why aren't you saying anything?"

Jack's eyes held only regret.

"Because you can't go, Taylor." Izzy's voice was firm. "They'll have people watching the funeral. You're their last link now, remember?"

Taylor took a step back, carefully removing herself from all contact with Jack. "You think that matters to me? My friend is *dead*. She'll never belay another rope, never struggle up another cliff. Maybe she was involved, maybe she wasn't, but I couldn't help her, not when she needed it most. Yet I can stand by her grave tomorrow. I can be there to remember her when they — when she's put into the ground to rest."

"Don't talk like that." Jack started toward her, but she took another step back, her body shaking.

"I have to talk like this. She had no family and only a few friends. She needed my help, but it wasn't enough." Taylor took a raw breath. Rage, grief, remorse churned through her, but none of them mattered.

What mattered was that her friend was dead.

"I'll do what you want afterward. Anything," she continued hoarsely. "I'll go hide in a monastery in Tibet for a year, if you want. But I'll be there for Candace first." Her chin rose, even as the tears came again. "You'll have to lock me up if you plan to prevent that."

Izzy muttered a curse. "Do you have any idea how dangerous it could be?"

"You'll be certain to tell me."

"Damn it, Taylor, this isn't a joke." Jack was behind her. She could almost feel the anger — and the fear — pour off him in waves. "They're bound to send people. They *want* you."

She looked at him with stony eyes. "Then see that they don't get me. It's your job, right? From the start, I was your job. It's time we both remembered that."

"You'd endanger yourself for a whim?" he growled.

"Not a whim." She made a slashing gesture in the air. "I'll be present to offer my respects to a woman who shouldn't be gone. And I'll be there to say good-bye, so she won't be lowered into the cold earth alone, without as many of her friends as possible."

Izzy crossed his arms. "I'd have to get permission."

"Then get it," Taylor snapped.

"You can't be serious." Jack whirled around, glaring at Izzy. "You can't possibly believe that this makes sense."

Izzy's face was unreadable. "She's not a prisoner, Jack. She has committed no crime. Admiral Braden suspected this situation might arise. Like it or not, I'll have to relay her request."

Jack muttered a short, graphic phrase.

"It's not a request," Taylor said flatly. "I'm going, one way or another. After that —" She shrugged. "I'll do whatever, whenever." She stood tensely, avoiding Jack's eyes, feeling too much pain to risk a glance that might make her resolve waver, even for a second.

Later. Not today. Not before she'd sent off her friend.

"This is crazy," Jack said harshly. "No, it's criminal. You both know that."

When he had no answer, he strode outside, and the front door banged hard.

"He's right," Izzy said quietly. "This is nothing short of insane."

Taylor stared down at her hands. They were

shaking, she noticed, damp and cold from her tears. "He's trying to protect me, Izzy. But he can't."

"So it's gotten personal between you?"

Taylor shrugged. "You'll have to ask Jack about that."

"I'm asking you."

She stacked coffee cups in the sink, then closed her eyes. "I think it's always been personal for me, since the first time I saw him balancing that stupid plank of stupid wood." She took a hard breath. "And that changes nothing. I'm going to Candace's funeral. We'll take precautions, I'll be alert, you can put men all around me, but — but I'm going."

"You're sure, Taylor? You need to be absolutely certain about this."

She nodded, her sharp words and anger suddenly gone. In their wake, all she felt was weakness and betrayal.

"In that case, I'll make the call."

"The chopper leaves in twenty minutes." Izzy stood on the porch of the casita, zipping up his jacket. The big aluminum case was gripped in his right hand.

Jack didn't answer, sitting on the bottom step, his face hard.

"McCall will drive me back."

Jack's hand clenched and unclenched. "Is she going?"

"Yes."

Jack shot to his feet. "You're all fools to allow it. She'll be a clear target for anything that moves, and you know it."

"I know it. You know it. She knows it." Izzy's voice tightened. "But orders are orders. If she wants to go, Braden says it's her right."

Jack kicked a stone across the courtyard. It *pinged* loudly against the far adobe wall. "Braden can take his orders and —" His breath caught hard and he turned back slowly. "This is Braden's doing, isn't it? By God, he's going to use her to set a trap for the Albanian."

Izzy stood unmoving in the darkness.

"That's why he had you tell her — and why he approved her visit at the funeral."

"We don't know that she'll be a target. There has been no new activity near her apartment and no sign of Rains."

"Bullshit. You know Lemka will send someone to monitor the funeral. Hell, he might even come himself." The words exploded off Jack's lips. "I'm calling Sam McKade. We'll have Braden overruled."

Izzy moved in front of him. "You'll torpedo any chance at a career in the Navy if you do."

Jack's jaw worked hard. "I'll take that chance."

"What if Braden pulls you out? What if he sends someone else to replace you? Do you want a stranger walking beside her when it only takes a split-second's distraction to leave her dead? Or don't you care about that?"

Jack's fist was rising before he knew it. With a curse, he reined in the hard right hook inches from Izzy's chin. "Okay, Teague, you've made your point. No stranger will be standing watch over Taylor tomorrow. But I want to know the *whole* damned story, not just the pieces that Braden wants me to hear."

"You're asking me to disobey mission directives?"

"I'm asking for the truth."

Izzy grimaced. "Same thing." He rubbed his neck, staring down at the case in his hand. "I'll tell you what I know, which isn't much. And you'd damned well better see that Taylor doesn't find out. Not yet."

Jack nodded.

Izzy sat down on the porch. Lightning flickered off to the north, but he didn't appear to notice. Resting the big case in his lap, he began to talk softly.

When Taylor walked out into the darkness five minutes later, her face was pale but composed, and she carried her single small suitcase. Her purse and all its contents had been secured in a protective case, to be delivered to the Navy's biohazard lab for a thorough inspection.

She watched lightning flicker over the horizon as she listened to the distant echo of coyotes up in the hills. For some reason, the low cries sounded like a warning. She shook away the thought, staring around her. It took her a few seconds to realize that Jack and Izzy were sitting nearby, motionless in the darkness.

"Am I disturbing something top secret out here?"

"We're done," Jack said, his voice grave as he stood up. "You're all packed?"

"Everything I came with." Her whole body felt cold as she faced him in the moonlight.

"Then let's go get Sheriff McCall." He started to take her arm, but she drew back.

"Not now," she said. "Not until this is all over."

After a moment, Jack nodded. Thunder rumbled in the distance as he opened the gate from the casita. "In that case, we'll fill you in on the arrangements as we walk."

Chapter Forty-two

The church was in a small delta town near Sacramento. The weather had turned gray, and rain threatened as the big black limousines pulled up in a row.

A good day for a funeral, Taylor thought. Candace hated to spend beautiful weather anywhere except outside climbing a sheer face of granite.

Except now she'd never climb again.

Rounding a curve, they crossed a vast green lawn that stretched to a winding drive. Beyond was a line of people dressed in jeans and dark parkas. Candace's climbing friends, Taylor realized.

She stared out at the gray sky. "Did Rains do it?"

Jack was at the opposite side of the seat, his face unreadable. "No. The man was identified by one of Candace's friends. He was a foreign national seen several weeks before in contact with an Albanian named Viktor Lemka."

"The man in Monterey," Taylor said quietly.

"So we believe."

Taylor watched the first limousine stop. The doors opened and half a dozen big men in suits got out. When they reached the little church, they remained outside.

"Yours?"

"Ours." Jack pulled a box from his pocket. "Come here."

"Why?"

"Just do it. For once, don't argue."

She moved warily, her face set, her eyes cool as he lifted her lapel carefully and pinned a rhinestone brooch in place. "Just in case," he said grimly.

"How about a ray gun and a secret handshake to go with it?"

He didn't answer, pulling a small wire out of his pocket.

"What's that for?"

"A lapel mic. I'll be able to hear whatever you say the whole time we're here." He slid the wire under her jacket and draped the cord down into her shirt pocket, where he clipped a small transceiver in place. "Looks like you're set. Remember, all our people will be wearing a lapel pin with the state flag of California. If you need them, use them."

"I'll remember." They were nearing the church, and Taylor felt a stab of pain when she saw the shiny hearse decorated with flowers.

Jack smoothed her lapel and touched her cheek, just for a second. "You're good to go, O'Toole. Break a leg."

The ceremony was grim, rain sheeting off the roof of the little church. A dozen mourners sat restless and uncomfortable, trying to ignore the rain as the minister spoke about happier rewards and the greater world beyond.

Taylor sat listening, dry-eyed and cold, almost numb. She hoped that Candace was in a place with granite slabs and perfect traverses. That would be her true idea of heaven.

She turned her head. Jack seemed to be listening to the minister, but his eyes shifted constantly. At a door halfway back, she saw Izzy, dressed in a raincoat with the collar turned up. So far there had been no men with machine guns, no sudden assaults by strangers bursting from an unmarked car. There were only a few people who sat uncomfortably, doing their best to mark the passage of a friend.

When Taylor looked up, she was surprised to see the minister had stopped speaking and people were filing out of the church. She stood up and turned, coming face-to-face with the woman she had met at the shopping gala.

"Martha Sorensen." The woman held out a hand. "When I heard, I — I couldn't believe it." Her voice broke and she looked away. "You know that Candace worked at my lab for five or six months. I still can't believe she's —" She took a shaky breath. "It was a nice ceremony, wasn't it?" The question seemed vacant, spoken not to Taylor or anyone else in particular.

As she put away her hymnal, Taylor heard the tinkle of metal and noticed Martha Sorensen was wearing a bracelet of small cats, just like the one that belonged to Candace.

"Candace had a bracelet like that."

"She loved that silly thing. One day at lunch she insisted that I buy one, too." Gently Martha touched the metal figures, one by one. "She was so young, so naïve. She didn't deserve . . . this. Nobody deserves what happened to her."

Taylor moved closer as they walked to the doorway of the church. "Had you seen her recently?"

"She came into the lab once, looking for Rains. If Harris Rains were here now, I'd kill him myself." The older woman's voice was raw.

"Maybe it wasn't Rains."

"What do you mean? Rains was behind this; I know it."

Taylor stared out at the sullen sky. "She was seen with a foreigner just before — before it happened."

"Who told you that?"

Taylor rubbed her neck. "I can't remember. Just a rumor, I suppose."

Martha turned, blocking her way. Her face was pale and blotchy, her eyes bloodshot.

From crying, Taylor realized.

"The police said nothing about her meeting a foreign man."

Taylor couldn't recall if this information was to be kept secret or not. "Maybe it was a mistake."

Martha nodded slowly. "A very big mistake, I'm afraid." Then she walked out into the gusting rain.

As Taylor stood in the doorway, Jack moved in behind her, flanked by a huge man with a broken nose who looked a lot like Vinnie de Vito's bodyguard. Sure enough, Sunny and her uncle were standing underneath umbrellas outside. When she saw Taylor, Sunny ran forward. "I was desperately worried about you," she said over a hug. "You didn't answer your phone, and you didn't answer your door. Then Uncle Vinnie heard about Candace. Even though we didn't know her, we wanted to be here for you, Taylor. I'm so sorry."

"So am I. It's all like a bad dream."

"What can I do to help?"

"Nothing, Sunny. I'm just tired. I'll be fine."

Sunny's uncle moved closer and touched Taylor's arm. "I offer my deepest condolences, my dear. To die young is the worst of tragedies."

Taylor didn't answer, a burning in her throat.

"We're worried about you," he said. "Very worried."

"I'll be fine. Really."

"I have a car. If you want to drive back to San Francisco with us, it would be our pleasure."

"We'll see." Taylor was vague, fairly certain that Jack would have other plans.

After a last look of sympathy, Sunny's uncle moved back outside, his arm on Sunny's waist.

They made a sad group, straggling over the wet grass toward a square of naked earth not

516

far from the church. Underneath his umbrella, the minister intoned the final ritual.

Dust to dust.

But there was no dust here. Only rain and tears, Taylor thought, as the simple brown casket was lowered into the wet earth.

And then it was done.

Taylor closed her eyes. Some part of her was unable to believe that death was so close. Almost like a sleepwalker, she found Jack's arm.

"You okay?"

She didn't answer, turning back toward the cars, frozen through nerve and bone.

"We'll go now."

She nodded numbly, noticing a cluster of people near the path to the church. She saw a flash of light and realized they were reporters.

A woman waved her arms, talking loudly as she strode closer. "Ms. O'Toole? You were her friend, Ms. O'Toole. Have the police told you anything? Did Candace know her killer?"

"You'll have to ask the police that," Taylor said dully.

"Do the police have any leads?"

"You'd have to ask them about that, too." When Taylor started to move past her, the woman tried to grab her arm, but Jack pushed her firmly out of the way, which only made her more angry.

"What about Harris Rains? The word is, he was involved."

"I don't know what you're talking about."

"Are you certain of that, Ms. O'Toole?" the reporter said, her voice shrill. "I'm told that you and Harris Rains were having an affair."

Taylor swung around, her hands closing into fists. "Are you completely crazy as well as a monster? We're at the woman's funeral. She's *gone*. Don't come here with your obscene questions. Let her have her peace."

"But —"

Jack shoved the journalist aside and then they strode on toward the church. "Do you want me to go back and punch her?"

Taylor smiled grimly. "A pleasant thought."

"Don't worry, it's almost over."

"All her friends were here," Taylor said quietly. "Candace would have liked that." She kept walking, not feeling the rain against her face. The cold didn't seem to matter now. Up ahead she saw the minister come out of the church, carrying an umbrella. He waved once and started toward her. As he did, several reporters broke away from the crowd by the road.

"Damned vultures." Jack moved to Taylor's side to block their way.

One man charged ahead, shouting questions, and Jack knocked him to the ground. Suddenly, more reporters sprinted over the grass.

Would Candace have no peace, even now?

Taylor saw the minister with his back turned. He shook his head as the scuffling continued. "This is an outrage, an absolute outrage." His voice sounded tense with disapproval. "Why don't you come with me into the church, my dear? It will be more quiet there."

Sighing in relief, Taylor followed.

Jack held the struggling reporter on the ground and motioned to a nearby agent. "See that he's removed," Jack said grimly.

"Yes, sir."

"Where's Izzy?"

"Near the limousine."

Jack nodded and looked up. Taylor was a few feet away under an umbrella, talking with the minister, her head lowered. Maybe that would be good for her. She hadn't talked during the whole trip from Arizona, and he knew the pain was eating away inside her.

With it came the guilt, as if she had been somehow to blame for Candace's death.

He touched his earpiece, frowning as he heard Izzy's voice.

"I'm at the car. Let's move."

"Copy." Jack turned back toward the church and cursed.

Taylor was gone.

"The flowers were nice." Taylor walked to the front of the empty church, passing sprays of white lilies, yellow roses, and one elegant orchid, the only warmth on a cold day. "She would have loved them."

The minister moved along the pews, then shook his umbrella and set it carefully on a pew. "She was so young, so much alive. And then a thing like this."

He turned. As he did, Taylor felt fear wedge in her throat. This wasn't the man who had spoken in the church and offered the eulogy at the gravesite. This man had hard eyes, a thin, cold mouth, just like the man in the photo Jack had shown her in Monterey.

He was the Albanian, Viktor Lemka.

She whirled, running for the door. "Jack," she blurted. "Help —"

But she got no farther. Caught hard, she felt her arms shoved behind her, her mouth covered by a thick cloth. She felt a prick at her neck, kicked blindly, hearing the Albanian curse.

He was pulling at her coat as she fought him, his eyes pale and eager, as if he was enjoying her pain.

Then the room spun around her, and the flowers were gone.

Jack was running to the church when he heard Taylor's voice, a murmur nearly drowned by static. Where was she? Had she fainted?

Then the side door opened, and Taylor emerged, umbrella over her head. She walked slowly, a bouquet of white lilies in her hands.

He sprinted toward her, relieved. Out of the corner of his eye, he saw the hearse lumber along the gravel path beyond the church, heading back toward the road. "Taylor, stop."

She just kept walking.

He jumped a low stone fence, grabbing her arm. When he turned her around, someone else stared back at him beneath the umbrella, a woman with heavy features and sullen eyes, who was wearing Taylor's coat and her black hat.

"Izzy, Taylor's gone. Get back to the church."

Jack was at the front steps when the door burst open and Martha Sorensen ran toward him, her face bruised. "He killed my sister. Candace — she was my sister, all I had. I was a fool not to see it before, but — he'll kill again if you don't stop him. Don't you see?" She struggled to hold Jack. "Your friend — she's there, in the car with him. He's hidden her in the coffin."

Chapter Forty-three

Jack was running hard.

In front of him, the hearse swung sharply and swerved onto the main road along the river, the driver's face out of sight. Jack slid into a two-handed firing stance and shot out the right front tire.

The hearse fishtailed over the wet road, but kept on moving.

"Izzy, get me a rifle. I'm going after him."

Izzy sprinted up with sniper gear, and Jack dropped to one knee, sighted, then took out two more tires. This time the big car shook, crashing through a row of oleander bushes.

"Remember, he's to be taken down alive if possible."

"I'll remember," Jack growled. "Get your people into position past the bridge. I'm stopping him there."

Izzy burst into a hail of sharp orders as Jack sprinted toward the little stone bridge that crossed a branch of the river. By crossing the marsh, he made a shortcut that would put him at the bridge ahead of Lemka. A bullet whined past the SEAL's head as he zigzagged through the reeds and up the final slope.

The hearse rocketed toward him, Viktor

Lemka's angry face glaring through the windshield.

Still moving, Jack shot out the last tire. The hearse slowed but didn't stop, momentum driving it straight toward the bridge. As bullets whipped past, Jack dropped, using the bridge for cover so he could shoot out the windshield.

The glass exploded into small chunks that blew back into the car. When the last fragments fell, Lemka emerged into view, shouting curses and firing over the wheel.

Suddenly the passenger door jerked open and a man rolled out, firing as he hit the grass. Instantly, one of Izzy's men took him down with a clean headshot.

Lemka turned the hearse sharply, nosing toward the water. Screened from Jack's view, he jumped clear, clawing his way along the steep bank.

Jack sprinted around the bridge and put a bullet in the Albanian's knee, then shot the gun from his hand while Izzy shouted and half a dozen men poured forward over the grass in pursuit. Jack was ahead of them, almost at the hearse when it struck a stone barrier at the water's edge, shuddered, then flipped to one side, rolling down the slope and pinning the Albanian against a row of boulders.

He screamed shrilly, then sobbed as his body was caught and slowly crushed, inch by inch, beneath the plunging steel frame.

Jack heard the distant wail of sirens as he hit

the water. Seconds behind the out-of-control hearse, he fought through icy currents, thick with silt and reeds. Cursing the lack of visibility, he shrugged off his jacket and jackknifed down through the shifting darkness until he felt the outline of the hearse's back door.

A pocket of air had gathered inside, and Jack heard Taylor's muffled shouts carried through the silty water as he swam in closer. Barely able to see, he shattered the side window with a rock and found his way up into the precariously shifting pocket of air near the back door.

"I've got you, Taylor. Hold on."

The lid shuddered. Her hand emerged from the open coffin. "H-help me."

"I'm right here. Stay in the air pocket while I get the back open."

"H-hurry. Not much left." She was fighting to hold the coffin open as the hearse shook, nosing downward.

Jack took a breath and worked his way outside to the back door. After two tries, he freed the handle and wrenched open the door.

The hearse pitched forward sharply. Instantly, the coffin slid down, bubbles churning as the air pocket vanished. Still holding his breath, Jack found the top of the coffin and pulled it up, seizing Taylor's arm as icy water poured around them.

Suddenly she tensed, jerked from his arms. He felt her straining wildly, kicking against the water below him in a fury of small bubbles.

Her air was gone.

He shot to the surface, grabbed a breath, then dove down again, holding her head as he found her mouth and blew hard. Then he squeezed her arm and kicked downward, searching for the barrier that held her. Precious seconds passed before he felt one of her legs tangled in the curtain rope from the sinking hearse, dragging her down. He dug into his pocket for his knife, slashing at the heavy strands as she was pulled relentlessly to the muddy bottom.

Her moan was muffled in the cold currents.

Again he shot to the surface, where Izzy was waiting in a rowboat. He tossed Jack a big police flashlight. "What else do you need?"

"Get an ambulance up here with oxygen. Blankets, too."

He wasted no more time, gasping as he dragged in air, then plunged down into the darkness again. When he found Taylor, she was drifting sluggishly, and he tilted her head to give her more air, then kicked down, holding the light as he hacked away the last cords of twisted silk. The deadly tendrils fell away like black wings, drifting in the murky light.

Jack caught Taylor's body, kicking furiously toward the surface until they finally broke free into dim gray light. Helicopters roared overhead while an ambulance screamed from the riverbank. Reporters, held back behind a hasty barricade, waved cameras while they shouted questions.

None of it mattered to Jack as he swam toward the shore with Taylor limp in his arms. He pulled her up onto the grass, checked her airway, then flipped her over and gave a sharp thump on her back.

Nothing happened.

He tried again, kneeling close and shoving hard along her ribs, pressing her whole body into the grass.

She shuddered, coughed hard, lurching in spasms that shook her whole body.

When she was done, Jack turned her carefully, angling her head and brushing the wet hair back from her face. "Can you hear me, Taylor? Come on, talk to me, honey. Give me hell."

Her eyelids fluttered. She coughed painfully, staring up at the sky. Then her hands twisted, sliding around him. "You were r-right."

He closed his eyes on a prayer of thanks, holding her as close as they could get in their wet clothes. "Take it easy, love."

"Have to t-talk. So — scared. So cold."

"Shhhh." He kept stroking her hair, dimly aware of Izzy's shouts and the ambulance surging closer.

"He was too strong. He opened — coffin." She coughed brokenly. "The Albanian. D-dressed as minister."

"It's over. You're safe, Taylor."

"S-sorry." She clung tightly, shivering as Izzy put a blanket around her shoulders. "Sorry for Nancy Rodriguez." She was crying in a ragged voice, her body shaking. "Sorry I was a fool. So — damned sorry, Jack."

"Forget it." Jack drew her closer, kissing her cold face and wet hair, shivering a little himself.

She looked at him, frozen, bedraggled, and beautiful as she managed the ghost of a smile. "Never apologize for t-telling the truth. Someone very smart told me that once."

"Not so smart," Jack whispered. "And he was terrified he'd lost the thing he valued most." Then he gathered her in his arms and carried her up the wet, rocky bank toward the waiting ambulance and a circle of cheering agents.

Chapter Forty-four

"Captain Ryker, can you hear me?"

The big fishing trawler was quiet. No sounds drifted up from the engine room or from the deck as the woman in the Navy uniform flashed her light carefully through the hold, stopping on the small metal locker next to the wall. "Captain Ryker?"

She didn't really expect an answer. In cases of extreme trauma and extended captivity, victims lost the ability to respond, out of terror or confusion or both. It was her job to cut through that fog.

She checked the big metal door and saw that the lock was in place. Frowning, she pulled out a gun. She had heard that the trawler had been located thanks to a tip from an old man with serious mob connections, but Lieutenant Markowitz didn't believe the story. On the other hand, she didn't much care if the tip had come from the Kremlin, the Pope, or Mob Central. All she wanted was to find the Navy's top biohazard expert before it was too late.

"I'm going to shoot off the lock, Captain. It won't be long now."

Did she hear something shuffling inside?

She took aim, fired, and tore away the lock, then carefully opened the door, gun at her side in case the kidnapped scientist struck out in fear.

The stench caught her hard, but she put it away, stepping back for a clear view. It still took all her training not to gasp when she saw the blood, saw the flies, saw the tortured face staring up at her.

"It's okay, Captain. We've got a car waiting. Water, food, blankets. You're going home."

He didn't move, his eyes blind. Heaven knew how long he'd been stuffed in the metal locker, Markowitz thought grimly.

"Why don't you give me your hand?" She spoke softly. "Then we can go home. Your wife is waiting for you, Captain Ryker."

He blinked, his face shifting as if he was using muscles that were unfamiliar. "W-wife?"

"That's right. Angela is fine. She can't wait to see you."

"Didn't talk. Didn't help them." He closed his eyes on a dry sound of pain. "The man — he's going to kill her. Have to stop him." He hunched forward, trying to claw his way out of the squalid locker, and Markowitz helped him slowly to his feet. "Albanian," he rasped. "Viktor, his name is. He's working with Harris Rains. Going to kill my wife if I don't —"

"There's no need to worry about Viktor Lemka or Harris Rains. They're dead, Captain. And your wife is just fine." The lieutenant took his arm as they shuffled toward the stairs. "You can talk to her as soon as we get on deck. My phone is right here, and she's waiting for your call."

He ducked his head, shaking hard like an animal pulled awake and tossed into icy water. Markowitz waited in silence, eyes averted until the low sobbing stopped. Then the scientist stood up tall. He looked down and tried to smooth his torn, soiled uniform, frowning when he saw the bloody bandage around his left hand. "Let's go —" He turned to her, eyes narrowed. "Lieutenant — ?"

"Markowitz, sir. Pleased to make your acquaintance. Very pleased. Believe me, a lot of people want to welcome you home, sir."

Ryker took a breath, blinking as she guided him to the open stairway. And he smiled awkwardly when he saw the sky for the first time in almost five weeks.

"So beautiful," he whispered. "Alive. Going home."

Epilogue

"*You* are a complete wreck."

Taylor stared at her face in the mirror while the words echoed painfully in the quiet room. Her hair was a bright flow of auburn and copper, her dress a shimmer of black silk — and her hands were trembling.

Not because of the reporters camped outside her apartment building, harassing her whenever she went in or out. Not because of the mayor, who was waiting for her in the lobby.

Because of Jack. The man had her tied up in painful little knots.

She frowned at her reflection. "Okay, you're terrified. What if he doesn't come tonight?"

Her eyes narrowed. "What if he *does?*"

With a strangled sound, Taylor sank into a chair in the ladies' room of the exquisite downtown hotel. It had been almost six weeks since Candace's funeral. Six weeks since the underwater struggle that still woke her up sweating and terrified at night.

Martha Sorensen had been arrested that same afternoon, and once behind bars she had spun a sordid tale. As the manager of Rains' lab, she had been in a perfect position to report back to the South American crime syndicate hell-bent on acquiring Rains' new biological weapon.

Along with its vaccine.

Martha's contact had been Viktor Lemka, who had researched every detail of Rains' schedule, his lab projects, work habits, and all his contacts. When Rains vanished from the boat in Oregon, Lemka's search was stymied, and the Albanian had ordered his men to squeeze Candace for information in the belief that Rains would contact his lover for help, as he had in the past.

No one knew then that Martha and Candace were sisters, separated in their teens and shunted through a series of indifferent foster homes until Martha was old enough to support them.

Taylor closed her eyes, remembering Martha's face as she had filled in the details of the simple plan that had raged out of control, resulting in the loss of the only thing she'd ever loved — her sister.

It had been a simple matter for Candace to seduce Rains within days of their meeting at the lab. The affair had been strictly business for her, a means to keep Harris Rains under her thumb and open to her scrutiny. This part of the plan had been Martha's, conceived when she saw Rains' interest in her sister. But the climbing episode with Taylor had been Candace's brainchild, a risky but meticulously planned *accident* that would cast suspicion on Rains, who had begun to turn secretive and suspicious, even with Candace. Next had come the funeral wreath, sent to Taylor to reinforce the fiction that she was also at risk from Rains, who had tried to murder his lover but failed.

When the South Americans had cornered Rains on the street several days before the convenience store incident, they had warned him how completely he was caught in their web; if he decided to approach the police, Candace would produce her evidence about how Rains had engineered her climbing fall.

The Albanian had been insane with fury at any delays, knowing his employer would not tolerate mistakes. After Rains escaped from the boat, Lemka demanded that Candace contact Taylor, who was also unreachable, thanks to Jack. Trapped and cornered, with no more options, Lemka had seen his final chance to draw Taylor out of hiding — through Candace's death. Martha hadn't realized the connection until Taylor's comment at the funeral. Later Lemka had carelessly mentioned the bracelet Candace had worn the day she vanished. In the days that followed, guilt had driven Martha to the brink of insanity, but she had laid bare every detail of the long and secret dealings between Rains and his South American contacts.

Taylor felt a stab of pain. Her whole image of Candace had been false, carefully created to foster the web of lies meant to trap Rains. But somehow Taylor found it hard to think of Rains as a victim. His greed and arrogance had led him to ruin more effectively than any of

Candace's manipulations.

Meanwhile, Martha faced years in jail, racked by remorse for the sister she had drawn into danger and ultimately to a brutal death. Neither of the women had expected Rains to be so resourceful — or Lemka to be so inhuman.

Taylor felt her knees go weak as she remembered how Lemka had cornered her in the church. She had come painfully close to death that day, probably as a captive in some isolated cabin or boat while Lemka exercised his unholy skills. Only Jack's bravery had saved her from that unthinkable ordeal.

As music drifted from the room next door, Taylor thought about her dead friend. Candace had been reckless, ambitious, and manipulative. She had betrayed Taylor and come close to causing Taylor's death. What if Taylor had seen through the betrayal sooner? Could she have changed the outcome?

It was a question Taylor would never be able to answer. That meant one more demon to add to her collection.

Outside, the music grew louder. Sixty of the mayor's handpicked guests were sipping champagne and dancing by candlelight, but Taylor couldn't summon up the enthusiasm to join them.

She looked up as the door opened. A petite woman with long brown hair strode inside, her eyes dark and very tense. Odd, Taylor thought. Why was she wearing a pantsuit and sandals rather than evening clothes?

"I've been trying to reach you, Ms. O'Toole." She had the hint of an accent. Dutch? German? "Don't you ever return your phone calls?"

Not another journalist.

Taylor closer her eyes and sighed.

The danger was over, but she still felt no sense of relief or completion. She had lost a friend, had seen her sister threatened, and had nearly died herself, and all of these memories were as sharp as if they'd happened minutes before.

And the reporters were still digging, hoping for blood and secrets, because blood and secrets sold papers.

Taylor turned away. "Only when I like who's calling." She started toward the door, but the reporter blocked her way.

"You're not slipping out so fast. A lot of people want to know what happened between you and Harris Rains after that convenience store robbery. The man was a hero, and now he's dead. Some people think you were involved." Her eyes narrowed. "*Very* involved."

"That sounds like a story for one of my books, Ms. Hall." Taylor remembered the woman's name from the badge she'd worn during the press interviews after the robbery. Come to think of it, the woman had been there in the throng at Candace's funeral, too. "Maybe you need to rein in your oversized imagination."

"Listen, Ms. Taylor —"

"No, *you* listen. Harris Rains and I had no connection, personal or otherwise." Taylor kept to the story that Jack and Izzy had hammered out for her. "We were both in the wrong place at the wrong time during that robbery. That's the long and short of it."

Taylor started toward the door again, and this time the reporter gripped her arm. "So you insist that you two weren't lovers?"

Who knew that the woman's attractive face and intelligent eyes hid such callousness? "Do you journalists take deaf lessons? The answer is no, we weren't."

"And you also insist that you aren't involved with organized crime? That would be amusing, given that your friendship with Vinnie de Vito is a matter of public knowledge."

Taylor had had enough. "Go away, Ms. Hall. Or maybe you want to spend some quality time inside a garbage bin?"

"Are you threatening me?"

"You bet I am." Taylor's hands fisted. She was in the mood for some good, clean blood-shed. Taking on this reporter would be a pleasant exercise after all her recent sleepless nights.

Of course, fighting would only add to her problems.

That thought calmed her down before she could throw the first punch. "Look, there's no story here. Rains had a string of bad luck, and so did I. That's all I can tell you."

Footsteps clattered outside, and the door banged open. Sunny de Vito burst in, her fuchsia silk tunic flying. "What's going on, Taylor? Everyone's out there waiting for you."

Everyone? Did that include an incredibly sexy Navy SEAL named Jack Broussard?

Taylor pointed to her inquisitor. "Ms. Hall here is from the Oakland *Tribune*. Apparently, she believes that Harris Rains and I were lovers — and that we were knee-deep in organized crime."

Sunny's eyes narrowed on the reporter. "What makes her think a crazy thing like that? Oh, right. Because you're a friend of mine. If someone has an Italian name, it means they must be in the Mob."

The reporter frowned and took a step back. "You're Sunny de Vito. You're the niece of Vinnie de Vito."

"That's right." Sunny's voice was a rough purr. "That's d-e V-i-t-o. Be sure you spell it correctly. Of course, if you decide to write about me or my friend, it may be the last writing you ever do."

The reporter shoved her notebook into her purse. "Is that a threat of bodily harm, Ms. de Vito? Maybe I can quote you on that."

Sunny stepped in closer, right in her face. "Harass my friend again, and you'll find yourself scribbling obituaries somewhere in Kansas."

The journalist clutched her purse to her chest. "But my story — my rights. The freedom of the press —"

"Ends when you harass and intimidate innocent people," Sunny snapped. "When you invade a funeral and desecrate the memory of a friend." She poked a finger at the reporter's chest. "I can find out where you live. Maybe I'll have a few of my uncle's friends camp out on *your* doorstep and take pictures night and day, the way you people do. No privacy, not ever. I wonder how much you'll like *that?*"

"You can't —"

Taylor glared at the reporter. "Direct any other questions to my lawyer." She was rattling off the name of San Francisco's most prestigious law firm when her eyes narrowed at a delicious thought. "On the other hand, maybe I should put you in my next book. You'll be the reporter who stumbles on a hot tip from an ex-gangbanger in San Jose. While she's busy trying to figure a way to boost her career based on the information, four civilians and a police officer are shot, leaving her to answer why she didn't act sooner. Sorry to say, but her story ends badly."

"You can't write that about me."

Taylor raised an eyebrow. "I'd never be so stupid as to use your real name, for heaven's sake. But everyone would know it was you."

The journalist looked uncertain. "My source told me —"

"Check again. Your source is all wrong this time."

"My source is never wrong." The reporter shouldered her purse and stormed to the door. "You haven't heard the last of me."

Taylor watched the door close, shaking her head. "Is it just me, or are all reporters vultures?"

"Both." Sunny patted her arm. "Now tell me why you're hiding in here, looking like death on a stick."

"I do not look like —"

"Is something wrong between you and Jack?"

"What could be wrong?" Taylor said, wondering why her voice sounded shrill.

"Isn't he coming tonight?"

"Only if he can get away."

"So he's doing something hush-hush." Sunny studied Taylor. "And that bothers you."

"First the reporter, now you." Taylor dug in her evening bag, found a comb, and attacked her hair. "Okay, I'm nervous, and that bothers me. I'm not used to being nervous about men." Sighing, she slapped her comb down on the polished marble table. "It's been two months, Sunny."

"Two months since what?" Sunny looked mystified.

"Since I met Jack. And things are getting serious."

Sunny still looked mystified. "Which means?"

"Which means it won't be long until we're at six months."

Sunny ran her tongue across her teeth. "Do you turn into a pumpkin at six months?"

Taylor's face was pale, her voice shaky. "I've never made it to six months before. Not with *anyone.*"

"Not ever?"

Taylor shook her head.

"So Jack will be the first. Great. Enjoy it and stop worrying."

"I can't stop worrying. Things are getting complicated, Sunny. Not that he's given me a ring or anything like that," she said hastily. "Then I'd really melt down. But he's thinking about it. And I'm thinking about him thinking about it."

"Now you've got me thinking about it." Sunny's brow rose. "So what do we think about you and Jack and a ring?"

"On the one hand, it's amazing." Taylor took a deep breath. "On the other, it's awful, agonizing, and completely out of the question."

"Because you're afraid you'll screw things up," Sunny said astutely.

Taylor covered her face with her hands. "It isn't as if I've shown great judgment about people, Sunny. Look at Candace and Martha."

"We all make mistakes. Suck it in, O'Toole. You've got a great man who's crazy in love with you. Get out of this bathroom and go deal with that."

"I can't. I'm . . . paralyzed." Taylor sat down slowly. "Jack's not like any man I've ever known. I can never predict when he'll have leave, so I can't make any plans. When he's gone, I don't know where he is or if he's even alive. I don't think I can live this way."

"It's spelled l-i-f-e, Taylor. Close your eyes and jump in. You'll figure it out as you go along."

"What if I can't? And what if Jack gets bored with me — or I get bored with him? What if this relationship blows up in my face, like all the others?"

"Welcome to the human race, honey. Everyone's asking the same questions, but we seem to muddle along in spite of all that. You will, too. On one condition." Sunny's eyes narrowed. "Do you love him? Back in high school, you fell in love every week. My job was consoling them after you dumped them, remember? Of course, that experience had its moments," she said wryly.

Taylor looked in the mirror and searched the image she saw there. "Yes," she said quietly. "No question about that. I love him beyond imagining."

"What about Jack?"

"The same. At least that's what he says."

"And you believe him?"

"When I'm not suffering from bouts of acute paranoia."

"And you dare to call *me* dysfunctional."

Sunny tossed Taylor a tissue. "Use that. If you start crying, you'll ruin your eyes. Then I'll start crying, and we'll both be a mess. Jack pulled you out of that river, and you should be celebrating, not quaking here in terror."

"But how do I know if everything's going to work out?"

"You don't," Sunny said gravely. "You can guess and plan, but you don't ever know. So you just get on with life, because that's the only way to find out."

Taylor dabbed at her eyes. "So I'll have to go outside? See the mayor — maybe meet Jack?"

"That's the general idea. Some of the most important people in San Francisco are waiting outside, not to mention my uncle and his whole reading club."

"Uncle Vinnie brought his reading group? That's so sweet." Taylor took a shaky breath, smoothing her dress. "I suppose it won't be so bad. If Jack comes, fine. If not, that's fine, too. I can handle a little uncertainty in my life. Being chased, threatened, shot at, and nearly drowned makes a woman tough."

"That's the spirit."

Taylor smiled at her friend. "Anybody ever tell you you're pretty damned smart?"

"All the time." Sunny pointed to the door. "Now get going. Your therapy session just ended."

Taylor slung her beaded silk scarf over one shoulder. "On my way. I just needed to work though one last crisis. Thanks for being here, Sunny."

"Anytime. Break a leg."

The music soared. "I'll try." Taylor squared her shoulders, then vanished outside.

"You won't thank me tomorrow," Sunny called. "Not when the new shipment of Green Goddess drinks arrives."

Taylor hadn't gotten twenty feet before Sunny's uncle zeroed in on her. "Is anything wrong?"

"Not anymore." Surprisingly, it was true. Sunny's speech had helped throw Taylor's anxiety into perspective. She wouldn't hide from the changes in her life. Instead, she would celebrate them as doors to new opportunity. "Sunny says you brought your whole reading club."

"Right over there, all fifteen of them." Vinnie pointed to a well-dressed, athletic-looking group of men. "We were going to read the new John Grisham this month, but that idea got voted down. We decided to reread your first book instead."

Touched, Taylor waved at a short man with a deep tan, perfect white teeth, and a broken nose. The man waved back at her, smiling broadly.

"That's Anthony Delveccio. He used to be an accountant in Atlantic City, and now he's our club treasurer. Smart fellow."

Taylor sensed a story screaming there somewhere, but she didn't have time to pursue it because the mayor closed in, two photographers in his wake.

"Ms. O'Toole, I'm so pleased you could come. I have a dozen people hoping to meet you." His voice fell as he bent his head closer. "Of course, they know nothing about what really happened, even though the press has gotten wind that Harris Rains was involved in something big and possibly nasty."

"So I hear. One of them just cornered me in the ladies' room."

The mayor gestured sharply to his side. "I'll put a stop to that." He said a few words and the aide vanished. "I'll see that her press privileges are revoked and she is escorted from the premises." Camera bulbs flashed and the mayor angled his head, smiling confidently for the first of the evening's photographs.

Taylor smiled back, trying to hide her anxiety as she scanned the crowd.

She was searching for a Navy uniform and a pair of strong, broad shoulders as more flash-bulbs went off around her.

Taylor was on her third glass of champagne an hour later, but there was still no sign of Jack. She'd met all the mayor's friends and listened to their stories. She'd danced with a CEO from Walnut Creek and a Pulitzer-winning journalist from Berkeley. Her feet ached, she was tired, and she wanted to go home.

Where was Jack?

As a waiter passed, she scooped up her fourth glass of champagne. At least she wouldn't be feeling any pain tonight when she went home to her lonely apartment and her empty bed.

"No more champagne for you."

Taylor glared at the man in the pristine white waiter's uniform. "The least you can let me do is get drunk. The danger's over, remember?"

Izzy searched her face, remaining cool and distinguished even while dressed as a waiter. "So it appears."

"What happened to Jack?"

"He's tied up. Paperwork."

Taylor frowned. "And Lemka was definitely the one behind Candace's murder?"

"No doubt about it. We've impounded all of Rains' papers from the lab in Mexico, and his staff there is being interrogated as we speak. No material made it out to his employers in South America," he added quietly. "We caught Lemka's men in time."

Taylor breathed a sigh of relief. "Thank God. The last thing we need is a new biological weapon unleashed on the world."

"The government owes you for all your help, Taylor. I expect you'll be receiving a personal call to that effect in the next few days."

"There's no need to thank me." Taylor was staring at the crowd, mulling over something

Izzy had said. "Wait a minute. How can you be so sure that none of the recombinant ricin got through to South America?"

Izzy didn't answer.

The truth came to Taylor in a horrifying flash. "You know because a team went down and set up surveillance. They probably monitored all phone calls and radio traffic." The image made her knees go weak. "Jack was with them, wasn't he?" The words were a whisper. "That's why he's not here — because something happened down there."

Izzy measured the emotions playing over her face. "I didn't say that."

"You didn't have to say it. We both know that dangerous missions are Jack's specialty. Because this was personal, he'd be the first to volunteer."

Izzy set her champagne glass down on a nearby table. "He definitely wanted to be here. The mayor pulled all the strings he could, but they weren't enough. Jack's part of an important team, Taylor. They have experience in areas that make them unique."

Taylor wanted to ask what kind of areas.

But she didn't. Izzy's face told her this was another topic he wasn't free to discuss.

She drew her scarf slowly around her shoulders. "I thought I knew what I was getting into with Jack. I thought I could handle the questions and the worry. Now I'm not so sure." She pulled the scarf tighter. "Meanwhile, I have two questions. Who was the inside leak?"

"Agent Rodriguez's partner, I'm afraid."

"Last question: Did Rains ever threaten Candace?"

"Not according to Martha."

"So that was a lie, too." Taylor felt the cold taste of betrayal. She had swallowed Candace's tale of woe completely. "So she slept with Rains for money."

"Maybe she had some feelings for the man."

It was a weak lie, and they both knew it.

Taylor shivered. "I don't feel very good, Izzy. I — I think I'd better go."

"I'll take you."

"No need. I can catch a cab."

"I'll take you," he repeated, his tone inviting no argument. He waited while she said her good-byes, then escorted her to the front door, where the wind whipped up from the bay, sharp and cold.

"Give yourself some time," he said quietly, motioning to a car nearby.

When the dark sedan pulled up, its driver jumped out, and Izzy opened Taylor's door. "He's a good man, Taylor, but you're both going to have to make some serious changes. Jack has always gone by the book, and following the rules isn't exactly your strong point."

"So we're oil and water. Tell me something I don't know."

As she slid into the seat, Izzy glanced across

at her. "Oil and water make a great salad, just as long as you handle them properly. Shake them up a little, add the right spices, and they're a killer combo."

"Is this a cooking lesson or Relationships 101?"

"Neither. Just some friendly advice from someone who has seen too many people walk away without trying. I like you both too much to see that happen."

Taylor's eyes narrowed. "I don't see *you* wearing a ring."

Izzy grinned. "Hell, no." He started the car and slid smoothly out into traffic. "Just because I dish out great advice doesn't mean I take it myself."

They didn't talk on the drive. Taylor was busy trying to hide her disappointment at Jack's absence, and Izzy was too polite to mention the sprinkling of tears she'd brushed away in the car.

"I know Jack. He doesn't do things lightly." Izzy parked and escorted Taylor inside, stopping outside her door. "Give yourself time to see where the relationship is headed before you jump ship."

"I've never been strong on patience." Taylor opened her door and waved as Izzy got back on the elevator. Her feet were aching with a vengeance now, and she sighed as she dropped her keys on the table by the door.

Stepping out of her stiletto heels was going to be an orgasmic experience.

"Hold it right there."

Hard hands gripped her waist. Taylor froze, her heart pumping as callused fingers moved along her waist, then tightened, turning her slowly.

She took a racing breath. "You *made* it."

Jack was wearing his white dress uniform, his face shadowed in the darkness. "It wasn't easy." He pulled her closer, inhaling. "You smell incredible."

For a moment, Taylor was tongue-tied. She had forgotten how tall he was, how commanding his presence. How much she loved him.

"How did you get in?"

"Mrs. Pulaski saw me downstairs and loaned me her key. She said to have fun."

"Do you charm *every* woman you meet?"

"It took me a long time to get close to one, and she was the only woman who mattered." Jack touched her face, then held out a thick envelope. "The doorman asked me to bring this up. A courier dropped it off after you left tonight."

Taylor glanced at the address label.

The lawyer. More questions she couldn't answer.

Taylor held the envelope for a moment, then dropped it on her desk. She still hadn't decided what to do about her search for her birth parents. No matter what she chose, someone would be betrayed. "I'll look at it later."

"No decision yet?"

Taylor shook her head. Discussing her adoption conflicts was the last thing she wanted to do now that Jack was here. "Are you okay? You look exhausted."

"It was a long flight." He looked at her dress and frowned. "Look, I'm sorry I missed the mayor's dinner tonight, but things didn't . . . work out."

Taylor bit back a dozen questions and slid her arms around his neck. "No problem. You would have been dead bored inside ten minutes."

"Not with you in the same room."

"I think we can come up with something better than chitchat and handshakes over champagne cocktails."

His eyes darkened. "Is that an offer?"

"What do you think?" She tilted her head, brushing his lips lightly with hers until Jack made a rough sound and pulled her closer, his strong arms closing around her.

She ran a hand along his chest and saw his jaw tighten. "Did something happen to you, Jack?"

"I told you, I'm fine. Come see what I brought you."

He was probably lying, which didn't surprise Taylor since the man would never admit to weakness or pain. But before the night was over, she'd find out the truth about how badly he'd been hurt, and God help him if he expected to play macho tough guy with a serious wound.

Taylor was surprised when he held out a handwoven bag the size of her palm. "You had time to shop?"

"Not exactly. It was pretty strange. We were miles from any town, up in the hills near —" He stopped, shook his head. "Doesn't matter where, just in some hills. Suddenly this old lady appears out of the fog, her face lined and dark like a walnut. After what feels like forever, she reaches into her pocket and pulls out this bag. At first she says something in a dialect I don't understand, then she switches to Spanish. 'For the woman of your heart,' she says. 'Let them carry her sadness now.'" Jack looked into the darkness and Taylor felt him slip back to that distant place he couldn't tell her about. "Something about her voice made my skin itch. She had a wild sort of laugh, and she refused to take the bag back. She wouldn't accept any money, either." He pressed the bright fabric into Taylor's hand. "So here it is."

"Am I what she said?"

"Woman of my heart." Jack's fingers tightened on Taylor's hand. "Always. There's no going back, not for me."

Suddenly the bag felt very heavy in Taylor's hand. She had to make him see all the problems looming before them.

She took a deep breath. "I've never made it

to six months before, Jack."

"Never?"

She shook her head. "My record at relationships isn't exactly promising. Actually, it's hopeless."

He seemed pleased by the news. "So we'll start with a clean slate. If something works, we keep it. If not, it gets tossed."

"It's not that easy. People always have emotional baggage. Heaven knows, I have a closet full." Taylor opened the small bag, stunned at the beautifully made set of seven bright dolls. Each had a distinctive face sewn with tiny stitches, along with matching hair and clothes. In the darkness, they looked amazingly lifelike.

"One sadness every night," Jack said. "That's what the old lady said."

Taylor slid the exquisite little dolls back into the bag. "They're lovely, Jack. But —"

"We start with a clean slate, Taylor. Try it and see what happens."

He watched her as he bent his head, kissing her hard until she went boneless against him. As his hands closed on her hair, he took a deep breath.

Being here felt like a dream after the last eight days in hell. The mission had been harder than expected, and one of his team had been badly wounded. In spite of that, the operation had been a success, bringing definitive proof that Harris Rains' discoveries had not left the U.S. Jack was still hurting where he'd been kicked by a goon who had appeared out of no-where while the team was hunkered down, waiting for extraction. The man and his friends had been high on peyote and gut-busting local tequila, and they'd been hard to subdue without attracting unwanted attention.

Jack didn't want Taylor to see the bruise that covered most of his side, so he figured he'd work fast and keep her distracted. "About that offer you made . . ."

Taylor's voice was thready with passion. "I have some wine around here, if you want."

When she touched his right side, he managed to bite back a hiss of pain. "Forget the wine." He brought her hand to his mouth and kissed her open palm. "All I want is you naked, be-neath me in that big bed, surrounded by blue pillows."

Her dress slid free and fluttered to the floor, a wave of silk and crystal beads that shimmered in the moonlight. "How's that?"

"Words fail me."

"You're sure you're up to this?" Taylor asked softly.

He gave her a slow, cocky grin. "Ask me that question in ten minutes."

Taylor pulled open the top button on his shirt. "Something tells me I won't have to."

Jack swung her up into his arms. When he sank down on top of her, she touched his face gently. "As far as I can tell, everything seems to be in working order."

"Maybe you need firsthand evidence of that."

"Good idea." She slid her body slowly over his.

"God, you take my breath away." He skimmed her skin inch by inch, stopping at the shadow above her thighs. "Every night I saw you in my mind, just like this."

"Then why am I the only one naked here?"

"Because I'm trying to take my time about this."

She drew him down toward her. "You can take your time later." Taylor found his zipper and eased him free, teasing him between her warm fingers.

Jack frowned. "I swore tonight would be controlled, gentle, full of finesse. I wanted that for you. For *us*."

"When I want gentle, I'll tell you." Taylor levered her body against his, her eyes dark with challenge.

"Hell." Jack buried his fingers in her hair and sank deep, feeling her body shiver beneath his. His control was fraying, and he couldn't get deep enough, close enough. He needed her panting, just as desperate as he was.

A moment later he got his wish. Taylor's nails dug into his back, tiny bursts of pain in perfect counterpoint to the mind-shredding slide of her body rising against his.

Need snarled, driving him right to the edge, and Jack barely winced as her arm struck his bruised ribs.

He didn't feel the pain. There was only Taylor and the magic their bodies wove in the darkness.

Their fingers slid together, clenched hard. When she gasped his name and rocked against him, Jack felt his heart slam against his chest.

Then there was only the smell of her perfume, the heat of her skin, and finally the reckless urgency as he lost himself deep inside her.

Taylor didn't move.

Jack lay motionless beside her, his breathing slow and even. When she was certain he was asleep, she rose carefully on one elbow, studying his naked body in the moonlight.

A shallow scar ran along his collarbone. A huge bruise mottled his right side. Both were new, courtesy of his last mission.

How could she ever get used to this shadow world he lived in, with its dangers that he could never discuss?

More questions.

She eased to her feet, moonlight spilling cold and clear around her. On the bed Jack muttered, curling his body toward the warm spot she had just left, one hand opening over her pillow.

She closed her eyes, hit by slivers of pain. Love wasn't the problem. Trust wasn't in question, either. Men didn't come more honorable than Jack. But Taylor wasn't sixteen anymore, wasn't young and fresh and malleable. How could a stubborn, independent woman change enough to meet an equally stubborn, independent man halfway?

She stared down at her wounded hero, asleep in the moonlight. He had loved her with grim desperation, as if to wipe away haunting memories. Sensing the depth of his need, she had offered herself completely, holding nothing back. She had never been so focused in the physical, so vulnerable to the emotions racing through her.

No going back.

She picked up one of the dolls from their bag near the open window and whispered just how much she loved him and how frightened she was of failing at the one relationship that mattered. Around her the curtains moved, drifting high, touching her bare shoulders like a cool caress. The tiny face looked back at her, calm and infinitely wise.

She slid her hand over Jack's uniform jacket, ghostly in the light from the window. His collar was folded and one shoulder dangled low on the back of the chair where he'd hung it. Carefully, Taylor gathered the crisp fabric against her skin, inhaling the faint male scent of his body. And in that moment, she knew.

She *knew* with the same clear certainty that she recognized the pace of her breath and the beat of her own heart.

There was no going back. She would be contrary when he needed a good fight, and she would hold him when his memories were too grim to bear alone. She would try not to ask too many questions.

Through the window, a foghorn droned, hidden somewhere out in the mist. She must have heard the sound hundreds of times before but had paid no attention, perpetually caught up with an endless stream of day-to-day worries and decisions rather than what was really important. How could she have missed the small constant things that slid beneath the surface and fed the true mystery of life?

The sound came again, clear in the three a.m. silence.

Each low drone lingered like a message. Taylor wasn't sure what the message said, but the sound made her feel grounded, anchored in a world she could no longer see clearly.

She smoothed Jack's uniform and hung it up gently, a lump at her throat. Tomorrow she'd call the lawyer and start the search for her birth parents. She was finally ready to face the answers she might uncover. Tomorrow she'd also call Annie and come clean about her adoption, even if they argued all night and crashed another golf cart in the process of making peace between them.

But tonight she would curl up here, touching a man with weary eyes and callused hands, a man who gave her his best again and again without conditions or expectations.

Jack's eyes opened as she sat on the bed. "I missed you."

"No way. You were lost to the world, my friend."

"You think?" He gave a slow smile, pulling her across him so that Taylor felt the unmistakable force of his need.

Her breath caught. "Maybe you did miss me after all."

"Let me show you how much." His hands were gentle, the fit of his body perfect, and the depths of her emotion left Taylor shuddering as they came to the edge of a place she didn't recognize.

"What are we doing, Jack? Where are we going?"

"Wherever feels right," he said quietly. "Forget the wondering and the worries. Go by how it feels." He slid his fingers through her hair, studying her face in the moonlight. "How does it feel now?"

"Perfect." She shivered as he brought himself deeper in slow, powerful strokes. "Better than perfect."

"I like those shoes you were wearing when you came in. Maybe you could wear them for me later — without anything else."

She gave a silken laugh. "I might consider it. With the right inducement." He moved again, and she closed her eyes. "Do that again, and I'll wear anything you want, Navy."

"I'll hold you to that."

Taylor closed her eyes, hearing the foghorn drone somewhere in the mist. She understood its message now, a deep truth that echoed through her life, marking the moment that her questions fell away, irrelevant before the fierce knowledge of what this quiet warrior meant to her.

She blinked as tears stirred. "I don't have a clue what we're doing, but suddenly I don't care. I'm with you, Jack."

He kissed the curve of her jaw, then shifted. "Stay with me, love."

Her answer was a low sound of pleasure and the fluid rise of her body against him, and suddenly he was all the way where she wanted him to be, the pleasure climbing in shuddering waves, his hands tight, clenched on her hair as he whispered against her face in the darkness.

There in the night, shadows stirred. The old demons reared their heads and howled — but this time, Taylor didn't even hear them.

Author's Note

Thanks so much for joining Taylor on her wild ride! No one is better at finding trouble than this stubborn woman. Of course, that's probably why she has become one of my all-time favorite heroines. (Not to mention that her writing process is so completely bizarre. In case you're wondering, I *do* wear big, orange headphones when I write, and no, I do not wear maternity clothes to get in the right mood. As for the rest of Taylor's eccentric writing traits, I plead the Fifth Amendment!)

In case you were intrigued by the monarch butterfly sanctuary in Carmel, you can find more information online at *www.pgmonarchs.org*. It is hard to imagine that these delicate creatures fly to a small stretch of coastal microclimate every year in a journey of thousands of miles. To see the trees filled with their glowing golden wings is truly a miraculous sight. For more information about the monarchs and the beautiful Monterey landscape, try the wonderfully informative *Monterey Bay Shoreline Guide* by Jerry Emory (Berkeley and Los Angeles: University of California Press, 1999). If you're in the area, be sure to stop by the Monterey Bay Aquarium, which is full of fun activities and ever-changing exhibits. You'll come away with a new appreciation for the richness of this rugged part of the California coast. If you can't visit, you can bring up their live webcam for a peek at the bay scenery and the antics of the otters. As of the time of publication, their bay webcam was running at the following link: *http://www.mbayaq.org/vi/vi_aquarium/vi_monterey_cam.asp*. The otters are guaranteed to make you smile!

If you're looking for one of the best guides to San Francisco, try *San Francisco* (London: Dorling Kindersley, 2000). The street-by-street tours are great resources, and the maps alone are worth the price of this wonderful book.

In case you missed the story of Taylor's sister Annie and her hunky SEAL husband, look for *My Spy*, which is set at a beautiful spa on the rugged California coast. Wounded when he saved a busload of children, Sam McKade needs time — and a safe place — to heal. Although he doesn't recognize Annie, she *definitely* remembers him!

Does Izzy seem familiar by now? He should! The man has charmed his way into four of my books already, beginning with *The Perfect Gift* and continuing through *Going Overboard*, *My Spy*, and *Hot Pursuit*. Yes, I do plan a book for him one day soon. Stay tuned to my website *(www.christinaskye.com)* for breaking news on that front.

Meanwhile, I'm laughing out loud at a whole new crew of stiff-necked characters, people who give the word *dysfunctional* new and interesting meaning! My heroine is dealing with a missing ferret, death threats, and a May wedding in stunningly beautiful Carmel, California.

But a wedding is the last place Summer wants to be. For her, weddings are very dangerous things. They always make Summer turn warm and fuzzy and go a little crazy. . . . Now she's thinking about what would happen if she forgot the rule book, kicked back and tried out an over-the-top, no-strings-attached affair.

With probably the most gorgeous man she's ever seen.

For Gabe Morgan, Navy SEAL, one week undercover at a lush seaside estate is a plum vacation with pay. Doing a favor for an old friend makes perfect sense when a senator's family may be at risk. Gabe can juggle snooty guests and the laughably neurotic members of the bride's family without missing a beat, even if the bride and groom *do* seem to argue a lot. The real problem is that weddings bore Gabe stiff. Eloping would be more his style — the faster and simpler the better. Not that marriage is *anywhere* on his radar screen.

But that's before Gabe gets a look at Summer.

As the big day draws closer, the chemistry between Summer and Gabe is off the charts, simply too strong to resist. Keeping their hands off each other may be their hardest assignment yet!

Stop by my website for a sneak preview early in the summer. Meanwhile, happy reading. I guarantee plenty of exciting news!

Christina Skye

Christina Skye

About the Author

Award-winning author Christina Skye lives on the western slope of the McDowell Mountains in Arizona. *Hot Pursuit* is her seventeenth novel.

Be sure to visit her online at *www.christinaskye.com* for updates on Taylor and Jack, Izzy and the wonderful folks in Almost. Watch for her new book, coming in the Spring of 2004.

The employees of Thorndike Press hope you have enjoyed this Large Print book. All our Thorndike and Wheeler Large Print titles are designed for easy reading, and all our books are made to last. Other Thorndike Press Large Print books are available at your library, through selected bookstores, or directly from us.

For information about titles, please call:

(800) 223-1244

or visit our Web site at:

www.gale.com/thorndike
www.gale.com/wheeler

To share your comments, please write:

Publisher
Thorndike Press
295 Kennedy Memorial Drive
Waterville, ME   04901